LIFE DRAWING

"With the ease of a natural storyteller, Emily Arnold creates an elegantly drawn portrait of an eccentric, artistic family as she explores the limits of love and art and family ties in this accomplished and original novel."
—Alice Hoffman, author of *Fortune's Daughter*

"Emily Arnold has the storyteller's gift and the painter's eye. Characters and scenes are brushed onto the page full of vibrancy and color and life."
—Julia Markus, author of *Friends Along the Way* and *Uncle*

"*LIFE DRAWING* is like a fine painting that stirs a certain mood. Its words cast a poetic glow."
—*The Pittsburgh Press*

"Filled with poetic, flowing language and beautiful allusions to art, Arnold's novel should appeal to writers, artists, and generally to people interested in knowing more about children who grow up coping."
—*Grand Rapids Press*

"Not since *A Tree Grows in Brooklyn* has a writer enticed readers into a character so successfully. . . . There is an emotional pitch that is maintained almost to the point of pain. There is an intellectual challenge that is equally painful."
—*The Jersey Journal*

"Emily Arnold has delineated the vistas of a young artist's life and fashioned an accomplished landscape."
—*The Philadelphia Inquirer*

By Emily Arnold:

A CRAVING
LIFE DRAWING

Life Drawing

Emily Arnold

Published by
Dell Publishing
a division of
The Bantam Doubleday Dell Publishing Group, Inc.
1 Dag Hammarskjold Plaza
New York, New York 10017

Laurel ® TM 674623, Dell Publishing Co., Inc.

ISBN: 0-440-20025-3

Reprinted by arrangement with Delacorte Press

Printed in the United States of America

March 1988

10 9 8 7 6 5 4 3 2 1

OPM

"Reason respects the differences and imagination the similitude of things."

SHELLEY

"All great artists had unhappy childhoods. Someday you'll thank me."

MURIEL HEALY GEER

1

When I was nine and already toughened to carry the burden of expectation people had of me in a life made precarious by my parents' incompetence to manage it, I lay in my bed one night listening to them damage each other downstairs, waiting for my little sister Portia to break down.

I knew she was awake, and imagining her state of mind relieved mine. Portia's sweet, absorbent nature gave her endurance. I had found out how long she could fend off tears. A moonbeam, veering through the branches of the linden tree, shone on one of her hands clutching the covers and the other a doll. The small mound of her body was as still as it was when she played dead and I stood over her with a smoking cap pistol until she gasped convulsively and raised her own gun.

Her face was obscured, but I figured her eyes were staring. They were large, round, honest blue, and with her blond ringlets she looked like a doll herself. People noticed how much she took after Muriel, our mother, whose face was implacable too. I had our father's lank reddish-brown hair and close-set eyes, a color that shifted with the light but was usually a shade of green.

I had extinguished my little flashlight a few minutes before and was analyzing the hues throbbing in the dim corners of the room. There was red, brown, blue, even green and yellow, if I kept from blinking. Concentrating, it was possible to trace the methods used in the Great Paintings book I pored over every afternoon. One Impressionist had gone so far as to paint scarlet shadows. The depths and mysteries of color were ambiguous and engulfing, but I had been drawing for years and with a black pencil could work at recreating what I saw, or, rather, what lay waiting to be grasped and rendered. Drawing meant "drawing out"—seeing implied obligation, finding form and relationship—and was a complicated, moral act.

I had been drawing that night. At the top of the page I had written, "Expressive Faces." These imaginary heads, in full-face and profile, looked very real. Most were male because I could use a male head any way I wished, without restraint on my penchant for the grotesque. They grimaced, laughed, menaced, were sorrowful, surprised, and grim. Their features made up a kind of catalog too: They were Human Types. I had no idea where they came from, but they must match reality somewhere. The paper and flashlight were shoved under my bed when the wrangle began below.

Their voices rose together, stopped abruptly, and erupted again, his self-consciously modulated—Desmond delivered himself of remarks, even in rage—hers darting and thrusting and heedless, although she strove equally for effect. There was a crash, as if a chair had been knocked over. Portia and I liked to do that, too, out in the shed, in our Wild West game. We had taken furniture stored there and set up a saloon, which we demolished in raids. Someone stomped across the room, Desmond shouted, and for the first time we could distinguish his words: "Who do you think you are, MRS. GOD?"

The remark hung in the air. Then she started to shriek—long, eviscerating cries that beseeched us: This was our mother!

"*Do* something!" Portia cried at last. "We have to go down!"

She thrust little bare feet over the side of her bed. The doll tipped forward in her lap seemed to mimic her alarm. I gazed back at her coldly. I was frightened, but my sympathies scuttled from one to another of us. The schism between Mother and Father that had rent our universe and made all choices dire, opened a bottomless pit. Either parent was capable of hurling me into it. Portia had never taken sides and could witness the clash without affecting its outcome. She ran over noiselessly and tugged at my arm.

"We have to go! She's hurt!"

I shook my head. But then Muriel screamed my name.

"MIRANDA, MIRANDA, HELP!"

Portia let me shoot ahead. We ran along the carpet in the hall and down the steep back stairs. Was he killing her this time?

At the bottom was the side door that led to the driveway, and next to it a little metal hatch for milk deliveries that had figured in many a game. A short corridor lined with pantry cupboards led to the kitchen, which we entered, breathing hard. Portia let go of her doll and it landed with a soft thunk.

Desmond stood at the far end of the room. His right arm was raised over his head, and I noticed the angles cut by his shoulder and elbow and the corresponding field of umber his gesture projected onto the pale yellow cabinet behind him. I felt the tension in his muscles and how they worked, and, working, looked. I felt the grip of the bread knife in his fingers and palm and the lines of force leading over to Muriel, who cowered in the other corner, one hand on her breast, the other crooked behind her back, her shoulders tipped away and her mouth wide open. The lamp with its conical shade swung over the table, and light lapped their torsos in turn. It was terrifically exciting to see—I felt as if I were making up the scene myself, and in fact, I had already used a few of its conventions when I illustrated radio programs in progress: "The Shadow knows. . . ."

Desmond lowered his arm when he saw us, and it seemed to remove support from his face. Everything collapsed—eyes, brow, mouth. With an effort he reconstituted his charming smile. Portia and I hadn't laid eyes on him for two days, when he had been his usual mild self, puttering over his coffee, forgetting two cigarettes in two ashtrays, gathering up sheafs of notes and the crossword puzzles he worked before dawn when he couldn't sleep and tiptoed out of his little room at the back of the house to sit in the kitchen alone. He had been wearing a tweed jacket that morning, gray flannel pants, and a mustard-colored silk pocket handkerchief. His hair had just been combed with lots of water and he had a pencil mustache ("Like a stage bounder," he said, doing his little soft-shoe routine that we loved). He had whistled through his teeth and called "Cheerio, darlings" to us before he left for the city on the rackety train. We had watched from the window seat as he sauntered up the street, whittling on a little stick for relaxation, as

he always did while walking. We could pick out his figure
blocks away, among the men whose arms swung at their sides.

"Ah, the little girls," he said now, running the words together. "Now look what you've done." Muriel snorted disgustedly. He took a step toward us and Portia gasped. I stood my
ground, shielding her. I was aware of my hands—there was no
place on my pajamas to put them. We were trying to do the
right thing, but Desmond clearly disapproved of our coming.

"You leave them alone!" Muriel enjoined.

He smiled slackly and raked at his hair. His eyes narrowed.
"Don't use them for your purposes," he said. "Pour out your
venom on me, but not them. Now, Miranda, Portia, I'm not
going to hurt anyone. We're sorry we woke you up."

"Look what he's doing! Miranda, you look! This is the father
you admire so much!"

Desmond carefully placed the knife on the counter, stared at
it, opened a drawer and put it inside. "There is no good nor evil,
but thinking makes it so," he said, and fell into a fit of coughing. Phlegm churned as he worked to raise it. He doubled over
and his face grew livid. When he had recovered a little, he
looked helplessly in my direction. There were deep lines around
his eyes, and they seemed bigger than usual. I realized he
wasn't wearing his glasses and the depressions they had dug at
the bridge of his nose were dark.

"She's afraid of me," he said, and laughed soundlessly. I
loved him, but even his normal routines were mysterious to me.
Whatever was the violent attraction between them that threw
all of us together and somehow accounted for my existence but
guaranteed no good?

He stretched his mouth and eyes until his whole scalp
shifted. Then he shook his head and shot searching glances over
the surfaces of the room. "I really can't see," he observed.

"What do you think, Miranda?" Muriel asked waspishly.
"Oh, my God . . ." I had the feeling that we had been summoned not to rescue her, but to fortify her attack. She seemed
refreshed. "He's been out buying rounds for the cronies who
take credit for his work," she informed us briskly. "Mr. Bigshot. They all take advantage of his so-called generosity, don't
they? Everyone knows it makes him feel so good. What he can't
see is his family barely scraping by." She set one row of teeth

exactly on the other, lips parted. That was her look when the things that tormented her seemed also to bring the most satisfaction. Her theories aggravated her until they were confirmed. "Hail blithe spirit, bird thou never *wert*," Desmond had teased her. Muriel fussed at Portia and me and at everything she surrounded herself with, pulling it all into line with her notions.

"You suck the life out of me," Desmond said now, bowing. This threw him off balance. His white shirt was spotted and loose, and most amazing of all, his fly was unzipped and a little flag of white poked out of it. Muriel crossed toward us on the far side of the table. I saw that she had his glasses in her hand.

He discovered his cigarette pack on the counter, took one out, lighted it, and dropped the flaming match to the floor. We watched it burn.

"You'll set the house on fire," she said.

He stomped on the match. "You'd have me pay to breathe . . . for my every *inspiration*," he said. He waved his arm, and the cigarette, stuck deep in the notch between his fingers, left fat circles of smoke in the air. He shambled forward and Portia popped out from behind me to throw her arms around Muriel's waist.

Mother embraced her hard. There were tears in her eyes, and the veins rose in her throat. "What are we to do?" she gasped. "How are we to live?" She cupped Portia's face in her hand and I could see one eye staring out.

"Oh, come," Desmond said. "Let us just get a grip on ourselves. . . ." He shook his head humbly, and I thought of going to put an arm around him, too, but he started to cough again. Turning his back, he stumbled to the sink, took up a glass, ran water into it, and drank. A stream ran down his chin, and he spilled what remained in the glass when he set it down. Mother muttered a sound of disgust and pushed Portia aside. She snatched up a sponge and dabbed at the spills. Desmond watched her crouching at his feet with a rueful little smile.

"What's the use?" Muriel asked, standing. She pulled a tissue from the sleeve of her old sweater and wiped her eyes. "I've taken all I can. He thinks that because he's clever he can do anything he wants." It didn't seem to me that he took such liberties. She grabbed Portia's hand and pulled her toward the door. "Are you staying here, Miranda? Or are you coming with me?'' Startled, I looked from her to him and back. She waited, eyes gleaming. It seemed mean of her to suggest I thought I had a choice. She and Portia went out of the room and I ran after them. Would Desmond be all right? Would he be himself to-morrow?

"He'll set the place on fire," Muriel told us again on the stairs. Portia, two steps above, flashed me a stricken look. What could I do? Muriel hurried into her bedroom and we hovered in the doorway while she flung open her closet.

"When have I been able to buy myself anything to wear?" she muttered, and pulled out a small suitcase. "Go get dressed! What are you waiting for? We have to get out of here." She unbuttoned her skirt and hauled it up. When it covered her face, with her arms crooked over it, we ran.

We raced along the hall, away from the warm light of her room, and I yanked the cord that hung from the ceiling of ours. The sight of our belongings—her dolls, our balls and bats, my desk and canister of pens, pencils, and brushes, the book-shelves, an antique microscope I'd found in the shed when we'd moved to this house, Portia's bag of leotards and ballet shoes—all of this checked us for a minute and had enough reality to contravene the adult derangement we had fled. Couldn't we just slip into our beds and go to sleep?

But we could hear Mother speaking in the honeyed tones she used on the telephone, and then she came in, carrying her suit-case. She slammed it down on my bed. "Hurry! What have you been up to? Put your nightgowns in here. Fold them . . . and your toothbrushes. Get dressed, girls! And I mean a dress, Mi-randa! Your blue velveteen."

I protested. The dress, which was her handiwork, was ugly and inhibiting, with a little lace collar and puffed sleeves that chafed my armpits. I had spent agonized hours in it being fitted, Muriel on the floor with a mouthful of pins, poking and pull-ing, but so far I'd avoided wearing it out of the house. I would have to put on patent leather shoes, too, which I hated nearly as much. Where were we going?

"I *mean* it!" she added, flying out again, and we obeyed. Portia liked to look fancy, and I eyed her resentfully while she but-toned her sky blue dress and buckled its matching belt. My dress was dark, almost navy. Muriel had chosen it in an effort

to make me look sophisticated and teach me style, but I thought
of it as redeemed to the extent that it looked like a sailor uniform. I was still struggling with a snap when Muriel came back
with a brush and began violently to arrange my hair. She had
painted her face and wore a shiny mauve dress with scalloped
sleeves that showed her pale upper arms. Her shoes were fragile
and high-heeled, with ankle straps, and although she stayed in
one spot, she kept taking little corrective steps as she brushed.
A rhinestone necklace glinted on her breast, where a big square
of flesh was heaving with her exertions. She had two barrettes
between her carmine lips. A dizzying cloud of perfume settled
about my head. I usually avoided her face—of all the things I
saw every day, it was the only blur. But now I couldn't help
looking. Muriel was ravishing. Her eyes were avid and their
color had deepened within the penciled outlines and reminded
me of the sky at dusk. Her cheeks were a soft rose. She had
combed her hair up and sprayed it, and her restless way of
moving that seemed arbitrary and intrusive in ordinary life, was
now thrilling. I leaned forward to touch her breast with my
cheek. She gave my hair a last savage swipe and pushed me
aside to begin on Portia's. With her she was gentler, and I understood that it was because she had more to work with and I
had never willingly submitted.

She gave us a look: We were ready. In the hall I remembered
my pencil and pad and ran back, over her objections, to get
them. The absence of pockets in my outfit meant that I had to
carry my materials, but I couldn't face the unknown without
something to draw on.

We went down the front stairs this time, clattering in our
shoes, and Portia and I put on our gray spring coats and waited
while Muriel transferred the contents of one purse to another
and threw on a white, square-shouldered jacket, glancing from
time to time out the window.

The living room was dark, and the door leading to the pantry
and kitchen was shut. I pictured the pale striped fleur-de-lis
wallpaper in the living room, the window seat, bookshelves,
flowered wing chair, fireplace, the corner in the dining room
where I sprawled to sketch beneath a window—just as if we
had gone away on a trip back to Grandma's in Illinois before
she died and I were drawing on memory to ease homesickness.

How far were we going now? We had packed, it seemed, for just a night, and that must be nearly over. But then the clock on the mantel struck eleven times, correcting me. There was no sound from the kitchen. I wondered what Desmond was doing. I couldn't smell smoke, but we might never see this place whole again. Why didn't we stay and protect it? I glanced at Portia, whose eyes were cast down. We were like partisans behind the lines. If captured, we would know nothing, not even each other.

Muriel said, "Here he is," and we followed her out the door. There was a taxi at the curb shedding light on the deserted street. The neighbors' houses were dark. The cool, clear air carried a faint scent from the lilacs blossoming next to the shed. Our feet crunched on the walk. I looked at the Studebaker sitting in the driveway, outsized and inert. It was a sign of Muriel's vexation that she felt entitled to a taxi and was leaving the car behind. There was no chance that Desmond would hop into it and give chase. He was the only Daddy around who never drove. In fact, we had lived uniquely without a car, shopping for groceries with an old toy wagon until recently, when Muriel made a deal and bought this showroom model, which was the color of Pepto-Bismol and humiliating to be seen in.

In the taxi I had the righthand window on the sidewalk and a full view of our squat stucco house. I had drawn it so often that I could have done so with my eyes shut, and my regard for it was almost without sentiment.

Muriel said, "Take us to the hotel." The driver hadn't shown his face—just the prickly back of his head above a wrinkled jacket collar. Muriel sat back and smoothed her skirt. "If he knows what's good for him, he'll sleep it off," she added. I prayed she would not expose more of our troubles, and hunched down in the seat so the driver wouldn't see me if he did turn around.

"Someday you'll understand," Muriel asserted. "Oh, God," she wept briefly. "You girls are all I have. . . . I wish you were a little older. . . . I'm doing the best I can. . . ." Portia, squeezed between us, put her arm across Muriel's lap. "He flings his money to waiters and deadbeats because it makes him feel important. . . ." She blew her nose loudly. "All I care about is that neither of you makes the mistake I did. You'll have to be able to take care of yourselves."

We passed beneath a streetlight and I sank lower. Another time she'd have ordered me to sit up straight, but now she ignored me. The driver cleared his throat and hummed a song.

We passed stately homes set across easy lawns. Our side of town was congested and had a strident look, and Muriel envied these people. I wished she had more pride. There were few lighted windows—people went to bed early and slept peacefully. Once, a man standing meditatively, waiting while his dog struck a cringing pose in the gutter, looked up at us, surprised. He wore a light cardigan sweater and I noticed by the way it hung lower in the front, that its drape suggested a mood.

Muriel sniffed. It was disarming to ride along with her just a passenger, as if we all shared the same fate. "What will become of us?" she murmured. I wanted to know what she had done with Desmond's glasses, but was afraid a question would attract her enmity to me.

At the center of town was a wide intersection where a traffic light had recently been installed, and we waited there, although no one else was abroad.

To our left lay a street of smart shops and a few businesses, mostly real estate and insurance agencies. To the right was the boulevard that ascended Hotel Hill. The hotel had been built toward the end of the last century, when the village was a country retreat for sportsmen from New York City, twenty miles south. People used to stay there when the races met, just outside of town. Now there were plans to turn the track into one of the first shopping centers, but the hotel still operated and was used for celebrations. Muriel would read in the paper about people we knew by reputation whose sons and daughters had wedding parties in the ballroom.

The driver hummed softly. The taxi smelled of stale smoke and seemed out of place in the pretty, tranquil town where everyone had their own cars.

We turned onto the curving drive that wound through a park. The hotel at its center was lit like a fanciful ship, four stories high, with battlements, wings, and additions of pink sandstone, and a pair of crenellated towers flanking the entrance. From a distance at night it was just a mass riding the hillside, with cheerful windows. As we drew closer, we heard orchestra music. Portia and I strained to see.

A few feet from the door the driver sped up, then stomped on the brake and we skidded to a stop. Muriel took a long time settling the fare. She, unlike Desmond, was chary with tips. When we had disembarked, the driver inched forward, parked, and struck up a conversation with a uniformed man who stood smoking in the shadows. Muriel gave them a dirty look, and I thought she must have expected one of them to carry her overnight bag into the hotel.

"I'll take it," I said, reaching. I shoved my pad of paper and pencil into my coat pocket. She surrendered the bag, and we followed her up two broad steps into the gleaming lobby. She moved briskly, her head held imperiously above her squared shoulders, and Portia and I had to struggle to keep up. The orchestra came to a blaring climax, and there was applause.

A few people in dark suits and long dresses drifted out of a wide doorway to our left. The women wore corsages and clutched little purses. Portia had taken a handful of my coat and was peering around me. I shook free. Muriel marched to the desk without looking at anyone. A young man waiting there came to attention and adjusted the knot in his tie.

I set the suitcase on the marble floor. The couples strolled about, smiling at each other and chatting. I looked up at the vaulted ceiling, where the pinkish air seemed to thicken with altitude. A few men and women separated and slipped through doors marked Ladies and Gentlemen. I felt a twinge in my bladder and willed it away. Muriel stood with her weight on one foot, the toe of the other pointed down to the floor. There was a burst of laughter and clapping inside the big doorway.

"Look!" Portia whispered, gesturing. I turned. Four giants with ruddy faces wearing firemen hats, slickers, and boots were coming in the front entrance. We froze. I whirled to see if Muriel had noticed. Her back was still to us and her head bent close to the clerk's as they studied a paper on the desk. The four huge men cased the lobby and smiled at us. I took Portia's hand. Now they would break the news and we would have to tell Muriel. Maybe we would live here in the hotel from now on. Then I thought, *Did our father burn up with the house? Why are they smiling?*

"What long faces, little misses. What's the trouble?" one of the firemen asked, bending with his hands on his great knees. I could not declare myself. He turned to his companions, who gathered around us too.

"Stood up, maybe," another suggested.

"What? Who would stand up pretty girls like these? I don't believe it. Is that the truth?" Their great black shapes, like comic book insects who carried children off to cliffside caves, threw shadows all around us on the floor. Our pocket of air filled with the odors of rubber and after-shave lotion.

"Be a gentleman, Billy. That's what you do. Be a gentleman and ask the lady for a date."

Billy grinned. He was well past childhood, but seemed almost one of us, with no sign of beard.

"Hey, now, who was here first?" Another fireman lifted his hat and bowed. His curly blond head was ridged, and a line ran across his forehead where his hat had rested. Tendrils of hair shot from his open collar, and beads of moisture glinted above his mouth.

"Little ladies, may we have the pleasure—" He stopped. In her distress, Portia had begun to hiccough. Her face went crimson and she jerked helplessly.

"Get her a glass of water."

But none of them wanted to leave her. "Hold your breath, missy. Take a good deep one; that's right. Hold it." Portia's great blue eyes bugged obediently.

"Wait a minute." The curly fireman crouched, ducked behind her, and then popped out, waving his arms. *"Booooo!"*

"Girls! What's going on?" The firemen parted for Muriel.

"Firemen," I said. "I think the house burned down."

"No!" Muriel searched their faces.

"We don't know a thing about it, lady."

"Just got here, ma'am. We've had no calls."

"Really, girls," Muriel said after a moment. She glowered at me. "They're overexcited," she explained.

Portia released the air she'd been holding and waited. *"Hic!"*

"Well," said Billy, who hadn't relaxed his grin. He clapped one of the others on the back. "I think we could all use a wee one, what do you say?"

The tallest one held his hat to his chest. "We didn't mean to frighten them, ma'am. Look, we'd be honored if you—and your husband and the girls—joined us for a glass of champagne in-

side." He tilted his head modestly. "We're part of the cere-
mony. They promised us all we could drink."

Then that thing that sometimes happened to Muriel in the
presence of other people and so amazed us every time happened
again. The mask of suspicion fell from her face, and instead of
grudgingly taking things in, she began putting them out. Her
cheeks dimpled, she gave a push to her bunched-up hair, bright
thoughts danced across her brow, and her eyes sparkled.

"I ought to put the girls to bed," she said. "We're here by
ourselves this evening and it's getting late."

"Oh, let them have a dance! It's just once a year!" The fireman leaned toward her, pleading. Then he picked up the suitcase and gestured with it toward the doorway as if it were no
more burden than a pair of gloves. "What do you say?"

"It's the Fireman's Ball," Muriel informed us. "He told me at
the desk."

Just then the orchestra struck up again. Billy took Portia's
hands and led her in a circle in two-four time. The tall fireman
read consent in Muriel's face, and offered her his arm. We all
moved toward the ballroom. Portia held a hand to her mouth,
but little spasms rocked her from head to toe.

I couldn't see past the press of people lounging in the doorway, only the crystal chandeliers overhead and streams of cigarette smoke rising toward them. A short cheer went up over the
blare of the music, and our firemen bowed and waved. Muriel
laughed and clapped her hands together. We filed in, the crowd
parted, and we halted at a long table covered with a white cloth
and chairs placed haphazardly around it. A man in a pink jacket
and a little black bow tie sat talking intently to a sloe-eyed
woman with severe black bangs and a gardenia over one ear.
She watched our arrival dully, whispered something to the
man, and left. He shrugged, rose, and began pulling chairs out
from the table so we could sit down. Portia yawned, clapped
her hand to her mouth, and grinned at me. "They've stopped!"
she told me. Her cheeks dimpled just like Muriel's.

The firemen threw their hats and slickers over the empty
chairs. They all wore white shirts, dark pants, and red suspend-
ers. Billy rubbed his hands together. The tallest one poured
champagne into a row of glasses and presented one to Muriel.

"Sit down, why don't you?" the man in pink said to me. *"Have a ball!"* he chortled, and plunged away through the crowd.

I slid into a chair. "Take off your coat," Muriel said, on her way to the end of the table. I shook my head. Portia permitted the blond fireman to remove hers and tipped her head coyly when he praised her dress. I shoved my hands into my coat pockets and the fingers of my drawing hand curled around my pencil. I stuck out my jaw, blew a strand of hair away from my eyes, and stared ahead.

Muriel stood with one hand on her hip, the other wielding her glass. She talked in a low, rapid way, and two men in dark suits leaned toward her, interested in what she was saying. Beyond them were rows of white-covered tables. People sat here and there or roamed the room or leaned aside to let others pass. Opposite the door was a mirrored wall, and against it, the bandstand. The bandleader had bright red hair and wore a clownish plaid jacket that hung nearly to his knees. He jiggled his right hand to keep the beat and executed bouncy little steps. The silhouettes cut by the musicians behind their shielded chairs, the sunbursts from the chandeliers, and the dancers' bobbing heads were reflected in the mirror. It was a turbulent, unnerving scene, and I turned my attention instead to figures nearby.

A man at the next table nursed a glass, rubbing it against his cheek as if to soothe a burn. He had a long donkey nose and pockmarked skin stretched over craggy bones. Because his lashes were scant and bags hung beneath them, his eyes looked inverted, like trick pictures in a puzzle book I had. He shifted his apathetic gaze to me, and I pretended I'd been looking past him.

Muriel gave a supple laugh. I turned and saw her set down her glass and run her hands over her skirt. One of the men crooked his arm for her and set off toward the dance floor. Portia sat on the edge of the table and the blond fireman knelt like a prince before her.

"Well, I'll tell you why," I heard him say. "It's because I like the way a dog looks at you. . . ."

Muriel disappeared into the crowd. It worried me when she tried to enjoy herself. The necessary loosening of constraint made her seem vulnerable, ready to be duped by her own

desires, and indeed, the small pleasures never lasted—she was
always disappointed. But her sense of fun was as regenerative
as a weed in a roadbed, and this music, this crush of dancers,
this champagne were straight out of the stories she told us of
life before my birth. I stared for a while at the spot where she
had been swallowed up and then, unwittingly at first but with
the little flush of exhilaration that always launched me, I took
out my pad and pencil and began a portrait of the pockmarked,
dog-nosed man's beautiful face.

Before long he realized what I was doing. First he shook a
finger at me and held a napkin over his face. Then he peeked
out and turned a theatrical profile. I drew that.

"Will you look at her!" said a voice behind me. "Hey,
Haeffner, she's got you cold! Every ugly inch!" I felt spectators
gather.

Haeffner himself came over to see. "That's me, all right," he
pronounced. "Terrific. How about doing wisemouth, here?
Come on, Georgie, get over here and sit down for your portrait."

Georgie was plump, with big ears. He tilted his head to a
three-quarter view, and I had to work to keep the proportions
correct and suggest three dimensions. Practice paid off. I finished and let him see. He snatched up the paper and showed
everyone. "It's amazing! Imagine doing that!"

"She makes it look easy!"

"I always wanted to draw, but I never . . ."

I smiled carefully, modestly. It always amazed *me* that people
were so easily persuaded by lines I set down. The drawings
were good likenesses, but they could have been better. Yet I
also knew that I was more cannily accurate when I worked fast,
under pressure. Laboring would erase spirit, even if each feature
had verisimilitude.

By this time there was quite a crowd. Several men brought
their wives or dates to be sketched. When Muriel returned, an
orderly line had already formed. Someone must have said,
"Here, let me buy this—" I was busy with my pencil and the
bits of paper people shoved at me. Muriel sent to the front desk
for proper paper and made a sign: PORTRAITS $1.

I barely paused between pictures. My hand cramped and
each new face triggered a fresh spurt of anxiety and excitement.

The women expected to be flattered, I supposed, and compromising what I saw was more tiring than struggling for the truth. Whenever I could, I insisted on profiles, which were quicker and surer. Cries of recognition from those waiting convinced each subject even before he rose to take a look and broke into a slow, marveling smile. Muriel asked a few people to lend their pictures and hung them on a line she tied between two chairs on a table. This display attracted more customers, including the hotel manager, who stood with a look of long suffering, I thought. Muriel told him, ". . . since she was three years old. I recognized it then and worked with her. . . ."

"She's a real artist," someone said.

I was aware of the band playing and people rustling and commenting, but I dared not look away from my work. Once, when my wayward hair fell over my eye and I shook it back, I glimpsed Portia, her face serene as a little cat's, revolving slowly at arm's length with the blond fireman. Dancing in their vicinity had been suspended to give them room; the tune was a romantic waltz, and they looked oblivious, as if the moment and the space they occupied were exempt and out of this world.

Finally there were just two customers left. My hand ached and the heel was sore where I'd rubbed it against so many sheets of paper, but I gave the last as much effort as I had the first.

The room emptied gradually and the orchestra played a spiritless "Goodnight, Ladies." The musicians rose wearily and put away their instruments. The bandleader scanned the dance floor, took a flask from behind one of the shields, and tipped it to his mouth. He smacked his lips and wiped them with the back of his hand. I did a quick sketch, just for myself. Someone left the crowd at the door and crouched under my table, looking for something. A woman removed a shoe and hopped away with it in her hand.

Muriel hurried over with a metal box and scooped all the dollar bills into it. "I'll let you count it," she promised. "And then we'll talk about what you should do with it." She looked tired; her lips had faded, the color creeping into the tiny crevices around her mouth. Her eyes were smudged and her hair had loosened. But in her animated state, the lateness of the hour and the champagne giving a certain punch to her gestures, she was still remarkably pretty. The firemen stood around, persistently amused by her. They helped her take down the display line and then everyone sorted out coats.

Portia's head had sunk to the table where she sat. Her plump cheek billowed out and little bubbly exhalations fluttered her lips as she dozed. A faint frown knit her brow. Someone had stuck a gardenia in her curls, and it lay, wilting, over her forehead.

The firemen held a hurried conference while Muriel roused Portia. They appeared to arrive at a compromise, and escorted us out of the room with chivalrous gestures. Portia had revived to a surprising degree, but I was exhausted and grumpy. Muriel allowed them to lead us into a dim cocktail lounge off the lobby, where everything was bloodred and a piano tinkled insinuatingly. I sprawled on a banquette. Muriel opened the cash box. It seemed to me that I must have drawn everyone at the Ball, but there was just sixty-seven dollars.

"Some of them left more than a dollar," Muriel said. "You couldn't have drawn that many. But I guess you're a professional," she smiled. "I'm very proud of you."

"Why don't we call Daddy?" I demanded.

She tossed her head. "We're going to teach him a lesson." It was the sort of thing she said about me. I picked up a peanut and threw it at Portia. The blond fireman threw one at me. A waitress in a short black skirt and fishnet stockings came up, clucking her tongue good-naturedly. The tall fireman ordered highballs and Shirley Temples for Portia and me. When it came, I accepted mine with an urbane sneer, but I felt that we had lifted the tent flap of the world, sitting there at that time and that place, and were breathing its festering, rowdy smells.

The blond fireman was telling a story; Muriel listened with an eager smile: "So I see Dennis everywhere with all these gorgeous women—at Flannagan's, on the train, on the street—and then he up and announces his engagement to Marilyn. So I say to him, 'But, Dennis, how is it you're getting married? I always see you with these beautiful women.' 'Yes,' he says, 'it makes Marilyn crazy with jealousy. I don't know what to do about it. . . .'" Everyone screamed with laughter.

I gave Portia a punch. She glowered and moved away.

"Miranda! You watch yourself!" Muriel cried. "Every single

time I come close to enjoying myself, this happens," she confided to one and all. "I'm sorry. It looks as if I'll have to excuse us and say good night."

I got up and went to the doorway to wait while she elaborated on her farewell. Then, so tired it was like a dream, I floated with her and Portia into the elevator, rose, got out, and traipsed after the elevator operator, to a door. He opened it with his key, winking at Portia and me as if it were a trick. He set the suitcase inside and backed out, shutting the door. The room was a field of beige—chairs, bedspreads, dresser, walls, curtains. Muriel was still fuming.

"Why can't we call Daddy?" Portia asked.

"Oh, all right," Muriel snapped. She waited a long time for the switchboard to respond, and gave our number. Portia and I watched from our bed. "No answer," Muriel reported. "No doubt he's in the arms of Morpheus." Portia looked at me and I shrugged. "We'll all go to sleep now," Muriel said.

Portia and I lay stiffly in one bed and Muriel in the other. It must have been dawn, but the windows were covered with heavy drapes. When I closed my eyes, a parade of faces passed before them, daring me to reproduce them.

Muriel spoke. "I want to tell you something about your father, Miranda. He lacks nerve. He's always done his best work for other people, his best for people who will settle for junk. He's never done it for himself, never realized his talent. All he wants is to please those chumps and be flattered in return."

She lay back and began to breathe heavily. Portia and I fought briefly for territory, and then we slept too.

2

I woke to see Muriel ripping open the curtains. Noon's rallying light poured into the room. She was already dressed and stood tapping her foot while Portia and I scrambled to get ready too.

I thought of surrendering as we descended to the lobby, of coming out of the elevator with our hands up, the way Portia and I did when routed from a stronghold in the room over the shed: "Throw your irons over there; now vamoose." But the desk clerk ignored us, and a runny-eyed old man at the door smiled down as if our visit had been personally gratifying.

"I'll buy you a breakfast out," Muriel said expansively. "But we can't dawdle over it. There's too much to do at home." We were glad of the treat and the extended outing. I never felt, in town, like a common citizen, and that day I marched along (carrying the suitcase, like Muriel's page) with stagey aplomb.

It was Saturday, and many shoppers were at large. Muriel, too, wore a disdainful expression, perhaps to ward off anyone who might recognize us; but except for a child from my grade at school, who cast us a furtive, incurious glance, all were strangers. The little block of shops and the luncheonette where we had pancakes were too tame to sustain my bumptious fantasies for long. I wished I were in the city, with Desmond.

We went home on a bus and Muriel said to me, "I think you should use your money for art lessons. We can go see Basil Peake—maybe he'll give you some professional pointers."

When I was three, as Muriel recalled it, I began to draw, almost compulsively and with amazing accuracy people said, everything I saw. Recognizing a force to be harnessed, she'd sat with me while I drilled at making ears, noses, eyes, feet, hands, whole clothed figures with pockets and cuffs and wrinkles. She'd have liked for me to practice bowls, flowers, pitchers, and landscapes, but early on I began to concentrate on the human figure, preferably in action, but at its least foreshortened.

It was the maidenly passion, too, of Miss Hill, my current teacher, to foster my talent. She was a tilting, attenuated woman with fuzzy pinkish hair flying from its pins, and pale, beseeching eyes. She had suggested I seek audience with Peake, who painted sporting scenes for *Field and Stream* and had turned himself into a local celebrity by lecturing to clubs and school-children.

Miss Hill had exempted me from most classwork and sent me off to the library to study on my own, or set me up with brushes and paints to make backdrops for concerts and plays or murals for the hallways. It was impossible not to relish this in part. Performance was the key to Muriel's approval and perhaps everyone else's. But I craved ordinary acceptance.

Despite her prodding and promoting of us, Muriel wanted it too. In midwinter the PTA had sponsored a Family Hobby Show, and she insisted we enter a display. We were to present ourselves as a normal family—what were our hobbies? Muriel had spent her last year of college in Paris, the first midwestern girl to win a certain French prize that carried a scholarship. She'd picked up the Parisian custom of having paper books bound in leather, and the result was her shelf of the works of Anatole France, Zola, and most fascinating to me because Doré had illustrated them, twin volumes of Rabelais. She would be a "collector of fine editions." Since my hobby was my vocation, altogether for real, I had to choose another activity, and settled on rock collecting. Portia kept an album of ballerina pictures. Desmond, who could pen a neat Gothic script, was made to write labels for my rocks and captions for Portia's album. Muriel decreed that his hobby would be calligraphy. The night of the show we set ourselves up with the other families in the gym, and when people wandered by with questions, Muriel did the talking. I think Desmond and Portia were as embarrassed as I was, but Muriel seemed to feel we were not poor fakes, but simply versatile, as adept at this suburban game as any.

Now, trudging up from the bus stop, we found the house still standing, but deserted. I went to look at Desmond's room and found his bed neatly made. Then I ran back down to hang around Muriel, as Portia did too. For once we weren't looking for an excuse to hide from her on a Saturday. When school was out, we were subjected to routines which were like a family curse. Although it seemed to torture her, Muriel was unable to shake off the auld sod tradition she'd been raised on, and regularly took up the rugs for beating, scrubbed the floors, the windows, and the upholstery. She repaired and altered, refinished and transplanted, in angry fits, obliging us to suffer along with her. The quality of the work Portia and I put in was never satisfactory—Muriel's dive-bombing inspections concentrated on the shortcuts we tried to get away with. But we had an unspoken advantage, knowing she took shortcuts too. She was teaching us necessary skills, she insisted, a little sadistically, as if settling the score with her own tormentors.

The radio program Desmond was currently writing with his partner, Lou Gregorian, was called *Clapper's Corners* and revolved around a small-town barber shop. Before it was moved to Sunday evenings, where it led off the Comedy Cavalcade, he had often been home on Saturdays. Muriel hectored him too. But when Desmond took up a hammer, he whacked his thumb. When he spaded the earth, it triggered an old back injury. When he tried to open a jammed window, his elbows shot through the glass and streamed with blood. All along the street we could see fathers perched competently on ladders or bending over the hoods of their cars or manfully hosing grass seed. He must have felt that Muriel's furious, volcanic (and oddly voluptuous—she was no puritan) labors were meant to ward off something.

Now, this Saturday, I felt burdened, vicariously, by the weight of Muriel's loneliness and a commission to ease it. She had made herself another cup of coffee and sat at the kitchen table with a little pile of clippings she'd saved—theater reviews, travel articles, tips for handymen, merchandise at bargain prices. Portia and I slumped against the counters, almost eager for our assignments. The cat we called Nobody, who had simply walked in the front door one day and been adopted by Muriel, meowed from outside, and I let her in. She sidled over to Muriel and wrapped herself around her legs, purring. Muriel looked us up and down.

"Well, haven't you anything to do?"

"What do you want us to do?"

"For heaven's sake. I'd think you were old enough to make *some* decisions for yourselves," she said wearily. "If I were you, Miranda, I'd work on my drawing for a while and see what I'd learned from all this. There must be lots of people in town who would like their portraits drawn. We could put an ad in the newspaper." She sipped her coffee. "Portia, we'll have to cut your hair today. I thought about it all night."

Portia went out the side door and rode away on her bicycle. She had pals a few blocks off, and I suspected her of conforming to common standards with them, of throwing off her real life and insinuating herself contentedly into other, more complacent ones. She was learning the ropes somewhere, and got along better with everyone than I did. Portia's pale, artless face turned instinctively toward the light, and she was always changing, I thought, while I didn't seem to at all. I had possessed the same nature since I was born (Muriel confirmed this) and could not escape the house, or Mother, or even Father, but carried their infection everywhere, picking it over in my mind for clues, afraid that I would miss something crucial. There was a concrete parallel in my habit of filling my pockets, everytime I went out, with the things I might need: a knife, pencil, notebook, length of string.

I didn't feel like drawing and went up to the attic, where boxes of papers and photographs were stored. There were also stacks of magazines—*Life, The Saturday Evening Post, American Mercury*—which I pored over so much that the world that had existed before I arrived had more coherence than the one I was in. I had added a few of these magazines to the copies I'd made of Luks, Glackens, Sloan, and Hopper, which I put up for sale at an orange crate newsstand at the end of our driveway. Customers could pick a periodical or a piece of my artwork—I wasn't willing to stake a business on art alone.

The boxes contained Desmond's unproduced play scripts and other writings, including a few diaries and packets of letters he and Muriel had written to each other. At nine I contented myself with speculating about the old pictures.

I picked up one of Muriel, aged seventeen or so when she'd been, she said, a "soubrette." She wore a flamenco dancer's dress, black and lacy, that hugged her hips and swirled out below. She held a fan and castanets, which were still with us down in the piano bench. Once in a while she brought them out and demonstrated how she'd used them in her famous routine, back in Babylon, Illinois. She had a dimpled grin and a look of easy mischief in her eyes. Her figure was curvacious, but with a doll-like economy, and a flagrant headliner's smile. She was standing in a grassy backyard—the weathered siding of a little shed showed at the edge of the picture—her pose as innocent as wholehearted efforts usually are, but hopeless too: flamenco out there in the boonies? Her father, the Irish barber in that smugly Protestant town, must have snapped the picture and he must have been proud. Any number of traveling showmen had wanted to take her on when she was a girl, and she won singing contests all over the state. Boys were mad for her.

Here was a snapshot of the young Desmond. His ankles and wrists shot out of a bellhop's uniform, the little round cap perched on a shock of hair lighter than it was now. He had blinked as the picture was snapped, and his smile was so broad I could almost hear him laugh. He was dressed up to play Toby, the perennial rube.

"All right, girls, take my hands, get into line . . . here we go. . . ." After dinner, when we were little, he used to show us his soft-shoe, bandy-legged, clacking his heels at the end and rolling his eyes. He'd gone to the Gladstone Hotel in Kansas City every summer during college, where the tent-show managers made their bookings, near where the tents themselves were manufactured and the candy and popcorn distributed. He'd had to fill in everywhere, not just act: He could play the harmonica, juggle oranges, make coins vanish and pop out again from our ears, and before its strings rotted away, show us how he'd played his two tunes on the fiddle—"Goodnight, Sweetheart," which closed every show, and "Pop Goes the Weasel."

"We played opera houses," he told us. "That's what they were called because opera was respectable and theater had an onus." He held his nose comically. "To this day, you'll find the booboisie of the land supporting grand opera but not stage plays. It's that old fundamentalist fear of getting too close to life. I don't want you girls to be respectable."

He did imitations of the candyman, pitching from the stage, which was laden with prizes, and before long we saw that reproduced on television, as we had recognized Toby *("Is anybody mad at me?")* in the hero of *Clapper's Corners* on the radio. "I got invaluable experience as a writer," he said. He had written two centennial plays for little towns and the preachy speeches the managers gave before the final act of every show. "I found I could write anything. It made a professional out of me."

When he told us the company was expected to take on the local baseball teams in the towns they visited, Portia and I listened skeptically. We knew that Desmond was no ball player. The fathers who worked on their houses and yards played ball, but he never did. "I was a lightning base runner," he insisted. But we were demon athletes ourselves, and there was evidence in his bearing and fastidiousness that Desmond might almost have been a sissy.

I found two pictures of Desmond and Muriel together, still young, but with an airy sophistication, a lightheartedness that made my throat catch. In the first they stood on the deck of an ocean liner. Muriel had one hand on top of her head, holding a hat in place. The other was stuck between Desmond's arm and his ribs. He held a glass of champagne aloft. Everyone in the background was looking at them; all were smiling broadly. The other picture had been taken indoors, in a parlor I didn't recognize, although pieces of furniture were familiar—Muriel was sprawled in a chair we had downstairs in our living room now. Her mouth was wide open, her head thrown back. Desmond stood behind her, laughing too. They were watching a plump, blurred figure apparently flinging himself across the room. A message was scrawled across the back: "Two phrases I'll never forget—'Where's the _____ gin?' and 'Is anybody mad at me?' With affection and gratitude, _____." I couldn't make out the name.

Portia's head appeared suddenly at the top of the stairs.

"Miranda!" she cried. "We forgot!"

"Forgot what?" I shoved the pictures back into their box.

"Tomorrow is Mother's birthday!"

About a month before, we had made a plan and put together our earnings from my newsstand and the wager Portia won when some teenagers on the block had pooled two dollars and bet her she wouldn't jump off the little roof over the neighbor's back door. We'd bought a pin the shape of a grace note to honor Muriel's singing and a square plaid kerchief for her to wear while she did her chores.

Muriel loved violets. "They bloom every year on my birthday," she said, and we were struck by the complacency of the remark and the suggestion that she had made some kind of deal with the environment. Violets *were* blooming in our yard already, but there weren't nearly enough of them. We would have to find more.

"All right. We'll get up at dawn and do it," I said. "We can make a cake when we get back." Making something Muriel made expertly was risky, but we hoped we might distract her from the arbitrary forces that drove her.

We passed another evening without Desmond, each of us busy with our own works, and Portia and I went to bed early, leaving Muriel with a book and Nobody placid on her lap.

Early the next morning we slipped out of bed and tiptoed past her shut door. Outside I led the way in a crouch through the great woody mock orange bush behind the shed, into the Rieger's yard for the first time. We scanned the windows for signs of life and found none. Muriel chased children and dogs from our yard, which mortified us. Next door, on either side, the Murphys and the Cochranes were permissive, but back here we were dizzy with fear of being caught. On we went, nevertheless, snaking through hedges from yard to yard, in search of big gardens.

We were acquainted with everyone on our side of the block—next to the Murphys was old Mrs. Young, who took in stray cats. Portia and I had picked out kittens twice and taken them home to "play with for the afternoon," hoping Muriel would adopt them, and she did. But the Murphys' vicious boxer had killed them both. Muriel said Nobody had come to our house thinking it was Mrs. Young's. She could take care of herself and hadn't been threatened by the dog.

Beyond the Irwins lived the disheveled doctor and his mother. Their house had a porch with ripped screens, weedy vines, and big old chairs misshapen from exposure to rains. We had gone to him for vaccinations. He had wheezed and sweated and left huge white welts on our inner thighs that Muriel said were disfiguring. But when Portia had a fever of 104, she had called him and he carried her in a blanket to his car and drove her to the hospital. She was in bed for six weeks with nephritis. I brought her schoolwork home to her every day and Desmond brought puzzles and books and toys every night—more than we had ever seen. It was after Portia got well that he began to stay away from home until late at night, and then sometimes for days at a time.

Portia and I found the first sizable bed of violets in a shady spot two houses beyond the doctor's and on the other side of the block. We had to climb over a picket fence. Portia steadied me while I went first, and when my feet hit the ground, a dog growled. We froze, breathing hard. Portia's face looked as if it had been thrown at her from a distance. The growling stopped, and we lit across the yard to the violet patch, bent double, grabbing stems until each of us had a handful. We rested under the cover of a beech tree. This was a fanciful tent, its branches like Rackham's sinuous drawings, and the ground was soft and rich. A bird above us scolded, and a squirrel skittered along with a beady stare. There was no other sound. In all of the houses, everyone slept on.

"Partners in crime," I whispered, but I didn't feel like a real criminal. It seemed that this peaceable kingdom of stocky houses, well-tended yards, enveloping trees, flower beds, hedges, and fences which I could suddenly see as if I were soaring above, had mysteriously become ours as we submitted to its purpose and harvested its crop. We were free to explore people's protected places—the rules were suspended.

Everything I looked at made a picture: the big white house there, its porch, the bluish shadow cast by the roof, the dappled lawn, the girl next to me on her haunches with a branch curving at an angle crossing the angle of her back. Impossible to end our mission now, while we were at large and the world so safe!

We gathered up our wilting violets and threaded through another privet hedge, flattening against the springy leaves to get our bearings. Ahead was a magnificent flower bed, "ablaze with color"—the phrase pleased me. Tulips thrust up in a joyous crowd, batched in reds, yellows, pinks, whites, and even blacks. *Safety in numbers,* I thought, and a terrible greed possessed me. I didn't even glance at Portia, assuming she must follow, but checked the house—a Tudor pile with leaded panes and no human sign—and streaked for the flowers. Portia fidgeted behind me while I picked.

"Miranda, they'll *know.* Tulips don't grow back."

"They'll never miss them. Mother will love them."

She inched forward and took a yellow tulip.

We threw ourselves into it, breaking long, juicy stems close to the ground, where they crackled and dripped. We picked so many we had to cradle them in our arms. Each glorious cup was implacable, so much more spectacular than violets that I considered discarding mine, but then decided two bouquets were sensational. I looked at the mutilated mass of gently twisting, overlapping, flowerless leaves with a feeling of complete, horrific achievement, and dashed for the privet hedge.

We ran all the way home, and when we got there, both of us had scratches on our arms and faces, tangles in our hair, and rips in our clothes. Neither of us wanted to go into the house, but we were afraid to stay outdoors, and the flowers would die out of water.

In the kitchen we got down to business with a silent, logical collaboration that was a variant of Muriel's syncopated routines. I found a gigantic fluted vase and a little bowl, and Portia stuffed the flowers into them. We tried to duplicate a breakfast from an advertisement in *Life*: a slice of golden toast with a pat of butter melting squarely in its center, a two-minute egg perched on a little china throne, a glass of orange juice, a folded napkin, and a cup of milk—since we didn't know how to make coffee and Muriel was particular about it. Portia fetched an envelope from the desk in the hall to represent The Mail. I wrote "Many Happy Returns, 36," with flourishes, hearts, and butterflies on a piece of paper, stuck it inside, and addressed the envelope: "To Mrs. Desmond Geer."

The arrangement was a still life—just what Muriel urged me to draw. "Why do you do all those hideous men's faces? Why can't you make pictures that will please people?"

We went up, knocked on the bedroom door, and waited.

"Well, what is it? What are you doing out there? Come in."

She had yanked off the little mask she slept in because she was sensitive to morning light, and raised her head to peer around, vexation and vigilance already spread on her face. The delicate ruffles of her pink nightgown ringed her throat. Nobody lay beside her, regarding us narrowly. As we marched forward, Mother's expression changed—it was like watching water run off a plate—to surprise, wonder, and wonderfully, delight. She didn't look thirty-six to me, lying against her pillows, but more like a bedridden girl.

"What is this? Gracious! Will you look!"

"Happy birthday to youu, happy birthday to youu, happy birthday, dear Motherrrr, happy birthday to youu," we sang. Nobody's ears went back. She stretched and dropped to the floor.

"Where did you get those tulips?" Muriel smoothed a place on the bed for the tray. "There are so many."

"We got these too," Portia said, holding the violets at arm's length.

"There are dozens, dozens! Miranda, answer me!"

Portia and I looked helplessly at each other. She shrugged. I had done it. I would have to take the heat.

"We just picked them."

"Just picked them? Where?"

"People's houses."

"*People's houses?* These came from people's private gardens? Whose?"

I shrugged again. Muriel flashed me a look of disgust, and lay back to stare at the ceiling. Portia reached for Nobody, but the cat slid under the dust ruffle. I gave the breakfast tray a little shove.

"This will get cold, Mama."

Muriel spoke in her tone of browbeaten irony. "Did anyone see you?"

"Oh, no," I assured her. "There wasn't anyone up."

"Well, I hope not. I sincerely hope not. That's all I need right now." She studied her tray. "This is very elegant, girls. There must be an awful mess in the kitchen." Then she smiled slowly. "Whoever they are, they're in for a surprise, aren't they? It must look like a hurricane hit."

"Robin Hood of the flowers struck," I ventured to say, and Muriel chuckled. We hovered, like courtiers, at a levee.

"You haven't read your card."

"How do you like your breakfast?"

"Is your father downstairs?" she asked. We shook our heads. This was just as well, in my opinion. I felt that we had tenuous enough influence over Muriel's mood.

"You both look as if you've been in a brawl, or a tornado." She tapped her egg sharply with her spoon. "I don't understand you, Miranda. What do you think happens to children who burgle gardens? Get another vase, Portia. They're smothered, all jammed in there together. Let's at least try to make them last."

Portia ran out of the room, and I stood with my head bowed and my hands in my pockets while Muriel took a few bites of egg and toast. "I could use a cup of coffee," she remarked. "I'd like to go away on a trip. I wish we were in a little *pension* in Paris. They bring you your breakfast—a pot of coffee and a pot of hot milk and croissants with butter and jam. You sit and eat and look out on to a little walled garden. . . . After a while, you begin to think in French."

Portia and I loved talk like this, but it annoyed Desmond, whose only foreign tongue was schoolboy Latin, and who had never been abroad. He wasn't musical, either, and Muriel's repertoire of Italian arias, German lieder, and French cabaret songs nettled him. "She puts a lot of Correggio in that," he would say under his breath, or, "I'm no expert, girls, but I'm inclina knock musick." I tried to imagine being in Paris. I wished I could think in French. I had made a list in my notebook of skills I intended to master by the time I was twenty, including languages and verses committed to memory, so that I could move through the world autonomously, like a Renaissance man, like Leonardo, who also drew grotesque faces and inquired into how things worked. My power would be enhanced if I could think in French!

I gazed about Muriel's bedroom while she ate. There was a rose-colored love seat opposite the bed, covered with sewing. The fabric was rife with pins, and when I moved it aside to sit down, I pricked my fingers. The walls were hung with heavy, antique frames that had belonged to Desmond's parents. Muriel had put reproductions of her favorite paintings in them: Renoir's girls at the piano, Manet's *Olympia*, a Bonnard interior, and a photograph of herself taken when she'd given a concert, long ago in a Vanderbilt's parlor. She wore a beaded black dress, its deep V neckline echoed by her arms and clasped hands. Her face looked proud and serene.

Various surfaces were covered with scarves and throws and antimacassars crocheted and embroidered by her mother, who seemed to have taken a needle to every bit of fabric and toweling that had come her way. On the dresser, too, were bottles of perfume, a few of them dating all the way back to Paris, and a leather-covered jewelry box full of extravagant, valueless old pieces that Portia and I loved to play with. A wooden screen onto which Muriel had pasted reproductions of Japanese prints, stood in one corner, hiding a dressmaker's dummy. A straight-backed Victorian chair lacked a seat—she planned to recane it. Coffee tins covered with wallpaper held pencils, scissors, needles, and buttons.

"What time is it, anyway?" she asked lifelessly. I sprang to attention. The clock was gone from her bedtable, and she never wore her watch. "I'm one of those people who can't keep time," she would say. "It's the electric charges in my body." I took this to be an interesting boast. "The clock is under the bed," she said now. "Will you look?"

I pulled it out. "Ten forty-five."

"Well and Sunday," she sighed. "Your father must be having a high old time of it."

Portia came back with a vase, blushing. "I couldn't reach it," she said. "I got a chair." Muriel set to dividing the flowers.

I had an inspiration. "Tell us about Genevieve!"

"Oh, do you think about her?" she asked, brightening. Genevieve was her French seamstress friend who lived above an Italian restaurant in some remote city neighborhood. To visit her we had taken the train, then a subway that eventually burst into daylight on elevated tracks and ran past rows of low apartment houses with people leaning on their windowsills, watching us rattle by.

Genevieve's was a hard-luck story, and it seemed to appeal to Muriel for that reason, though she was a puckish, lively woman when we met her, with a captivating accent and clothes that clung to her body, shiny with wear at hip, buttock, and elbow, and carried, Muriel told us, with "panache." I had an idea that romantic and sordid went together and gave Genevieve that special sway.

"I met Genevieve," Muriel began, "when I was living at the Arts Club on West Eighty-seventh Street. You remember that it was founded by Mrs. Vanderbilt and some other ladies so that young women who needed to pursue their careers in New York could have a place to live and studios to paint or practice in. Everyone was serious, and it was an exciting place to be. I had a terrible time convincing your grandparents to let me live there. In a certain way, they'd have been content for me to stay at home and marry Hubbard Mosely, who had waited for me to come back from Paris. He eventually owned a hardware store.

"Genevieve was recommended to me by Lily, who lived down the hall and was studying to be a concert pianist. We were going to give a recital together, and I had to alter a gown at the last minute. We got along so well, and it was a way to keep up my French. I soon discovered that she was being 'kept,' and that was certainly not approved by most people, by a rich man. Her clothes were beautiful, she ate in the best restaurants and saw all the plays, even though she went on working, to keep up her dignity. But when she introduced us, I found that he had messy whiskers and was quite old—well, he wouldn't seem so old to me today, but he did then, and he would seem *very* old to you—and that he had a wooden leg!" She paused, her eyes round, and let us imagine the stump, the leg with its leather strap by the bed. "It can't have been easy for her. But he had promised to marry her when his mother died. Finally he admitted that it was his mean old mother who was the rich one and just gave him a big allowance. The old witch found out about Genevieve and said she wasn't good enough for him and he'd have to renounce her, or she'd write him out of her will and leave everything to her cats. So he gave her up. Genevieve never saw him again, and she'd put up with him for seven years."

There seemed to be more than one moral to the story: Bartering for a better life, if you were powerless, landed you in the drink, and men couldn't be trusted. Genevieve had survived, of course, and still made her living as a seamstress. She had taught Muriel the art of dressmaking.

Muriel shuffled the tulips with deft, violent gestures. "These flowers make me feel reckless," she said. "I do miss Genevieve. Let's go see her. You girls can play in the restaurant garden if you want and have tortoni—and now we can *drive!* We'll sing in the car and we won't get lost. What a lovely idea, Miranda."

"Oh, yes!" Portia and I cried, clapping our hands.

Muriel jumped out of bed and snapped her fingers over her head. "Girls, make yourselves presentable. Try and please your mother on her birthday."

"Wait!" We had forgotten her presents. I ran to get them from my bottom drawer. When I returned, Muriel had raised the window shades. Clouds were passing before the sun, and light came to a place on the carpet, vanished, and reappeared. She was holding a dress aloft on its hanger. It was an old blue crepe she was making over: White basting stitches loped along the seams at the neck, shoulder, and hem. She seemed to have hoarded all of her old clothes. "You can't find fabric like this anymore," she would say, and set to renovating. But she changed her mind so often, taking new tucks and darts and letting others out as fashions changed, that practically everything in her closet was in transition. She had tried to adapt a few of her things to my figure, but I wanted to wear Desmond's old sweaters, and jackets with pockets like his.

"Is this *ma costume pour aujourd'hui?*" Muriel sang in her art soprano.

"Look, Mama, we got these for you."

She unwrapped the packages and gave us a melting look. "How sweet, how pretty," she said, putting them on her dresser. "I'll have to wear something plain, I guess, something drab. Genevieve will see just what straits we are in. What's the weather like? Portia, we must do your hair—disguise it somehow, and I'll cut it tomorrow. Cheer up, girls!"

She launched into one of the songs we liked best because it was funny. We were all singing at the tops of our voices and it was hard to tell: Had a door slammed just as we finished? Muriel stood still. For an instant the house was so silent it seemed to be inflated and softly rising. Then we heard footsteps and whistling: "Pop Goes the Weasel."

Portia lunged jubilantly for the door, and Muriel snarled, "Shut that!"

Portia turned to look at her, and in the interval I leapt to obey. The latch clicked. But why? Now what did we do? The day was dissolving, just as we'd found a way to celebrate it.

"Don't say a word," Muriel snapped. She took a satin robe from her closet, put it on, and vehemently tied it around her waist. Nobody rubbed against her leg and began to clean herself.

We heard Desmond come upstairs, pause, walk down the hall and come back again.

"Hiho?" he called. I could imagine him shaking his head. "There is an air of mystery about this place," he said. "Darling? Are you in there?"

"What do you want?" Muriel said disgustedly. "Comforting? Did this one make off with your wallet? Infect you?"

"You wrong me," he said mildly. "Where are the girls?"

"They're in here with me. We're celebrating," she said, with bitterness that stung me.

Portia was frowning. I figured she, too, was trying to fathom the thing about his wallet. But she said, "Daddy, it's Mama's birthday." Muriel threw back her head and folded her arms.

"Well, Portia, I know it is," Desmond said. "That's why I'm here. Will you come out and help me make my presentation?"

Muriel gripped Portia's arm and held her tight.

"Come, now," Desmond called. "Pray open the door to your chamber. My hands are full."

"Mother?" I asked.

"*One* of you vestals must be able to open up. . . ."

"Tripe. Feeble, disgusting claptrap," Muriel shouted.

"Billingsgate wit. She's about to relent. The worm in the heart turns. . . ."

"Where the hell have you been?"

"I've been working," he replied, offended. "I slept on Lou's couch."

"This even happened the night you were born, Miranda," Muriel confided. "Have I ever told you?"

There were sounds of struggle, then the doorknob turned and he sidled in, pushing with his shoulder. He bore a big round tray covered with tiny cakes no more than a couple of inches square, glazed to a creamy gloss, with chocolate swirls and garlands and little pink candles that burned flutteringly. He had a flat box in fancy wrapping pressed to his ribs.

"Wow!" he exclaimed, looking at the tulips. "How many suitors have been here before me?" He wore his bright yellow bow tie and a hound's-tooth jacket. His eyes, behind his spare glasses, the tortoiseshell ones, were dark hollows.

He and Muriel stood facing each other until she sighed and sat down. He put the tray next to her on the bed.

"Well, where did you get these?" she asked.

"Secret." I noticed the tray had a crown and the name of a hotel on it.

"Blow," Desmond commanded.

"Help me, girls," she said. "I assume there are thirty-six of these?"

"Naturally."

We all bent and blew the candles out.

"These are petit fours, girls," he said. "Only a day old. Quite a coup." We remembered our plan to bake a cake. Desmond handed Muriel the box. She pursed her lips and shook her head as she took it.

There were several layers of tissue, but the suspense was cruel because she pulled out only a pale blue garment trimmed in lace and ribbon and rosettes, with narrow straps. She stood and pressed it eagerly to her body.

"It's luscious. But Des, it must have cost—"

He smiled, took off his glasses and polished them on his handkerchief. " 'So far as my coin would stretch, and when it would not, I have used my credit!' " How blind he looked without his glasses!

"Your *credit*!" she scoffed.

He replaced his glasses and sneezed. "Is that cursed kitty in here?" Portia bent, drew Nobody from under the bed, and threw her out into the hall.

"There's more," he said, and drew a smaller box from a pocket.

"Perfume," she cried.

"Indeed. *Coup de Foudre.*" She snorted. But she wore a little smile, tipped the bottle onto her finger, and dabbed scent on her neck, elbows, and chest. The whole room seemed to reek. "Miranda, come over here and be feminine."

"Never." But Portia allowed herself to be odorized.

> "To throw perfume on the violet
> To smooth the ice, or add another hue
> Unto the rainbow, or with taper-light
> To seek the beauteous eye of heaven to garnish
> Is wasteful and ridiculous excess,"

Desmond recited, looking tenderly at me. "Miranda will find her own perfume." I went hot with pleasure. But then he said, "Girls, will you leave us alone, please? Your mother and I have some private matters to attend to."

"Oh, no, we don't," Muriel said.

"But we do."

I felt sliced in two by this exchange. I had committed a crime that day and I wasn't sorry—but where was the profit in it now? He said, "The newspapers are downstairs. Take a look. Later we'll all go out somewhere in that pink tank."

Muriel held the blue thing tenderly in her lap. "Miranda," she said in a fruity voice, "will you make me a picture? The best present is one you make yourself."

I nodded. Portia and I shut the door behind us. Downstairs in the front hall were the five city newspapers, four of them with comic sections that we usually spent all of Sunday morning with. I liked to draw my own dramatic scenes, using the inky black shadows that the Prince Valiant artist used. I ran down the stairs, picked up the papers, and hurled them into the living room, where they scattered over the floor and couch.

"What are you doing?" Portia cried, her mouth huge, the sounds coming out of it tiny. Muriel's door opened above. We both stared up. Desmond carried the tulips out and set them down on the floor.

"Sneezing to beat the band," he explained. "Must be the pollen." He went back inside.

"Oh, my God," Portia said, sounding just like Muriel. "Miranda, you'd better clean those up. What if they come?"

"They're not coming down," I said darkly. "You can do whatever you want, they won't care."

"Please, Miranda," she begged, but I waved her off and went down the hall to the side door. She would probably go in and pick up the newspapers herself.

I wheeled my bicycle out of the shed. Heated talk wafted from Muriel's window. Their inconsistency enraged me. I rode to our school a few blocks away and climbed up the stone blocks at the corner of the building, four stories, and heaved myself over the little wall at the top. I ran on the roof from one end of the building to the other, over the science room, the music room, and the third and fourth grade classrooms. I could see all the way to Brixton Road and to the railroad and the cement factory.

I narrowed my eyes and set my gaze to a point in the air just beyond my nose, but without letting any of the distant view go entirely out of focus. The result was the illusion of motion—I seemed to be sailing along through the atmosphere, and the trees and houses to be moving, too, but at a different speed. I tipped my head back and saw the clouds zipping along so fast I was dizzy and fell back to the roof in a heap. When I had lain still for a while, I felt refreshed enough to climb down. I didn't want to go home, but there wasn't anywhere else I could go instead.

Muriel was on the telephone. I went silently upstairs.

Portia was sitting on our bed. "You could have gone with Daddy to the city," she said. "They had another fight and he left. I cleaned up the newspaper. You really are dumb."

In the kitchen Muriel said, "Don't ever run off like that without telling me. I was worried sick." But she seemed exhausted, to me. "I have a headache," she said. "I'm going to rest for a while. We have an appointment with Mr. Peake tomorrow at four. Come straight home from school."

A wispy woman wearing an apron and a scolding expression led us into Basil Peake's cottage, which nestled behind a row of high cedars on a dirt road at the eastern edge of town. Muriel had supervised my selection of pictures to show him—tame scenes, including a series of illustrations for *Tom Sawyer* and some horses I had copied from one of his own books, in the school library. She had made me put on a dress, and self-consciousness inhibited my powers of observation.

"Look around. Here is how an artist lives," she instructed when the woman stomped away to tell Peake we had arrived.

The cedars, which hid the cottage from the road, also prevented much light from entering the wood-paneled front room. Everything was dark brown, except for some masculine plaids and paisleys covering the lumpy pillow-strewn chairs and couch. Portraits of racehorses and duck hunting scenes hung on the walls. Muriel gave it all a glance, sighed, found a mirror and looked into that. I studied three old rifles on hooks over the mantel.

The housekeeper beckoned to us from the doorway, and we trailed down a hall, past two closed doors and a kitchen, to a bright skylighted studio. I could see a stream, a pond, and a waterwheel outside, and they so enchanted me that Muriel had to pinch my arm to get my attention. She was not going to speak in peremptory tones now.

Peake was very fat and slumped in a swivel chair, as if the celebrity and ease his vocation bought also gave him leave to go to pot. He wore a flannel shirt, bush jacket, twill pants, and a little visored cap over shaggy salt and pepper hair. I could imagine him, in his chair, training one of the rifles through the window at ducks on the pond.

The whole time we were there he never fully opened his pallid eyes, but stared stuporously out from beneath their lids. A cigarette jutted from between two fingers, but he seldom took a puff or flicked the ash, which grew to over an inch in length without falling as I watched it, fascinated.

Muriel shoved the small of my back, nearly pitching me into his lap. "Show Mr. Peake your pictures," she commanded, and rattled on to him about my various achievements and ambitions. I placed them on his big table and leafed through them as quickly as I could. He made a few rumbling noises. Then he heaved himself forward and took up a pencil sharpened to a needle point.

"Pictures are worthless if they don't have life," he said in a deep, ragged voice. "Here's what you do." Muriel edged forward behind me and breathed across the top of my head. She was always consulting experts. Desmond seemed to take the opposite approach and was always questioning their authority.

He was an expert, after all. Neither practice seemed to ensure a broadening of abilities or successful enterprise.

Peake made a quick sketch of a running horse, scratching away rapidly, putting down many lines. His ham hand surrounded the pencil lovingly.

"This is the start. Rough. Spontaneous. Now you get yourself a pad of cheap, thin, see-through paper, like this." He looked at Muriel. "You don't have to spend a fortune on this, don't listen to anyone who says you do." He picked up a pad. "You take a sheet of this stuff and put it over your first drawing and trace another one, more refined. But you keep the life in it, see?" He worked over the horse, selecting a few key lines and cleaning up the drawing considerably. "Now you take another sheet and put it right over that one. And you keep going, until you have your final picture." He swiveled in the chair and pulled a book from a laden shelf behind him. There, drawn with the precision I admired in his work, was the same horse. "Keep it spontaneous, do you see what I mean? That's the method." He squinted up at me. "You stop at the drugstore down the road on the way home, buy yourself a pad like this, and try it, young lady. And good luck to you."

In the car Muriel remarked. "*Life* is just what your pictures have! He didn't even really look at them. They have life and drama, that's what comes naturally to you." We drove along and she seemed to struggle for tact. I was, after all, a child, and impressions were formative. "Well, he is not a great man," she said. "I think Miss Hill exaggerated his importance."

"I already do that, what he said," I told her, always eager for a chance to prove my competence. I took onionskin paper from the living room desk for my tracings.

"Do you? Maybe you're just as well off working on your own. You have the advantage of an artistic household. Perhaps mentors are for children who don't have that privilege. Even I never had a real one, just people who praised me." She turned into the parking lot behind the supermarket and my heart sank. What a trick! Now I would have to push the cart for her and hang around while she tried to beat the system here.

"You must do what's right for you. Follow your nature's dictates," she said, opening her door. "Come on, Miranda, we don't have all day."

I looked at the women getting in and out of other, more respectable vehicles, and at the back of the row of shops. It seemed impossible that our family must yield to this place or last very long here. But for the moment I had no choice but to tag along after her.

3

"They're not quite at a civilized age," Desmond cried. "What was it Bob Benchley used to say? 'There are two ways to travel —first class and with children.'" He winked over his shoulder at Portia and tossed his stub of cigarette out the car window.

She and I were crammed into the backseat with Lou Gregorian, Desmond's old partner from *Clapper's Corners* days. However I tried to contract my body, my right thigh pressed his left one; perspiration seeped in my armpits and I was afraid he could smell it. I was no longer a child; I was fourteen and Portia was twelve. We hadn't seen Lou for three years, since he'd used to give us the paraphernalia for sound effects to play with in the control room while we waited for the show to start. Lou had been like an uncle, a calm, indulgent, brownish, treelike man we could lean on while paler Desmond darted about, the keen showman. Sitting so close to Lou now made me feel explosive and uncertain, and Desmond's remark was humiliating. He was still obliviously busy putting on a show.

Desmond had amazed us by arranging our first and last family vacation. His friend Jules Levy invited us to spend a couple of weeks upstate in Old Chatham, a haunt for New York City artists and theatre people. Jules had composed incidental music for some of Desmond's programs and recently struck it rich with a hit tune, "Drop in the Bucket," which Portia and I heard moving up the charts on the Hit Parade on Saturday mornings while we washed windows.

"It's a crime," Muriel remarked. "His serious pieces have never been appreciated."

Jules and Lou were writing a musical comedy about Adah Isaacs Menken, the nineteenth century flamboyante. *Clapper's Corners* had long been cancelled. Responding to criticism that radio had become a pitchman's medium, the station had scheduled public affairs programs on Sundays, and Desmond wrote many of them. We had heard him and Muriel wrangling over Jules's invitation to him to help out with the book for the musical. Menken was one of Desmond's favorite characters. Muriel asked him how he felt, seeing that an idea he might have had was going to enrich someone else. Why hadn't *Desmond* begun the book? "He can't finish the show without me," Desmond had said.

The summons to Old Chatham, his inclusion in the project as "play doctor," seemed to flatter him. There was grateful grandiosity in his desire to take us along. I realized later that he must have been desperate, that his career was crumbling. But the visible battle was always waged with Muriel. Because I fought it, too, and avoided her, too, I was blind to his private pain. A part of me didn't want to go on this trip. My own temperament consumed me and made separation from what I was used to an imposition.

Muriel had packed clothes, cleaned up the yard, and closed and sealed the house as if we were leaving for years. I recognized the grim preparations as a hedge against hope. Her dependence on Desmond was tethered to the expectation that each new opportunity would end with another loss.

Years ago they had breezed away to country houses and been valued for their gaiety and charm, which I imagined lay in mothballs now in her closet, along with all the clothes she had worn. She was grudging on our behalf. "Miranda, you'll have to keep working on your painting," she told me. "Portia, take along your French book." Portia was a superior student, a whiz at French, able to accommodate herself to Muriel's vagaries at home and attract a following at school. I would glimpse her in her crowd of kids down a hall, animated, like a brush stroke.

I spent most of my time alone, my course clearer than my contemporaries'. Work qualified all other experience. For a year Muriel took me to painting classes at the Museum of Modern

Art. I disdained most of the museum's collection and was relieved when the instructor let me paint the dramatic situations I favored. I illustrated my favorite books and sometimes stories I had made up. It pleased me to look upon my vigorous strokes, apart from the forms they shaped.

I made a studio upstairs in the shed and earned spending money making pastel portraits of children and peoples' houses and designing Christmas cards, which Portia peddled when she baby-sat. Muriel harped on the subject of art school for me and college for Portia. We were fated to survive on our brains and talent and win scholarships.

Of the trip to Old Chatham, she said, "It's a wild goose chase. What producer will take a chance on Jules, with his reputation?" Jules had written incidental music for radio under an assumed name because he was on an industry blacklist. "You have to have real connections, not a gang of misfits who'll turn you in the first time someone looks cross-eyed at them." Desmond defended Jules, and I knew Muriel's harsh attitude came from scorn for his accusers. "He was naive," she said—it was her strongest denunciation of anyone—"but I suppose he's moved up in the world with that song." Yet she took an astringent interest in the project. Jules telephoned to say that he hoped she would help them out by singing the score as they worked. Her voice and interpretation would give them a feel for a song's effectiveness. She set to altering a sunsuit and some summer dresses of prewar cotton.

We had met Lou at the train station, where he stood in the shadow of the overhang, his suitcase at his feet. He looked rueful and boyish, and Muriel greeted him with the guilty exasperation of a mother who has forgotten, until now, that her child is waiting to be picked up. He went around to her window to give her a penitent-seeming peck, and I wondered if we'd seen so little of him because Muriel made him pay for something that might have happened between them once. But for all we knew, Lou was just a bad influence on Desmond, without practical sense, with an apartment in the city and a string of women who fussed over him. Muriel showed him a complaining solicitude, herself. "Give Lou some room back there, girls," she scolded, and that was when Desmond quoted Benchley.

I saw Muriel's eyes on Lou in the rearview mirror, cold blue
sentries patroling a Maginot Line. He looked just the same—a
pockmarked, kindly face, and spiky black hair. He spoke in the
sad, flat, cultivated cadence of Maine. He gripped his long legs
at the knees and leaned forward.

Muriel's head was fixed and her shoulders squared. Desmond's head bobbed like a plastic bird he had brought home
when Portia was sick, and set to drinking by itself out of a
cocktail glass, illustrating some principle of physics. We drove
to the Hawthorne Circle and Desmond sonorously recited all
the signs pointing to places we could go from there. We headed
north and came to a rise where the air temperature dropped and
the broad view of meadows and fields bounded by curly trees
with still shadows and blue, hazy mountains, made everyone
gasp.

Desmond waved his cigarette and told us about his previous
visit to Old Chatham. Did Lou recall when Dick Bassett had
that idea to track down the true American painters whose careers were skewed by the Armory Show? Desmond was assigned to George Luks—I, of course, had heard this tale before.
It was Desmond's patriotic interest that fostered my own in the
Henri/Ashcan circle. Desmond had found Luks in a rented cottage on the outskirts of town. They'd passed many an hour
drinking the sun down on the veranda of a former speakeasy
called The Rubicam. "His working days were virtually over,
though. We never did do the broadcast. Every now and then
he'd persuade a crone with a chicken to pose for him. But no
one really understood him up there."

Muriel snorted. "He was drunk as a lord. He could hardly
hold a brush."

Lou smiled at me. "Are you inspired by the countryside, Miranda?" he asked, and I went limp with gratitude. His kindness
in turning our attention to my art made me nervous, though. I
had prickly views. The incessant green of the countryside bored
me. I fished for a worthy response. Muriel shot a look like an
evil spell at Desmond.

"You never do mention what happened on the way home
from that jaunt," she said through set teeth.

"Muriel, darling—"

"The girls might be interested. They wonder why it is I have to drive the car everywhere. . . ."

He raised his hand. "Muriel, don't. How many times have we—"

Lou cleared his throat. "Listen, folks," he began. His arm was pressed against mine and I tried to move away. "Miranda, quit it!" Portia protested. I prayed that Muriel and Desmond would drop the issue. He'd had to surrender his driver's license on the way home from Old Chatham—we knew that. We could put two and two together. She fell silent. Lou said, "The light up here is different."

I might have explained to him that it was tiresome to draw trees with thousands of leaves, or to paint a whole canvas in variations of the same limey color. The jumbled villages we passed through did interest me. I wanted to paint the worn sidings of barns, and houses with tipsy porches along winding dirt roads, and leather-faced farmers in baggy overalls. I was struck by the picturesque. I wanted to wander around making pictures like Luks. But Muriel made that kind of life seem frivolous. How would I eat?

Luks and I had in common a talent for likeness. He had earned his living as a staff artist and caricaturist for several newspapers. He had believed himself, Desmond said, to be, along with Franz Hals, one of the "only two great artists in the world," and when his paintings began to sell—before he abandoned the city for Old Chatham—he portrayed himself romantically as an ex-boxer and war correspondent. However it had ended, his artist's life had been full of adventure.

"I can tell you about country living," Muriel chimed in, and told the story of her father swinging a chicken over his head to break its neck in their backyard in Babylon and then decapitating it with a hatchet, and how she'd refused to eat supper that night. Portia gasped as she always did when she heard that story.

We passed a large pond and I wanted to get out and sit at its edge, dreaming. Neither Muriel nor Desmond could swim—that was another way we children had been cheated of normal parents. Muriel's struggles to contain nature and Desmond's indifference to it contributed to the tension between them. I imagined swimming out to the middle of that pond, where they couldn't follow.

Desmond and Portia took turns reading road signs: SKUNK HOLLOW, BREAKWIND FARM, TURKEY TROT, RIGOR HILL. He recited his favorite Burma Shave verse: "She raced her chariot at eighty per/They scraped from the roadway/What had Ben Hur."

We stopped for lunch. I looked at Lou, but his gaze was on a field beyond a rail fence. He stood and strolled away to lean on it. A cow ambled across the field to meet him. "Will you look at that!" Desmond cried. "Soul mates!"

In the car he consulted a slip of paper. "It's not much farther. Take the next left, then a right."

Muriel halted instead next to a barnyard, and hailed a sun-burned boy about my age who was hitching a plow to a tractor.

"Which way to Old Chatham? We're looking for the Levy place," she shrieked. The youth peered at all of our faces, catching mine before I could duck, and pointed unhurriedly up the hill.

"This is it," he said. "Center of town's just over the rise."

"For Christ sake," Desmond said. Muriel thanked the boy crisply and we pulled away. I turned to look back and saw him staring after us.

We entered a dusty little square. Three barefoot girls wearing faded dresses squatted over a pile of sticks and stones they were playing with, and a pair of dogs frisked in the bright sunlight. On a white frame building morning glories climbed toward a big black-lettered sign: OLD CHATHAM INN FOOD GROG. Across from it was a general store with wide steps to a porch, and an ancient gas pump. Three roads led away, all lined with splendid trees casting deep shade.

Like a new character Desmond might have written in, a woman came out of the store carrying a bag of groceries. She saw us and gave a shout. "You're here!"

"Poppy!"

It was Jules's wife. "We're just around the corner," she said. Desmond got out and embraced her. The little girls in the dirt stared at them and at the car, which had been washed and simonized weekly in our driveway and was just as pink as ever. Poppy wore a long cotton skirt and she moved lightly, although her figure was statuesque. Her skin was very tan and her long dark hair hung down her back in a braid. She and Desmond set forth, arm in arm, and we nosed after them. Desmond had on a white shirt and trousers, and had slung his white jacket over his shoulder.

The road curved, and we crossed a little bridge over a hurtling stream that ran from a pond where a couple of boys were fishing and then coursed down a rocky incline. Portia leaned far out of her window and Lou sat with his arms crossed, pressed against the seat back to give me room to look. We breathed a damp fragrance. The houses along the road were set close together, but at arbitrary angles, as if they'd been dropped from a box. Everywhere we looked there were nooks and crannies. Portia and I might have invented the place, it was so cozy and diverting.

Poppy and Desmond vanished behind a lilac hedge and reappeared on a sheltered, rocky bank planted with succulents and ferns and leading to the wide porch of a brown shingled house. When Muriel stopped the car, I could hear the stream roar and saw, at one end of the mossy light-dappled yard, a chasm and a waterfall.

The front door flew open and Jules plunged out of it, his teeth gleaming under his dark mustache. He was physically imposing, like Poppy, but jumpy and indecisive, and his clothes looked too small for him. His welcome was full of worry: "We were afraid you were lost. I asked Poppy if she'd been clear about that turn off Forty-one—well, you must be baking."

Two girls, each a year older than Portia and me, appeared in the doorway. They were Rebecca and Charlotte. The latter hopped down to greet Portia with a big shy smile, but Rebecca remained on the porch, her hair a dense black cloud, her eyes stony, a burning cigarette in one hand and a book in the other. Boredom froze her features. I shrank in my seat. Muriel noticed, then, that I was still in the car, and ordered me to get out. Lou strolled around, stretching his long legs, a little smile on his lips.

Charlotte took Portia off to the room they would share. Rebecca leaned on the porch railing with one arm cocked and her hand in her hair, the cigarette poking out of it, Rita Hayworth. She stared at me speculatively and took a drag. "Shall I show you your room?" she drawled. "It's not really a room, but you have it to yourself." I followed her inside with my suitcase and paint box.

"Mark won't be here until tomorrow," I heard Jules say.

"Mark and Sybill," Poppy said.

"Mark who?" Desmond asked.

"You know, Yates, the actor, didn't I mention him to you?"

"Ah, an actor."

"And writer," Jules added. "He's just spent three months at that colony up the pike. Working on a novel. Very gifted guy. I thought we'd get his ideas too."

I turned to see Desmond's face in the doorway. He looked as if he'd swallowed something vile. *His ideas!* I imagined him thinking. An actor who calls himself a writer! An art colony! How Desmond would thrive at an art colony! What contempt Muriel would have for it!

Rebecca led the way along a hall to the back of the house. She wore some perfume and I followed its scent like an animal.

"What are you reading these days?" she inquired.

There was a lot of dark wood and white plaster hung with photographs of all the Levys and framed copies of Jules's sheet music. We came to an alcove with a single window and a narrow couch beneath it. "This is it," she said. "Take it or leave it." She flung herself onto the bed and watched me set my paint box and suitcase on the floor. "Well?" she asked. "*Do* you read?"

"Um, yes." I felt robbed of my reputation, unused to working at impressing anyone new. My thoughts clouded. "*For Whom the Bell Tolls,*" I muttered.

"Good Lord."

"*Tender Is the Night.*"

"You should read George Eliot," she said, and stood up. "But of course you paint. Who are your painters?"

She had me on the run, and I couldn't bear to be fatuous on this subject. I raced mentally along the corridors of the Metropolitan and the Frick, turned the pages of my book on Impressionists, my book of Americans, the engraved volumes on the leather-bound shelf. My painter was different every week. So far, I had had trouble with Cezanne, because his bathers were ineptly drawn. But my pantheon was crammed with others. I even thought of Basil Peake and of George Luks. I had rattled from one idiom to another. Now I hesitated too long. Just as Rebecca spoke again, I hit on the perfect choice: Caravaggio! But she beat me to it.

"Are you following the Abstract Expressionists? Aren't they getting at something exciting and pure?"

Abstract Expressionists definitely didn't interest me and I said so. "I like paintings of real things, subjects, dramas."

Rebecca didn't bat an eye. "But you must adore Titian," she said. "For what he dared to do—with paint and theme. *The Rape of Europa,* for instance." She pronounced the title with relish. "Well, let me know when you're ready. We have to set the table. Charlotte and Portia clear." She went out, then poked her head back in. "That's a highly original haircut," she said.

Under the window was a washstand with two books set on it between a stone and a brick: *Daniel Deronda* and *Pride and Prejudice.* I had already read the second one. That gave me a stab of triumph.

We assembled for dinner. I couldn't remember when I had last seen Muriel and Desmond sitting at table, eating, drinking wine, and laughing. When Poppy set out her platters and dishes, Desmond remarked on the "groaning board." I saw Rebecca stare at his lips, as if his corny good humor bore serious study. Poppy was an excellent cook—the real article. Muriel's efforts at home, which she linked to her exposure to Parisian cuisine all those years ago, seemed mere imitative gestures. Jules hopped up and down, checking on details, like a novice innkeeper. Muriel had nothing to do, although she offered repeatedly to help, and her gaiety grew shrill. I wondered how on earth she would manage here without her litany of tasks.

When we had finished our cold soup, chicken and aspic, and salads, the room was dim and Jules lighted a row of candles that dripped a rainbow of colors. Desmond's face glowed in the flickering light. He was keyed up to the point of indiscretion, reaching out to the company so ardently. I was afraid he would cast himself adrift. Muriel ignored him and shared some joke with Lou. She smiled tolerantly into his melancholy, ironic face, and released her hold on Desmond, Portia, and me. She softened, grew large and still, but Desmond bore down on the rest of the table like a freight train.

By that summer I had read most of the journals and fiction he had stashed in our attic. I knew things about his mind that I kept to myself, keeping count, but hoping that some benevolence in me would cancel the notes before they fell due. *A writer pays a terrible price for fatherhood,* he had written. *I sit here while the little girls splash in their bath, their voices like the voices of angels playing, and the sound exiles me from everything that has ever sustained my soul. They remind me of my mortality. I cannot write.*

Jules poured more wine. He tipped his chair back and Charlotte climbed into his lap and nestled against his big chest.

Desmond told the story of how he had named his daughters. Portia rolled her eyes at me. Muriel had told me that they had been so certain I was a boy, they'd told everyone I was called Timothy. Once, at the radio station, Desmond had introduced us to a comedian we worshipped as "Scylla and Charybdis." Now he told everyone that he and Muriel had waited so long for a first child, he'd felt like Prospero when a daughter finally came. But what a squalling, colicky, willful infant I had turned out to be! Hardly his idea of Miranda. He had made a mistake, sticking that one on to the first girl. To rectify it, when the second daughter came, he named her Portia, for contentiousness. But this Portia—he reached for her, nearly upsetting his wineglass—had shown herself to be the sweetest, most tractable of Mirandas. He had unwittingly reversed our order and meddled with our fates. Ah, what a determining fate inheritance was, and just think, the product of no more than mindless, brute coupling.

Muriel's head shot up.

"Brute?" Lou asked mildly.

"Mindless," Desmond repeated. Rebecca nodded sagely.

Charlotte and Portia cleared the table. Jules cornered Poppy and threw his arms around her. Everyone else drifted into the living room. Jules called out to Desmond, "Well, old man, we've laid it out roughly and we await your refining hand!" Desmond bowed. Lou and Muriel were bent over a scrapbook. Jules sat down to play. Soon, Muriel was standing with a hand on his shoulder, hesitantly sight-reading. Desmond sank into a deep wicker rocking chair with a book of Pope's verses and a highball glass.

"Come to the porch," Rebecca said to me. "We'll have plenty of chances to listen to that." Outside, crickets and tree frogs made a steady racket and the stream splashed prettily. Muriel trilled a few bars, fell silent, laughed, and picked up the phrase again. We could see the lights of a neighboring house through the sharp black silhouettes of trees. Rebecca lit her after-dinner cigarette.

"We owe a lot to your father," she said, sucking in smoke. "My dad was an unfriendly witness and no one else would hire him for over two years."

There was an interval during which she puffed and we stared fixedly at the inky depths between looming shapes. Rebecca alluded to something horrible and I cursed my ignorance, but I was pleased to hear Desmond praised. Muriel thought he was just a soft touch, with too much self-love. If he lived by his principles, they weren't rewarding him very richly. "A man of principle is bound to fail," I had heard him say once. What, exactly, was Jules asking him to do here? Was it possible that Desmond could help them write a hit show and turn our lives around completely? I shivered a little, with the excitement of that thought. Rebecca stubbed out her cigarette and said, "Come upstairs with me. We can read for a while."

I supposed she expected me to fetch one of the books in my room, and to be polite, I did. But when I appeared with *Daniel Deronda,* I found her already curled up with *Marjorie Morningstar.* She raised an eyebrow. "I'm working on a novella," she explained. "And there are some days when I can't think of anything but sex. He handles it rather well, in this." She returned to her page.

I laughed, but it was hard to attend to my thick book, and I knew hers wasn't as demanding. Sex had claimed me, too, lately, but I hadn't articulated my curiosity. I had made pictures. They were sacred, private explorations of the male physique. My drawings of bound, naked slaves after Michelangelo, of Saint Sebastian writhing at his post, the arrows sticking out around the scant cloth that covered his penis, of wounded prisoners twisting in agony culminating at the crotch, were hidden under my dresser.

Our mutual silence was broken from time to time by Rebecca's sharp laughter, which she unloosed without telling me what was funny. It seemed gratuitously to exclude me. But her hauteur and her patronizing interest in me kept my attention half on her until I was sleepy.

"I'll be writing in the morning," she said when I stood. "I can see you after that."

I intended to be gone all day with my paint box, part of a fraternity Rebecca couldn't join. Right now I would go down and open the box and finger the tubes and brushes, smell the oil and turpentine, name the painter's colors: vermilion, alizarin, magenta, cerulean, prussian, ochre, cobalt, thalo, cadmium, manganese, titanium.

I stopped to say good night to the grownups. Their laughter sounded dangerous, and broke off abruptly when I entered. The five chairs were drawn close in the gloom, as for a conference of minor gods. Muriel gave me a bright, blind look and Desmond wheezed and waved his glass. The house and people seemed suddenly so strange that I felt I could lose my mind. Their droning voices did send spectres dancing through my dreams when I finally slept.

The birds woke me, and I dressed quickly and went to the kitchen. It was only six o'clock, but Poppy was already there, making muffins. She didn't seem surprised to see me, nor to hear that I was off to work. She offered the cheerful, conspiring encouragement becoming to a mother and helped me pack a lunch. I lingered a while with her, until the muffins were out of the oven.

Outside I went to look at the gorge. Sparkling water, clear to the point of magnification, coursed over rocks, the patterns of its movement repeated exactly, so that I could draw it as if it were still. Sunlight spotted the streambed. I made some pencil sketches, with Leonardo's notebooks in mind.

A skinny man in an apron was setting out vegetables on sawhorse tables when I passed the general store. We exchanged a smile and a wave. I took the road veering away from the inn, up a little hill and down. A clump of willows in a hollow marked a stream. The spot was a jagged accent in the broad field. I thought about the attraction sheltering places had for me. I did love to climb and oversee the cutout shapes that lay between solid objects, defining them. But I was also stirred by the dense bower and its particulars. I worked too fast, greedy for the whole picture, and detail helped slow me down.

The desires to surrender and render raged with equal force. It seemed that I must paint what I saw not just because I wanted to, but because I could. All the drawings and paintings I had ever seen exhorted me. I stood in an artist's landscape, with an unruly empathy for it.

A dirt track led off the road. I walked along its sunny spine through a tunnel of trees. The course ahead looked endless. I flung myself down and squinted up through the layers of leaves. The rapt, kindled figure of Bernini's St. Theresa flew into my head.

It was dispelled in an instant by the sound of a nearby engine. I scrambled up and peered through a break in the trees. A boy on a tractor was cutting hay in a field, his brown back swiveled as he eyed the rig behind him and extended his arm forward to steer. His face presented a simple profile, shaded by a straw hat. This was significant form, an image revived repeatedly in my sources for pictures. I ran in a crouch along the hedgerow to get a better view. It was almost too easy: He was perfectly beautiful.

I made a few vigorous, suggestive strokes to work over later from memory and my instinct for his body's gesture. Insects dived at me and hay tickled my nose. Heat throbbed from below and pounded from above.

The noise stopped. He hopped down and crashed toward me. "What are you doing?" he demanded. It was the boy Muriel had accosted on our way into town. "You drawing my picture?" he asked, and lunged for my pad. I held it to my breast and tried to rise. "You give that here!" I fled. He chased me along the edge of the field. The grasses released humid fumes as we crushed them. It was hard to breathe. I stumbled and he caught my waist.

"Let me go!" I cried, truly frightened. His skin against my neck and arm was slippery. His face came around my shoulder, scowling. "You can't just do that," he said.

"I can too. I'm an artist. I can draw whatever I want."

He let go of me and laughed. "You're a girl. I wasn't sure at first, with that hair. You're the girl in the pink car. Let me see that."

I yielded the pad and touched my hair, which was cut for action. I wasn't insulted. What mattered now was the drawing.

He squinted at it and took off his hat. "That's me? Well, it resembles me." He struck a comical pose. "I'll model for you. We'll do like they do in art school."

We both knew this was a ribald suggestion. He stared hard for a moment at my face. "You're with the summer people in town. You want me to show you things?" I nodded.

He let me draw him while he worked unaffectedly, and then he took me exploring, along a stream where fish darted to a large flat rock he lay down on, grinning up at me. We saw a cave where porcupines lived, but did not appear, and a pond with a nest of goslings whose parents jeered, but let us approach. He was tender toward everything we saw.

His name was Eugene W. Boice. He and his father farmed six hundred acres with two occasional hired men. He was a grade ahead of me, but when he was needed on the farm he skipped school. His brother had died at the age of three and his mother hadn't been the same since. But recently they'd had a miracle in the family. His grandmother's heart had stopped beating. They rushed her to the hospital and got it pumping again. She had told Eugene that while she was dead a beautiful glowing light shone all around her and celestial music played. It rid her of the fear of dying. She was ready to go again, any time.

I loved the way his overalls looked, the little twist to his mouth when he spoke, and his husky, manly voice. His feathery hair was the color of the dirt in the road where the sun baked it. We moved fast because he didn't have much time. There was always work, and his father kept a sharp eye on him. "But you come tomorrow," he said, pointing to a stile. "I'll be right there at noon, when I'm done with the barn."

On the way back I passed Rebecca leaning on her bicycle and talking across a picket fence to a stout elderly woman with a sharp face under a great floppy hat. Rebecca hailed me. The woman said something about my paint box in a thick accent. Rebecca interpreted. "Do you study, Madame wants to know."

I told her about the museum class. The woman grunted. "That is the beginning," she said. "To copy the Masters." Rebecca told her we'd better be going and that she looked forward to sorrel soup. They shook hands and I thrust mine out too.

Rebecca wheeled her bike along beside me. "Did you realize who that was?" she asked.

"Madame Deltail, a French woman." Muriel would want to know about her.

"Deltail's widow—the dealer," she said. "And before that she was married to *two* of the greatest painters of the twentieth century!" She named them and I knew who they were, but wasn't greatly impressed. "Think of it!" Rebecca said. "What a career! She has slept with three geniuses! You ought to pick her brain. It's as if I had a chance to meet Frieda Lawrence. She's coming on the Fourth. She always does. Last summer we had two Broadway stars and a member of ASCAP." This year they were going to all that trouble just for us. The Levys celebrated the Fourth very grandly, with a barbecue and fireworks, not just firecrackers and sparklers, but every kind of exploding radiance in the sky. Portia and I had heard all about it.

"Where have you been all day?" Rebecca asked.

"Drawing."

"Oh, may I see? I have an eye."

I wished, in a way, that she might see with her eye into my depths and fall back in awe, but I dared not share my experience with her. Nearly all my day's work was pictures of Eugene.

"They're not ready," I said.

"I understand . . . Mark Yates is here, and Sybill. They're having a tiff. I saw her weeping in the garden. I'm following them, for material. He looks like the hero of a novel."

We could hear the piano and Muriel singing in the house. On the porch a handsome young man was backed up against a corner post. His face wore a pained, obliging look, as if he were struggling to hear. But Desmond, leaning into him, an arm upraised, was in full cry.

"Oh, don't be modest," he was saying. "*Someone* has to scale the walls of convention. We *do* need new forms, I agree completely. The age of Tolstoy, Flaubert, Hardy, even Proust, for Christ sake, is over and done. What can they possibly tell us about our lives?" His voice dripped irony.

Yates saw us coming, and with a strained little smile, ducked around Desmond, who gulped from a glass, tracking his quarry over its rim with mordant eyes. Rebecca introduced me breathlessly. Yates's neat features looked weatherworn close up, and his eyes darted past me to the yard. A young woman swayed in the distance, a bunch of wildflowers in her arms, her long skirt brushing the grass. "Let me just see . . ." Yates muttered, and jogged down to her. He put his arm around her shoulder and swayed with her while we all watched.

"Have a good day, darling?" Desmond asked. "See many scenes out there?" He sat heavily down.

I went into the house. Muriel was next to Jules at the piano, singing a few phrases over and over, frowning with concentration. Jules's big hands moved nimbly up and down the keys and his gentle voice prompted her. Lou lounged off in a corner, his feet outstretched, fingers laced over his belly and a seraphic smile on his lips. He tipped his head to me as I passed.

Portia and Charlotte poked their heads over the stair railing. "Miranda, how does the general keep up his sleevies?" I stared at them. "With his *armies*!" they chorused, and fell back out of sight.

"God, Portia," I said.

At dinner Jules raised his glass to Muriel. "Our girl is still a star." I felt a choking pleasure. They fell to gossiping, Lou and Desmond, Muriel, Poppy and Jules, and I let their voices wash over me. Portia and Charlotte went ouside to play hide 'n' seek with children up the road. I sat on the windowseat, drawing the room and everyone in it. Muriel read the script. Desmond spoke insistently to Lou about someone.

"He's all right."

"Yes, he's all right."

"He's not a bastard."

"No, he's not."

"He'd *like* to be a bastard. . . ."

Sybill, pale and preoccupied, walked up and down before the bookshelves, plucking out a volume here and there, leafing through it, sighing, putting it back. Finally she drifted upstairs. Yates marked time for a few minutes, then followed.

"Who is Sy-y-bill, who is she?" Desmond sang, softly.

Before I went to sleep, I got out all of my drawings and looked them over. These might be studies for a major work: I had a model, a theme, like the Masters. Painting was surely the most privileged of vocations!

In the morning Jules, Desmond, and Lou shut off the living room and went to work. Desmond emerged carrying a sheaf of papers and his glasses. He had set up his typewriter in a little garden shed, covered with wisteria, behind the house.

Muriel clattered downstairs. "I'm late," she told me. "I stayed up way too long. Miranda, this role is so demanding—he's making something extraordinary." She threw a glance toward the kitchen. "Are you being helpful to Poppy? We mustn't leave all this work to her."

A little chill came over me and I didn't know why. Muriel knocked on the living room door, opened it and slipped inside. I wandered back to the kitchen, but Poppy wasn't there. Out back Desmond pecked at his old Remington. I crept to the door of the shed. His spine curved over the machine and a cigarette hung from his lips. He squinted against the smoke. A finger of each hand leapt at the keys.

"Hello," came a faint voice behind me. It was Sybill.

"Hi."

"Your father writes with such passion," she said, her face stupidly blank. "I like to see a man work. I hate it when they can't." She gestured with a pale, thin arm. She seemed immaterial, disconcerting, and needy.

"I'm a poet," she confided. "I don't think these people like me. Are you the one who paints? One of you is a poet too—that dark girl. I hate it when they all talk about politics. My parents are like that, but in a different way. They put all their feeling into some single issue, usually me." She picked up a piece of her skirt and dropped it. "I don't think artists can expect to have personal happiness in life." She looked straight at me for the first time. "I don't mean to depress you."

"Ah, Sybill," Desmond exclaimed from his bower. "The bleak and sinuous Sybill." She laughed and glided toward him. "This young woman writes poetry, but she looks to me like some contemporary muse." A crescendo sounded in the house. "Where is your Mark?" he asked conspiratorially. "Is he in there with them? They were going to ask him in. I don't think musical comedy is exactly his medium." He removed his glasses and rubbed his eyes. "He and I had a dispute," he said humbly.

A little breeze rustled the wisteria, surrounding us with its thick odor. "Well, Miranda," he said. "I'm working on a pretty funny passage. I think you'll like it. They've made me a doctor." He turned and reentered the shed. Sybill fingered her skirt and I hesitated, uncertain what was expected of me.

"Don't mind me, please," she said.

I hurried to the kitchen to look at the clock. It was two minutes to twelve! I raced to my alcove, grabbed my paint box, and set out for the stile, running nearly all the way, throwing the box from hand to hand. I climbed up and perched there, commanding the field. Eugene was nowhere to be seen. I waited for an hour or so, as I judged by the sun. It was hot and still, and eventually I felt betrayed. He had tricked me, but I was too ashamed to hunt him down and demand an explanation. Butterflies fluttered insolently under my face and flies glued themselves to my skin.

I wandered along the road and came to a steep rise. Beyond it lay a hamlet of four neat white houses and a little cemetery. A few yards away an old man sat under an oak tree. I saw that he was painting. He turned to peer from beneath his floppy hat and grinned. His eyes were milky and his mouth loose with ravaged teeth.

"Hello, hello," he cried. "Magnificent light, isn't there? It reminds me, actually, of Provence. Now, would you expect that?"

The smell of his paints lured me. Twisted little tubes lay in a box like mine, with bottles of linseed oil and turpentine. He was painting the scene of gravestones and houses, working now on puddles of blue shadow. He dabbed at his old palette. "What do you suggest? A little of this cobalt, perhaps?" He looked around opaquely at my chest. I watched him deepen the shadow. "Here's something amusing," he said. "I'll be buried right down there before long. Everything I'm recording will outlive me. Those apple trees were planted before I was born. Are children interested in such things?" He indicated my paint box. "Have you been painting? I haven't seen you about."

I told him I was visiting the Levys. "Well, then you haven't time to look long enough. I've painted this glorious view many times and it still has things to teach me. You're welcome to sit right here and join in, if you like."

But my interest in him was grudging and aimless. Perhaps I could sit apart and do a sketch of him—but no, I shrugged that notion away. His hand shook. The boundless view was made shrunken and equivocal by his palsied, deliberate strokes to the canvas. Heartlessly I left him, and he waved me on without looking up.

Children were riding bikes and throwing sticks to a couple of dogs in the square. I sat under my cloud on the steps of the store and no one paid me any attention. The sun glared off the white walls of the inn. Its door stood open, a little black abyss, and every now and then laughter drifted out of it. There were three battered cars parked in front, gleaming in the sunlight, and I wondered who could be idling there at this hour.

Hollyhocks bloomed behind a fence to one side of the building and I wandered over to examine them. When I neared the door, I heard Desmond say, "Admire as much as you can—most people don't admire enough—"

I hastened through the door. The room behind was dim as limbo, and people sat on stools along the bar, their heads and shoulders lurking in the mirror above the tiers of bottles. I spotted Desmond's steep profile at once, and then Sybill's. Her wispy hair glowed and her head was bent modestly. Desmond was turned away from her, gesturing to a bald-headed man in a shiny suit and skimpy tie. He didn't see me until I had marched all the way to the middle of the bar.

"Miranda!" He glanced behind me. "Are you looking for me?" I shook my head. "Well, I want you to meet Mr. Eigenbrodt. Mr. Eigenbrodt, this is my elder daughter. She is one of those who will command admiration. She is an artist already." We shook hands, and Desmond beamed. "Mr. Eigenbrodt has a proposition and I like it very much. He thinks we need a real hotel in these parts, and what interests me particularly is the idea of entertainments—a stock company, cabaret, out of town tryouts of new plays. Think of it, good food, good drink, we could persuade some of the writers and poets around, have speakers, our own little Chatauqua, our own little lyceum. The audience is here. The money is here. The talent is here. We're discussing his idea."

I stared into the eye of a stuffed buck hanging over the bar. Beyond Mr. Eigenbrodt a couple of slack-jawed men in overalls sat and peered shamelessly at us, nodding and grinning and fondling their sweaty beer glasses. The bartender leaned on a pile of napkins, ticking off items on a list in a folded newspaper.

"Your mother doesn't know I'm here, does she?" Desmond asked. I shook my head. "She has warmed to her role," he said gently. "She's yearned for something like this for a long time. I hope you don't feel neglected. It gives her so much pleasure."

"I don't."

Sybill slid off her stool and went to the jukebox. "Play us a tune," Desmond called, fishing in his pockets. Mr. Eigenbrodt came up with a coin and gave it to her. She looked over the music menu.

Desmond drained his glass and held it at arm's length for study. "Well, Mr. Eigenbrodt," he said, setting it down, "we must talk again. I think it's a grand scheme. I want to be part of it. It's an excellent investment, in every way."

Eigenbrodt produced a business card and gave it to Desmond. "We can put together an operation you people will be proud of," he said. "Locally owned shares and management. I'm pleased to be dealing with as distinguished a gentleman as yourself. This is very promising, very much so."

They stood with their hands linked, and then Desmond made an arc of his arm for me to walk under. Sybill came along behind us.

The sunlight outside was blinding. We all blinked, and Desmond groped for his pocketknife and a bit of wood.

"I don't think we need to mention this to anyone," he said. "I like these sincere, shady types. It's good to find out what they're up to, occasionally." We ambled along, and I noticed that he wasn't completely steady on his feet.

"Let's take a look at the water," he said when we could hear it splash. "Let's rinse our minds." To my relief, Sybill drifted on toward the house. Desmond and I ducked under some branches and leaned on the partial wall above the gorge. It was cool, and we had to raise our voices over the roar of the waterfall, which lent complicity to the moment. The pool was so clear we could see every immaculate stone.

"How deep is that, I wonder," he said.

"I can't tell. The light bends. I can ask Rebecca."

"Ummmm." He picked up a pebble and dropped it. We watched it settle on the bottom. "Do you know that people used to decide guilt and innocence by ordeal?" he asked. "A person accused of a crime was thrown into a body of water. It was presumed that God would make the water accept him if he was innocent. So if he sank, he went free—that is, if they fished him out in time. Judgment by one's peers is a modern idea."

"People make mistakes," I said.

"We're not infallible. We suppose we're rational. We don't wait for God's judgment. But there are those who think that if a man sinks, these days, he's guilty. It's a complicated question. You'll work it out for yourself in time."

The stream poured a ceaseless flow into the basin. It startled me to hear Desmond speak of God's judgment. He hated superstition and had told me he'd been converted by college philosophy courses to lifelong atheism. The few times I'd been dragged to church by Muriel, who put in stints with three different choirs, I had stood with my lips sealed when prayers were recited, preserving my integrity as a nonbeliever.

"Well, we'd better finish what we've started," Desmond said. "You know, Miranda, I am very proud of you. You will come to have pity for life and the living."

I reddened—he was practically shouting—and froze while he turned and walked off. Then I hurried after him, and might have thrown myself around his waist, but he was already on the lawn, in full view of the house. "I'll just get some coffee," he said, and went to the kitchen door.

Muriel was in a corner of the porch rocking, with a script on her lap. She smiled at me, "Are you having fun? I must get out for a walk, at least. I haven't had to work so hard in years." She lowered her voice. "They've decided to give a concert of some of the songs on the Fourth. Like a backer's audition for the neighbors. An audition for me too. God, this music might have been written for me, Miranda."

Her words fluttered to my brain, like leaves on a drain. "You mean, you think they might want you to do it—in New York? In a real show? On Broadway?"

"Well, I don't *know*," she said irritably. "All I can do is give my all. They haven't said a thing about casting yet."

She looked different—perhaps it was just the scarlet scarf tied around her forehead and the girlish anklets in her sandals which were incongruous with the old rocking chair. She pursed her lips. "Did you see that Sybill slithering past? She always looks as if she doesn't know where her next meal is coming from. She's supposed to be some kind of poet. What on earth can Mark Yates see in her?" She snorted. "Some men get so taken over. They lose all sense."

"She said she didn't think you liked her."

"She what? I haven't said a word to her! Incredible!"

She scanned a few lines of the script and I withdrew. "Miranda," she called. I returned. "I wish you'd spend more time with Rebecca. That was what we planned, and it looks snotty for you not to. Portia is having a good time with Charlotte. I'm tired of always having to count on her. Take advantage of this opportunity to have a friend, if nothing else."

Rebecca was not in the house. I put my paint box in my alcove and gazed despairingly out the window. The backyard, hemmed in by woods, looked like a trysting place. The carpet of fine grass was lush. From the shed came the clatter of the typewriter, but not for very long at a stretch, and with extended intervals of silence. I saw a flash of color in the wall of green, and stared at the spot. In a moment Eugene's face bobbed up, a few feet away. He moved warily, with a foolish look of commission, apparently spying. I ducked away from the window, ran out the front door and past Muriel without attracting her attention.

I looked along the road for a path into the woods. Here and there, through the trees, the house showed up. Then I saw Eugene's blue shirt. He was sidling along behind the shed. The typing had stopped altogether, and only his concentration prevented his hearing my approach.

"You're breaking the law," I said.

"Gosh!" he exclaimed in a hoarse whisper. "What in heck are you doing here? I was trying to see if you was in the house or not." He beckoned and skittered back to cover.

"What do you care if I'm in the house or not?"

"What? What do you think I care?"

I glowered at him. I wanted solacing or an admission of wrongdoing.

"You don't go peeping at peoples' houses."

"But I was looking for you!" His hands waved from his buttoned sleeves.

"Why don't you ring the doorbell then? Why don't you telephone?"

He shook his head impatiently. "I couldn't do that. I've never been inside that house." He glared back at me. "We lost a calf this morning. I couldn't get away."

I began to walk. He didn't follow. The claims on his time were humiliating to me. I had attached myself to an idea of my own allure beyond all reason and seen it exploded by the plain facts, briefly escaping my mundane existence only to be at the mercy of his.

He sighed and plunged after me, splintering twigs underfoot. "Did you wait at the stile?" he asked. "Is that what's got your goat?"

"I was there for a while. I had other things to do."

"Well, I'm sorry. Daisy calved and we saw something was wrong. The baby was born dead. It took hours. Dad cut it up but we couldn't see what was the matter."

I recoiled from the repulsive image.

"Is that your father in there?" He nodded toward the shed. "Yes."

"He was typing. Now I guess your mother's gone to him."

I held my silence. "It's bad luck," he said. "Third one we've lost this season." I was unmoved. He drove his fist into his palm and looked away through the trees. Then he ran his hand through his hair. I knew this repertoire of gesture well—my Tom Sawyer, my Huck Finn, my Lancelot, had all used it when discomfitted by events.

"Look here," he pleaded. "If you're just going to be mad—"

"I'm not mad." His eyebrows rose and the planes of his cheeks gleamed. A few little whiskers showed beside his ears, and a goat's beard of fuzz under his chin.

"I came all this way just to tell you . . ." He jammed his hands into his pockets and blew out his cheeks. I knew that what I wanted was impossible and unfair. He could not make himself available to me whenever I willed it. He could not be my secret companion and show himself at the Levys too.

"So, I got to go," he muttered. "You don't want to see me anyhow." He lifted his chin to see how I took that.

I reached for his hand. He drew closer. "I'm being mean," I said, all nerve. "Wait a minute. I don't want you to feel bad." The sound of this was rich and soothing.

His eyes went molten. I nearly laughed, but though my deliv-

ery and his syrupy expression were like playacting, the force of
something ineluctable lay behind them. I stared gravely into his
eyes, and he immediately shut them. He looked so innocent, I
had a twinge of impatience. Eugene was no savage I had stumbled over; he was tamer than I was, a boy out of one of the
stories I had used to make up and illustrate, a farmer's son with
his whole life coiled inside him, ready to roll, like the suc-
ceeding contours of a plowed field.

I took his head in my hands and grazed his lips with mine.
His eyes flew open. A little grunt escaped him, and he fixed a
look of inert magnetism on me. I felt an almost world-weary
calm. "Eugene," I said, direct from my chest, and held out my
arms.

He gripped me around my waist, stooping a little, and
pressed his damp face into my neck. My body felt huge, but he
lifted it and carried me a few steps, as if the challenge of the
moment called for a feat of strength. Then he set me down and
butted my face all over with his soft mouth, his hands spread
on the small of my back.

He had me in a powerful clinch, but I was protected not just
by my origins—who I was, and what I knew—but by my future, as well. I had a ticket to wherever I wanted to go, absolute
freedom. I felt like Winged Victory. With a virtuoso's finesse, I
softened my lips and offered them up. He adjusted the pressure
he put on them. Signals flew between our mouths. It was as if
we were performing a delicate task with only our lips and
tongues—untying a wet knot or picking a lock.

When my vitals shifted and throbbed, I was unprepared for
the feeling. We parted for an exchange of stuporous looks. Our
mouths fastened again, sucked the sinew from our legs, and we
sank to the earth, still kissing.

But when we landed, he pulled away and shook his head like
a dog struggling out of a pond. "Oh, Miranda," he whispered.
"I got to go, I got to go, my dad—" His look of abject gratitude
seemed out of keeping with events. We were *both* getting something out of this, and I felt as if we were sharing a lethal, fascinating toy.

He got to his knees and spoke earnestly. "I can't get back
here today. Tomorrow we hay all the fields past Cochrane's.
But Miranda, if we had a signal, I could throw a stone, say, at

your window, when I get a chance to come. Show me which one it is."

"I can't just sit by my window all the time," I said indignantly.

He frowned. "No. Maybe you could come find me. But if my dad sees you, he'll have my—" he blushed. "You try it, though. Come to the stile tomorrow around five."

I agreed. There was no point in holding out because he had let me down once. What I could have from Eugene, now, was sensational.

After he left I wandered in the woods for a while. I was relieved to be alone, physically numb and content with my immediate memories. I had a taste for blind pleasure. Love and oblivion were one.

4

When I emerged from the woods, Portia was standing forlornly in the middle of the road, calling my name. She had found Desmond, apparently dead, his head lolling over the back of his chair. Afraid to approach him alone, she had come to find me.

"You're hysterical," I told her, but dread underlay my impatience. We tiptoed into the shed. He reeked of whiskey. "Dad, Dad," we said, shaking him, and then gave up trying to rouse him and worried instead about what excuse we'd make when he didn't show up for dinner. But he did show up, his gestures and speech elaborate. Everyone seemed to give him a wide berth, even Muriel, who was in a brittle, gleeful mood.

The next day Jules and Lou passed under my window, arguing.

"I've tried to pin him down. But you know how he can be, evasive and promising the moon and the stars. . . ."

"Well, Jules—"

"It's a game."

"You know better than that. Look at the Swinburne scene. It's brilliant."

"I want to talk to Muriel—"

"No! Leave her out of it. She hasn't been so happy for years." They crossed the yard. It startled me to hear Lou speak passionately and so solicitously of Muriel. He almost played the tender husband's part. It reproached me. I wanted nothing to do with Desmond's difficulties and there wasn't anything I could give Muriel, nor anything I wanted from her.

I remembered an afternoon when I was five and we still lived in the city. Muriel had taken Portia and me shopping. When we came out of the subway, tired and cranky, it was raining hard and she ordered us, astonishingly, to take off our patent leather shoes, to preserve them. She hustled us gaily along, holding a newspaper over our heads, and called a halt at a corner when a siren wailed.

"Look, girls," she cried. "Fire engines!"

But the fire engines had careened around an earlier corner and we waited there in vain for the treat. I had pitied her for this plain, futile attempt to please us. Small moments of that sort were already in contrast to the larger reality, which consisted so often of struggle and unhappiness. When Portia and I got into the bathtub together at home, the water ran pink with blood from the cuts on our feet. But what I remembered afterward, when I thought of the day she had let us go barefoot in New York City, was Muriel's disappointed cry at the fire engines failure to come our way. When I was five, or six or seven years old, and saw her buffing her nails or putting up her hair to go to the theatre, or clipping tips from periodicals to make easier the tasks that filled her mortal hours, I wanted assurance that something could make her happy. She did nearly everything alone, and that was how anyone had to live and work, finally. How achingly poignant it was. Desmond had left us to her, left her with only children for companions. Now she rehearsed for her "audition" and catered to Jules. I stayed away from her.

Rebecca seemed to avoid me too. She affected concentration on her notebooks when I passed, but I noticed she narrowed her eyes at me sometimes. She didn't seem to be any lonelier than I ever was, but still, I knew I had disappointed her by finding my own way.

I saw Eugene just once in those three days. We were shy and circled one another uncertainly, until he acknowledged that he was pressed, as usual, and had only a minute. With that clear he let me know what was on his mind.

"You got a boyfriend at home? Do you do this with him?"

This was irrelevant, in my opinion, but I understood it and could reassure him. He kissed me in thanks, and we pawed at one another until we heard a tractor approach.

"Hide in the grass!" he ordered, and ran like a rabbit.

I peeked out and saw an immense, red-faced farmer in a vi-sored cap and overalls that fell open at the top, revealing rolls of fat as colorless as the moon. He stopped his machine when Eugene ran up, and let him climb up behind. They drove away, neither one looking back. Eugene had put his arm around the man's neck—could that be his father, the one so gross, with a braying mouth, and the other lean, with lips that had stirred mine? I shuddered at the thought, but it tickled me too. Eugene's caution was justified, and our drama deepened.

The Levys began to prepare for the holiday. Jules drove somewhere one morning and returned with cartons of fire-works. Poppy hummed over pots of vegetables, pâtés, and bar-becue sauces. Sometimes Sybill hung about the kitchen, debat-ing in a whiny voice whether she ought to return to the colony or go to New York or take a cabin alone near the ocean, which stimulated her imagination, but made her sad. Yates was sched-uled to read from his novel, and he sat polishing it under a tree out by the road, where an occasional car dusted him.

Eugene left me a note at the stile, written in block letters. It was a romantic gesture and gave me something to keep, so I overlooked its clumsiness. He would come get me after it got dark. I should meet him at the waterfall and we could watch the fireworks together. Exclamation points, X's, and hearts. I put the note in my paint box. I had done very little work, so I made a self-portrait for July Fourth, compromising nothing—hair still cropped like an urchin's, and each eye with a slightly different cast, the way everyone's are.

The Fourth was the hottest day yet, and a group trooped over to the pond in late morning to cool off. Portia, Charlotte, and Rebecca swam near the bridge, but I stood leaning on its rail, protecting my body from acute sensation. Lou stroked effort-lessly back and forth for a few minutes and went back to the house, where Jules and Desmond were said to be putting the finishing touches to their songs. Mark Yates, beautiful in a bathing suit, and Sybill, wraithlike but with long floppy breasts, sloshed in waist-deep water, talking in undertones. I felt restless and ran off down the road. Portia called after me and I pretended not to hear.

There was already a hint of festival in town—more cars than

usual and a little crowd talking on the store steps. A girl passed
on horseback, her face blank and her body rolling with the
animal's gait, absorbing its shocks. I discovered an alley I hadn't
noticed before, alongside the store, and followed it past an
overgrown field to a little shanty and barn so crowded together
that plants and buildings seemed to obey the same natural law.
A little fence ran from the barn to a well, and another enclosed
the shanty. All along the fence whirligigs were perched, their
blades causing woodsmen to swing axes, donkeys to buck,
monkeys to leap, cows to be milked, owls to spoon in pairs.
Miniature wooden farm animals grazed among the flowers too
—roosters, hens, chickens, pigs, goats, and rabbits. There were
two tiny windmills, and rocks painted like pieces of candy. At
first I didn't see an old man, who had been kneeling, then he
popped up near the well, holding a trowel, a sleeveless under-
shirt draped on his sinewy torso. He squinted at me and opened
a mouth empty of teeth. I couldn't wait to draw him. An old
woman holding a yellow cat in her arms appeared in the doorway of the shanty and looked down through the rents in the
screen. Her jaw worked as if to suppress an outburst of tears.
But her eyes had a leaden, unwelcoming gaze, and I thought
that perhaps children had tormented them.

Then, as I reentered the square, a pickup truck loaded with
country boys screeched to a stop in front of the inn. They
climbed out, making a racket and swaggering. A few of them
wore hats decked out with stars and stripes. They formed a
little knot, all leaning over the dusty ground, and suddenly
scattered. A firecracker exploded, then another, and they
cheered. They milled around, slapping each other, laughing in
twangy voices. Two on the outskirts looked over at me, poked
each other and called something I couldn't understand. I lowered my eyes and tried to pass, but a big-bellied boy posted
himself in my path.

"Here's a real firecracker, I bet," he said, and looked around
to see the others laugh.

"How would you know, Dwayne?" someone jeered.

"When you going to set her off?" another said, and I didn't
understand the joke.

A man came to the door of the inn and chided them. "Hold
on, there, boys, keep the peace. I'm running a business here."

One of the boys reached into the truck and waggled a bottle of beer at the innkeeper, who swore and raised his fist. Some of the boys climbed into the truck. I sprinted for the bridge.

Thank God Eugene wasn't like them, I thought, and immediately suspected he would be, in time. They were two or three years older, and this was where he lived. What would prevent cocky self-importance and its stupidity from creeping into his manner?

"You're different," he had said in reverent tones. I did want to be different, and also unpredictable. But I required Eugene, too, to be uncommon. How long would that last?

We set up sawhorse tables on the lawn and spread checkered cloths over them. Jules sent Portia and Charlotte and me scattering into the woods for kindling. Rebecca was his chosen partner in firemaking. They set about lighting the pile. Lou played three-handed catch with Portia and Charlotte. He had changed into white shirt and shorts, and his long brown toes in sandals were like intimate parts—I couldn't take my eyes off them. He threw me a surprise toss; I fielded it and lobbed it back. He whistled appreciatively and that sent me happily away, my mastery of an old skill intact.

In the kitchen Poppy brushed damp hair off her face with her wrist. "Put towels over these trays and put them outside on the tables, will you, love?" she said. Jules's music was neatly stacked on the piano when I passed, and someone had arranged chairs and pillows for an audience. Upstairs, water ran in a shower.

The guests began to come into the yard, women in long summer skirts, men with wetly combed hair, and a multitude of little children scampering. Charlotte and Portia corralled some of them and started a badminton game. Jules fanned the fire, now wearing a chef's toque and apron. Mme. Deltail, with a fringed shawl draped over her shoulders, glided to the porch, bearing a tureen. Poppy ran to meet her and they exchanged kisses on both cheeks while the tureen changed hands.

"Ah, the sorrel," Poppy cried. Mme. Deltail went to sit in a big wooden lawn chair under an elm tree. A pair of nearly identical young men squatted at her knees to talk.

"Oh, for an American summer!" I heard Desmond say from the porch, where he stood with a glass in his hand.

Poppy gave me a tray of little sausages to pass. Mme. Deltail had put on sunglasses. She accepted a sausage. "You are the young painter," she said. The young men eyed me indifferently. "Have you a vision?" I blushed. She poked one man's arm with her finger. "I have been so much *painted*. For Pierre, I never changed, for thirty years. That is vision. Always the body of a young girl." She looked down at herself spread in the chair, and chuckled. "I was his idiom. He painted from the inside, not the outside."

I shifted from one foot to the other. She chewed.

"How is your house, Mme. Deltail?" one of the men asked.

"Oh, it is much better, much. I have made contact with the spirits. I live alone, with less fear than before."

Rebecca was strolling with a skinny boy at least six feet tall, his hands clasped behind his back, spectacles reflecting the late sun, like one of Daumier's connoisseurs. He was talking earnestly to her and she listened with unbecoming deference. I felt a twinge of envy. "No more, my darling," Mme. Deltail said, dismissing my tray.

Jules's face was red. He talked distractedly to a paunchy man in plaid shorts, with a great round forehead, sharp nose, and sloping chin. "We've raised some of the money," Jules said. "But thank God that's not my job." He shifted the grill, and fat dripped into the fire, sending a cloud of smoke into their faces. He spotted me. "Go get Poppy, will you, sweetheart? Tell her I need her."

A swarm of children chased a kitten up a tree. Rebecca was in the kitchen. "I'm in despair," she said. "George—did you see him?—is very accomplished. He edits the literary magazine at Groton. My concentration is way off. It's as if you were trying to draw a dog, and instead you drew a half-assed horse and then tried to make it a decent horse. I can *see* the dog, but I can't *write* the dog. God, I do envy you."

"I'm sure you'll be good," I said. I wasn't sure if she'd meant that my work was easier than hers.

"George likes me, but he's so *funny*," she said, lighting a cigarette. "How can a boy be intellectual and immature, at the same time? His tongue practically hangs out. Do you know what's so subtle about people? After they get to know you a little better and are comfortable with you, they start to show you that spe-

cial little charm, and you realize what attracted them to you in
the first place . . . what they think they can get from you.
. . . George wants me to be his goddamn *mother*, I think. . . ."

We wandered out to the porch. A few raggedy country children were standing in the road, holding hands and staring at us.
A car slowed so that its passengers could look too.

Muriel emerged from the house in makeup and a diaphanous
dress with pale pink and orange flowers printed on it.

"You look pretty," I said. She gave me a sparing smile.

"What can we do about all these children? Poppy never said
there'd be so many."

Her eyes swept critically over the party scene and then to her
watch. I was surprised to see it on her wrist—she hadn't worn it
in years. "Well, it will be dark after the readings. They'll surely
be put to bed."

"They came for the fireworks," I pointed out.

"Oh, God, you're right. We'll have to keep them outside."
She went back into the house.

Jules organized a brigade to pass out platters of sliced beef.
His face was sooty, save where sweat had made shiny pink
rivulets. Poppy carried cold dishes to the tables. Mme. Deltail
presided over her tureen, ladling soup to adults. "This is *not* for
children," she said when one little girl held out a bowl.

When the talk slowed during dinner, we could hear band
music coming from the inn. The sun had fallen to the trees and
in its spreading, slanting rays, the scene had a staged, heroic
look. People got up and moved languidly; the light was yellow
and damp, as in a Watteau.

I realized I hadn't seen Desmond since he'd appeared on the
porch. His comings and goings were always whimsical—wasn't
it like him to disappear into the inn, and tell us later he'd picked
up local color, some dialogue, gotten a feel for real people? But
he mustn't miss the party. I went into the house to look for
him.

He was sitting upstairs in the front window, looking down
like Zeus on the party, his profile particular and elegant against
the sky, which had deepened by this time to a Maxfield Parrish
blue.

"Hello, darling," he said. "I wondered where you'd gotten
to."

"I was down there eating with everyone. Couldn't you see me?"

"Are they getting ready for our show?"

I stood at his shoulder and looked down. Poppy had lighted little hurricane lamps, and the guests were trooping into the door below. Children dozed on their father's shoulders, women leaned on each other's arms, laughing. Jules's voice rang up the stairwell. He evoked peals of laughter, then scuffling, as chairs were shifted.

"Yates will be leading off," Desmond said, his head cocked. We heard the actor's studied accents, muffled by the floor. "Don't let me keep you from hearing him, darling," he whispered archly. "But I must warn you, he is an experimental artist. He told me so, almost inadvertently. He's gone beyond realism, or beyond naturalism, beyond the beyond." He took off his glasses and peered through them. "He thinks there is something new, under the sun."

He picked up a little pile of papers from the window seat. "It's a rare gift, to sense what people want, to represent the passions and currents of the times in an entertaining and clarifying way. Everything new derives from something old." He shuffled the pages in a practiced way. "There is rapaciousness in pioneering. I am intrigued by what limits people."

Applause sounded below. "Come on, Daddy," I pleaded.

He led the way. Rebecca was speaking now, enunciating stridently, her sentences rising, then falling off abruptly. Desmond and I picked our way down the dim stair, he grasping the banister with one hand, his manuscript with the other. He was making far too much noise. People in the back turned to see what it was. Rebecca was next to the piano, in the light of a single lamp. She fell silent and waited until we had reached the bottom, her face inclement. One moment too many was allowed to pass, and Desmond waved his hand, calling, "I have something to read to you—something for the occasion. A very long poem!"

"Shhhh!" "What on earth—" "Desmond!"

Lou managed to squeeze through, and lunged for Desmond's arm. "Just wait your turn, old man," he said. Muriel's face glowed strangely. I looked miserably at Rebecca. I think that Charlotte giggled, but Portia beside her had pitched forward and was holding her face in her hands.

"Good lord, forgive me," Desmond said as Lou shoved him down onto the lower steps of the stair. "I had no idea, Rebecca—" He rose to appeal to her. "When you finish, please, Rebecca . . . I beg your pardon—" He set his pages carefully down, clasped his knees and shut his eyes.

She had to be coaxed, but not much. Muriel reached over with a consoling hand and whispered some incantation into Rebecca's ear that removed the scowl from her face. The sight of that sent me into turmoil—here was Rebecca, the center of everyone's attention, and Muriel's especially—and yet I could not honestly envy her. I waited to make my escape.

Rebecca finished her poem, and when the applause had stopped, Desmond stood, went to her and kissed her hand.

He told us that he would read a light piece. It was one of his wittiest, the sort of thing he could toss off so easily, full of puns and featuring the Levys, all the children, Muriel, Lou, even Mme. Deltail, and one or two other guests I hadn't known he'd even met. He was interrupted often by laughter. Lou leaned against the wall near me and I heard him say, "So that's what he's been up to out there."

Like a kleptomaniac who, after a blank moment, finds the goods in his pocket, I suddenly found myself outside the kitchen door, alone in the night, with Desmond reciting and the people tittering within. Eugene wasn't due for ten minutes or so, but I couldn't wait.

The way to the gorge in the dark was tangled, humming with insect noises that resembled words. The sound of the water led me on. The low moon was a mere sliver. Finally I arrived at the rocks over the gorge. Thudding water obliterated all other sound. I went to a spot above the falls where there were pine needles to sit on. After a few minutes I heard a branch snap.

"Miranda?"

"Yes." Eugene stepped from the trees and stood bashfully, just out of reach.

"You're here."

"Yes." He coughed and sat down beside me.

"Are they starting soon?"

"There's a reading."

"A reading?"

"People read things they've written." We were quiet.

"I used to sneak over, when I was little. They're really good.
As good as the Fireman's Picnic at Copake."

"Eugene?" I said, as my voice croaked.

"What?" he answered instantly.

"I'm sad." I could feel the warmth of his body next to mine.
He wore a light plaid shirt with the collar turned up. His hair
was slicked back with oil or water and his face looked flattened
by scrubbing. He rested his wrists on his bent knees.

"Sad? Why?"

"It's just life, I guess," I said woefully. "Just not knowing."

"Well . . ." He was at a loss. The complexity of my feelings
was beyond articulating. I remembered Rebecca's submissive
eyes on George. Had she been meeting him these last days? I
rested my cheek on Eugene's shoulder and he put an arm
around me. He kissed my forehead. I let myself be limp and he
began to knead my shoulders and arms. In time his thumbs
worked around to press at my breasts. He sighed.

"Cover me!" I blurted, and cowered in a position Muriel recommended for relief of gas pains. He crawled over me on his
hands and knees. I shut my eyes and made myself a tight coil
and he sheltered me completely. Afterward I thought that it
was a posture he must have seen animals assume while mating.
But he was graceful and tender then, and did just what I asked.
The weight and warmth of him calmed me, and after a while I
threw him off and we lay face to face, kissing.

"Oh, you are the one," he whispered, caressing me in a progressive way, and I saw that it was to be my body we explored,
not his. There was plenty for me to discover about my own
responses, so I cooperated, but suddenly he fell back, groaning.
"Oh, no!"

"What's the matter?" I straightened my shirt.

"Miranda, you're a nice girl," he said.

"Eugene, don't say that! It's a cliché!"

"A what?" I threw myself onto him. "Don't worry, Eugene."

He lay stiffly, his hands on my back. "I love you, you know
that?" he murmured miserably. He worked his hands to my
chest and stroked it. I felt a great wave of self-congratulating
generosity. He pulled up my shirt.

"No!" I cried, rolling away from him. "Leave me something!"

"I'm sorry," he said. "You see? I can't help it. We got to stop."

"I just don't want to lose control—"

"Well, neither do I!" he said indignantly.

Someone laughed a few yards away. Instantly we were on our knees, scanning the dark. He put a restraining hand on my thigh. I gripped his arm. A man's voice rumbled, then a woman's, muffled by the water. There was rustling and crackling, throaty laughter, then a splash, silence, and a scream.

"Somebody's fallen in!" Eugene cried, already on his feet and running. I struggled up and stumbled after him.

A figure stood wailing over the gorge. "Help, help," she said. It was Sybill. The noise of the water was deafening. Eugene scrambled down the rocks to the pool.

"He jumped!" Sybill exclaimed. "He was right beside me, talking, and then he jumped! Oh!" She threw herself against me. I wondered if she had tormented Yates to the edge of sanity. We shivered together, although the night was humid.

Footsteps sounded in the yard. "What happened?" Lou demanded, materializing out of the darkness. Others followed close behind. "What is it?" "What's happened?"

Lou knew before I did. "The bastard," he said softly. Eugene groped up the side of the gorge, supporting Desmond, whose legs worked like a puppet's. Hands reached down to assist them.

"Clumsy," Desmond said.

"You bet," Lou snapped, taking over his support and marching him toward the house. The rest of us stood looking at each other. Someone congratulated Eugene and asked if he were all right. He grinned diffidently. Sybill had vanished. Eugene was given a dry shirt and he rubbed his hair with it. I might have claimed him then, but that would have required my claiming Desmond too. I kept to the sidelines, hoping I was invisible. People straggled back to the house and Eugene went with them. I could hear Poppy fuss over him on the porch. He insisted he was fine, very politely; he had to get home.

"But the fireworks," she cried. He shook his head sadly.

The windows of the house glowed. Gradually voices lifted and the party was restored. I crouched next to the porch steps. The audience clamored for Muriel and Jules to get on with the show.

Eugene clattered down the steps, looking around.

"Here I am," I whispered.

He laced his fingers together. "I got to go," he said. "I think the world of you." He pecked my cheek. "I shouldn't be here. Your folks are going to have a fit."

"That was my father!" I cried, and turned away in shame.

"I know," he said. "He hasn't had a chance to think it out yet, but when he does, he'll want to wallop me."

"Why on earth would he?" I cried, but he just shook his head. "Eugene, please stay—" He touched my cheek sadly and walked away toward the road. I dragged myself up the steps and leaned on the door frame.

Muriel was sitting next to the piano with her hands in her lap, her body fixed, so that I knew she hadn't moved from the spot, but had taken in all the ruckus, the insult, and the interruption from right there, wearing a gallant trooper's face, as if she'd already weathered every kind of disappointment show business had to dish up over the years.

Jules sat down at the piano, smiling and flexing his fingers. He launched into the overture of *Adah*. He played with such ease, and the snatches of melody were so captivating, the whole room fell under his spell. He was a virtuoso, disarmingly modest, utterly undemanding, an agent of pure pleasure. He ducked his head, signaling Muriel to get ready, and she began to sing.

The self-conscious part of me that usually resisted her performances and found them strident and grimacing, was disarmed that night. After the first number she and Jules did a little dialogue that gave a hint of the plot and characterization. I heard Desmond's hand—he'd been telling us stories about Adah for years. The songs were clever, and Muriel sang sincerely, and the buoyant artifice of the musical comedy form drew us all together again, resurrecting the innocence of the occasion. There really was magic in a witty song. I remembered how often Muriel had exclaimed, even after she'd yoked her energies to domestic routine, "Oh, there's nothing like a show!" and there wasn't. Jules and Muriel smiled at each other—they were *showing* us. I caught Rebecca's eye and smiled. She returned a look ironic and indulgent, and then we both looked back to our parents.

They finished to wild applause and I thought they really might have a hit, after all. Jules wiped at his head with a hand-

kerchief, grinning and thanking us, as happily breathless as if
he'd been running all that time.

"Now for the act to top it!" he called and went out to where
the fireworks waited behind a barrier of fruit boxes to keep
little children away. We gathered at a distance, docile and alert.

He set off a few duds, but we waited patiently and cheerfully. A hush fell over the crowd after each launching, then,
with the burst of whorls and fountains and sparks, and the
little gulf of silence, we gasped and sighed in chorus. A baby
cried, and that made us laugh. Every face was turned to the
heavens, and it was Muriel's I kept seeing. She beamed like a
girl, refreshed and expectant, and I wished we could be sealed
into the night forever. Tomorrow was going to be terrible.

When the show ended, much too soon, to our plaintive cries,
guests strolled in little groups, saying good night, collecting
crockery and offspring, moving toward the road, where here
and there cars started, headlights shone on the trees, then
veered off toward town. Muriel stood surrounded by new fans
and I heard her rich laughter spill out into the night. I wondered
if Desmond lay in his bed inside, smoking, reflecting on
Muriel's moment of glory, or if he'd fallen asleep.

Jules, poking around in the grass for duds, listened to the
paunchy man ask how he could invest in the show. Jules was
clearly surprised. "Well, Joe, I'm delighted, really. I'll put you in
touch with Todd." The man said something I missed. Jules responded, "Oh, well, we're hoping for Merman, who else?" He
bent and ran his hand over the ground. "We've put out feelers,
you have to use middlemen, of course. But we think she's interested. It's a natural for her."

Over the heads of the yawning company, beyond the
farewells, the humming, mumbling, easy rumble, Muriel's
laugh rang out again.

5

I wore a strapless black satin top with bones to keep it erect and
a scarlet and black plaid skirt that fell, not to the tops of spike-
heeled shoes, as my neighbors' pastel tulle ones did, but to mid-
calf, revealing patterned black lace stockings and sandals with
heels I could walk in without hobbling. I could run in them, if
necessary. My gloves were not the common little white ones,
but were also of intricate black lace that reached up over my
elbows. Muriel had bought them during her year in Paris, and
part of my consciousness was tuned to preserving them. I had
slicked my hair back and sprayed it until it felt like a helmet.
My makeup was a few deft strokes of crimson on my mouth
and a smudge of Payne's gray over my eyes. I knew I looked
distinctive.

There wasn't anyone I wanted to talk to, but I'd have danced
if any of the boys had asked me. This was a senior class party,
everyone invited, given by Judy Griffin's parents, who had
commandeered the country club. That meant there were even
more uncertain, possibly tortured souls, milling around than
was usual at a dance, but I was as aloof from them, as I was
from the eager beavers who were good at parties. I had reigned
all these years as class artist and now as class bohemian, and I
still commanded a certain respect, but we were nearly at the
end of our school careers and my hermetical ways made me
irrelevant, a bizarre souvenir that had been around so long no
one paid attention to it.

I overheard Judy, Sandy, and Linda exchange bulletins about

the "crashers" from St. Bart's School. Linda knew the boys by name, and that was how I learned who Jock LeMieux was when he caught my eye from across the floor, lifted his chin with charming insolence, lowered it when I tipped my head and strode toward me. The atmosphere shifted as before an electrical storm.

His tuxedo was ill-fitting enough to give him an I-don't-give-a-damn look. His hair was slicked back, but not sprayed, and locks of it bounced to his forehead. When he tossed them back, his rimless glasses sparked. There were pink patches on his cheeks, the Gallic complexion. He held my eyes, even as his flickered over everyone to either side of me.

"Hey, Linda," he said as he passed her, and stopped in front of me. I met his stare, hoping to look indomitably sexy. The girls in the vicinity shut up and openly listened.

"Jock LeMieux," he said, sticking out his hand. "Want to dance?" I couldn't decide, for a moment, whether or not to peel off my glove. Finally I put my palm to his and he held it long enough for me to feel moisture seep through the lace.

I could see over his right shoulder. The batch of boys who had crashed stared at us with insouciant curiosity.

"Your secret is safe with me," I said. It was a typical non sequitur, and people who knew me no longer bothered to puzzle them out. Jock blinked, looked at the ceiling, shot his cuffs and wheezed, "Okay, we'll just do the steps. I don't need to know who you are."

I took his arm and we strolled onto the floor, where bouffant skirts filled every gap and dancers concentrated grimly, as if accountable to absent masters. Jock held me so that he could look down on my face, quite in contrast to the bashful burrowing of other boys. He really could dance, too, and I was grateful at last to Muriel for all the nerve-wracking practice drills we'd held in the kitchen in case Portia and I became belles and the ball were ever revived. How intractable we'd been, stomping out box steps and counting like drill sergeants, but some of it had registered. Jock and I whirled around stylishly, without a hitch, each challenging the other to invent, hitting our peak with the tango. A few kids had stopped dead to watch us by the time it was over. I let my gaze wander over the room to couples sitting at little round tables, and in a raised alcove, erupting with alcoholic merriment, the Griffins and their friends, who were chaperons.

The music stopped and a few couples clapped, the girls' gloves thudding dully.

"Let's get out of here and talk," Jock said, and steered me to a glassed veranda with potted trees and latticework. It looked deserted at first, but soon we encountered couples pressed together in shadowy intervals along the walls. Jock held my hand and pulled me along to the foyer, past a locked office, to an empty cloakroom. He leaned against the counter, took a pack of Gauloises from his jacket, shook it at me, and lit one for himself. The cloud of smoke put me on edge.

"Are your folks members of this joint?" he asked. I said no, adding a laugh he ignored.

"Hardly worth the dough, is it?" He told me he hated St. Bart's, where dances were even more of a drag, present company excepted, and had been forced to transfer from Exeter. "Grades," he explained. "I was involved with a woman." He sucked his smoke. "She took a lot of time. Couldn't do my work. I met her over the summer. When school started and I had to leave her, I was pretty broken up."

I looked away. Obviously I should ask if he were still so in love. But I didn't.

"There are some quite adequate teachers. But a very low level of sophistication. The good thing is, I can go home to the city on weekends."

He told me the LeMieux's owned a chateau in France, an apartment on Fifth Avenue, and a "camp" in the Adirondacks. The woman he had wooed was Swiss; he met her in Geneva and she was forty years old. It was over, yes. His uncle Guy was a film producer. I heard names that Muriel lovingly savored drop at my feet like peanut shells: Darrieux, Jouvet, Barrault, Gabin. He mentioned the "auteur system" and I knew what he was talking about. We were both gratified.

"Do you like to take risks?" he asked slyly.

What might he ask me to do? "It depends."

"I'm absolutely driven to take them. Last summer I tried something very interesting. I took my cousin's Jag to seventy-five miles an hour in the mountains, steering through binoculars." He let that sink in. "What do you think that does to your

depth of field?" I shook my head. "Well, it shoots hell out of it.
The ground crawls. You don't have any idea how fast you're
really going. Unfortunately, David was insanely jealous and
ratted on me. Now I'm not allowed to drive. My grandmother
was upset. She's very brittle. Chicago bourgeois. She and Papa
hate each other. But they all live together. Remind me not to do
that with my life."

I was more sparing with my disclosures, and embroidered
Desmond's accomplishments so as to give the impression he
was an enduring bigshot. The fact that he had left us and the
station a year before to teach at an upstate college, and now
lived with a woman scarcely older than I, allowed me to make
up anything I wanted. I hadn't seen him and had received only
a dozen or so letters. I usually tried not to think about him.

I told Jock that I was a painter. I had favorite masters I could
toss at him: Piero, Caravaggio, Watteau, Courbet, Manet. I
worked for pleasure, had once done portraits, but my object
now was to develop in other directions. I spoke of visits to the
Metropolitan Museum.

"I live across the street," Jock said. "And we have quite a
good collection at home. Papa buys contemporaries. Do you
know DeKooning? Newman? He goes right to their studios. But
there are lots of Impressionists. You'd be interested."

Could this be true? My feelings rose and fell. Disapproval
(from Muriel), envy, doubt—but his manner gave him cre-
dence. He also made me feel competitive, as most strange phe-
nomena did, but I kept quiet so that he'd go on talking. I
wanted him to like me, to find me pliant enough for affection
and steadfast enough for respect.

We went back along the corridor toward the music. He suggested a last dance. We glided over the floor, took switchbacks
and hairpin turns, dipped and spun, our faces impassive. I
hoped he wouldn't tire of me. I hoped that he would kiss me
when it was over and make plans to see me again and ask for
my telephone number (I'd have to think of something—he
mustn't call my home). He did none of those things, and instead walked me to the vestibule, where we shook hands with
everyone thronging around.

It was drizzling, and parents dashed up to the door with umbrellas, ordered their kids to hurry it up, and the kids jostled,

dawdled and cast backward looks. I saw most of those looks. My version of lofty reserve was to allow the crowd to hurtle past me. Once Muriel's page, I was now a spy, lurking, seeing more than anyone on the move could see.

The breathless, chattering girls flowed like lemmings. I waited for my prearranged ride with Jane Dexter's father. Out under the porte-cochere Jock bobbed with the St. Bart's group. Headlights glowed through sheets of mist. A long black car drew up, windshield wipers silently flashing, a driver in uniform at the wheel. He belonged to one of Jock's friends, a well-proportioned little fellow with blond hair and a perfectly fitted tuxedo, so that he looked like a doll, not a boy growing up. The boys climbed into the backseat, and the car slid away.

"Miranda!" Jane shrieked from the steps below. I nudged through the throng, my hands buried in my trench coat pockets, and rode home.

The following Wednesday I received a message from Jock via Linda. *Do you still do portraits? My parents want you to paint my mug. It was super at the dance. Come over to school tomorrow afternoon. I'll be waiting on the track. J.*

Linda watched me read. I folded the note and put it back into its envelope. "Thank you," I said, and spun the combination on my locker. Linda folded her arms. She was joined by Judy and Sandy, a trio in pale, fuzzy sweaters.

"Well?" Linda asked. "What did he *say*, Miranda?"

"He wants his portrait done."

"Uh-huh." Giggles. "So you're going to. Is he posing in his bedroom, with his bedroom eyes? His penthouse? I heard he has a penthouse."

I gave them a dismissing glance and walked down the hall. Their eyes on my back were like an unfavorable wind. *It's a professional arrangement,* I thought, but what sort of date was that? I had told him I didn't *do* portraits any more. I felt a little patronized. No wonder, he had become my patron.

The walk up Hotel Hill and beyond to the St. Bart's athletic field seemed endless in the chilly fall wind. The football team was scrimmaging in its white and scarlet uniforms. An irregular line of runners appeared on the surrounding track. To one side a huge youth prepared to hurl a medicine ball. This was masculine, absorbing activity, and I approached shyly, but as soon as

Jock noticed me, he veered off the cinders with a wave of the arm to follow. We met behind the bleachers, where there was a slatted privacy. Everyone on the field had seen him defect to a girl. He stood panting and smiling wonderfully, his hands on his hips. Even in the partial shelter wind whipped our hair and clothing and carried off some of our phrases. His cheeks were red. He looked like an illustration in a children's book.

We started to negotiate, barking out terms. He asked about media. I insisted on pastels, not oils, arguing that they were permanent enough, sprayed with fixative. The truth was, I was afraid to paint him in oils—a good likeness depended on spontaneity. Jock objected that he had seen pastel pictures of vaporous little girls somewhere, but I convinced him he'd be virile.

We came to the question of a fee. Neither of us, at first, was willing to name one. What was I worth? What did I want? What if his parents were not satisfied—whose fault would that be? As the true patrons they forced me to evaluate myself in practical terms. And Muriel—what would *she* have to say if I were cheaply had, or too dear for my own good?

Jock finally admitted that he'd been "empowered" to offer me one hundred dollars. I was staggered, yet it was a figure that seemed on reflection to be fair. I didn't realize until afterward that the portrait must have been his idea and that he'd asked for a little extra allowance to pay for it. The sum, piddling to them, was enormous to me. Jock had arranged for us to use a classroom in "Old Whimsey," the main St. Bart's building, every day from four o'clock until the light was gone—a little more than an hour. I told him I could do the portrait in a week.

"I'll see you tomorrow," I said crisply. I was thinking: *A week —that's all I have to make something of this.* "Wear whatever you want immortalized," I said.

He jogged backward after shaking my hand again, and I could feel his eyes on me when I turned away. The wind made my nose run, I was out of my element.

I came to envy Jock for many things, but none more keenly than St. Bart's, for all of its shortcomings. It was a small school, and for him a distinct comedown, but I'd have rejoiced to go there. Whatever it was that clogged his classmates' pipes and put pebbles in their mouths and icy fingers at the backs of their

necks—that stuffiness—would have sparked fires in me. I'd
have loved to be a boy at a boys' school. Whimsic was a big
square soiled-yellow brick building with an archway and gate.
Its prototype stood at Oxford or Cambridge—one of those
places, Jock said. I pretended, as we entered, that I was a young
subject of an English king. I had a reverence for old buildings
and for hardheaded learning, such as took place, I supposed, at
a boys' school with men for teachers. Inside, all was lavishly
shabby. Great paneled corridors connected outsized paneled
classrooms. The few desks inside were never lined up but left in
disorderly little huddles, surrounded by huge amounts of
empty space. Such profligacy seemed right to me, as if all the
extra room encouraged the expansion of ideas.

We used Heinz Shritt's big science room for the sittings because it had a sink. I glimpsed him the first afternoon, gathering
papers into a pile at his lectern. Tall, blond, and bent, he gave
me a sweet smile. With his little spectacles, a pink-tipped nose
that looked as if he had drawn it out of a scabbard, and the
inward frown that followed the smile, he reminded me of a
Breughel alchemist.

I put Jock next to one of the long, high windows, near the
gadget counter. Outside a handful of tiny figures, looking as
knights on a drill would look from a castle keep, ran, drifted
dreamily, and reversed themselves, following a ball. The late
fall afternoon was thick with damp that intensified the scarlet
on their shirts. Beyond them a woods of oranges, yellows, and
greens was gradually diluted. That scene filled me with longing.
The boys looked both free and safe. Their exercise, and even
their competition, took place within a snug enclosure, secure
and yet challenging. How might I enter such a world? Perhaps
on the arm of one of its own. I turned to Jock and adjusted his
head.

I explained that the pose was based on Flemish portraits of
prominent young men set next to windows overlooking the
territory they commanded, and he said he knew that. Yes, it
would amuse his parents.

He was cheerful at first and told me stories about his uncle's
film stars. The LeMieux males had a weakness for actresses.
The family fortune was established by his French grandfather,
who had set up a company in Paris and profited when an em-

ployee invented an electronic device that became essential to the manufacture of telephones, telegraphs, and yes! broadcast equipment. I let him chatter while I sketched his torso, the window, and suggestions of the landscape. When I had a soft charcoal outline, I told him he'd have to shut up and began on his face.

"Where do you think you'll go on to school?" he asked through clenched teeth, like a ventriloquist.

"Don't talk. Swarthmore." Rebecca Levy was at Swarthmore College. She had written rapturously to me about her classes and the brilliant friends she'd made. I read her letters over and over, moved by the wit she invested in me and seething with a desire to be there too.

"I'm headed for Colgate or Hamilton, then the London School of Economics, says the papa."

"Don't talk." I was surprised. He was as much at the mercy of someone's expectations as I, but he didn't sound rebellious. He had a successful tradition to continue, whereas I felt I must break from the past. For a few moments I experienced a mean envy, Muriel's dismissal of people who had "an easy time of it." Then I fell to working with such absorption that, in a sense, I forgot he was there. When he leapt from his stool and ran around to see how "pretty" he was, I was startled and annoyed. But his mischief made his face lively, and distracted me, too, so that my exasperation kept me from dwelling on what I was doing, freed my hand from my brain, and made possible the delicate marks that rendered exactly that intangible—a likeness.

"It's good," he said, behind me.

"Get back over there."

"My, what a tough girl."

Part of the inspiration in making a portrait, or drawing any subject, was a feeling of possession. Perhaps Jock chafed a little, sensing that, or perhaps it gave him pleasure. My great empathy for what I drew had a disconcerting element—it was almost like sexual conquest, or what I imagined that to be. It drew me closer and yet gave me distance. The more I studied him and put him down on the flat surface, the more at ease I felt. It wasn't the commonality of a mutual acquaintance, but better. He'd have overwhelmed me had we been in different circumstances.

I set down my chalk. If I worked any longer I might make too much, obscuring what was already in place. We packed up my easel and paint box. On the way out of the building I asked him why he had chosen me. Was it because I had boasted? Of course, he said. Exactly that. But how did he know I was any good? He hadn't. He had taken a chance.

I was stung. But halfway down the hill he took my arm and made me face him. "You're famous, don't you know that? Everyone said you'd do a great job. I saw some of your things at your school and over in the Municipal Building. One of the guys had a portrait at home that you did of his sister, and I looked at it. What do you think I am? Don't you know all this, really?"

I hadn't known. My victories must be won again and again—*I* must be won over and over. There could be no resting on laurels. I had thirsted for his respect.

The portrait took two weeks. Jock pretended to be so sick of sitting he would pay for an "unfinished slave." But sometimes he was gracious, and took me into town for coffee or a soda, where we were seen together by some of my classmates. This brought me a delicious new notoriety—when had I ever been remarked for my company? He made casual references now and then to a film we might go to, or to paintings he wanted me to see at home, but we never made any dates. When we crossed streets, however, I took his arm and moved with a pleasant thickness and lazy eyes.

Making his portrait involved acting and being acted upon. It was tempting to assume that the feelings growing in me as the image took shape were reciprocated. Reality lay in the relating and my aim was to get a perfect likeness. The concrete details I observed were put to paper, where they influenced one another and prompted new impulses in me—as he did too. His being and his image instructed me, and so did experiences stored in my brain, so did habitual motions of my hand. The process was sensational, not intellectual and bound to raise my feeling. I was drawn to him as I drew him; he was object and subject and my labor was to fill the gap between those two. I used him for my work, submitted to him in order to see him—and hoped that he, in some other way, was submitting and seeing too.

I hated to call the portrait finished. Finally it was clear that additional fiddling would stiffen it, so I signed and handed it over. Jock did kiss me then, on either cheek, while I stood with my lips puckered. I began to suspect how much he could hurt me.

Days passed and I heard nothing from him and nothing from his parents. I missed him and missed the portrait, too, to look at and further perfect in my mind. I wanted to know what they'd thought of it.

One afternoon Muriel asked why I was dragging myself around "like an orphan." Lately she had been wearing a shapeless housedress until afternoon and her hair frizzed out in all directions. The sun glaring through the window gave her an aureole. I straightened my back.

"I'm not."

"Your fancy friend hasn't called, has he?" I didn't answer. "Maybe you were as blah with him as you are with me."

"Oh, God, Mother." All her sensitivity must have been in her antennae. She often denounced my friends, and the worst of it was that what she said often had some truth. It turned out that she was feeling the strain of our circumstances and wanted me to take on more informed responsibility.

"I want to talk something over with you. You're the oldest and I have no choice but to rely on you. Your father hasn't sent any money in months. We may have to sell the house. It's worth twice what we paid for it. We can move to a smaller one and live more cheaply." I saw that she had a collection of real estate ads laid out on the table.

In a way, I didn't care. I would be gone in a few months. But Portia had a year and a half left. Self-possessed, she was still soft to look at, with dimpled prettiness, fine curly hair, and an encouraging laugh. She'd always been noted for her self-discipline, and, in her own way, she was as ambitious as I was, yet more at ease. She had told me that she felt unloved, sometimes, in our house because she hadn't a marked talent. But it was plain to me that Muriel and Desmond loved her for herself, and I envied her that. She was a model student and citizen, with scores of admiring friends. Sometimes she surprised me. "God, I'd like to go to a place like Samoa," she'd said. "I'd like to be with people who've never seen civilization." She shoved a book under my nose, open to a photograph. "Look at those faces.

They're so smart and happy! They're completely trusting! Completely curious! What if we could live in a cave and only have to be brave. Think how simple it is to face danger."

Just now Portia appeared in the doorway behind Muriel. She pantomimed obligation to be elsewhere. A little frown, gone in a flash, told me she was grateful to me for taking the heat, whatever it was. A car horn sounded. Muriel started out of her chair. "Portia? Was that for her?" But she had gone.

Muriel sighed. "We have to tighten our belts. I have an idea I can get a teaching certificate. Until then, I can only substitute." The refrigerator hummed. She pulled her hair back from her face with both hands, drawing the skin tight. For a moment she was the performer she'd always wanted to be. Her power over me was so great I could never imagine the failure of nerve that must have left her dreams to evaporate.

She began talking of my plans for next year. "You'll make a portfolio and apply to an art school in the city."

"But I want a liberal arts education, college—"

"What matters is that you have a talent. You have to develop it. No one is going to take care of you. Don't be naive."

"I don't want anyone to take care of me! Dad wants me to go to college, I'm sure."

"What interest is he taking in us at all?"

"Maybe he's doing the best he can—"

"Liberal arts will do you no good," she said. "Unless you want to teach—but you'll be qualified to teach art if you go to someplace like Pratt anyway." I stood up and walked to the sink and leaned on it, blood heating my face. "Liberal arts are for self-important people like your father. He and his cronies can wax nostalgic over the alma mater. He can teach little snobs Fine Writing." The room began to swim, my fury was so great. It was Muriel, after all, who had culture, high-flown taste, who had earned straight A's and a scholarship to France, who loved classical music and classical actors—Maurice Evans playing Hamlet to Desmond's Fred Allen. She used to go to a play every other week in town; Desmond would reminisce about burlesque. Now she was actually willing to throw aside the banner she had carried with such pride, in order to link Desmond to the liberal arts and thereby discredit them! It was inconceivable.

It wasn't even a betrayal of me. But I was the one who would suffer.

"You have to be independent," Muriel said. "You have to have training. You've just had a lesson in being taken advantage of, haven't you? This boy dropped you." Tears sprang to my eyes. I *was* hurt. She'd found a way to sting me more. "And look at your father's pals. Where are the ones who cared about us? Where is Lou, to name one?" She made it sound short for "lewd."

"You're wrong," I howled. "You don't know what you're talking about!"

But maybe she did.

"Don't be foolish. Someday you'll appreciate advice you don't want to hear. You never seem to think of anyone but yourself, but even at that, you're not practical."

I thought I'd explode. There was nothing more to say. I ran to my room and sobbed into my pillow.

I thought about Lou. I longed to prove Muriel wrong, most of all wrong that nobody cared about me. Lou had always shown fondness for me, and I for him. I knew, as surely as instinct and experience could tell me anything about another person, that he was not fickle or callous. It was entirely possible that he no longer cared for Muriel, and why should he? She had ridiculed him many times behind his back. Love was reciprocal. Love was inside me, waiting for its mate. My life had a shape, including the past, including Lou.

I decided to see him. I remembered once when Desmond hauled me off to a restaurant after a brawl with Muriel. We'd marched to the train and in his impatience we'd gotten off at an obscure station short of the city, blundering a few blocks through a rundown business district to a hole in the wall with an Italian menu, booths and red benches with stuffing dripping out of slashes in the plastic. I'd ordered veal Parmesan, and I still liked to order it. It symbolized a sad loyalty to him. After he'd cooled off, we went home and I was left to my own devices. I wrote out a plan to run away with him for good, hid it in my dresser, and eventually Muriel found it. She wasn't as angry as my misbehaviors usually made her—she was frightened and wounded. Now I was dreaming of running away to Lou. What would he do with me?

6

He sat at a table for two by the plate-glass window, the only customer in the place. I remembered picking him up at the railroad station on our way to the Levys three years before, and thought, *Lou is always alone.*

He stood and ambled toward me. The room was gloomy and smelled of masculine spices and strong coffee. This was probably one of Lou's bachelor haunts, more an Armenian club than a public place. His hand was raised to midriff level and looked as if he were slowing me down: I had changed so much more than he.

I'd walked from the subway at Thirty-fourth Street, looking out for the broad upstairs window with a neon light and unmarked doorway he had described, passing lofts and shops crammed with lace, hat trimmings, ribbon and rickrack—places where savvy Muriel used to buy her supplies. She almost never came into the city anymore, not even to the theatre.

"You look perfectly charming," Lou said, his down east accent as strong as ever. "What a treat this is. I'm so grateful." He kissed my cheek and dropped a hand to my shoulder. I felt the rasp of his whiskers and his warm breath, saw the pits on his skin. "You really can't hide that fierce little girl"—he smiled—"but I do salute the young woman."

I had had little traffic with grown men since Desmond left. My art teacher at school gave my work a thorough scrutiny, but he never seemed to look at me, and I was unused to compliments to my person.

A swarthy, grinning man in an apron seated me, and Lou looked me up and down with a smile that covered his teeth. My fall outfit had been put together from Muriel's closet—that enduring fabric and fine workmanship we could no longer buy. The shoulders of the tweed jacket were padded and their extravagance sharpened my carriage. The navy blue skirt, snug at the hips, flared when I walked. Even my shoes were Muriel's, handmade in Italy, over twenty years old. The clothes hadn't been worn in years. They fit a character frozen in time.

"This is Miss Geer, Ben," Lou said. "I've known her all her life."

Ben shook his head incredulously. "Wine on the house!" he declared. Four elderly men who were like fixtures of the room played cards in a dim corner near the kitchen, and a snowy-haired, stooping waiter set glasses in rows on a side table, polishing each one first with a napkin. The pale pink neon sign pulsed outside, tinting half of Lou's face at regular intervals, like a heartbeat monitored with dye. His hair was gray in places, but otherwise he looked the same.

He examined me with such pleasure, I could scarcely sit still. "What did you do today, were you in town?" he asked in his thrifty voice, just as if we'd had breakfast together that morning. His wanting to imagine my experience before we met gave it an added, flattering dimension. But without a clear conscience I couldn't be casual. Calling him had been a childish gesture requiring grown-up guile. Now that I was with him, I was tongue-tied. Concealing the dinner, I realized, would not be enough. Whatever it generated between us must also be concealed.

"I went to the Hopper show at the Midtown," I said, and he had to ask me to repeat it. At once I was drawn into an interior analysis of *why* I had gone to the Hopper show. I had outgrown him, after all—Lou would get the wrong idea about me. Should I also tell him I had gone to the public library to read the Swarthmore College catalog and send for an application? I decided to postpone mention of that until I could take his measure, or he mine.

I described the paintings I had seen and told him what I'd thought. ". . . and they seemed static, bits of people's lives that never went anywhere."

He tipped back in his chair. "I know what you mean. In fact, I don't know why anyone your age would like them. They do take you back to a bleak place. There isn't any change, as you say. He cheated a little, choosing subjects like that, so that what he says about them will always be true."

"Yes," I said. "I felt like a voyeur—and I used to copy them all the time, like a peeping Tom." He smiled—it was the expression of a kindly physician. If he asked me to take off my blouse so that he could listen to my lungs, I would do it! But then I thought disconcertingly of Jock. I had told Muriel I was meeting him to go to a movie. I'd looked up the review in the *Times* so that I could tell her about it when I got home. It made me uneasy that Jock didn't know of the deception. I wished I could alert him.

"I've been studying Renaissance painters," I told Lou, who was curious about all of my interests. "Mantegna, Piero—I want so much to go to Italy. Have you been there?"

He shook his head. "Not even the Levant. Your dad would be pleased. He loved history, and he never went abroad either." I was startled—he invoked Desmond as if he were dead. "We're a provincial pair," he added gently. "But don't stray too far from the present. You have too much talent to waste any of it."

I was deflated. The occasion called for something more graphic than fatherly advice. Still, he was showing that he did care for me. How angry Muriel would be if she could see me now! Surely the contempt she expressed for Lou was the result of injured feelings. It contained a kernel of coyness, an impurity that made it especially volatile. Injury, coyness, inaction. She was a still center, making sweeping judgments, like the searchlight of a becalmed ship, turning and turning in the choppy sea. If she regretted that Lou had drifted away, she would never admit it, nor find out why, nor ask him to come back. But if she discovered this defection of mine, she'd find a way to make me pay.

"I'll order for us both, if you don't mind," Lou said. Ben had returned with a bottle of wine and poured, nodding while Lou recited our order.

"Your father would make a toast," he said when Ben had gone, "but I'm lousy at clever summations. He was the lyricist, you'll remember." I nodded vaguely. "And I don't really know you, do I? We'll save it for next time." He drank, his eyes on my face. "What do you hear from him?"

I had expected Lou to provide news of Desmond. Muriel claimed he was comforted by a conspiracy of their old friends. Had Lou really not been in touch with him either? It was hard to bring the story up to date without seeming to complain.

"He's okay," I said. "He doesn't write very often. He's teaching upstate—you knew that?" He nodded. "I hear Jules is teaching at Julliard," I added. My source was Rebecca, of course.

"He's quite the distinguished professor," Lou said. "I suspect it's what he was cut out for. He profited from a setback and I admire that. It's a better life for all of them."

I straightened my back. Muriel, however immaterial, had squeezed herself into my chair and was pinching my thigh. *Wasn't it Lou who profited?* she whispered.

Jules's show hadn't survived its out-of-town booking, but it was said to have a loyal following in the business, to be one of those sacrificial works of real quality that keep everyone feeling smug about the theatre. The then unknown star had gone on to make a name for herself as a singer/comedienne, but she had been too young to make a convincing Adah. Desmond had not, as far as I knew, made any further contributions to the book. Lou left radio shortly afterward and went into television. For a while he wrote and produced highly acclaimed dramas broadcast live. Muriel never missed one.

"Maybe daddy is a good teacher," I suggested.

"Of course he is. He was very drawn to the Ivory Tower, but he feared being corrupted—you know the sly jokes he used to make about it. There is a side to him that wants to leave its mark in the encouraging of young minds."

I stared at my plate. The characterization of my father was not credible. "I like your Playhouse show," I said finally. Did that compromise anyone?

"Thank you."

"He's living with a girl," I blurted.

"I knew that. Do you disapprove? May–December isn't very dignified, is it?"

My heart hammered. He reached across the table and put his

hand over mine. When I met his eyes, the compassion in them made me feel more fraudulent than ever.

"I guess that's not what I meant to say. I meant, it must be difficult for you. A man my age, a girl yours—a little older . . . we're not supposed to cast so wide a net."

"I don't think that," I stammered. "He's my father, he's not you. I mean, not someone else—anyone." He removed his hand.

"Your father is a casualty," he said. "He was one of the finest writers in the business. You know that, I hope. It's not just my opinion. You can mention him to anyone who was around. There are good memories, in some quarters." His voice sounded far away. He cupped his glass with the hand that had sprawled over mine. I remembered how he had defended Desmond to Jules.

"I know he's good," I said. "It's a waste for him to teach Expository Writing." I thought of the clever lyrics he had written for Portia and me to sing while we washed the dishes; the puns, the games, the stories. Was that all wasted, too, just idle play? I had leafed through the boxes in the attic many times. The well-crafted speeches called attention to themselves. Who needed a specialist like Desmond anymore? He plied a quaint trade. And how could a child in front of a television set have drawn pictures of worlds created by language, as I had by the radio?

In a similar way abstract painters didn't have to be able to draw. Painted blobs and blurs looked arbitrary to me. I had no desire to make them and no way to evaluate them. Had painting become merely outsized and empty? If a painter could make anything he wanted, let it assume any form or none at all, what was the point? How could that be the work of an artist looking conscientiously at the world? I felt like a casualty, too, ready to flee already to an upstate campus, terrified that nothing would be expected of me any more and that I would not know what to do.

"He gave up," I cried. "When they stopped wanting him and telling him what to do, he gave up."

"Let me tell you something," Lou said sternly. "He helped shape the standards. He was a mentor to many, many younger writers, directors, some who are executives now. There wasn't anything we could do. You mustn't blame him." He seemed to have startled himself. He frowned, collected his thoughts, and reminisced again. "We were all so excited by radio—the ideas we would bring to people, the national community it would make—of course, all of it beamed from New York City, the seat of power. . . ." I could smell meat broiling and it made my stomach contract. I had skipped lunch to save money. Lou glanced out of the window. "We had our nerve. We were young. Des loves this country. He loves the heart of it. But he hated provincialism—'I'm intolerant of the intolerant' he said, do you remember? His sympathies weakened him, though."

There was a clattering in the kitchen. Lou stared over my head. "Nostalgia weakened him too. If you fail to do what you believed you would when you started out, nostalgia will get you. It's people who become more than they ever expected to who aren't tempted by it. Many of them aren't tempted to be gentlemen either, but he was. . . ." He rubbed his chin. "Des was so interested in failure. Who was it who said promise can never be fulfilled, by definition?"

I remembered standing in the front room over the Levys' door when Desmond had told me he was moved by what limited people and then blundered into Rebecca's reading. Lou coughed behind his hand. "So. Television will level us all. In a way, he was lucky to be out of it."

Ben arrived with plates of lamb and vegetables. At the same moment eerie, discordant music began issuing from a wall speaker, the same few bars repeated endlessly on a shrill, stringed instrument.

"Get yourself a glass, Ben," Lou said. The aromas rising to my nose made me slightly giddy. Ben came back with a glass, poured, and lifted it high. "My dear young lady friend, my dear old friend Lou Gregorian, we drink to times past and times present." Saliva glistened on his lips and his black eyes flashed. "The things we lose will increase us!" He tossed back his wine. Lou and I sipped. Ben backed away, smiling.

We ate. "Lou, do you remember when Portia and I used to come to the studio?"

"Of course."

"I loved it. I miss it." A dreamlike memory—*nostalgia*—wafted through my mind: The room with its console of buttons and switches, the big glass wall overlooking the actors holding scripts and standing in front of microphones, everyone wearing headphones. Portia and I had been informed; we had known what was going on, were known, ourselves.

"It was fun, wasn't it? We all played. . . ." he said.

"That's what I loved—grown-ups playing. Even the work was fooling people, making trains and galloping horses and creaking doors with a bunch of wooden blocks and straps and whistles and things. You could never imagine what the studio was really like from listening to the radio."

"You and Portia in your little dresses with puffy sleeves, your faces pressed to the glass . . . You were drawing, weren't you?"

We smiled at each other. Whenever I thought about striking out on my own, putting myself at risk in the world, I remembered the control room. It had been packed with experts, and yet there was playfulness, too, and the grown-ups had accepted us completely. Lou proved that. I had belonged. It was the only club I wanted to join, the one behind the scenes, the secret order. The actors were known to outsiders, but the people behind the big window were really in control. Where would I find the equivalent now? Muriel insisted that success depended on who you knew, what your breaks were, learning the password. But even though she'd been an insider, she'd failed to put herself forward to see how far her luck would carry her. She pushed Portia and me forward now.

"Your mother," Lou began, as if reading my mind. His voice caught and he cleared his throat. "Does she still have a garden?"

I nodded, chewing. I had been shanghaied into gardening too many Saturdays. It was rather a sore point.

"My father was a gardener, a professional one, when he first arrived in this country. He worked on an estate in Westchester, a very famous family in those days. He thought they mistook him for an Italian, the day he showed up. He hadn't learned English, but he learned gardening. Once he threw a peach pit to the ground and it rooted. Years later he showed me the tree, bent with fruit."

"You never told me that," I said politely.

He leaned toward me. My eye fell to the knot of his tie and the buttoned points of his shirt collar. Desmond had bought all of his clothes at Harvey French. Did Lou buy his at the same store? Were all men creatures of habit? How did Lou take care of himself? I imagined watching him lay out his clothes and put them on, assembling the man I knew.

"Miranda, I've always been very fond of you and Portia. Your mother may not accept this, but I feel a . . . responsibility." I raised my eyes. "She used to love a good time. When we all first came to New York, she struck me as the perfect bohemian."

I laughed, but the image, which Muriel herself had planted, often haunted me. The young and carefree Muriel—who had she been? The more she jigged through my reconstructions of the past, the more I was checked. Somehow an equivalency had formed: I wasn't free until I paid for her sacrifice. How had I been made to feel that?

"And Desmond refused to be a lousy person," Lou said mysteriously. "And I—" He shook his head. "Well, it's past."

Now is the moment, I thought. *Help me.* But wasn't Lou too entangled in my parents' lives to help me escape them? I saw him stretched out in the Levys' chair, his long legs overlapped at the ankles, while Muriel crooned. The scene was like a poster warning me. Muriel's singing had led nowhere. Her passionate, rankling marriage had ended, and whatever had happened to Desmond infected my blood.

"Mother could move to the city," I said. "She's wanted to, ever since I can remember, and now that she can, she won't."

"She might need time," he said. "She's a strict woman—morally, I mean, it's not easy for her to do what she wants. You remind me of her."

I was stung. "I'm wearing her clothes," I muttered.

He peered at me. "Are you? Well, I didn't mean that. I meant that you have a code. She's lived for you girls for a long time, now."

"Yes," I said sullenly. His approach to our lives seemed too honorable to permit him to imagine what the phrase meant to me. What a temptation it was to tell him that Muriel had driven Desmond off and clung to me. Lou would be shocked; he would think me ungrateful. But guilt threatened to bind me to my parents forever. Abruptly, I thought of Jock. The past fell away when I was with him, and the painful complications of the present faded. Where did the portrait hang? I wondered. What was the apartment like? How filthy rich was he? Wouldn't it be a relief to go there and see!

Lou speared a hunk of meat. "Aren't you hungry? Ben will be after you to fatten up."

I drank some wine and picked up my fork.

"I've been wondering whether you've fallen in love," I heard Lou say, and for an instant I thought he meant fallen in love with him.

"No!" I cried, my mouth full.

"No one at all?" He smiled, teasing. "Boys these days—an ordinary lot, I expect?"

I chewed my lamb. It was not a topic I cared to pursue.

"I feel awkward," he said. "I feel I'm being too gingerly— you're nearly grown. I don't know what you expected, or even why you called. I wonder if you know. So much time has passed. There's so much to say, where do we begin?" The room seemed to shrink around us. There were a few shaded lamps set on the walls, but they shed little light. Lou looked washed with umber.

"When I went to the network to do the first teleplay, the boss sent down an order: 'Let me see pores.' He was right. It was the medium. Everything is revealed in the face. There isn't time to do what Des and I used to do. Things fly past, images. People don't even talk the way they used to. We have a new language, new signals. Don't laugh at me, but my life is still changing—"

"I'm not."

"I feel young enough to start over yet again. There are experiences left—" He stared at me, through me.

"How is everything?" Ben's face gleamed. Neither of us had seen him approach. "You know, young lady, what we have for you if you eat your dinner? Baklava—you ever have it?" I shook my head.

"In a minute, Ben," Lou said, and Ben retreated. "God. Well, your mother used to say he was like a two-bit M.C. He can't leave well enough alone, and his timing is terrible."

I felt my skin shrink. "When was *she* here?"

His face had already registered alarm. The music came out of the walls, the ceiling, from under the table. He held up his hands, surrendering. "I wasn't sure whether she'd said anything." I kept my gaze steady. "She came in to see a play now

and then. I'm sure you knew that. We would have dinner together. . . . Look, I loved her." He shut his eyes, and without
their dark brilliance his face was lifeless. "I asked her to marry
me, to leave him. I wanted all three of you. I wanted to make
you happy. But she wouldn't make the break. She was bitter."

He opened his eyes. "I couldn't have helped Desmond. She
wouldn't believe that. Do you understand? Because I stayed,
she thought I was in management's pocket. Desmond was
courtly, he helped people, he stood for enduring standards.
Someone like that is always the first to go. And he never made a
peep of protest, as far as I know. We did—but no one could stop
what was happening. It was a sea change in the industry. Now
that you're here—you see what I mean, about beginning again."

I was shocked. So much was suddenly explained, but there
were too many loose ends. Wasn't Lou himself "courtly," and
didn't he stand for "quality"? How *had* he been spared?

Then I thought of what life might have been like if she had
married Lou. When had all this happened? When I was six, in
the first grade? Or nine, when we went to the Fireman's Ball?
Later, at home, I would match dates, memories—there were
even old calendars, in some box, marked up with Muriel's ap-
pointments. A little cloak of righteousness draped itself over
my shoulders. Maybe I'd have left home to live with Desmond
—I'd wanted to very badly. Why would I have tolerated Lou's
marriage to Muriel? He was my friend, not my father. *I* was the
one who had cared enough to stay in touch. I hunched forward,
watching his mouth. Poor, sad Lou. I wanted to get out of the
restaurant and away from him.

He reached across to take my hand, and I offered it stiffly.

"You have your life," he said. "I've watched you for a long
time, haven't I? You want to make a leap, for the sake of your
creativity, your sanity. . . ."

There was a long silence. "Have you talked to mother?" I
asked, too loudly.

"She won't talk to me," he said. I remembered once when
he'd brought me a rag doll. I hadn't liked dolls much, but that
one had gone everywhere with me. What an uncle he had been.
I wished I had left well enough alone. Why couldn't I call Jock
right now, see the portrait, meet his parents, hear them sing my
praises, sit in their parlor—as Lou said, start over?

"Miranda," Lou said carefully, "now that you're here, I can say something to you. I've saved quite a bit of money. What I'm doing now is absurdly lucrative." He gave me an apologetic look. "I have no family, no one close." I half rose, half turned, to locate the telephone. Lou started up from his chair. "She might never permit this, if she knew. . . . I want you to have some. I want to help you, to make it possible for you to do what you need to do. . . ."

I dropped into my chair. "I want to go to Swarthmore College. That's what I need to do."

He sighed. "Good. Of course you do. That's something we can work out." He looked very relieved. But I felt hooked. Just as I had tried to escape, he'd found this bait. What would I owe him? How would we work it out, how conceal it from Muriel? Or did he think he could persuade her that he was worthy? Was this a bribe?

"There is so much hurt behind us," he said. "It doesn't have to be all we ever know about each other."

I thought that if I were to sketch Lou then, he'd be a Hopper figure, all right, alone at a table with a white cloth in a nearly deserted restaurant with ochre walls somewhere in the night city. His private sorrows were so naked, there was little else to see. I didn't know what to do. I had wanted advice from him, and comforting. I had valued his neutrality, and destroyed it. Who was left for me to consult?

"Excuse me, I'm sorry," I mumbled, standing. "Ladies room." His face was blank. I bolted. Ben, behind the counter, pulled out a tray of pastries when he saw me coming. I asked him where the bathroom was, and he pointed down a narrow passage stinking of burned fat. I fumbled in my purse for a nickel. Surprisingly, Jock himself answered the telephone.

"It's me."

Silence. "Miranda? It's Miranda?"

Oh, relief, joy, at the pleasure in his callow voice! "Yes. I'm in town for the evening. With a friend. We've finished dinner. I wondered if maybe I could come over and see the portrait."

"Oh, gosh! Terrific! I almost wasn't here. I took Grandmama to a train and nearly went over to the Garden for a fight. So it's lucky. Where are you?"

The passage was hot, and I worried that my voice would

carry. "Downtown. I can get the subway. It'll be half an hour, I think."

"The subway! Take a cab, for God's sake."

He made me laugh. In the ladies room I washed my face and powdered it.

Lou stood when I returned, but I didn't sit down.

"You're not comfortable here, are you?" he asked humbly. "I was going to suggest—it's only five blocks from here—why don't we go to my apartment? It's a warm evening, after all. Don't look so frightened. This isn't a battle for your soul. I'm your father's oldest friend. I want you to have something from me because I care for you."

"I can't, Lou! I'm sorry! I'm very grateful. I can't." I began to cry. He took me into his arms and held me after my tears stopped. The music had stopped too. The room rang with quiet.

"It's all right," he soothed.

"Thank you." I couldn't wait to be gone. Did I remind him of Muriel now?

"I love you, Lou," I whispered. He tipped his head—he hadn't understood—but I did not repeat it.

On the street I looked in both directions, hoping a cab would draw up and suck me inside.

"Where are you going?" he asked, and I was surprised he hadn't assumed it was to a train and home.

"Uptown. In a cab," I said, ashamed.

"We'll walk to the corner." He stood a few feet out in the street, vulnerable, intent, with the grave dignity I had always admired. A cab appeared and Lou stopped it, his arm in the air, his coat flying. He brushed my cheek with his lips as I got in. He shut the door very carefully.

"So?" the driver said.

"Fifth Avenue," I said, and the address. I felt rescued, then, by my own spirit. Onward! The cab pulled away and raced north. I tried to put Lou and the restaurant and everything we had said out of my mind. Gazing out at the lights and movement of the city, I imagined a scene of welcome: Jock's mother would kiss me, her perfume subtle and powerful, her necklace grazing my own throat. His father would certainly put lips to my hand. Words would fly in two languages. They would approve—adults liked me.

We pulled up in front of the building and I struggled with bills and coins while a doorman waited. I glanced across the street to the Metropolitan Museum, which I had never before seen at night—hulking, black, all the art inside, locked away forever.

The doorman made me give my name. I'd rather have gone to the delivery entrance and been ignored than pass muster with him. But he let me into the lobby, which was furnished like someone's grand house. A flower arrangement three feet high sat in front of a mirror, and couches lined the way to the elevator, where a short, elderly, distinguished-looking man dozed on his feet inside the car. It had enough glossy brass and wood for an Edwardian men's club, and there was even a velvet bench to ride on. I glimpsed myself in another mirror, hastily avoiding my own eyes.

"Yes?" the little man asked.

"LeMieux, please."

He pulled the gate shut. "What time is it, please?" I asked.

He jerked around. "Best time of your life!" he shot, grinned, and dug for a pocket watch. "Twenty to eleven."

That was terribly late. How was I to get home at a reasonable hour? We rose smoothly to a little square chamber with two doors, more flowers, and on one wall, an exquisite landscape. I wondered if it was real—how careless to hang it there. I rang a bell and waited for a maid or Jock's mother or whoever would open one of the doors.

Footsteps sounded, followed by a teasing silence. Finally the door on the left flew open and Jock stood grinning at me. He wore a dressing gown, patent leather slippers, and carried a brandy snifter. A long dim hall stretched behind him with dark, fissured reflections.

He posed for a second, and we both laughed. "Come on in!" he cried. "As you see, I've just been enjoying a quiet evening at home."

We walked along between the smoked mirrors and came to a whole wall painted to create the illusion that one stood inside a villa, with a view to the sea, far below.

"That's a Sert," Jock said. "They rented that place once, in Portugal, and invited him. He made this as a present afterward." He swirled the brandy in his glass, walking backward, watching my face.

We entered a large bright room with a creamy carpet, a cartouche in its center and festoons of flowers and baskets around the borders. Jock saw me staring at it. "Savonnerie," he murmured close to my ear. The walls were painted spruce green and the woodwork was cream with gold stripes marking each panel. Tapestry chairs sat here and there, and hanging on the walls, in such profusion that my eyes avoided them at first, were paintings, one above another. It was a *cabinet de peinture.* When I could begin to look systematically, I recognized a few. They were, all of them, dazzling.

"My God. You *own* these! You live with them!"

"These are just the old guys. I thought you'd dig them."

Right in front of me was Gauguin—horsemen on a beach. It reminded me, as I studied it, of an early Picasso. Had Picasso seen this painting too? The thought made me shiver. I regarded Picasso almost as a rival. The old rascal got away with just the sort of audacious virtuosity I wished I could permit myself. He borrowed freely, he invented whatever he liked, and he made more than just a good living. I had heard that if he sketched one's face in a café and made a gift of the scrap, it was worth a fortune. His maddening masculinity was the key. There were hints that his inspiration came from devouring women. He could not have been raised as I was, to worry about pleasing other people.

Below the Gauguin was a Boudin beach scene—some Le-Mieux had made a witty juxtaposition. Fashionably dressed families, daubed daintily and adroitly, huddled in high-backed chairs or under umbrellas—vivid blots of color in a field between paired triangles of creamy sand and azure sky. Next to that was a Manet—I couldn't believe it! Three Parisians squeezed together in a café, seeming to submit to the painter's eye, but disdainful, too, boulevardiers, like Manet himself. It was such a fleeting moment. Another Manet had been painted in Venice. When had he gone there? Oh, how I longed to travel! Bright blue and white poles spiraled out of the sparkling water of the Grand Canal. I stumbled on, gasping aloud. Jock leaned against a chair, smiling down his nose, his cheeks pink, a French schoolboy acting a part in a play.

I saw a Matisse, it must be, but how gray! Two women strolled down a rainy hillside between bare sticks of trees. Farther along, a Degas dancer made my own body respond to the perfect symmetry of the composition as if I'd been struck. Jock stepped discreetly closer. He might have been presenting me with these paintings, making a lavish gift.

But that was far from the case. I had breeched someone else's inner sanctum. LeMieux choices surrounded me. Democracy and art were not complementary; society didn't even seem to *value* art. No wonder it wound up out of sight, with individuals who did. But still, wasn't the collection a display of excessive greed? Why should a mere businessman hoard so many ennobling works? I knew little of patronage, and nothing at all of investments.

Every picture bowled me over. I would take away nothing but memories. Maybe I'd never be back. (I stole a look at Jock, who immediately struck another waggish pose in his drawing room comedy getup.)

"Where did these come from?" I asked.

"Oh, Grandfather got most of them. He was more or less on the scene. Sometimes he was paid off in art. . . ."

Halfway around the room I pulled up short. "I don't believe it!" A Hopper hung over a little carved chest. It was a sad girl, ironing.

"You don't like?" Jock called from the sideboard, where he was pouring brandy.

"I love it! I love all of them! It's the night of all nights!" (Oh, faithless—the night had been Lou's until a short while ago. He had promised me far more than this.)

"I even love the still lifes," I went on, pleased to hear myself say it. "Look at this lemon on a plate, and this bunch of asparagus. All they're about is painting well. It took me a long time to see that, to realize lemons aren't boring to paint. Oh, I'd give anything for this to be my life!" I meant *painting*, of course, but Jock may have thought I meant his way of life. Perhaps I did.

He bounded over and handed me a glass of brandy. I drank, watching his glass swallow his face. His eyes swam behind the liquid. "Come along," he said. I heard a door click softly shut.

"Where are your parents?" We hadn't seen the portrait.

"We have the place to ourselves, as it happens," he said. "They had to go out—away."

"There's nobody here?"

"Yes. No. Are you frightened?" He cocked his head.

"I heard someone, just now."

"Just Magdalena, going to bed. We don't have to sit around being polite to the old folks. I think it's terrifically lucky. Aren't you glad?"

Awe and ignorance put me at a disadvantage, but I was determined that he not see that.

He took my hand. "I've dreamed of your coming here," he said. "Really," he added, reading my face. "Of just showing you and not having to explain everything. You can *see*, you know? It's simpler. I couldn't have planned it better. We're in the hands of fate." He bowed his head. "They can be pretty rough on people."

"But where's the portrait? Didn't they like it?"

"It's being framed," he said brightly. "I forgot to tell you. They absolutely adore it. Come see something else." He pulled me down another hall, past a salon with hideous tubular furniture and enormous, violent abstract canvases on the walls. "Papa's," he said, over his shoulder.

We stopped at the door of a bedroom and he darted inside. The room, (its walls a brushed rose), glowed alluringly. The headboard of an outsized bed ascended to the ceiling, trailing satin drapes. The matching coverlet was embroidered, scalloped, and forbidding. Jock crooked his finger. I tiptoed a few steps. It was a sacrosanct place, too carefully designed to hide secrets I might stumble over, but too grand for casual trespass. I wished he hadn't led me into it.

"There they be," he said, pointing. "In absentia, so you know what you're missing." A pair of portraits hung between glass-doored bookcases. They were remarkable for twinned severity of expression. Both mother and father looked pinched and guarded. Jock took after his father—there was a resemblance of essential bone under his prettier flesh. His mother wore a look of proud martyrdom, and in fancying that I saw through her, I believed I saw the portrait's weakness: The painter had ridiculed and exalted her at the same time. She looked physically flattered and painfully aware of it.

"Okay, we've made our duty call. Now for the treats." He beckoned me to a wall where a small drawing in black chalk and sepia wash was hung. "Like it? It's a Fragonard, of course."

A half-naked woman, her robes fallen open and off her flanks, bent over a man in a Romantic's white blouse. His curly head burrowed at her bare breasts and his hand groped below her belly. They tussled on a vast pillow-strewn bed with trailing curtains. A little plaque on the frame read: *La Résistance Inutile*.

I could feel Jock's eyes on me. Then his fingers wound around my upper arm. "They had their bed made after the drawing, it's such a favorite," he said, and the improbability of that distracted me for a moment. "Gorgeous, isn't it?" he prompted. He held his breath while we looked some more.

The drawing stirred me, the more so for being unforeseen. I felt subject to Jock's strategies, suspended between attraction and suspicion. Suddenly my stomach lurched so violently that I tottered to a chair and leaned on it.

"What's the matter?" I shook my head. "You need to lie down," he said. "I've got more to show you. They're really fine."

He hurried to a little casement window set in the wall and pulled out a book so heavy he had to carry it in both hands. "Come over here. You'll appreciate these. Make yourself comfortable." He heaved the book up onto the bed and climbed after it, kicking off his slippers and scooting to the center. He plopped back against the mound of pillows with an expression of feline satisfaction.

My bowels growled and clutched at themselves with iron fingers. I hung onto the chair for a moment longer, praying for relief, and the spasms abated. But I felt feeble.

"Come on," Jock crooned. The great book lay on his lap. He patted the coverlet next to him with a droll smile.

I groaned involuntarily and walked to the bed, pausing again to shore myself up. Jock held out his hand and shifted an inch or two. I took off my shoes and stretched out beside him. The fabric was slippery and dense. The view I now had of the room seemed unnatural. I lay stiffly, prepared to ward off attack, but he only touched my thigh lightly and asked if I didn't feel better.

"Here are my treasures." He opened the book to a scene of another bed, not a Fragonard—it hadn't the Master's effortless knack—but set in his time. Gradually I saw, too, that this picture was far more explicit. The man sat on the floor, one knee bent, and the woman on the bed above, exposing her genitals full to his straining face and distended tongue. His penis thrust out of his shirt. I reddened. My pulse raced.

Jock flipped a page. Another partially clad eighteenth century rake loomed over a plump, vivacious harlot with rouged cheeks. She pulled at his member as if it were a throttle, hauling him over her onto a couch. Again, in spite of myself, my head reeled, as blood flooded my face and my nether parts. It throbbed there, demanding that I look at more. Jock peeked sideways at me, and I glowered stubbornly at the page.

I was marveling that great artists had yielded to this impulse, too, as I had, with my St. Sebastiane and my bound slaves. These pictures were, no question, far more advanced than mine. Jock ran the tips of his fingers over my neck and down my arm. He raised his eyebrows, leaned over, and kissed me lightly, a delicate, sucking little fish's kiss. Instantly I succumbed to an unprecedented wave of urgency that washed away will, or rather sent it raging. Jock shut the book over his finger. I could see the title now—Fuchs: *Erotische Kunst.*

"This is our *enfer* collection," he whispered. "They don't know I know about it." He brushed my cheek with his lips. "What do you think of it?"

"I think it's funny that grown men, who could sell their paintings to anyone, who were great painters, would make these."

"Funny . . ." He chuckled indulgently, snuggling against me and reopening the book. We studied more scenes. One involved serial coupling, among a group of Victorians on a picnic, wielding dildoes, which Jock identified and explained to me.

"Here's a Grandeville," he said, turning to a drawing of young ladies gathered to observe as two held the legs of another apart so that a fourth could kneel between them. He turned to an Oriental section, where the heterosexual pair was restored in great variety. We had begun to stroke each other, almost unconsciously.

"Ahhhhh," he groaned abruptly, pressing the book against his lap. "It's getting me. I need your help, Miranda."

He rolled over onto me, and I tried to shift under his weight so as to be touched in the places that demanded it.

"Put your hand there," he muttered, and drew it to the hard mound at his crotch. I rubbed tentatively. His head lolled next to mine on the pillow. I thrust one leg over his and ground against his thigh. A wave of nausea rose from my gut and I gulped for air.

He raised his head. "You okay?"

"Yes," I swallowed. "Please touch me too."

He put his hand between my legs and sawed back and forth. We were the two arms of a machine. "Yes, yes," he sighed, hauled his body onto mine and set to bouncing rhythmically. The bed was so soft it offered no resistance and our movements were erratically syncopated. It was like wrestling on a cloud. Elusive sensations tantalized me. I tried to fix my position so as to meet his intermittent descents, and he stiffened his arms, ramming his pelvis against mine. He dropped his damp face to my neck and panted there.

"I really care for you, you know that," he rasped in my ear. "You're so great. I . . . respect . . . you. Listen, do you want to?"

He slid up and down my body and I clung to his buttocks. We had been making a lot of noise and slithering over the satin, perilously close to the edge. My heart pounded so that it seemed to drown out my consciousness, but I heard him tell me he cared for me and was touched, relieved, even proud. I must certainly care for him, for his hands, molding me as a sculptor would, with love.

"Yes?" he asked, lifting himself. I arched my back to follow, abandoned, dazed, a reply gurgling in my throat when suddenly the hummock that had pressed so voluptuously to my pudendum dissolved—squashed, like a grape underfoot. He rolled off me and uttered a sob. Then he shook the hair from his forehead, sat up, and said formally, "I'm sorry. Believe me, that will never happen again."

I didn't know what had happened, exactly. Had I inadvertently blundered to some source of pain? Had his clothing chafed when I pulled on it? What had I done? My nausea, having teased me long enough, now arrived in full force. I threw myself off the bed, gasping, "Bathroom—."

He raised an arm and pointed. I yanked open the door and fell to a praying position in front of the toilet. A tidal wave of dinner and brandy coursed into the bowl and splattered its rim. After I'd been evacuated and added a few dry heaves, I sat back in harrowed calm. All was silent.

Two doors slammed. Footsteps sounded and a woman's sharp, low, scolding voice; a masculine mumble, a feminine blast and more, louder treading of the floor. Before I could scramble to my feet, they were all in the room, eyeing Jock with consternation as he pulled at his robe and slid to the floor.

I stood next to the toilet, afraid to flush it. Papa's back was to me. A woman's shoulder leaned in the doorway, and peering over that was the brown face of a girl, her eyes huge and overwhelmed, staring directly at me. M. LeMieux turned almost casually to see what she saw. When he started toward me, I pulled the flush handle and water roared, removing all matter, but not its aromas.

"What? What is happening?" Jock's mother cried, having come all the way into the room. Both hands flew to her bosom. She seemed to beseech, not to reproach.

"This is Miranda," Jock said very loudly. "Miranda, the parents." He groped on the bed for his glasses. "She's the one who made my portrait."

"Very nice, very nice job," M. LeMieux murmured, looking away from my face. He turned to his wife and coughed delicately but insistently.

She turned to the girl in the doorway. "Thank you, Magdalena. You may go to bed now."

Jock loosed a theatrical sigh. His mother silenced him with her eyes. She turned to where I cowered. Jock did a little puppetlike shuffle. I had been waiting for him to offer some explanation, but he clearly had no intention of doing so, at least not as long as I was present. That must mean I would be blamed after I'd gone. He clutched at his robe, head bowed penitently, and kicked the book, by degrees, under the bed.

"Where do you live, Miss—" his mother asked. Before I could answer, she said to her husband, "We'll send her in the car. You'd better ring down to Jean-Luc right now." He winced and exited.

I told her I lived near St. Bart's. I had planned to take the train. She waved me off impatiently. What difference did it make to her—this was what Jean-Luc was for, to get me out of her sight in a responsible manner. It was the method these people used to deal with messy situations. I shifted from one foot to the other, weak, my mouth puckered and vile-tasting. What time must it be? I wondered. The realization that I must call Muriel gave me strength.

"By all means. Use the one down the hall, if you please." When I went out, I heard her voice, then Jock's, intense and controlled so that I wouldn't catch their words.

"Do you know what time it is?" Muriel asked, her tones, naturally rich in sarcasm, made querulous by the dinky French phone. I told her I was chez LeMieux, and that diverted her right away.

"What's it like?" she demanded to know. "I want you to *observe* your surroundings, this time." I told her I'd been sick, which didn't please her. "My God, they must have loved that!" she said. "I'm not surprised. You never regulate yourself properly." I said I'd be home as soon as the limousine could take me.

"It's already after two. I'll wait up. This will never happen again." That was just what Jock had said.

Papa LeMieux escorted me to the car in embarrassed silence. Jock looked up and gave a wave that seemed mocking to me, but was a gesture of complicity, perhaps, though hardly comforting. His father and I marched stiffly along the corridors, and when we got to the parlor I tried to look again at every painting, like someone starved, desperate, foolish.

7

I had cashed the check Jock gave me; now I imagined it coming back to him from the bank, along with the one from the frame shop. I heard nothing further from him. The money pleased me —I put it into a college fund—but I was otherwise chagrined. I had foolishly let him tempt me, thinking I could attach myself to something dazzling and alien.

By spring I felt inured to his ilk, and vowed to stick to people who needed to be sensitive, who were short on cash and had to barter when it came to feelings.

My rumpled art teacher, Mr. Pearl, called my attention to an article in *Art News* about a "society portraitist."

"The human face and figure are the noblest subjects," he said gruffly, jabbing at the page with a square fingertip. I was grateful to him for confiding his disgust. "Just look at the shallow treatment he gives them. I don't care what the subject asked for. Who will remember his fee?" The man really got his goat, and I could see why. We shared a few moments of companionable distress. Mr. Pearl had once been a painter. His school teacher's salary and the indifference of most students must have discouraged him.

Muriel recovered interest in her life. She dieted until her clothes fit and even bought a sharp-looking suit at the Saks branch in the village. A copy of *Vogue* turned up on top of her pile of periodicals, and she pored over it with more interest than envy. I was still afraid she would telephone Lou, or he her, but his name didn't come up, even when I was in danger of nervously blurting it myself. She looked for houses for sale and this became a regular, involving recreation. Her guide was Clement Gunther, a realtor, and therefore an escort always a telephone call away; in fact, always calling her. Gunther had a large round head and hair cut so close to his scalp it looked like a sprinkling of mica. He was short of breath and long of phrase, and Muriel boasted that he found her an ideal client—bright and educable. His son Mike was in my class at school, but neither Gunther nor I ever mentioned the connection and our mutual reticence made his outings with my mother seem vaguely illicit. He usually carried a pair of gloves in one hand and with the other popped mint Lifesavers into his mouth, peeling them off the roll with his thumb. After a while he took to waiting in his long car for Muriel, out at the curb, playing the radio and drumming on the steering wheel, gloves and file folder on the seat beside him. I would wave when I came home, and turn a precise corner into the driveway, which brought a grin from him. Muriel bustled out of the front door looking as if *this* would be the day she'd find a place. He leapt from the car and ran around to open the passenger door. When he got back in, their laughter was muffled, then obliterated by the growl of the engine. I would have the house to myself for a few hours.

I mailed my application to Swarthmore without saying anything to her, and asked three teachers to write letters of recommendation. Life had taken a conservative turn, I wrote Rebecca. I felt responsible, but dull. I could *smell* my independence ripening.

One day in early February, Linda and Judy cornered me at the lockers.

"Have you seen the new artist?" Judy asked, looking at me sideways.

"Hugh something," Linda added, twirling her pearls.

"Really cute." Judy sniffed. "Incredible. He's a junior. Everybody's crazy about the way he draws." She stared squirrel-like at me. "Ronnie sits behind him in history and he did these doodles she just couldn't believe. . . ."

"You two should get together," Linda said officiously.

Portia mentioned him next. I was in the art room after school, drawing the cement factory from the window, using colored pencils, slowing myself down with meticulous technique. I

glanced up and saw her lovely, gallant smile through the glass
in the door. I hadn't felt the proper gratitude for those glimpses
of a face as familiar as my own, while we shared a school. I
waved her in without stopping my work.

"He moved out from the city—The Bronx," she informed me.
"He wants to meet you. Sam says he's smart, but extremely
shy."

She pointed him out—a slight, tense boy standing apart from
the throng filling buses at the north door. He was the only one
without school books and his hands were jammed into the
pockets of an ochre-colored corduroy jacket much too light for
the weather. His collar stood up against his neck and he
squinted as if he'd just taken off dark glasses. His eyebrows
were nearly invisible on his pale face, but they arched up, an
expression of pained indecision. So this was the new artist, the
new gun. I was curious. "He wants to meet you," Portia said
again.

I was invited to another party, in Suzanne Winston's basement, which we entered through a bulkhead, following signs
stuck in the yard. An anxious face flashed in the kitchen window when I descended to the smoke and din of rock 'n' roll
records. Suzanne had forbidden her parents to interfere and
they were complying. She lived just a block away from me, but
we had never been friendly. Now, in the middle of senior year,
the social crowd had become sentimental about the rest of us
and embraced the whole class. There was a new tone to our
exchanges, gushing and breathless, the prelude to good-bye.

The few lamps in the room were draped with towels and
scarves. Dancers bobbed like goblins and stags straight-armed
their way along the knotty pine, beer bottles aloft, sloshing the
heads of certain girls, calling out their positions like gunboats.
Boys I had known since grade school gave me the once-over,
their eyes congealed. I leaned on a door frame. The room
throbbed with noise.

A couple stomped in front of me, shiny with sweat. On the
walls, photographs of Suzanne and her horse bounced to the
beat. I had seen her, not long before, tearfully tell a clutch of
sympathetic girls that Big Ben had been sold. All those rosettes
on the molding were show ribbons.

"Do you come here often?" said a voice in my ear. It was the new artist, leaning on the other side of the door frame, in an unlighted tool room. For a moment I couldn't place his face. He sipped from a glass, not a bottle, and eyed me over its rim.

I laughed. "I've heard all about you," I said. "I hear we have something in common." I began to compose my letter to Rebecca: *Things are picking up here. . . .*

"In common," he repeated. "You don't hang around with her, do you? Our horsetess?"

"I've known her all my life. Just don't ride her too hard."

He stepped back. His voice was hollow and only his feet were visible. "Came to read the gas meter. Been trapped in here for days."

The record that had been playing came to an end. We watched the dancers' discharging motions. "Do you want something?" he asked. I said, "Soda." He pushed through the crowd. More guests were shooting down the bulkhead steps to be greeted with screams or indifference. A boy knocked a can of beer from another's hand, drenching his partner's dress. "Oh oh oh oh, God," she cried, her face like someone in a Last Judgment fresco. Then she laughed explosively, turning crimson, and covered her face with her hands. Three girls led her away like nurses.

Hugh returned, holding glass and bottle over his head. "Such a display," he said. I wondered what he was drinking. He caught me staring at his glass. "Elixir," he said. What did I care?

"I'd ask you to dance, but my gout," he said. We drank. His arm grazed mine. I inhaled the vapors of after-shave lotion and was touched by the suggestion of vanity. "Who's that by the couch?" he asked.

"Dwight Sawyer. He plays football and trombone and when he was little he was incredibly fat."

"I wouldn't want to mess with him now. Who's that dancing with what's-his-name, Tom?"

"Doreen Lawson. Why?" Doreen was gorgeous, already crossed over the line from decorative to predatory.

"She's peaking. You know what I mean? Life will be downhill for her from now on." I looked at his face. "Man comes down the road," he went on in the same tone, "sees a farmer lift up his pigs, one by one, to an apple tree, to eat the apples. Man says, 'Say, doesn't that take an awful lot of time, feeding the pigs like that?' Farmer answers, 'What's time to a pig?' " Hugh drew a finger across his throat, *cut*, the way Lou used to in the control room.

So we passed the evening, exchanging observations and wise-cracks, out of place by choice, content to stand on the sidelines. I had learned to banter from listening to Desmond's puns and pointed colloquialisms, those models of oblique self-expression. I knew that such tricks protected me from people I already felt distanced from. Now they linked me to Hugh, who had his own repertoire. His was another nimble imagination dodging its ene-mies, entertaining its friend. We even kept quiet about our pas-sion for art—discretion would help us establish trust. We pre-served and lubricated an assumed but unproven understanding. Everything we learned about each other was indirect.

We stayed until the very end. He walked me home at two, and on our doorstep, under the light Muriel had left burning (was she watching or sleeping behind her dark front window?), he pulled a paper from his pocket and handed it to me. I un-folded it. It was a pencil drawing of two wrestlers, very sensu-ously drawn. The figures' sexes were not clear and the act might have been, I thought at startled first glance, coitus. I looked closer and concluded that the subject was athletic, not sexual, but his line was powerfully erotic.

"*The Struggle*," he said. "It's for you. I made it for you." He squinted. His eyebrows climbed his skull and he shoved his hands into his pockets.

"Thank you," I said. I was moved. The gift was significant, and the drawing was wonderful. It was not my place to, but I began to feel proud of him. I urged him to help me on the staff of the school literary magazine or the newspaper. He would not do that, would not join any staff. He made me feel foolish. He only doodled, that was the extent of it, that was the use of it, no more. It was a private thing. I decided he must be unwilling to test himself in an arena. But the way he spoke made me shut up. I sensed that he was the sort who would not fight, but would withdraw.

For a week his face, with its self-conscious tough mask, stole my mind from the French Revolution or the dishes in the sink or the need to go to sleep. I imagined his ripe lips, thought of kissing them, leaning my cheek on the shoulder of his soft jacket or against his blond curls. I wanted to believe, on the evidence of lips and silences and iconography (*The Struggle*), that he harbored passions and I would, in time, discover them. Most people my age had a "personality," a set of prejudices used like a snowplow to push drifts to either side. The pull between Hugh and me was certainly deeper than personality.

"You were out late," Muriel observed. "I was awake until after one and you hadn't come in." Her glance fell over me to the floor. She asked no questions. Was I free?

I didn't lay eyes on Hugh, but that didn't worry me. I did look for him, craning my neck in the hallways between classes, hurrying from door to door when the last bell rang, hoping to head him off. Yet I relished the waiting; it provided a transition. This episode in my life was going to be strange, I could tell.

One afternoon I walked along Brixton Road, past the cement factory, to get a closer look at it. Hugh popped up in my path. He didn't smile.

"We meet at last."

"What I was thinking."

"It's no coincidence."

"You being here?"

"*You* being here. I have something to show you." He stuck out his hand, and I gave him mine.

This was the edge of town—the houses had shrunk to bungalow size, and the factory lay just across the line. A railroad spur ran next to it, and another old commuter line, long out of service, veered toward a sharp drop where it crossed the underpass for County 9, which ran into town and became the main shopping route. Years ago I had ridden my bicycle up here to visit a little woods that had been the grounds of an estate, the untended specimen plantings giving the plot a wild, magical feeling. Now the golden bones of houses under construction had replaced them. I felt bereaved, looking across the plain. Hugh loped along beside me, bouncing on the balls of his feet, squinting, his breath steaming, wearing just his usual jacket against the cold.

At the end of the street we followed a footpath trailing below the tracks to the county road. Next to the underpass was a steep embankment with a grudging display of brown grasses, bottles, cans, wire, and an old boot. The roof of the Meridian Avenue

Station loomed, rust colored against the ponderous gray sky. Hugh let go of my hand and flung himself up the bank.

I followed his jackknifing arms and legs. We grasped at the ground, panting, our shoes slipping and scraping. Smoke from the factory coated my lips and tongue and cinders embedded themselves in my palms.

He got to the top first and looked down at me with an indecipherable expression. I lunged past him and took three leaps over the rusty rails and bent weeds in the trackbed. He walked to the station and held up his hands like a safecracker. Large sheets of plywood were nailed over the windows.

The landscape fell away on all sides; the track ran on a narrow ridge. Cars entered the underpass below and emerged on the other side, tiny and silent. The wind up high was loud. These tracks hadn't been used since I'd lived in town. The main line was the one Desmond had taken, within walking distance of our house. For an instant I could see him, his elbows crooked, whittling, walking at a good clip, a trim figure Portia and I waited for, before we were allowed to go off the block. The sun set behind him.

Hugh flexed his fingers. "What are you doing?" I asked. If we were caught trespassing, my trouble would be greater than his. He was a spellbinder, responsible to no one, but I had a reputation to protect.

He lifted one of the plywood panels from a side window—it hadn't been secured at all. "Come in," he said, and went over the sill. I scanned the horizon again and followed him.

He lit a match and then a candle, took it around the room and lighted more candles, all set into little cans full of sand. There was a wood stove in the center of the room and benches lined up on either side of it. My eyes were slow to adjust to the gloom. I saw a pile of pillows on the floor, sketchbooks, and a backpack.

"So. What will they say when they excavate this dump?" he asked. I turned in a slow circle, blinking at the walls, not quite sure I could believe what I was seeing.

"Bear in mind," he added, "the human senses apprehend only about ten percent of reality. The rest is lost."

Two broad walls were covered with murals. I picked up a candle and stepped closer to one. Grotesque figures leapt, embraced, lifted fanciful weapons, and at intervals, surrounded three of Hugh's self-portraits. They gazed dourly out at me; their eyes followed me when I moved, and two were attached to animal trunks; one donkey, one prancing goat. The landscape was as disconcerting as his face: gigantic trees, laden with fruits and blossoms, towered over men and women who lay beneath them, feeding each other. Dwarves stuck their toes into their own mouths, stood on their heads, lay in clamshells, rode turtles or peered from the halves of eggs. Here and there an imp pulled down his trousers and a tart bared her breast. The wall was crammed full of things to look at; every element seemed related to every other in some way, all of it puzzling, the solutions proposed by the clues also eluding them. I hadn't the slightest idea what it could all mean. There was an aquatic look to the landscape—cold tones at the center, warmer ones at the outer edges. He had used aerial perspective, which made it all dreamlike. The most violent images were rendered in delicate, pastel hues, and the most fantastic drawn with a loving realism. It was alarming and compelling.

Finally I said, "How did you do all this?"

"What's time to a pig?" I was rebuked. But what was the right thing to say? He stood watching me, glowering down his nose.

"They look like dreams." I moved along the wall. "No, they remind me of something else—it's Bosch! That's it, isn't it? And this part looks like Goya, right?" I turned my exuberant face to his. I was immensely relieved.

He was coldly furious.

"I mean it as a compliment," I said, my voice rising. "They're so good, is what I mean—like Old Masters—and these scenes are like nothing else—" I was at sea with my references.

"I don't copy anybody. I don't know what you're talking about." He turned his back to me. "I did them for you." I stared at his back. Could he be sniggering, stifling mocking laughter? Did he really not know? Had genius made its spontaneous appearance in an abandoned railroad station? The images were so like ones I had been awed by, assumed were unique, and stored away in the past.

"I wouldn't let anyone else in here," he muttered.

"I hope not. You'd be arrested. This isn't public property."

He was making me stupid. I turned, frowning, to the second painted wall. It was more peaceful, with rocks, flowers, thorny little trees, and a glow in the distance that might have been the setting sun, or might have been a fire. I wondered abjectly what Hugh had thought of my childish murals still on the walls at school, with their banal, curricular subjects. Behind me, he made a clatter. He had opened the stove and was stuffing it with newspaper.

"Someone will see the smoke," I said.

"Nobody has in the last two months." He smiled lazily, in a new mood. "It just blends in with the crap from over the town line. Listen, Miranda, I haven't vandalized this place. I've improved it. When they break in after we're dead, they'll charge admission to people."

"After we're dead?"

"In the next century." He lit the newspaper and blew on it. The fire caught with a suck. "This keeps me sane," he confided, standing and stretching. "I had a little place in the city, a shed behind a store. The guy let me stay there any time."

"And you painted?" I pictured myself in my shed, safe and busy.

"Yes. Made some drawings. Listened to the radio . . ."

This was wrenching to think of. It drew me to him, mingled the things that had made us conscious. "I used to listen to all those mysteries and draw. My dad wrote *Clapper's Corners.*"

He looked blank. I named some more shows. "I tuned in music," he said, shortly. "Midnight to dawn."

He said his father, who had been a lineman for the telephone company, was injured and transferred to a desk job. They had moved to their present house. "It makes him touchy. He hardly ever opens his mouth. He wants me to fight." Hugh made fists. "We spar. I let him hit me. He seems to feel better. I lift weights. But I need my hands. I can't box."

"Your father doesn't care about your painting?"

He laughed and turned away. "So," he said. "I'm giving you the other two walls."

"What?"

"Those. You paint on them. Then we'll have our own museum."

"I can't do that." I didn't know what to say. The idea was

outlandish, wasn't it? I had more important things to do. My life was more serious than this. . . . "The police are going to come in here one day and—"

"Look, it's just playing," he said. "There's no law against that. You're too serious. Nobody needs this place."

"I'm sure there's a law," I said stiffly. What *was* I afraid of? Was it having to choose something to paint when these amazing images were already in place? He had painted dreams, dreamily, without hesitation. What did I want to work on that would never be seen by anyone?

"You want people to find these, I know it," I said.

"I do not. I don't want anyone here but you."

"You said 'excavation.' "

"We won't be around for that."

Hugh shot me a sharp pale look. I was ashamed of my resistance.

"Let's go, Hugh." I stamped my feet and stuck each hand in its opposite armpit. "It's freezing and I have to get home."

He sat on a bench, stretched out his legs, and laced his fingers behind his head. "What about it?"

"I'm thinking about it. I can't afford to get caught. I want to graduate. I don't have so much time. I want to go to college. People trust me."

"Go ahead, then," he said, curling his lips. "I'm staying. I don't have to be anywhere."

I left, angry that I must walk through that end of town alone, must climb ignominiously out the window first, while Hugh lolled on the bench, sneering.

On Saturday Muriel put me to work waxing the floors downstairs. She had begun to sort clothing and fabric for disposal and instructed Portia and me to go over our things and thin them out. She hurried up and down the stairs with a scarf over her hair, humming tunelessly, the joyless sound rising and falling all day long. Portia scrubbed the walls of the upstairs hall. I was on my hands and knees in the dining room when the doorbell rang.

Muriel flew past with an armload of curtains. I heard her speak in an amiable tone and then chortle. She called my name. I stepped over my waxed triangle. Hugh was lounging in the doorway, his eyebrows at a cocky angle, his eyes clear as glass and narrowed to slits.

Muriel cried, "We're getting acquainted. Your friend is willing to help me out in the cellar. We've inspected his muscles." She gave him a fluttering glance. "He's staying for lunch." Hugh's gaze was steady, but he battled twitches about his mouth. "I think you'd better buff that," Muriel said to me, leading him away.

I heard him going up and down the cellar stairs. Portia came down and whispered, "What's he doing here?" I had never brought a boyfriend home before and Muriel had instantly possessed this one. Several times I heard her go to him and then laugh richly, the sound of it rolling through the house. Hugh's manner with me had been languid. With Muriel he was a charming engine of industry.

Finally I went down to the cellar to see what he was doing. The cupboard at the foot of the stairs stood open, displaying the old Norman Rockwell *Freedom from Fear* poster, with its craggy, kindly American faces. I kicked the door shut.

Hugh had taken off his shirt and was cleaning out a coal bin. His muscles, like ropes over his bones, so much more developed, in their way, than his face, gleamed under a coating of sinister pitch. He grinned. "Is she always like this?"

"You shouldn't let her bully you. You're not her son."

"I have to have lunch somewhere. She said 'lentil soup.' What's that?"

"Oh, for God's sake," I said. "We never have that."

When we sat down at the table, Muriel scolded Hugh and sent him upstairs to the bathroom Portia and I shared to wash off more of the grime on his arms and neck. I went hot and cold, thinking of his penetration into the house. He returned. "I'm stained," he said. "It's permanent."

"And if I find dirt on that towel, I'll skin the stain off you," she said. Portia shook her head at me, as if to say, "Now you see why I tell them to honk and wait for me outside." Muriel was playing Aunt Polly, whom I had drawn, dragging Tom by his ear. She was fashioning quite a complex entertainment for Hugh.

We all ate the soup and she interrogated him. We learned that his mother could sew. "Can she *really*!" Muriel exclaimed, as if it were a lost art. "She likes to enter those contests in the paper," Hugh added. "She wants to travel."

"Brava," Muriel commented. "Well, I like to enter those contests too. We'll have to compete with each other, though, your mother and I." She propped her chin in her hand. "Where does your mother want to go?"

"I really don't know. She has a sister in Florida. She said something once about Hawaii."

"I see," Muriel said. "Hugh, you haven't said a word about the lentil soup. How do you like it?"

Her tone would have alerted a moron. "I think it's an acquired taste," Hugh said, deadpan. "I don't think it'll go over in America."

Portia and I looked at Muriel. "I think you'll grow to appreciate it, after you've had a few bowls," she said. Then she refilled his to the brim. "I'll take that as a personal challenge."

She liked him. She had exposed his weaknesses, mostly to do with an undistinguished background and with ignorance, and found his sense of humor. It meant I could probably spend as much time with him as I liked, as long as he came home with me occasionally to banter with Muriel. No friend of mine had ever been so welcome.

At the end of the day Muriel pronounced his work satisfactory and Portia and I let our mouths drop open at how easily he got off. In a flash I thought I understood what this was all about: Muriel's flirting had the poignancy of futile longing. She had wanted a son. Hugh's response to her was instinctively tolerant, but Portia's eyes glazed as she watched them. Our instincts were those of women raging to get away from their own kind.

Before Hugh left he asked me to take a drive with him after supper. He was only sixteen; I knew it wasn't legal. Muriel gave me leave without a question. He drove his father's stout green Buick as if we were delivering explosives. The seat was so wide I chattered to fill up the gap between us. We parked on a dead-end road where trees were bunched in the glow from a single streetlight. Our shifting on our seat made a comic noise. The night was black. I couldn't see Hugh's face. The air inside the car was warm. A door banged shut somewhere; a boy called a dog.

"Ever go fishing?" he asked. I said no. "We go to a cabin in the Thousand Islands. My dad taught me to fish. We both prefer our own company now." Across the street the lights in a house were extinguished, one by one. "There's a castle on one of the islands, abandoned now, but it belonged to a rich guy a long time ago, a huge, pile of a place. I found an open window in the cellar and I used to explore. I was scared to death, shaking the whole time, but I moved on from room to room. There was a lot of heavy furniture—oak, mahogany, a table twenty people could eat at, big couches, moose heads, deer heads, fish, of course, guns, paintings, silver platters, chandeliers. The kitchen was a block long and in the basement. They sent food up on a dumbwaiter. The paintings had so much varnish, they were all the same color. Mountain scenes, mostly, but some white-water stuff. Gold leaf frames. Everywhere I went, I thought somebody was following me. I've never been so scared. I mean, forty, fifty rooms." He had reached over and was softly kneading my shoulder. His voice was monotonous.

"It was depressing, in addition to scary. I didn't go back until the next summer—I was eleven, I think. The place was different, I could tell right away, but I didn't know why. Then I realized there wasn't as much stuff. A few beds were gone, a few couches, a table here and there, a painting. In a few weeks I went back and there were *no* paintings, no silver, no beds. I was scared, but I couldn't stay away. The next time almost everything was gone. It was more cheerful, in a way. I actually liked it better. I wanted to live there. It was as if they were moving out so I could move in. But I never saw anybody. It never looked as if anybody had been there in years and years, and they hadn't. Finally one day I went inside and the place was bare as a bone. I thought, Somebody must look after this place —what's going on? Am I the only person who notices? On Labor Day the scandal broke. Everybody was talking about the big heist at the castle. It had dawned on them, somebody had gotten away with everything. How did they do it, everyone was asking. How did they get that much stuff out without anybody seeing? They called it The Great Loot." He kneaded my shoulder, then drew his fingertips along the inner surface of my arm, my ribs, his knuckles barely grazing my breast. "It reminds me of that thing in science, where they put a frog in water and heat

it up slowly until it boils to death without ever feeling a thing."
He looked at me. "So they say . . ." His fingers increased their
pressure.

I pulled away. "That's something I hate about human beings," I said. He cocked his head.

"What do you hate?"

"That we're so adaptable. People get used to anything, adjust
to anything. It's supposed to be a strength, and I guess it can be,
but it scares me. We can put up with such terrible things, with
cruelty and suffering and wickedness and ugliness. It makes me
mad that we're so soft and foolish."

He leaned over so quickly, my lips were still parted for "foolish." His kiss was a luring, provoking one and made me strain
toward him. He drew me, his hands fluttering over my back and
my arms.

It was our kissing I thought about when I found him at the
station the next day. But we stood several feet apart, and he
bent broodingly over a sheet of butcher paper spread on the
floor. His inattention to me was mesmerizing. I waited to see
what he would do. He knelt with a conté crayon and drew,
making wide strokes over the whole page. Waves spewed foam.
An island rose from a jetty of rocks. A building went up.

"The castle?" I asked. He grunted. I decided to sketch him
while he worked. I had finished two drawings in my little notebook when he added himself to his scene, a tiny figure in a boat
tossed by gigantic waves. He looked back at me over his shoulder.

"It looks like a Homer," I said.

"Don't draw me."

"Why not?"

"Paint your walls."

"I don't know what to paint. They're so blank."

"What difference does it make?" He wiped his hands on his
pants and sprang up. He had seemed irritable and distant. Now
he faced me and said, "I love you, you know that, don't you?"

A sharp laugh pushed out of my mouth, and my hand flew
up, as if to plug it. "Well," I said. He sat next to me. His eyelids
were thick and a vein throbbed in his forehead. Tiny golden
hairs glistened around his mouth. I thought his expression and
gestures were like acting, not phony, but a parody of some

kind. I began to play against them, pretending to emotion I did not yet feel. I got up and walked to the window and leaned on it, conscious of how I looked. It was the first week in March and lemony shafts of sunlight thickened whatever they touched. I examined their effect on my arm at the sill.

Hugh coughed. I turned and looked at him. The room was hazy with light and dust. We were sixteen and seventeen. Recrossing the room could amount to nothing or be charged with significance. It all depended on my attitude, on how I swung my arms or narrowed my eyes. Fate had brought me this disturbing boy, his pictures, his distracting talent. I moistened my lips with my tongue. A little breeze blew in, lifting the edges of the butcher paper. The bare walls called for a frieze, didn't they —a pattern with repetition and a theme. Hugh had drawn from his life, just now. I remembered our stay in Old Chatham, the modest repetitions in Eugene's work and my anxious vigil in the buzzing heat, when I had thought he'd jilted me. Hugh seemed to work without thinking, certainly without afterthought. It all just happened, and by magic his subjects were the ones that great painters had chosen.

"Can you stay a little, Miranda?" he asked.

"I have to get home soon. I have to help out."

"I guess you do. Well, my mother wants to know if I'm alive every now and then, but that's all."

No wonder I was more cautious than he was! I would definitely be missed. "I don't have time to start anything now," I grumbled.

"Listen," he said softly. "Nobody gives a damn." He walked to my side and pressed his palms on my face, pulling it to his. My throat stretched and a line went taut the length of my body. He held me the way he drew, as if he'd practiced for years, and seeing and touching volume were almost the same. We kissed. I believed that he loved me and I could trust his wry lips and clever hands, the tactile sense that was standard equipment for us both. We knew the shape of the act; its image was in our brains. Love was an intersecting celebration that extended the reverence we already had for line, form, color, and relationship. We knew what the other was experiencing! This was no timid experiment, we were claiming a prize we had trained for. When I looked at Hugh, I drew him in my mind, and that response found its resolution when I made love to him. Our surrender to passion was complete enough to be important. Each of us had wanted our feelings and creations to be important, but we'd hesitated to declare them so. Sex was the perfect alternative. But it left us temporarily confused.

I arranged myself to go, dizzily remembering the rest of my life and its obligations. Hugh lay with his eyes clamped shut.

"Well, good-bye," I said. He smiled faintly, a smile that suggested a pinched nerve somewhere. He wouldn't look at me. I stood for a moment, wondering what could be the matter, and he rolled over with his face to the wall. I left, finally, with a sense of disadvantage. There had been no satisfying way for me to depart.

But I was mad to see him, the next day. We met at the station and every day afterward. When Muriel was through with me as the weather warmed, I raced to Hugh, and I simply got used to his strange ways. If I had a thought at all, it was that we really *were* artists, really did have bohemian souls, lying every which way with our tongues hanging out, like opium addicts. There was no wrong in any of it, I decided, and passion made adepts of us. Like Alice, we took two steps in one direction in order to arrive at another. Abandon led to skill, stupor to exquisite awareness. Neither of us had done anything like this before and we had everything to discover. Lust linked me at last to the human race.

But he was in control, after all, as any tireless lover must be. I was too complacent to understand. What concentration in his face, in his touch! What could I compare it to? He was the perfect lover, never spent, and just exactly what I deserved.

"Don't leave me," he whispered, and I promised not to. I was falling in love with something too. "We're away from everybody," he said. "It's just you and me. All the rest are out there, somewhere. We don't care. We're different. We're only like ourselves. I love being here with you."

I didn't tell him that I felt more carnally akin to other people than I ever had. My hair trailed on the floor, my blood gathered and burst again and again, and all of it had to happen, we were sure. Hugh was like the caretaker of an estate to which the owners would never return. He knew where everything was kept and what it needed, how to protect it, how to extend its life. He had a talent. I lay across him, the room upside down, the sky in the window, winter leeching away, spring about to arrive.

"I know what I'll paint," I said. "Just what's out there, as if there were no wall. The tracks, people waiting for the train, the illusion . . ." I was remembering the Sert in Jock's apartment.

". . . of a train bearing toward us on the track," Hugh said, his eyes shut.

"It's too corny? Too surreal? I just need an *idea*. Why wouldn't trompe l'oeil be a good exercise?"

"Trump what? Exercise?" His voice was lost in my flesh.

"I haven't met her parents," Muriel complained.

"We're working on something," I said. "I haven't either. It's a perspective problem. He has a studio. I'm painting a huge train, almost life-size. You stand in front of it and it seems to come right at you."

She examined me. "You two are so serious," she said. "When I was your age, we knew how to have fun. You have such long faces."

I sketched the train, the platform, and the commuters on a grid and transferred them to the wall. I was relieved to be busy again on a project. Hugh admired me. He stopped working to do so and for a few days his silent homage was agreeable. But I made errors in the perspective and distorted some of the figures in relation to the overhang of the station. He began to exasperate me. We couldn't wait to lie down together, but that was annoying, too, because it kept me from concentrating.

Hugh sprawled in a corner, smoking Lucky Strikes, and by the end of the week, sucking on a pint of Southern Comfort. "Come on," he urged me. "You'll like it. It's sweet."

"Why are you wasting your time this way?"

"What makes you think I'm wasting it?"

"Oh, come off it, Hugh." Hearing Muriel's words and tone come out of my own mouth only piqued me further.

He drew a few wrestler pictures, using an "ink" he mixed from cigarette ash, coffee, and water. I watched his progress out of the corner of my eye.

"Why don't you make things people will like?" I said. "You could sell your work." Didn't we spend too much time together? We couldn't be all things to each other. Why hadn't he made other friends? But the truth was, I'd have fought off any rivals. I disgusted myself.

"When can I meet your mother and father?" I asked. His face hardened at my tone.

"You don't want to do that. Believe me." He laughed cynically and suggested they were too cretinous to understand anything I might say to them. His father would just read the newspaper; I might never see his face. His mother would ask impertinent questions. "I'll draw them," he offered.

The cartoon made me cry out. "You *do* know something about art! You know Grant Wood, anyway."

"Who doesn't?" He ripped his picture in half. He frightened me. I felt burdened by his lack of interest in anything but me. Even so, I was afraid of losing him.

I had a respectable life centered on school, and I returned to its responsibilities while harboring my lurid interludes with Hugh. Now he waited for me after classes, leaning with studied indifference against the wall. When I chaired a meeting of the literary magazine, he sat in the back of the room, rubbing his chin and smiling ironically. After I'd finished my homework, he'd pick me up in the Buick for a "drive" before bed, and Muriel let me go, night after night. We found quiet places to park, and the constraints of the car's interior, like rules of form, intensified our passion. Rain sometimes beat on the roof, steam coated the windows, our hot breath made our heads swim.

One night in the rain a powerful light was suddenly beamed on us. It caused a metamorphosis. No longer perfect lovers, we were bums scrambling to cover ourselves, blinded, hiding our faces.

"Okay, lover boy, where's your license?" the cop asked. He had waited a minute or two for us to compose ourselves.

Hugh rummaged in his pockets. He hadn't been able to zip his pants and now, in the searchlight, he didn't bother to. I sat as far away from him as I could. The night air entering the open window dispelled the odors of love and made me feel clammy. Hugh chuckled to himself. He looked at the cop, who shrugged.

"You have to have a license to do this?"

"Come on, kid, cut the comedy. Let's see it."

"I didn't bring it. On my dresser."

The light wavered. "You got to carry your license when you

drive, buddy," the cop said. "Now you take the young lady home and be glad you're not in any worse trouble."

Hugh thought the incident was anticlimactic. He was keyed up. I didn't like his obstreperous reaction. We stopped at my corner and argued. My throat hurt when I finally got out of the car and walked to the driveway.

A light was on in Muriel's bedroom. "Miranda?" Portia whispered from the side door. She huddled in her nightgown. "Where have you been? You look a wreck. Mother's mad. She's afraid you've been in an accident or something. Here, comb your hair and fix yourself up and have a story ready."

I accepted the comb gratefully. Portia glided me off into the darkness of the back hall. I tidied myself and closed the door audibly, but not too loudly. Upstairs I greeted Muriel and offered apologies. We had run out of gas—what could be simpler? I coughed and winced in pain.

"I see you're coming down with something," she said, her face softening a little. "I hope you're not going to miss school tomorrow. This has been a very foolish episode. Don't repeat it."

"Thanks, Portia," I whispered in her doorway on the way to the bathroom. There was no answer.

I got sick. The infection ravaged my bronchial tubes, took away my voice, and sank to my lungs. I coughed the way Desmond used to, raising great residues of phlegm. I ached for Hugh, but I wanted him to be reliable again. My head was a sack of stones on the pillow, my neck a burning pipe, and my thoughts hallucinatory. When I could sit, Muriel held a mirror for me to comb my hair and I gasped at my gaunt face.

"Hugh has been calling," she said. "Poor thing. He's bereft, I guess, without your company. I asked him to clean out the shed on Saturday, and he was very sweet, but I hardly got a word out of him."

"He was here?"

"He couldn't see you, Miranda, you were raving." She gave me her exasperated look. "It's hard to understand what you two see in each other. . . ." But she *must*, I thought, praying I wouldn't have to pay.

Portia delivered a letter from Desmond, addressed to us both. *The railroad once passed through this place,* he wrote. *It was a jerkwater town then, and it's less than that now.* He provided the etymology of *jerkwater. I miss you, girls. I miss your thoughtful heads. Students here are born graceless, and the ones thirsting for more than we can give them will probably never get out of here. I see them caring for senile parents as their own heads turn gray. . . .* Call their bluff, *Miranda, Portia—whoever* THEY *turn out to be, in your lives,* CALL THEIR BLUFF. He said he was writing his magnum opus, a novel of society called *The Age of Nonsense.* "Is your mother selling that house? She hinted as much, on the phone."

I looked at Portia. "He calls here?"

"I guess so."

"*My God.*" *Is your mother selling that house?* he had written. Then, *I suppose I've ensured that we'll all mourn after it, despite the collective misery that's been staged there. It's a human quirk to be hopelessly attached to what has caused pain. Well, I'll see you soon, darlings. There are a few things I want to rescue. A few books, a few boxes.*

"You think he's okay?"

"He seems to be."

Muriel insisted I take a steam cure. She put me on a stool in front of the stove. The teakettle boiled with mentholated jelly, and I leaned over it in a newspaper tent, her steely fingers on my neck. I was gagging when Hugh came in and sat at the table. She let me turn to say hello. He played with a matchbook that said *Paradise Lounge.* Even with the sadistic twenty minutes I spent steaming, the scene felt cozy—daring for its coziness. I imagined us to be an exemplary family, three women alone in the world, and a brotherly suitor who kidded the mother affectionately. When she and Portia left the room, he came and leaned over my shoulder, ran his hands flutteringly down my arms, brushed my breasts, twisted his head to kiss my mouth and beat his tongue there until I broke away for breath.

"Hugh," Muriel called. "Will you come in here for a minute? I need your muscle."

In two days I was back at school, but Hugh was not. I expected to run into him in the halls, but never did. He didn't telephone me at night. I missed him terribly, and became alarmed that our intimacies had grown excessive and frightened him off. Whatever he was doing or whatever had happened to him, it was depriving me of the hidden, privileged existence that had already overshadowed my normal one.

I went to the station three times one day, but couldn't bear to linger there alone. The images on the walls seemed mad. I waited by the telephone at home, but would not call his house because he had been so snide about his parents. I was unwilling to expose myself to them. But how could they be the caricatures he had drawn? He was born when his mother was past forty, he had told me wryly. Would she not be a dignified matron?

Saturday night Portia went out to the high school. She was Sam's girl and waited for him while he played with his dance band. She was part of the action, but with nothing to do—all the musicians' girls primped and jiggled their feet, waiting. Portia complained about it. "This is not what I want out of life," she said.

Muriel was on the telephone in the coat closet by the front door, her voice insistent. I left her a note and set off at a run down deserted streets, under coldly twinkling stars. I kept to the center of the road and ran with more stamina than I ever had in daylight. The night clarified my desires. I'd been laid up so long my body pumped like a racehorse let out of a gate. Finally I had to stop, bent double, drawing broken breaths, at Hugh's corner.

His house was two stories high and almost identical to its neighbors. The green Buick was moored in the driveway. My heart leapt when I saw the car. Hugh was not out with another girl; the chances were good that he was inside the house, just a few feet away.

There was low shrubbery and a tender maple in the front yard. I crept to the azaleas beneath a wide picture window. Hugh was inside staring straight ahead, in perfect profile, skin stretched pale over his skull, an otherworldly light flickering from across the room. I could hear the muffled twaddle of the program rise and fall, but his expression never changed. My heart thudded so loudly I had to hold my breath to interpret a sudden sound. It had been the back door slamming. Footsteps followed. Someone was coming around the house. I ran off in a panic.

On Sunday I went back on my bike. The sky swelled with gray clouds, and I shivered in the damp wind whenever I stopped at an intersection. Daylight revealed a number of bare spots in Hugh's lawn. The shrubbery, too, was patchy, and the blossoms on the azaleas scant. But the house was without blemish, built not very long ago. The doorbell glowed with its own little bulb. I rang it and brought a face to the living room window. Hugh's mother opened the door. She was plump and pale, with the same faint brow, which I looked down on. She examined me and broke into a smile.

"You're Miranda." Her voice was childlike and she turned her lips in, as if she had been too brash. Plucking my sleeve, she called, "Howard, Howard, Hugh's Miranda is here."

"Hrmmmmmph," I heard. I followed her into the living room. She untied her apron in transit and tossed it onto a chair. I noticed the striped easy chair Hugh had been sitting in and a gray sofa, a glossy coffee table, a shelf of *Reader's Digest* condensed books, and a reproduction of a large earnest painting of a rushing stream bordered with birches. Hugh's father reposed in a reclining chair. He nodded, with what I took to be an appeal to ignore him. His large doughy face was crowned by thin, carefully combed reddish hair, and he held a newspaper spread wide. As soon as his wife spoke, he retreated behind it.

"We've heard so much about you." *What?* I had thought Hugh kept quiet at home, to protect himself. "He's not here," she said, as I listened with a fixed smile. "It's so sweet of you to come and see us. I've wanted to call your mother and get acquainted. Hugh has told us such interesting things about her, as well. But I'm a terrible slowpoke, he probably said . . ." She looked brightly at me. I thought how scornful Muriel would be. Aromas of pot roast and cabbage drifted from the kitchen. Houses I knew in the town smelled of chocolate chip cookies and air freshener.

Hugh's father shifted in his chair. I felt critical of him, in imitation, again, of Muriel. She didn't approve of people who sat around taking it easy in the middle of the afternoon. He was probably one of those husbands kept in the dark by an alliance of mother and son. If I lived here, I'd be on her side too. She was sharper than she sounded, I figured.

"Hugh is painfully shy. He gets it from me," she said. "He was the sensitive one from the day he was born. Oh, he feels pain. I remember rashes, little hurts, nothing ever broken, thank the Lord. You know, the way they just wrinkle up and scream.

He's too old for me to watch out for him now. Howard and I have a tendency to be overprotective, especially in a new town, my heart just goes out to Hugh . . . so much to learn about a place . . ."

She pulled a handkerchief from her pocket and mopped at her neck. "When Hugh told us who you were and all you've done to make him feel welcome, we thought it was the luckiest thing that ever happened. . . ." I squirmed under the ironic assaults of this speech. She took that for modesty and cocked her head appreciatively. The wattles of her upper arms shook when she clapped her hands in her lap. Hugh's father cleared his throat. A clock ticked, then a timer rang in the kitchen. She jumped up. "Excuse me, dear, I'll just be a minute."

Hugh's father lowered his newspaper and gave me a stern look. He cleared his throat again. "Where's your dad gone to?"

"New Caledonia," I said. "It's—"

"I know where it is." He restored his newspaper screen.

Hugh's mother hurried in, located her apron, and tied it around her waist. "I can't resist," she said. I waited expectantly. She ruminated a minute more, then made a little end run around the recliner, stooped to take something from a low cabinet, and brought it to me: a photograph album of maroon leather with gold stamping. She sat on the sofa and patted the cushion next to her. I sat next to her to look and smelled lily of the valley on her skin.

"Here he is, just what I was saying," she cried. Baby Hugh in a bonnet and dress screwed up his face and balled his little fists for the camera. His eyes set my heart pounding again. I wanted him desperately—that was why I had come, to find him, and he wasn't here. I must go elsewhere and look; I must leave this house.

"And look here," she laughed, throwing her head back. Now little Hugh toddled along a sidewalk and a female hand reached down from an upper corner of the snapshot to steady him. "Look, look,"—as if we were sharing these moments all over again or she were passing the torch of natural affection. I could think of no scene that would disgust him more: She really was oblivious in a terrible way, ready to betray his privacy and invade mine.

I told her I had to get home, and she urged me to wait for

Hugh. "I don't know when he'll be here . . . he usually calls.
. . ." I knew this to be a lie. Smugly I strode to the door. Howard grunted when I said good-bye.

"Thank you, I'm glad to have met you," I said on the step.
She pursed her lips and eyed both sides of the street. I felt her
fingers dig into my wrist.

"Listen, please tell me, do you think anyone will catch you
over at that station? Will there be trouble? You've lived here a
long time and Hugh doesn't realize—"

I felt as if she'd jabbed a gun into my back. "I don't think
anyone cares at all. I really don't know."

"Oh, but, oh—" Her little voice ascended to the bright new
leaves of the maple. "I never really worry about Hugh. He
doesn't *want* me to. . . ."

I gave her a wave like a traffic cop's, plodded to my bike, and
rode away. Pedaling to the station, I raged that she might have
had a glimpse of me at my most vulnerable, in unknowing
thrall to her little boy. The thought of Hugh confiding to her
about me in any way was chilling. I hadn't feared his taking
advantage of me until now, and his mother seemed eminently
capable of it.

I set about, almost without reflection, to erase all traces of my
collaboration in the station. The water ran in the janitor's sink,
and I found a bucket, a mop, and even an old sponge. I
scrubbed my drawings off the walls, taking pains to rinse the
streaks. It was a tremendous relief to remove them, as if I'd
been proven innocent after being implicated in a crime. When I
finished, I stared for a while at Hugh's paintings. They seemed,
not the flowering of art, but an inspired deception.

While I waited to cross Stratford Circle, a car loaded with
kids honked and swerved. Portia was inside, waving.

At the side door of our house I heard simple chords and a soft
melody played on the piano. Then Muriel's voice was added,
lilting and sad. I went to the dining room and listened from the
threshold. Her back was to me; her neck rose white from her
collar. She didn't hear my approach.

"Beautiful dreamer, wake unto me," she sang, "out of the sea
. . . wild Lor-a-leeee . . ." Tears sprang to my eyes. I wanted
to rescue her, to send her back to the world for some pleasure. I

wanted her to be happy at last, so that I could stop worrying about her.

When she turned and found me standing there, she wasn't startled or annoyed. "I've been so blue," she confessed with a laugh. "There's nothing for supper. Are you starved?"

"I could go out and get something," I said, eager to provide.

"Good. Go to the White Castle. What a good idea."

She had fond feelings for this outfit, whose stores were tiled in gleaming white. The burgers were so cheap, Portia and I could eat five or ten at a sitting.

"I was thinking," she said. "Do you remember the girls at the Arts Club? I remember Jeanie—Stephen Foster made me think of her. When we were living there, they were doing Rockefeller Center. We went once to see Diego Rivera painting those murals that were removed, when the Rockefellers saw what he was up to. There was a party. He was a glorious man, huge and energetic. We were introduced to his wife, Jeanie and I—she was *tiny*. I remember Jeanie looked at him and then she looked at her, and she pulled me aside and whispered, in a shocked, amazed way, 'It's not *possible!*' " Muriel laughed. "Perhaps I shouldn't have told you that story," she said. "It was so funny at the time." She glanced to the living room door. "Well, before you go, I'd better show you." She walked to the door and stepped down the two steps to the other room. "I've sorted everything, deciding what we should save, which is next to nothing, if we keep our senses."

The floor was covered with boxes, papers, photographs, books, cardboard files with marbled covers—all the stuff I had rooted through in the dusky, suggestive attic, was laid out there like the casualties of war.

"This is all to be sold," she said, indicating an area cordoned off with string. She bent and picked up a batch of letters tied with ribbon. "There's some valuable material. I called around and found a dealer. Of course, he may not show up. Look, this is Mencken. Here is Edgar Lee Masters, Irving Berlin. Some of them are personal, in a way. It's the signatures that are worth anything, he said. Well, here's a gem." She handed me an envelope, with a wry look.

. . . *returning to sources of inspiration is like trying to revive an old love affair (I mean very old). You consider me successful. I won't be coy, dear boy. I see myself as a flop.* The letter went on to discuss the creative process. I couldn't read it. The signature embarrassed me: It was someone we had studied in school.

"New Caledonia, for God's sake," Muriel muttered, fishing at a box.

"Mother, you can't do this without letting him come and take what he wants."

"Can't I?" She sounded almost bored. "Look at this! Old Jack Benny scripts. I remember how that happened. And Toscanini, autographed. Did I ever tell you about the Maestro's mistress, as we used to call her? She lived next door to the Levys, on West Seventy-eighth Street. An incredible creature—used to lie in wait for anyone who came to their door. She would waylay and interrogate them. It had something to do with a fixation about Poppy, of all people—the way she threw a coat over her shoulders, or the way she kissed someone hello in the doorway. I don't know—"

"Daddy wrote to us. He said he was coming to get his things."

"Did he? We'll see." She crossed the room, bent like a beach-comber. "Here is your archive," she said. "Everything you ever put to paper, or I'm a liar." I watched her lift drawings, one after another, leaf through sketchbooks, unroll friezes, recalling the circumstances of their composition. There were even class notebooks I had doodled in.

"I had no idea you'd saved these," I said.

"I'm not surprised. Some day you'll appreciate it. Someday you'll want them. Meanwhile, they move with us. I'll go to all the trouble it takes to preserve them." She sighed.

I held up a drawing. "It looks inept."

"Well, it's not. It's extraordinary. No one your age was doing anything like it." The scene was of boys swimming off rocks, done in pastel on colored paper when I was nine. "See how natural those figures are. I just never understood your choice of subject matter."

"I remember this," I said, getting caught up in the spirit of things. "Miss Hill wanted me to do something for Memorial Day."

"By the way," Muriel said, "you had a telephone call." I

whirled on her. "It was your friend Jock. You haven't seen him, have you? I couldn't get much out of him. He's terribly stiff."

"Jock . . ."

"He wants you to go to a dance at St. Bart's. I thought you could wear that pale green dress Isabel Stoll handed down. I can take tucks under the arms and lengthen the straps—"

"I hate to wear other people's clothes."

"There's nothing to be ashamed of. It's beautiful, so well made. The things in the stores get sleazier and sleazier. It's wasteful not to use a perfectly good dress."

"Not now, Mother!" I cried. My eyes caught the packet of letters she had tossed to the floor. The things laid out belonged to me, as well as to Desmond. She couldn't pull them out from under me this way! Perhaps Portia and I could find a place to hide it all. I had no idea what it was worth, but probably not much.

After we ate our hamburgers I called Jock.

"I've been thinking of you inordinately lately," he said. "I want you to come to this dance. I told you what they're like at school. But we'll go to my friend's house later, a bunch of us."

"Jock, I don't think I want—"

"Miranda, let's let bygones be bygones, what do you say? It was a once in a lifetime occurrence, believe me. The dance is the weekend after next. The band is really competent. I know, because I'm chairman of the committee. Everybody's going."

I kept my mouth shut for a few seconds and he tolerated the silence. "Okay. What time will you come get me?"

"Oh, great! About eight o'clock. I'll be in the limo. Ha, ha. Wait and see, baby. What color gown will you wear?"

"Probably putrid green."

"Okay, I won't forget. See you, Miranda. À bientôt."

I lay in my darkened room, lulled by the spooky crisscrossing branches at my window, when a sharp crack sounded on the glass where it had been struck. I looked out. There was Hugh in a pool of pallid moonlight, gazing up. I stared back, withdrew, and pulled on a sweater and jeans. I moved carelessly, but my breast was bursting. I ought to be furious at him, and I still was, but desire was more powerful. Desire had lured me into lying and deceiving for so long that discovery would uncover, not just what I did in secret, but who I secretly was.

He nodded toward the house. "All sleeping in there?"

"Yes." We walked to the shed, slipped into the side door, and climbed the little stair. He sat on the cot under the front window. Its old gray cover shone in the moonlight. He tried to pull me down beside him.

"I hear you met my folks," he said hoarsely.

"It was humiliating."

"I warned you."

"Hugh, where have you been? Why didn't you call me?"

"I had to be by myself for a while. It wasn't anything. Come on . . ." But I wouldn't budge. "You washed our drawings off."

I stared incredulously at him. "You won't explain yourself? Not at all? Your mother *knows* about us, in the station and everything. What did you tell her?"

He got up and put his arms around me. I ducked out from under them. "Look, I told her we were painting the walls. She doesn't care. She doesn't understand. She just wants to be in on it."

"*In* on it! But why didn't you tell me you'd told her? Do you let her in on everything we do?" My voice shook.

"Of course not." He was sneering. "Jesus, Miranda, you saw him. You saw her. She's just lonely. Have a heart. It's crazy to—"

"It *is* crazy. It makes me feel crazy." I recognized his technique—to turn things around, accuse the accuser, and I knew the self-pity that lay behind it.

"Ahhhh," he crooned, stroking my back. I let my anger fade. But did he think he could do whatever he pleased? Perhaps by cloaking meaningless behavior in mystery he made a work out of nothing. I hated to participate but what choice had I unless I broke off with him now?

"I missed you," he murmured. "You have to believe me." He caressed my body, eased his onto the cot and pulled me over him. "I dreamed we were in a canoe, gliding along, the water was black."

"Hugh, what are you going to do?"

"Do?"

"With your life. I'm going away to college next year. What are you doing after you graduate? What about your painting?"

He turned his head with a dismissing sigh. I didn't press him.
He had no answer. He never gave a thought to the future. I was
really worrying about myself. He pleaded with me, quietly,
pressing me, gently touching. My mindful self rose from my
body, leaving it to its singular purpose.

Miss Holmes, an alumna and social worker, conducted the
area interviews for the Swarthmore Admissions Office. I met
her at her agency. She had a sharp but compliant expression,
practical hair, and bright, loose, embroidered clothing.

"I got an extraordinary education," she said. "The comrade-
ship is what stands out most, as I look back—I mean between
students and faculty. It was a revolutionary place. Those days
are over; the philosophy is proven effective, the traditions are
set. But things still happen there, I'm told, that couldn't happen
anywhere else."

She had majored in anthropology and spent her vacations
digging in Mexico. For the agency she was writing a book
meant to correct popular misconceptions about foster children.
"We're finding that most are really very happy in the homes
where they've been placed. Not only that, but they usually go
on to become high achievers. Not at all the dreary stuff of fairy
tales." I examined a strident plant blooming on her windowsill.
She told me it was a bromeliad. There were so many worlds I
knew nothing of.

"This is very good," she said of my dossier. "But I wonder
why you're not going to an art school? The arts aren't treated as
seriously at the college as in some places, like Sarah Lawrence
and Bennington."

"I want the liberal arts," I said. "I want to be as broad as
possible." I couldn't tell her that I was afraid to commit myself
to an art school. There was more to it than a refusal to be
steered where Muriel wanted me to go. I was afraid of being
swallowed, or worse, of being *unable* to be swallowed. An artist
was more than a person who could draw well or even paint
well. An artist was a person who could do nothing but paint,
who lived to paint, and I suspected that this drive, a quality
that I thought of as absolute, was missing in me. If I went to an
art school, I wasn't sure what I would do there to justify my
presence. The question didn't arise in regard to college.

Several days later, I saw Muriel waiting in the living room window when I turned into the driveway after school.

"Something astonishing has happened," she said grimly, her eyes gleaming. She handed me an envelope addressed to her. It was from Lou. My hands shook and she sighed while I fumbled with the paper.

"He's set up a trust for you and Portia," she said impatiently. "For your education. I'm thunderstruck. God, I'd like to see Desmond's face when he hears this. I could hardly believe my eyes."

"You think we should accept?"

"Of course I do. You're damned lucky, getting something out of the wreck of our lives. We'd be fools not to accept."

"I want to go to college."

"You're misguided, Miranda. If you don't develop your talent now, you never will. You'll be a hobbyist and you could be great. But I'm not going to dictate your choices. It's up to you."

Portia came home and whooped at the news. It turned out she had an announcement too. She had gotten permission from a friend's mother to store Desmond's boxes in their garage. I looked at her in amazement. The matter had flown from my mind. Hers was so retentive and magnanimous.

"All right," Muriel conceded. "I have no desire to be vindictive."

Our dinner was silent. Later I would drive out with Hugh. I would be leaving for good before long and could do as I wanted, as he seemed to. No one would sit in judgment of me. Muriel looked preoccupied too. "He really is a passionate man," she said, clearing the table. Portia and I didn't ask, but we assumed she meant Lou.

After dinner she and I washed the dishes. "It's so exciting," she said. "I'm so happy for you."

"You'll get your chance," I said. "You know, I think maybe Lou would like to get together with Mother."

"Really?"

"I have a feeling."

Muriel bustled in. "I'm not going to work with Clem any more," she announced, brandishing a sheaf of ads. "I wish you girls would sit down with me and help go through some list-ings. There are decisions to make. I don't want to make them alone. I wish for once you would cooperate with me. . . ."

"Why won't you work with Clem?" Portia asked.

"He's a fool."

We spent an hour on real estate. We argued that she ought to leave the town, go back to the city and take advantage of all the things she loved to do there. But she clung to her plan.

"I've been here too long to leave now. I have to have some security. I can teach in the schools."

I worried about her. What if she wasn't able to support herself? And I wanted her to be happy. How could she be, alone in the town?

"If you don't want to help, why sit here?" Muriel said. I got up to leave. She had more to say. "I can't stop you from doing what you think you want. If any good comes of it, it will be that you separate yourself from Hugh." She had taken me by surprise.

"I thought you liked Hugh."

"That's not the point at all. I do like him. But you must outgrow him, one way or another, or you'll pay a terrible price."

I looked away. She went on. "Lou's money will take care of tuition, but there are plenty of other expenses. You'll have to find a job."

"I know. Rebecca says there are lots."

"Oh, what does she know about work?"

Hugh and I spent more and more time together as the end of the school year approached. I felt I was using him up, that he would cease to exist when he ceased to be what I needed. The subtle conversion of appetite to dependency was not apparent to me. I didn't tell him about the dance at St. Bart's and justified the omission as necessary to spare his feelings. But some excuse was called for—we were together every night. The right line never occurred to me, though, and on Saturday, when Jock called for me in a limousine after all ("Isn't that the limit?" Muriel said)—I thought that this time I was disappearing and it served Hugh right.

Jock was elaborately courteous, offering his arm when we entered the gym and introducing me as "Miss Geer, the artist."

He danced with his usual flattering panache. I felt I could take on the whole crowd, and many of his friends did cut in. They were all glib; I had hardly to make an effort. Everyone was a stranger to me and I was strange to all of them. I felt glamorous, but supposed the feeling would vanish at midnight. What the hell.

"Honey, we're splitting," Jock said to me after two hours or so.

"Already?"

"The guys are waiting. Rudy has his car. I told you."

"I don't want to leave."

"We have booze. Come on, this is for kids." I was dancing with a boy. He retained his hold on me, but stepped back to let Jock and me conduct our exchange. Jock said, "Cripes," and hurried off. My partner reined me in again. He gave me a sympathetic look.

"You want to stay? I don't know. I mean, you're his date. Maybe I could get you another ride later, though. . . ."

"That's nice of you. I think I have to go."

Jock gestured like an impressario, filling Rudy's car. I squeezed into the backseat. The boys did all the talking, using unnaturally deep voices and passing a flask around.

We made it, over twisting roads, to the house. All the lights blazed and it looked wide as a city block. Rudy hopped out and stood in the foyer, ushering us inside. I asked where the bathroom was.

A girl sat contemplating her image in the mirror. When I came in she picked up a lipstick and ran it around and around her mouth.

"Hi," I said. "How did you get here?"

"Tony," she said. "We skipped the dance."

There was a pink chaise I wanted to lie down on. Instead I sat, miserably, my hands in my lap. I was wearing the green dress. It didn't look bad, but I wasn't comfortable. Hugh must be waiting for me. I couldn't get him out of my mind, now that we were away from the dance.

"So, how long have you known Rudy?" she asked, turning to stare at me.

"I just met him. I'm a friend of Jock's."

She rolled her eyes, blotted her lipstick on a tissue, and dropped it to the counter. "Are you going upstairs with him?"

It took me a minute to understand. "No."

She shrugged and walked to the door. "Well, all the luck, then," she said, and went out.

I considered telephoning Hugh and confessing my meanness, but I couldn't promise to come home promptly. Besides, he was probably lurking in our yard, waiting for me. I went to find Jock instead.

He was sprawled on a sofa with a glass in his hand. "This is excellent scotch," he said. "Will you have some?"

I walked to the end of the room and back. The windows were covered with drapes from ceiling to floor. The furniture was all knee high and very broad. There was a lamp on the table at his elbow, its base an ebony female nude with bronzed nipples and scarlet lips.

"Come sit by me," he said, his mouth loose.

"That's a truly remarkable lamp."

He smiled and reached for the lamp's breasts. "Doesn't do a thing for me." He patted his knees. I shook my head.

"What do these people do?"

"Rudy's pop is a doctor, a woman's doctor. Fixes female parts, delivers babies, that sort of thing." Someone started up a record player in another room. "They're dancing in the dining room," Jock said. "Let's go." He stood and offered me his arm. We walked down the entrance hall, past the bathroom. There was a door next to it. Jock stopped and jiggled the knob. "I'll bet this is locked." The door opened. "Aha!" He reached in and switched on a light. We saw a desk, two chairs, and another door. A doctor's white coat hung on a hook next to the desk, and Jock pulled it on.

"Vell, fraulein," he said, "vy don't you tell Herr Doktor vat iss de madder, like a gut madchen?" He ogled me, rubbing his palms together.

"I have a funny feeling, Doctor," I said. He advanced on me. I shrieked and made for the second door, which opened at a touch. An examination table took up most of the chamber. Jock chased me around it twice, tried to vault over it, and lay down on his back with his feet in the stirrups.

"It's cold, Doctor, it's cold," he whimpered. We laughed until we were blinded by tears.

He sat up abruptly. "Listen, Miranda. What about trying again, you and me? What about tapping all this passion? Don't you want to?"

I had to catch my breath. "I'm sorry. No."

"I'm really a better man. You like me, don't you? You want to see how I've reformed."

"I like you a lot."

"And there's somebody else," we said in unison, and laughed again. "If we could stay here, if it could just be this," I said, meaning it.

"Let's have a last dance, and I'll take you home."

We agreed that we were well suited, we had humor and cynicism and heaven knows what foul traits in common—the situation was terribly sad, like a Hemingway novel. He clutched his crotch, doomed to impotence by an old war wound. Tim and his girl were swaying like vines in the dark. They stopped and told us to shut up. "Time to beat it," Jock said.

In the car I told him I felt like a booby prize. I hated for him to have to drive so far to get rid of me and start over. "You don't even *drink*!" he cried. "I can't do *anything* with you!" His behavior was impeccable. He had more than made up for his earlier lapse. But what would I ever be able to do to make up for mine? I asked him to drop me at my corner, and he did that with gentlemanly resignation. We exchanged a dry kiss.

I crept around to the backyard at home. Hugh was sitting in a chair Muriel had left by the hedge.

"It's you," he said, looking like the sole survivor of some disaster. That expression irked me, but I let him rest his head against my breast, stood by the chair while he clutched at my hips. He seemed less like my disconcerting companion than a submerged part of myself, an imp able to sabotage whatever I might try thoughtfully to do.

8

In September I drove us to Swarthmore in the Studebaker. Portia came along to see college firsthand. Muriel fretted most of the way about new car noises. She had allowed a possibly incompetent mechanic to give it a tuneup for the trip.

At my dormitory she put my clothes in the dresser and closet the way she thought they ought to go. My roommate was late and I wondered how Muriel might have behaved before an audience. As it was, I heard a lot of insinuating advice, as if she, given this opportunity, would make more of it than I could. But it must have been wrenching to launch me that way and recall her own exit from Babylon.

At one point she unpacked a box I hadn't noticed. It contained a watercolor tray, tubes of paint, brushes, charcoal, and a sketchbook, selected as if for a beginner's kit.

"I didn't want to bring art materials," I protested.

"You're the limit, Miranda. How will anyone find out who you are? You can't squander your talent just because you're here." I put the materials away in the desk.

We walked the paths between green turf, among all the other parading families and keyed-up freshmen, and toured the pillared main building and the outdoor amphitheatre, where Muriel recalled for us her undergraduate acting career. Our progress was more and more aimless. Finally they were ready to leave, and as we spun out our last few minutes together, I was seized by a desire to jump into the car and drive home with them. Then I was alone, waving, wanly, at the receding pink car.

I took a deep breath and glanced around to see if anyone was paying me any attention, and of course no one was. I was on my own at last, on the threshold of an intellectual and spiritual odyssey, at liberty to try what I liked and find my own true path.

My roommate Sada and I examined the course offerings and made out our schedules.

"You're taking Lipper's course, I assume," she said. Barry Lipper was a new associate professor of Art History. He had been trained at the Warburg Institute and NYU, was a disciple of Panofsky, and already a star on the lecture circuit. He published in scholarly journals, but also in ones like *L'Oeil, Horizon, The Saturday Review*—he could be read by Muriel, at home!

" 'Art History 201: The Landscape of Rapture,' " Sada read in a come-hither tone. " 'We will examine the genre, concentrating on key moments: *The Garden of Earthly Delights,* the *Sacra Conversazione, Departure From the Island of Cythera, Sunday Afternoon on the Island of the Grande-Jatte.* Emphasis is on both iconography and connoisseurship. Emphasis is on islands. Permission of the instructor required.' Have you seen him?" she asked.

"No, why?"

"Oh, my God," she said.

We were both admitted to the course, which was fully subscribed. We lounged in the dark, looking at slides projected on twin screens, while Lipper darted from side to side, aiming a pointer at the pictures. He was mesmerizing, and indeed handsome. The course covered every bit of human history that interested me. His remarks and his gestures were all distinctive, and how my eyes and mind loved anything that was distinctive. Painted and sculpted forms endured by themselves, but they also submitted to analysis, they were not above that! The embers cooled, could be held, turned, examined. Paintings contained more than I had ever known they did—allusions, information, prophecy. There was plenty to keep me occupied for a lifetime of study. The class was like a camp meeting—I'd have run forward and spoken in tongues if he'd called on me to.

Lipper's slightly predatory masculine energy turned his words into rockets. The air was thick with them, an hour and a

half at a clip, three afternoons a week. My other courses were
chores compared to the hours I spent listening to Lipper on
fairies, witches, wildmen, the terrors of the forest, the bliss of
the walled garden, nature as property, the country squire, the
sky, Marie Antoinette, allegory, asymmetry, sensuality, harmony, shock, civilization, ruins. His cheeks glowed faintly blue
and slightly damp. His hair was black as pitch and always in
place. His eyes glowed and so did mine. The rest of the class
enjoyed the performance, but could they *feel* what it was like to
live for the visible world and remake it—the eternal bondage of
the artist? Lipper seemed to know—his own passion for art set
him apart. I longed to signal him and be recognized. The rest of
the faculty were forever yanking their ties loose, foraging in
their hair, earnestly—even apologetically—negotiating with
their students from the lectern, in the halls, on the pathways,
on the telephone, carrying their babies in halters, their groceries
in bicycle baskets, their briefcases and canes in their hands.
Lipper was a heroic, freestanding figure.

"We will be mindful of Matisse's observation," he said, "that
the great painter is one who finds a personal and enduring idiom in which to express his vision."

The Bosch lecture came early, climaxing with *The Garden of
Earthly Delights*. I anticipated it nervously, and when the picture
showed on the screen an old force filled me: part ambition, part
covetousness, part wonder. Roiling love for Bosch's mad genius
plucked and poked at me like his capering figures. But I had
invested so much feeling in the work without understanding it.
I had hovered at the edge of the garden, fearing to enter because
I might not belong inside and would have to retreat to a plainer
place. The paintings Hugh had made to resemble this one
seemed to be *folie* of some kind, or a trick.

"Many of the bizarre images we see owe their appearance to
The Sack of Constantinople," Lipper said, and showed us that a fish-
shaped boat was not Bosch's invention, but came from a Greek
seal he had somehow seen. One by one he nailed down the
sources of the strange images I had assumed were divinely inspired. But he also showed that, in a way, they had been.

"Here we see philosophical, theological, alchemical allusions
to the beliefs of a sect called 'The Free Spirit'. . . . The painting
is systematic, if you will—completely bizarre, to be sure, but

internally consistent. Here is the ultimate rendering of the desperation of medieval life, and at the same time, the landscape of the collective unconscious. . . ."

Was everyone as relieved as I was? I felt that in the daylight of my youth I had never really focused my attention. In here I could learn, encouraged by darkness, and learning, I was beginning to realize, would let me off the hook. Mysteries were unraveling that would absolve me of my obligation to make art. How wise I was to come here instead of art school, where I would have to make up images. Instead of hurling myself into a gulf of uncertainty, risking my consciousness, flailing wildly for subjects worthy of my efforts, worth putting into the world at all, I could sit high on the bank and observe the tides of influence on art that already existed. My reprieve was the History of Art, the museum of the mind. But a vibration in my groin made me long for Hugh. Had he seen Greek seals somewhere?

"As unsettling as this painting is," Lipper was saying, "it represents a view of the world. Sin is shown to lie in not following one's natural instincts, in not permitting an unrestrained expression of rapture, the ecstasy of God-given existence . . . slide, please . . . as in Marguerite Porete's *Miroir des Simples Ames*. . . . The soul is annihilated, made drunk by purifying sensuality. . . ."

I heard all this, that sin lay in not following one's natural instincts, and I nearly burst with the thrill of the words tagged to the images, but my interpretation was narrow. Rather than answer the call of my instincts, and open myself in every way, I decided to become an art historian. I made an appointment with Lipper, waiting in line behind the eager throng that always surrounded him after class, to discuss my candidacy for honors work.

"It's a little premature, isn't it?" he asked. "You have plenty of time. But tell me something about your background." Then, after I'd blurted a little of my enthusiasm for the Tuscan School, he said, "I do have something you might work on with me. You can get a little experience under your belt before you decide on a project."

I wanted to sound cosmopolitan, so I mentioned the LeMieux collection.

"You've seen that?" he asked, snapping to attention and pulling a small notebook from his breast pocket. "How the hell did you get in?"

"I'm a friend of their son's."

"Holy— What did you see?" He was ready to write.

I said that there had been a few landscapes, a significant Matisse, the Manet Venice scene, the Fragonard—then I began to blush and stammer.

"How often do you see the boy?"

"Well, I don't, really, anymore. . . ." I hated to disappoint him. He put his notebook away. "What I want," I began, struggling to express what I hoped would please him, "is to study one painter in depth. I want to understand one artist's worldview. I care about art that's *about* something."

"Well, here's what I propose," he said. "I'm doing a catalogue raisonné—the work of a neoclassical painter in Ingres's circle. Gouzot, do you know him? Well, never mind, he's pretty obscure. What you'll do is list his drawings and engravings, describe what they're about, and track down the antique sources for the figures. You say that you draw?"

"Yes, but I—"

"Good. That's what I need, an eye that can pick out the dispositions of the figures quickly, match them up with coins, engravings, and so on. You'll use the standard references—Ripa, emblem books. I have some of them here and the rest you can get at the museum library in town."

I swallowed hard. What an assignment! He was so brusque, and took my competence for granted. Scholarship had its tools and methods, its apprenticeship. Lipper had invited me into art history's control room!

Sada dropped out of the course after two weeks. "I want to look at pictures, I'll get a camera and take some," she said. "And I'll look at them with the lights on. In there I just go to sleep."

Nothing she ever said made me angry, though her views were Philistine. She was a banterer, but a good listener too. She loved life, just as it unrolled around her, and jeopardized her English major by scorning anything written before 1900. She had subscriptions to *Time* and *The New Yorker* and would lie in her bed, reading lines from some movie or book review that caught her fancy. People stood in our doorway to be brought up-to-date—

she strewed her belongings so lavishly on the floor and furniture that our room had a perverse attraction, but discouraged actual entry.

It was to Sada that I confided about Desmond and Lou and Hugh. She had a sentimental and practical grasp of human nature. "So, who doesn't go for the mysterious stranger, especially if you know him well?" she commented, after hearing my stories of Hugh.

"I've foresworn him," I told her.

"We'll see."

"I have!"

She thought that Lou's generosity toward me and Portia was something out of a fairy tale, and she read his letters so she could ensure that my replies were up to the mark. "I hope that man drops the torch he's carrying for your mother," she said. "He deserves some tenderness."

Desmond captured her imagination, although I spared no detail of what I considered his vagrancy. "God, you really love him, don't you?" she said soberly. "You're his kid, and you know it in your heart." This made me uncomfortable. I must have given her a skewed account, slighting Muriel, although she herself had told me often enough that I was "just like your father."

Sada said, "What's strange about that? He's romantic, doomed, driven, and charming."

I burst into tears. She waited with a sage expression while I got hold of myself. "I understand the man," she said. "It's not for nothing I'm a critic. He probably couldn't bear to create anything less than a masterpiece, so he excused himself from trying. He had to go on doing his work, though, so he preserved his standards by feeling superior to it."

I remembered a line from one of Desmond's journals: *I want to do some dramatic writing. I need something to say and the will to say it.* How appalling that had seemed, when I'd read it: It didn't sound adult, not the reflection of a man with two children, a wife, and years of experience in the world. How had he been trapped in that mute place?

I went to see Lipper. His office was locked and I waited in the hall. Suddenly he was beside me, seizing my arm above the elbow, pushing his key into the lock, steering me into the office.

"These will tickle you," he said. He had a box of slides for me to sort: Prix de Rome winners from the French Academy, 1790–1810. We peered at the huge overpopulated canvases and he identified the various biblical and historical subjects. I had never heard of any of them, and cursed my narrow education.

"This is what the nineteenth century rebelled against," he said. "Baudelaire wrote 'there are private subjects that are very much more heroic than these.'" Lipper glanced at me. "There was a great rush to escape the overly civilized. Delacroix is an example." He opened a second box of slides. "I'm curating a show of these in New York. It's the first time the French government has let any of them out of the country."

The second set of slides was of faces displaying various emotions. I was swept back to my childhood drawing. "I used to do collections of faces, just like these!"

"Did you? Well, this was a competition too. Facial Expression. The men histrionically stoical, the women histrionically hysterical. Catalogued conventions. Illustrates the hamstrung, overblown nature of a painter's schooling."

Sitting with him in his office was a test, every minute, but I felt privileged to be there. An orange sun was low in the sky outside the window and its rays baked my right cheek. I sat without moving, as if it were part of the trial I must undergo in order to win his confidence. I was reminded of riding in the car beside Lou, pretending to be disembodied, lest I offend him.

"We'll start the catalog as soon as I get back from New York next week," he said. "You can work right here. We'll arrange my office hours." He told me a story about a trip he'd taken to Louvain as a graduate student. He'd happened to arrive at the museum just as a Soviet curator escorted a Van Eyck altarpiece back to its home for an exhibition.

"You can imagine the excitement," he said. "No one in Belgium had laid eyes on it for half a century. The representative from the museum let me witness the unveiling—just the three of us, the Belgian, the lady Soviet, and me. She was one of those stocky, lugubrious bureaucrats, with a certain sexual air, not seductive, but massively female. She and I uncrated the picture with a crowbar while the Belgian guarded the door. It was three A.M. We toasted it with champagne." I could visualize the scene, like the radio programs I had illustrated for years—

the heroic figures, the political intrigue, the theatrical lighting.
It was pure Caravaggio!

"By the way," Lipper said, as I was leaving, "I have something to ask of you. . . ."

I wrote to Muriel bragging that Lipper found me, too, "bright
and educable." He told me personal tales about his travels and
his work. He asked me to do original research in my freshman
year! Furthermore, I was going to get a look at his house, which
was several miles from the campus, in defiance of college convention, and reputedly filled with fabulous art. Lipper had
asked me to look after his small son for a few afternoons while
his wife rode at a nearby stables. His confidence in me was
obviously comprehensive. The pay would supplement my
dishwashing earnings. Muriel would have to admit that I was
starting off with a bang.

Lipper's wife was to pick me up in her car, then I would drop
her at the stables, play with the boy at their house, and fetch
her at the end of the afternoon. I waited on the street outside
my dorm. A red Volkswagen crawled near and stopped a few
feet from me. A woman leaned out and stared wordlessly.

"Mrs. Lipper?"

"Maxine, please," she said. "So you're the new one."

I stood in confusion, and she beckoned impatiently. "The
new sitter, aren't you? Get in."

The child was standing in the backseat, waving a plastic machine gun with which he swiped at the back of my head when I
sat down. "Henry, cut that out!" Maxine cried. Then she
sighed. "I can't do a thing with him."

Loud sucking noises issued from behind us. I turned to look.
Henry had his thumb in his mouth and was gazing out the
window with wide, brown, innocent calf's eyes like his mother's. There were other resemblances: both had squashed features, thick umber hair, and short plump bodies. Her face, I
now saw, looked swollen, as if she'd been crying. She wore a
childish costume—stiff, round cap; collarless white shirt; jacket,
jodhpurs—all of them wrinkled and slightly soiled. In the toylike car mother and son looked like part of a family of circus
performers. She was in a touchy mood, but made an effort to be
friendly.

"Henry wants to say hello to the horses. He's a complete pain

in the ass if I don't let him, so bear with me. I'll give you
directions to the house. Stay out of the front rooms. Henry's
allowed in the tower and the kitchen, that's it. Barry is crazed
on the subject." Her pouty mouth worked around the words
and drew me more than her eyes did, with their vague, unsettling appeal.

"Go go go go," Henry yelled.

"Bugger off," Maxine retorted. "People think I'm crazy to do
this at my age," she said, driving with a suddenly expansive air.
"Only kids really have the nerve for it. Even the best riders
won't take jumps after they've grown. But I always wanted to
do this. My daddy got me a horse when I was twelve. But he
never let me jump her. So I'm doing it now. I'm going for a blue
ribbon at Devon, then I'll quit. Am I nuts?" She turned to me. I
shook my head. "Of course I am. I'm absolutely bloody terrified. But what discipline, working it out with the animal, negotiating every step of the way, learning the subtle signals—
where else can you get that? And then, there's the fence—over
you go, and all that control is either in your blood or it isn't.
Either you make it or you don't."

We parked near a small circular track, and when I opened my
door, Henry slithered under my arm and bolted for the fence.
Maxine shrieked, but he only darted an impish look back at
her. He crawled under the bottom rail and advanced on three
women in getups like Maxine's, riding enormous horses. One
reared when he spotted Henry, and the others pawed and
snorted. The women looked terrified. A young man with a clipboard ran forward, and so did Maxine. The horses seemed
ready to bolt. Maxine scooped Henry into her arms and carried
him back to me, scolding, "Henry, if you want to say hello to
Bouguereau you goddamn stay put. What an impression you're
making on poor Miranda."

She squeezed his tiny hand. He puckered up his face and it
flooded with blood as she tightened her grip. Moments passed,
and I wondered if he could hold his breath until he fainted.
Abruptly she released him, and kneeling, threw her arms
around him.

"Oh, Mommy's little nuisance, Mommy's little man," she
crooned, her eyes on the ring, where order was being restored.
"Look, Honeybear, here he comes."

A girl led a sleek black horse into the ring. Henry waved with all his might. "Boogie. Boogie!"

"God help me," Maxine said under her breath. Another figure had caught my eye. A tall, broad-shouldered woman with tousled, sun-bleached hair had ambled out of the stable. She was dressed in a loose shirt and jeans and conversed good-naturedly with her horse, who walked alongside her as docilely as a dog. She adjusted her saddle, swung aboard, and rode nimbly away toward a trail leading into some woods.

Maxine had opened the car door and thrown Henry inside. "Okay," she said, "he's all yours. Just don't stray out of the kitchen and you'll be able to control him. Here are the directions."

I got in behind the wheel. "Did you see that woman?" she asked. "The Lone Ranger? What I wouldn't give—that's Sarah Jenkins, the painter." I had never heard of her. "You're probably too young to remember her wild episode of celebrity. She even had her moment on the TV news. Bodily impressions in sand dunes, if I remember. She dropped out of sight, then, and now she turns up at my stables and teaching at the Philadelphia College of Art! But how in hell could I have ever predicted that *I'd* be here, either?" She gazed after the cantering figures, woman and horse, in such harmony. I felt a sharp twinge, myself. What had I given up, giving up painting? But underlying that was another feeling—that I hadn't, really. Maxine said, "She rides that way because she's from Utah or somewhere and ate buffalo meat as a child." Her swollen face assumed its pout. I wondered for an instant if she were fed up with *me*.

Henry was banging his fists on the car window.

The Lipper house sat in an area of estates surrounded by walls of rhododendron, but was itself the focus of a small bare plot. It was Victorian, with long windows, a tower, mansard roof, and a porch. Henry scampered to it, selected a car from the heap of toys there, and threw it over the side to the driveway. He pedaled around in it, yelling at the top of his lungs. I looked into the kitchen, which was large and geared to the needs of a professional chef. There was a play area for Henry behind a long counter. When he noticed that I had gone in, he followed and made for the jumble of canisters, sifters, pots and pans, spatulas, spoons, pillows, and even an old typewriter. He poured what appeared to be real flour and water together onto the floor and stirred them with his hands. "Pas'" he cried, showing me his gummy palms.

"Henry, are you supposed to—" He scrambled up at my tone and tried to dash past me to the door. I grabbed him and washed his hands under the faucet while he wriggled and kicked.

There was a high chair so I strapped him into it and asked him to point to a cupboard where I might find him a snack. After a number of gleeful false leads, he indicated a cupboard stuffed with crackers, pretzels, potato chips, and the like, and ordered one of each. He picked them up in turn and peeked coyly from behind them. When he was finally munching contentedly, I hurried to explore the out-of-bounds front rooms.

"Sorry, sorry," Henry called plaintively after me. I wondered what he thought he was sorry about. I pitied him, but the feeling was tempered by exasperation.

The front rooms were two, each square, painted creamy white, with long windows letting in a flood of light that bounced off the walls, blurring the objects and giving an impression of beatific opulence. When my eyes had adjusted, I saw that the furniture was austere, with odd juxtapositions: a Shaker table, a Biedermeier mirror, a basket on the floor, an American quilt in a heap in a corner, a carpet issuing in folds from a colonial blanket chest. The walls were hung with paintings. Their arrangement was spare—I had a sense of discriminating selection, not the helter-skelter display of the LeMieux apartment. Lipper was my mentor, now: I was disposed to be extremely respectful.

I gaped at a portrait of a swan-necked lady. It must be an Ingres! Next to it was a Corot landscape, then a Vigée-Lebrun, a Perronneau (identified with the help of a little metal plate on the frame), then a Rosa Bonheur of goats in a field. I glided past a pair of Hudson River landscapes, a Rosetti allegory, and a Remington cowboy. Henry screeched in the kitchen and I was afraid he would tip his chair over. I hurried away, a plunderer, stuffed to the gills, and shut the door behind me.

When I went to fetch Maxine, she insisted I hang around the house and get acquainted. "I have to do a paper for Political Science."

"Just for a few minutes," she said. "Indulge me."

"Your art collection is superb," I said hesitantly. "I peeked at it. And the furniture—it's one of the nicest houses I've ever seen."

She gave me a long stare, as if she'd never been presented with such a face as mine. "It's for show," she said finally.

In the kitchen she put Henry back in his chair, took a bottle of wine from a rack that ran the length of one wall, and opened it. She sipped from her glass. "This is Barry's pride and joy," she said in a flat voice, holding up the glass and in lieu of a toast. "He got this batch on his last trip to the Gothic cathedrals. It's just coming into its own. You're sure you won't?"

She sat on a stool at the counter, curling her toes around its dowels. She had asked me to bend over and pull off her boots, then thought better of the request and went upstairs to do it alone, returning flushed and grinning. "Next time, when we know each other better."

Henry gobbled pretzels. When he interrupted our talk, or rather hers, Maxine ignored him and increased her volume. I wondered if I were still responsible for him, but when I moved to attend to him she said sharply, "I'm trying not to spoil him. I'll need your cooperation."

She chewed on a variety of cheeses and imported crackers, and pumped me about people at the college. "Tell me what you've observed," she commanded. "You have such a credulous manner. What do you see? Have you been to the Allens? The Cunninghams? The Corvesis?"

I chose to misinterpret her desires and gave blank assessments of my courses, but that made her impatient. "No, no, *people*! Their *lives*! That Marcia Alden, for example—now, in her cups, she isn't above confiding that her family all think Frank might have been a little less dim in the attic." She went on about someone else. I was embarrassed. She had concluded that I had no set of clever observations, so she must give me some of hers.

"And so, what, exactly, is your work with Barry?" she asked suddenly, in the middle of a story about a cocktail party in the history department. I thought she was suggesting that I might

lack competence, and freely admitted that he was starting me
on something routine.

"I was his research assistant once," she said. "I know what it
means. Did he mention that, in your interview?" Her eyes were
steely.

I was shocked. "If you think I—"

"Did you know that you can get too old to be his assistant?
It's like working for an airline, as a stewardess."

I had blundered into a hornet's nest. Working for Lipper began to look downright dangerous. Maxine appeared to be molli-
fied when she took me home, but I was uneasy.

When Lipper asked me if I wanted some tea in his office a
few days later, I was so circumspect I could hardly move. "I'm
grateful to you for helping out with Henry," he said. "Maxine
is isolated out there. She suspended her doctoral course work
when I got this appointment. I assume she'll get around to re-
suming it." He stretched his lips over his teeth and frowned. "I
know an academic couple who commute between Buffalo and
Berkeley so they can both have tenured jobs. There's a limit, I
think."

His remark was ominous. A limit to what? I began to sympathize with Maxine, but it would be foolish to involve myself
further with a couple who were so at odds, and risk being
caught in the middle. And how could I be detached and be his
protégée?

I looked at the clock. "I have to meet your wife."

Dolly Spencer, a department major who always wore a black
sweater and a white silk aviator's scarf, was leaning, round-
shouldered, against the wall outside. I nodded to her and went
down the hall. Lipper's voice drifted after me and then his door
shut. When I turned, Dolly had disappeared.

During the afternoon I drew some portraits of Henry. He was
amused and sat motionless for nearly ten minutes, long after I'd
put down my pencil and urged him to go back to his play.

"But that's marvelous!" Maxine cried when I shyly showed
her the sketches. "And there are more! Let me see!" Her com-
ments were ones a drawing instructor might make, and she no
longer seemed so sullenly frivolous. She knew what she was
talking about and was genuinely appreciative. The day was

mild. We sat together on the porch steps and I drank a glass of wine, too, while Henry burrowed in the sandpile.

"Well, surely you're going to carry this talent further," she said. "You don't want to join the slag heap at some college."

"I don't want to make art—not seriously. I'm sort of burned out. I did too much too early—" She made a face at me. "I really want to study, to become learned."

"It's a man's world," she said. "Academic salaries are disgraceful. If I could do what you can, I'd be out of here in a flash, enjoying my autonomy. But let me tell you, at the risk of seeming a bitter old bitch, I was hooked on him, too, on all that pizzazz. He was a promising guy. I saw that. So I helped him do his thesis. I mean, I really worked on it. Not just the typing, but that too."

Henry stood and cradled a rubber dinosaur in his arms. "Don't cry, Birdie," he sang, threw it down, and jumped into the cockpit of his car.

"I was not just Barry's student; I was somebody else's wife. A mathematician. What do you think of that? And I had ambitions of my own: a Ph.D." She pronounced the initials as if they were obscene. "I was working on Persian miniatures, something Barry knew nothing about. It was all mine. I walked out on my marriage. I became Daddy's girl again. Daddy paid my tuition. Daddy furnished our place, for that matter." She waved her arm toward the two parlors. "I can see you're curious: Well, Barry filled up the walls." She put her forehead to her knees. "I convinced Daddy it was all for the best. Barry, of course, was poor as a church mouse. It's a classic tale of naked ambition." She laughed loudly.

Finally I asked, "Where did he get all those paintings? They must be worth a fortune."

She guffawed some more. Tears came to her eyes and she swiped at them with the back of her wrist. Wine slopped onto the steps. "On an academic's salary, you mean? An instructor?"

She leapt up and grabbed my hand. "Come here," she commanded. "Come on, I'll give you an education. That's what you're here for, I presume." She yanked me into the house and down the hall. We stood in the first doorway, before the resplendent works.

"Can't you guess?" she cried gaily. "Come on, take a stab!" I shook my head and focused on the Ingres.

"They're fakes!" she cried. "Isn't that grand?"

My mouth dropped open. "But they're beautiful—they look so real!" They'd made a fool of me.

"For God's sake, of course they do. Their owners couldn't tell the difference. Barry came along with his Ph.D. and told them they'd bought fakes, and they were so humiliated or so ticked off, they let him cart them away and hang them on *our* walls. It's quite a sideline, isn't it? He got them for a song—literally."

I was speechless. Maxine stared thoughtfully at the "Rosa Bonheur." "It's a way to make your education pay. But not everyone could pull it off. And Barry loves forgeries. He really admires them. He wouldn't accept any he didn't admire. In many ways, for him, they surpass the originals for their sheer power. I guess it's because *he* knows and ordinary people don't, and a beautiful painting worth nothing at all but cherished by some yahoo for its cachet is a comment on our absurd system of values. And the poor bastards who made them—well, you see the many layers of all this. . . ."

On the contrary, I felt a puritanical revulsion toward both cynical Lippers.

"Since Henry was born," Maxine said, turning suddenly on me, "you are Barry's third 'research assistant.' "

"Well, nothing is going on!" I said hotly. "I wouldn't do that. How could he? Wouldn't they fire him?"

"You're the first one he's sent home," she said bemusedly. "Some kind of distribution of his ego, territoriality." She laughed bitterly. "Christ! What must Henry be up to? Don't you run off." She clattered down the hall and looked to see if I was following. "I'm sorry I said that," she called. "I'm glad he sends you out. I'm very glad."

Henry was sitting placidly on the sandpile. Maxine ran over and hugged him, showing me her large bottom straining the seams of her jodhpurs.

"I have to go."

"Sit down for a minute. You can't run away after I've bared my soul to you. Listen." She sat down again and pulled my hand until I sank to the steps beside her. "Here, a little touch more." I held out my glass. She drank deeply from hers, filling her cheeks before she swallowed.

"You know," she said in a stage whisper, "they're scared shitless at the college that we're planning to run off to some university the first time Barry gets an offer. Some place with an endowed chair, a hunk of money, a stage for his routine. But they're wrong. He wants tenure here." She looked delightedly for my reaction. "He wants the comfortable life, where he's the only game in town. He can hide out on his country estate, has time to advise his clients, he can pluck delicious girls off the bushes—you've been thoroughly screened, all of you; you're the crème de la crème."

I had a paralyzing empathy for Maxine; after all, this was a variation of the tale I had gone to sleep to for most of my life. Would she let her story be carved in stone, as Muriel had, or would she wake up and take things into her own hands? I didn't want to warn her. It would have been presumptuous.

"I'm afraid I can't work for you anymore," I said miserably. I wasn't raised to flee my obligations. She looked stricken. "I'm sorry it's short notice. Studying is more time-consuming than I'd expected." I must have looked as foolish as I sounded.

She seemed to be summoning superior forces of her own. But then she said, "Barry's assigned you something. You'll be doing that."

"I think it's premature. I think I need some broader experience now." She chuckled. I did too. She drove me back to the college and squeezed my hand before I got out of the car.

Because I felt obscurely in the wrong, I prepared myself for an ugly exchange with Lipper, but he was in a jolly mood and even agreed that a general survey would benefit me more than the minutiae of scholarship. "Dolly can take over your project," he said easily.

I was about to scuttle off when he said, "I hope my wife didn't burden you. I hope that isn't why you're here." I shook my head. "She says you're a talented artist." He paused, apparently to give me a chance to affirm or deny it. I held my silence. "So, if it's simply a matter of time for your work, it's something I can't argue with. This is primarily an academic institution. The coursework is demanding."

His tone was unsettling, and I knew that Barry Lipper would

never show the interest Maxine had in my artwork. Art was a
kind of tool for him; artists could not be. I heard myself tell him
that it was true. I needed more time for drawing and painting.
My voice swelled with perverse pride. Inwardly I resolved to
continue with art history, but as a kind of fifth columnist, a
secret representative of the practitioners.

Toward the end of the semester Lipper lectured on fakes, and
he was just as enthusiastic as Maxine had said. They were not
equivalent to the real thing, of course, but they had their interest. The connoisseur's appreciation of art was not limited to
authentication.

As Barry Lipper's light waned for me, I lost patience with the
language and methods of his discipline. We talked in class as if
we were translating from a foreign tongue, and used preten-
tious phrases that seemed superfluous to me. Surely the works
said all that needed to be said. People talking about art without
ever having tried to make it were just blowing off steam, and
my earlier notion that Lipper understood as much about *making*
as he did about *explaining,* seemed callow. But I loved nothing
more than poring over the pictures in the extravagant volumes
that the library owned. In doing so, I recovered a trancelike
state that was akin to the painting one, but more soothing,
without a goal.

It was in the library one afternoon that I stumbled upon references to Gottfried Mind, an eighteenth century idiot in Berne,
acclaimed as the "cat's Raphael." His head and hands were so
oversized that he attracted jeering crowds when he walked in
the streets. His despairing father had peddled his drawings of
cats, deer, and rabbits in order to support him. These creatures
were rendered with singular radiance and collected all over Europe, even by royalty. I pitied Mind and I envied him. How
cruel was his fate, but it had relieved him of choice—he'd had
to enlist his particular gift just to survive. Of course it was a
freakish talent and appealed for that reason to his fashionable
contemporaries. The gap between dexterity of the moment and
the making of complex, meaningful works of art, was immense.
One could survive as a curiosity, especially if deformed or a
child—but how turn that peculiarity to greatness?

Perhaps, when I leafed through the indices of a few magazines, looking for *Jenkins, Sarah,* it was in search of a more natu-

ral kinship. But when I found a review of one of her shows, it
described landscapes, and I had never been drawn to them.
There were no reproductions in the article, and the usual obfuscations of art language abounded. Jenkins's work seemed to
*combine increasingly refined impulses of her own with an understanding of
basic pattern and change in nature*—whatever that meant. *Small percep-
tions built to a rendering of the whole that challenged one to see in ways that
were new, reverent, transforming.* The paintings were *humane and ambitious.* It amused me to think that I had glimpsed her at Maxine's
stables, that this lanky westerner might be a great artist, riding
at the remotest edge of my life.

There were other wise men on campus besides Barry Lipper.
One of the most legendary was Professor Juan Brava y Gravas,
whose seminar in comparative literature inspired me to make a
series of monotypes illustrating *Don Quixote.* I drew on pieces of
cardboard with crayon, inked them and pressed them to handmade papers in my room. It was a simple process that I could
manage without much equipment, and linked me to the Impressionists who had experimented with Oriental images. I considered sending them to Hugh because they reminded me of
him, too, but thought better of letting him think he was on my
mind.

Professor Brava, though tall and stiff in manner, seemed burdened by sadness, I assumed because of certain strains in the
Spanish character, and because the Civil War had driven him
from his homeland. Students were in awe of his erudition, his
candor, and his sorrow, which elicited rare devotion. He assured our class that the important questions could always be
simply phrased and must be addressed over and over again.
There was nothing new, he said, under the sun.

This encouraged me to go and see him in his office. I had been
reading Ortega's *The Dehumanization of Art* and had understood it
to doom the modern painter to alienated abstraction. When
Brava opened his door and ushered me inside with fluid, Old
World courtesy, my confused thoughts prevented me from
framing any kind of question, simple or not. My glance flew to
the tooled leather spines of the books ranged like regiments
behind him, and to the reproductions of *Las Meninas, St. Jerome,*
and *The Disasters of War.* I wondered if I could begin to tell him
about myself, starting from the beginning, omitting nothing,

like a village storyteller—but whose attention to every detail finally robs the tale of its point. He noticed that I was looking at the pictures, and remarked that our study of the rise of individualism made us alert to the self-consciousness of Velasquez painting himself in the mirror, painting the maidens.

I thought of a question then. It was certainly simple, certainly unsophisticated, but I asked it anyway. "Did they know he was great while he was alive? Did he struggle for commissions? Did the king realize that these pictures would live forever? How can you tell if art of your own time is great or simply fashionable?"

He nodded, frowning, his eyes filling with light. "In Spain, isn't it so, when we see a dancer perform, we know, as an audience, that she has, or does not have, what Garcia Lorca has called *el duende.* I speak of the dance because it is immediate and evanescent. We know from our reading of Coleridge's organic model about the essential nature of a work of art. It is from him that we draw our ideas about originality, spontaneity, authenticity, indeed, *self-expression.*" He stared thoughtfully at the El Greco and laced his long fingers.

"I recall a performance by Artur Rubinstein. The simplicity of his playing was almost naive. I was deeply moved. Out of nothing, he created everything. Not from passion, nor fortamento, nor to please us in any particular way, nor to meet standards we have imposed, but from his own pure concentration. He opened a window to us and spoke through it. He was an agent of the music, isn't that so? It poured out of him."

"I understand that. I understand being an agent of music. But Ortega says the painter is at the greatest distance from reality, from the essential 'lived' quality without which representation is impossible." I paused, and then blurted, "I feel so distant from life. I feel I've been looking at it and the looking sets me apart, as if appreciating how things appear and wanting to make them myself puts a sheet of glass between us."

"So you are a painter. I didn't know that," he said. "I hope you will show me your work."

"I'm not working now. I just want to learn now," I mumbled.

He nodded. "You will find your relation to the world. It is consciousness, is it not, that will bring about the necessary change. Persist in your looking. Take pleasure in your youth. You will need to draw on it later. We know that Rousseau and

Wordsworth wished to recover the innocence of childhood, not stifle it as civilization had done. It is a matter of art, rather than artifice, is it not? It changed everything, this idea of the unfettered child. We have gained the self in modern times, but the self can be a prison too."

This, of course, was true. But how could I recover what I had never experienced? The first drawings I had ever made were of things around me, and I had set about perfecting them at once. I'd never smeared finger paints like other children, never drawn a round sun with slashing rays, never a stick man or a lollipop tree. Where would I look to unearth my own innocence? Had it ever existed?

Muriel wrote that Portia was going to graduate a year early. She had taken extra courses and passed examinations that exempted her from others. They were already weighing various colleges. Almost as an afterthought, she added that Portia was going to visit Desmond in New Caledonia. This news struck me painfully. It was the first visit either of us had dared to make, for fear of betraying Muriel. I felt guilty and excluded. I also admired Portia's courage. My mind would go blank alone with Desmond. The contradictory feelings (he had abandoned us, but hadn't he deserved more love than we had ever shown him?) would abort the inconsequential pleasantries that might normally pass between father and daughter, and where would that leave us? I felt as unprepared for my parent's reality as I was for my own.

One Wednesday afternoon I got three messages that a male had called long distance, refusing to leave his name. I thought that was odd behavior for Desmond. Sada was in our room the next Friday, dressing for a date with Roger, when another yell came down the hall from the telephone booth.

"I bet it's Hugh," Sada said complacently. I ran out.

"Hi," he said. There was a roaring in the background, perhaps trucks on a highway. "Can you read me?"

"Where are you, Hugh?"

"Philly. I've come here to die."

"What are you up to?"

"I'm up to visiting you."

"Hugh—really? Are you really here?" He didn't deign to reply. "Well. Great. Do you want to stay here? Shall I ask at one of the men's—"

"Forget that. I've already cased the joint and it's not for me."

Was this likely? I supposed that it was, that he had come and skulked around the campus, trailed me to class, peeped into windows, and arrived at his own conclusions without speaking to a soul.

"I've taken a room. Can you sign out?"

"What kind of a room? Where?"

"The Ritz. That kind of a room."

I would have to take a chance on getting caught. The practice was to give a local address, someone's relative. Hugh's customary obscurities were not reassuring. He read from a train schedule, however. He was better prepared than usual. I could arrive at 5:03. After a long silence I agreed to come. We signed off.

"You were right," I told Sada. "He's in Philadelphia, at a hotel."

"My God," she said. "I am awestricken." I laughed and let myself feel wanton. "Roger would never do anything so inspired!" she said.

When I stuffed my Ortega, some underpants, and a shirt into a green book bag, she threw up her hands. "My God, you can't go like that! Where is your sense of style?" Her overnight case was under her bed. She shook it upside down and emptied it of hairpins, lint, Kleenex, and earrings. "Okay, take this and this and this," she commanded, grabbing a black negligee, lacy underpants, and perfume from drawer, closet, floor, and windowsill. The bag distracted me: it was bird's-egg blue with a satin lining, and looked like the one I had carried for Muriel into the hotel the night of the Fireman's Ball. I stared stuporously at it.

"This is what normal people use," Sada said, noticing my expression. "What the hell's the matter?"

I loved irony more than truth so I shrugged and said, "Nothing. I should send you instead. You have the knack."

Hugh was standing a few yards down the platform, his nose in the air, eyebrows cocked, hands in his jacket pockets. The pose even included a cigarette pasted to his lower lip.

I stood where I landed, while passengers picked their way past and waited for him to turn and acknowledge my arrival. Finally he did and frowned in his old mocking way. He took my elbow and the bag and we left the station. He had no luggage but a frayed paperback stuck out of one coat pocket. Stubble glinted on his cheeks but his hair was neat and shining and his clothes pressed. I silently accused his mother of getting him ready for this trip. Was it possible? What had he told her? What had he been doing all these months? I myself felt transformed.

We walked so out of step at first that we collided and begged pardon. The discomfort of reunion made me want to go at once to the hotel and make love, rub off the strangeness and tension like a layer of traveler's grime. Afterward we could go out and explore the city in unison.

"Coffee?" he asked.

"It's almost dinnertime," I said irritably. "Let's go to the room and then look for a place to eat."

He was craning his neck. "I have to make a call." He ducked into a storefront. I followed. The place was stocked with girlie magazines, comics, racing forms, movie star books. The local tabloid shrieked a macabre headline. I studied the pictures illustrators had made for the periodicals. Swarthmore seemed a remote and refined outpost. A woman behind the counter stared at me as though she could see through to my fears and pretensions.

Hugh spoke for a while in an undertone and hung up.

"Who was that?"

"A guy I have to meet on Monday. Gaylord." He opened the door. The woman watched us go out. "I said I'd call."

I was irritated by this show of reliability for someone I didn't know. Hugh's abbreviated, self-dramatizing talk seemed to emphasize our divergent interests. I wanted him to court me, to lure me back.

He said he was hungry. Perhaps that was a form of courting, to go to dinner, but he seemed reluctant to be alone with me. We were in a neighborhood of Italian restaurants and wandered into one with candles in Chianti bottles and plastic tablecloths. Two thick-necked men lounged in the doorway, watching passersby, but it was early for dinner and we were the only customers. Behind the kitchen door, a woman's voice cursed loudly. The door flew open, the cursing stopped abruptly and a waiter emerged. His cheeks had deep ravines, as if he'd been clawed. He reminded me of Michelangelo's flayed face in the

Last Judgment. I chose my old dish, veal Parmesan, feeling as much at the mercy of my companion as I had been when Desmond and I ate at that other Italian joint so many years before. Hugh read the menu from top to bottom, perhaps thinking of something entirely different. Finally he ordered lasagna.

He began to talk, self-consciously. "You'll want to meet Gaylord. His family has adopted me. They live in Harlem. Not what you might expect. Guards, doormen, gates, a courtyard, a huge bar, a baby grand. There isn't a white face for blocks." He gave me a smirk. "I'm Gaylord's valet."

"Where did you meet him?" The story sounded invented.

He grinned. "On the Bowery. He has a studio down there and he lets me work in it. He's in the education department at NYU. Going to be a teacher. He gave me some canvases and I paint them over and over. There's good light, but it's grubby."

"What do you paint?" This fantasy matched my old idea of a life in art. It was both incomplete and too good to be true.

"Self-portraits, since I'm available to pose. And what I see out the window. The bums. I go to cafés and draw." He stretched and looked around the restaurant. "You know."

A latter-day George Luks, indeed, making himself obscure so that people would leave him alone.

"What are you going to do when you graduate?"

"I don't know. I'm staying loose. Not school. I've had enough. I can wait on tables. There's one place where the owner will hang my work and give me a job. He'll do anything for people he likes—lend them money, let them crash in the back, feed them." He smiled. We stared at each other. Nothing happened. He pulled the book from his pocket. *The Flowers of Evil.* "Somebody said this was good," he said.

The hotel was on a sidestreet near Rittenhouse Square. On our way there it began to rain. We stood across the street looking at the smoky, double-glass doors and the sputtering neon sign. Hugh pressed a room key into my palm.

"You go on in first. I could only afford a single, so . . ."

I was alarmed. "Can't you go? They've already seen you—"

"I want to be sure you get in. Just play it cool." He gently punched my arm, a coaches' gesture he had always made fun of, and backed away from me, into the shadows. Someone came out of the hotel and we turned to look. The man felt the rain, turned up his collar, and walked away, whistling. A car passed, slowly, as if the driver were searching for someone. Hugh poked me again. He put Sada's bag down on the sidewalk and took a pack of Lucky Strikes from his pocket.

I crossed the street and entered the hotel. The lobby was bright as a clinic, with raggedly humming fluorescent tubing tacked to a tin ceiling. Couches of green vinyl and chromium tubing stood here and there on a gray linoleum floor. I had thought I was alone but a bald-headed man rose behind the counter, apparently searching the mailboxes. He turned and grinned. The elevator was down a little hall. I took a step toward it. "Evening," the man said. I halted.

"Evening." I waited, but he only stared at me. I sank onto one of the couches. The elevator door clanged open and a man and woman emerged, arguing bitterly. She grabbed his arm and he yanked it free. "I told you, this is no way to start, but you always—"

"You ain't seen him yet," the man snarled. "Quit reading people's minds." He pushed with his shoulder at the outside door. She carried an umbrella, and after a glance at the weather, shook it open angrily, gave me a look, and followed him out.

I stood up to see if the elevator car were still open. Hugh hadn't told me the room number and I was afraid to pull out the key to see. The clerk muttered to himself. Hugh's face showed in the blurred glass of the door. I shook my head at him and he faded away.

I picked up a travel folder from a pile on a shelf and studied a list of bus tours. With my eyes on the folder I walked to the elevator and punched "four." The door shut, and I looked at the key. Its tag read "thirty-six." I punched "three" and the car lurched to a stop. The hallway was dim, lit only by a bare bulb at the far end. The carpet was vaguely Persian, patterned in colors of midnight, mud, and dried blood. I found the door to the room and went in.

It was tiny, with a sink, a tub, and a toilet all behind a curtain hung on a curved rod attached to the ceiling. The lumpy bed stood high off the floor, and next to it a mission chair, a small table covered with oilcloth, and above that a ceiling light with a little glass shade. I pulled the string, shut the door, and opened the curtains at the window. I stared back at myself, reflected against a brick wall, and fell into the chair. Footsteps sounded next door, heavy, thudding. I imagined a hulking man confined to a similar room, someone with nowhere else to go.

I got up, washed my hands and hung my coat on one of the two wire hangers suspended from the curtain rod. I used the toilet. I wore no watch and there wasn't a telephone, just a curling card with instructions in case of fire.

Finally Hugh rapped on the door, and I sprang to open it.

"I had to wait—dudes were having a fight outside," he said. Water dripped from his head and shoulders onto the floor.

"This place is like something seamen go to on shore leave."

"I only had enough money—"

"It's all right, Hugh." I wanted to embrace him, but he circled the room in a jittery way, looking under the table, touching the bed. We were so far from home, as if waiting to be missed and rescued. Rain socked at the airshaft.

He had put the overnight bag on the table. I opened it. Hugh lay down on the bed and cradled his head in his hands.

"Put on that black number," he drawled. I whirled on him. "I took a look at it," he said.

"Well, I'm not going to wear it." It was not something I would ever wear. He seemed to have forgotten who I was. The illicit meeting had debased us. I took off my clothes and brushed my teeth in my underwear.

Hugh took a toothbrush from his breast pocket and stood beside me. We spit into the sink. "I'm sorry," he said.

"It's all right."

He turned back the bedspread and undressed very deliberately, almost fondling his clothes, and his long white body was a surprise, looked surprised itself to be so exposed. The milky skin was covered with pale blond hairs. I removed my underwear—it was the first time we had been wholly naked together —and hurried into bed without looking at him again. He reached up and pulled the light string, climbed in after me, and then we seized one another.

I woke in a state of terror. In the pitch dark, I was pressed against Hugh's bowed back; he had curved inward, childlike, to sleep. I was chilled through and through and the mattress smelled of choking mold. The man next door had wakened me with his wretched coughing. I gripped my sides. A vision of faces pierced the dark, entreating me to declare myself, or do something—I didn't know what. Dire or rewarding things were happening somewhere else and I should have been there to take part. Hopelessness and guilt that reached back all the way to the beginnings of my experience sucked me under. I longed for home. I longed for comfort for my conscious self, for a place to be that was the right place.

I pressed my cheek against Hugh's shoulder. "What's the trouble?" he whispered. I was surprised that he knew anything was. He turned over and gave me a hot, slack kiss.

"I want to be at the center," I said. "But I'm outside."

"I know," he said. "Me too."

He held me and rocked our bodies, and I was chagrined by my neglect of him. The spurious romance of this night derived from my rushing to experience, not to this other person. Hugh was, after all, tender, and his preoccupations had not prevented him from noticing my longing. I ought to have considered him, and I felt blessed that he wasn't wounded by my desire to be somewhere else.

The coughing began again, and suddenly I put a name to it—Desmond. He sounded the way Desmond had used to, in the night, in our house. I imagined him now, as if he were next door.

"Hugh," I murmured, "*home*."

"You'll have to make your own," he said. "Your mother's about to sell it."

"I didn't mean that. I don't know what I meant." If I'd ever felt at home, I'd never have wanted to run away from it. How I had hoped that out in the world I'd find a force, perhaps in the way I responded to some artist's passionate expression, that would shape my own work. It hadn't happened. I had protected myself from life and from art in the same way, afraid that letting go would result in my being overtaken. I could hear Lou saying that promise could never be fulfilled. Hugh began to make love to me. Someone else had said that pleasure moves out from the center of the body to its boundaries, and fear travels the same path in reverse.

We ate in a cafeteria the next morning and walked the city streets, moving through adjacent villages, almost as alone as we'd been in the room. After a day we were seasoned cheats, and entered and left the hotel together. I grew perversely fond of the place.

At the museum we parted for a time. Hugh stayed with the medieval paintings, but I wanted to study the Eakins. He said they were too deadpan for him, but their exactitude, their righteousness, fascinated me. How deeply Eakins had probed for truth to arrive at so finished a surface. I remembered that he had taught a Life class for young ladies at the Pennsylvania Academy and been fired when he removed the model's loincloth. It was not with the young ladies that I aligned myself, but with Eakins. A young woman was copying one of the paintings now. I did wish I were in her place. Eakins fired my ambition, but he also curbed it: The works had a sovereign perfection that warned me—don't take art lightly. Hugh came up beside me. He mentioned he had found a life drawing class at NYU that wasn't supervised on Saturday mornings and had crashed it. I understood his desire to take part but not be held accountable, and disparaged the same tendency in myself.

On Sunday we went to the train station and waited without speaking. Then when the train pulled in, we embraced fervently. I got aboard and found an empty seat on the aisle. When we left the station, I bent forward to look for him. He watched the windows pass, but gave no sign he saw me. The young man in the adjoining seat greeted me. He was Tom Batter, a Swarthmore student. I knew him by reputation. He was president of the student volunteer agency that had organized protests against the college's investments in South Africa. Now they were launching a campaign to force integration of the Woolworth lunch counters in Chester.

"I have to tell you," he said, "that was one hot farewell." I reddened. "I'm just teasing," he hastened to assure me. "Maybe I'm jealous." He removed his peaked cap.

"I didn't expect witnesses," I said. I remembered glimpsing Tom as he crossed the campus, trailed by a line of little children, like ducklings. They were orphans or chronically ill, someone had said. I mentioned the scene. "I admire you. It makes me feel ashamed that I don't take care of anyone."

"It's in my blood. I was raised to be virtuous." His expression was artless. "My dad runs a Quaker relief agency and my mom teaches deaf kids. I can sign as well as I can talk. But I can't do either outstandingly."

I laughed. "*I* was raised to be selfish and I'm not even excelling at that. I'm supposed to be driven. But I'm useless."

"What do you mean?" He turned to search my face. I was exhausted. I had better be careful—this young man took everything I said literally.

"I'm an artist. But I've put it aside."

"But that's a gift!" he protested. "I can't believe you said that! You're not useless. You may be singleminded. . . ."

We watched the back streets of towns roll past, and when the little stations appeared, like the Meridian Avenue one, I thought, I am rolling past, I am rolling past. I asked Tom about himself so that I wouldn't have to talk. He had planned to go to medical school, but now he wanted to teach. "Not college, little kids, where I can make a difference. I'm fascinated by them, babies on up. They're born perfect, and with only trial and error to guide them. They get taught and pushed and hurt. The family is a poor agent, these days, for the job. Even mine was, and I had a happy childhood."

"Is happiness what toughens you for life?"

"Toughens?" He made a face. "I'm talking about the system breaking down—members fighting for their own survival, hang the common good. Somebody starts to worry about his own future, and everybody else loses out. That's the way people are."

"I guess so," I said, and wondered how long his stamina would last. His self-assurance was a pleasure, though, after two days with Hugh. He was well disposed too—happiness must lie in disposition toward the world.

A week later a letter came from Portia. She told me she wanted to go to college as far from home as possible. Berkeley fit the bill.

I saw Dad. We missed you, she wrote. *He was rather vague, or maybe depressed. Adele has moved out and he never mentioned her—neither did I, needless to say. His house has library books literally covering every surface. I don't know how they let him go on borrowing them. He eats practically the same meal every night, usually cottage cheese. The freezer is full of cigarettes. He was almost too sober, does that make any sense?*

Desmond had never complained. His protest had taken the

form of flight—but I remembered some scenes of family life
where he played the genial husband, making a show of obliging
Muriel's whims. What did she think of him, if she ever did
anymore? Suppose Desmond pulled himself together and
breezed through the front door, scattering flowers and perfume,
and proposed that he and she take a trip together and after that
set themselves up in a little apartment in the city to enjoy life.
What would she do? Turn up her lip and stand with her hands
on her hips, or at her breast, covering her heart, and tell him he
was a greater fool than she had ever realized? Or would she
dimple and smile and lower her eyes while she thought it over,
all of her coquettishness restored in an instant?

Hugh had said he still visited her. He'd transplanted a rose of
Sharon tree and laid some tile in the bathroom. Portia knew all
about his friend Gaylord. Hugh was almost a member of the
family, now that I was gone. Family life was a mystery. It certainly wasn't over—it would take another shape, or I hadn't yet
seen its whole shape, or how it could be finished.

9

Rebecca had paid me a call when the upperclassmen arrived, a week after freshman orientation. She was plumper and wore a saronglike garment that gave her the composed, brainy look of an Indian exchange student. The visit felt social, rather than personal, as if my acquaintance with her distant past was potentially embarrassing. When she uttered her long, complicated sentences, her eyes strayed to the book upside down on my unmade bed. She told me her chief interest now was "the theatre." She had a genius boyfriend, Philip, and they collaborated: a dramatization of *The Waste Land,* some monosyllabic one-acts, a few spontaneous performances at different sites around campus. They had done some agitprop at one of Tom Batter's rallies the year before.

Afterward I would see Rebecca and Philip, who was sinewy and compact, with a fuzzy, ambiguous hairline, crossing the campus in a crowd of friends. They talked boisterously, not caring who might find them obnoxious. Sometimes she and he walked alone, arm in arm, their long, pushing-off strides perfectly matched, like skaters'; their eyes trained on the ground as they conferred. They were the highly visible artists, attracting a following of disciples and connoisseurs.

One night Rebecca accosted me in the dining hall while I was clearing dirty dishes off a table and Sada sat kibitzing.

"Philip and I have done a new adaptation of *Threepenny Opera,*" she told us. "We've gotten permission to stage an all-student production. Jack Lang is doing musical direction. You know, it's a fabulous piece—that music, the politics, humor, spectacle." She beamed at me. "I thought maybe you'd be interested."

"Interested?"

"In helping out, joining in. You have the background."

"Do you know who Jack Lang is?" Sada asked, when Rebecca left without a commitment from me. I shook my head. "You must be really tuned out," she said. "He's the best-looking thing in this town, to begin with. He can play anything on the piano, he's a composer, and he's expected to win a Fulbright to study composition in Rome next year."

I continued to load my tray. "We've got to do it!" she cried, her eyes burning.

"Got to do what?"

"Audition! Get plum parts! I've been dying to do a show. I never thought those pansies would get beyond *The Waste Land.* And I'm sick to death of the dance group and Satie."

"You were in shows in high school," I said. I'd heard a lot about *Pal Joey.* "I can't dance and I'm not a singer. Singing is artificial. It's like foot binding."

"That's Philistine. Anyway, it's not what Weill and Brecht are like."

"There isn't anything that calls attention to oneself like singing out loud," I continued. I wanted *not* to be conspicuous, but to emulate Rubinstein—to be a conduit, not a performer.

"You would sing like Lenya," Sada said. "Haven't you *listened* to my record? And it is not artificial to give yourself over to a character. If you're any good, you disappear, yourself. It's like any art, really," she said cleverly.

"My father doesn't care much for singing either," I said grumpily. "He used to say his favorite diva was a stripper named Stormy Petrel." Did I really want to be left out? Could I watch from the audience while Sada tripped across the stage, spend all those weeks on the sidelines while the company rehearsed? Before the evening was over, I had allowed her to persuade me.

We rehearsed to her Lenya record. "You're going to get Jenny Diver," she predicted.

Auditions were held one night after supper. We would-be actors moved uncertainly through the auditorium of the theatre, sat in scattered seats and waited to be called. Rebecca wore a scarf rolled around her forehead and ran repeatedly up and down the steps to the stage. Philip sat halfway back in the house with his feet thrown over the seats ahead and a clipboard propped on his thighs. Jack Lang, dark-haired and handsome as a movie star, amused himself at the piano. A girl in leotards and a long red jersey skirt leaned over him, talking while he doodled his songs. Everything she said made him laugh. I thought of Jules. But Jack wasn't distractable in the way Jules had been, with his household of women always a step ahead of him, making him seem lightly clownish, a man ripping one hat off his head and slamming another down in its place. Jack was good-looking and women followed him. I waited nervously for my turn. I had never learned to read music. It had not been on my list of essential life skills.

Sada lounged beside me, giving the candidates her shrewd attention. She loved this atmosphere. Although everyone had come to try and outshine everyone else, we were a group, and Sada submitted without conceding her individuality.

When she was called, she bounded to the stage, barked "Mack's Song" and the key she wanted Jack to play it in. She counted out a few beats. He grinned down at the keys. She began. Sada really couldn't sing, but got by with a patter, no trace of uncertainty, and was obviously tickled to be up there. She was a pleasure to behold. She danced, too, with an arch, wanton exuberance. Her daily motions were completely familiar to me, and these elegant turns were a revelation. Rebecca told me later that she decided on the spot to make Sada choreographer and give her a solo number to perform.

When my name was called, I shot out of my seat. Encouraging faces turned toward me as I went by—all of them had passed this initiation rite. I felt that I was begging to be admitted to a group for the first time and must demonstrate my sincerity with a feat. My heart pounded and my face burned.

" 'Surabaya' from *Happy End*," I said to Jack Lang, and he set a comfortable key. I sucked air into my lungs and belted out the song. My voice, ringing out the harsh lament, filled the house, as if it were something I was hurling with all my might. When I got to the place where I spoke in a low mournful tone, Jack stopped playing. I finished dizzy and confused, and walked backstage instead of down the steps. The little audience burst into applause.

They cast the principal roles that night. Sada and I went back to see them posted on the bulletin board. I was given Jenny Diver. We were far too agitated and happy to sleep, and stayed up talking for hours. When I finally lay down, the leap I had made on the stage played over and over in my mind. I remembered faces in the audience, remembered reaching out to them, fielding their response, and sending it back. This was the exulting exchange that Muriel had wanted to have with the world, and it must have been her failure to sustain it that colored her later years with bitter disappointment. I could sympathize; I could share her regret. The gratifications of performing seemed boundless. I was susceptible too.

But one has no hold on transcendence, and I needed to protect myself. What if Muriel saw me on stage and drew comparisons of her own? What if she were critical or grudging in praise? I decided not to tell her about the play, nor to tell anyone.

Rehearsals began. Even when not scheduled for scene work, cast members couldn't stay away from the theatre. Rebecca and Philip were serious as surgeons, but once the actors found their stride and could play, we were irrepressible. When I made what Rebecca called a "good choice" or invented some bit of business, it pleased everyone. We were a company, all for one and one for all. We loved to work.

I was mesmerized by Jack Lang. He treated everyone alike, with bemused, offhand tolerance. He was an effective coach and willing to set my songs in keys that made the most of my voice, so that my performance was enhanced. His fingers danced on the keys while he watched me on the stage. He never missed a note. Later in the evening the girl in leotards would usually arrive. She sat on the edge of the stage, dangling her legs. Jack stood between them, his hands on her thighs while she rested her arms on his shoulders and looked down at him with a lascivious smile. Performing had stimulated a desire for total involvement in me, and I burned with jealousy, watching them.

But satisfactions outweighed complaints. I mulled Jenny Diver over in my mind whenever I could. The show was like a

tableau vivant, and I worked at my part the way I blocked out a
figurative painting. People had always said that the expressions
I drew showed on my face and the poses in my stance. Charac-
terizations were built in layers, like a series of progressive
sketches. When I let my mind drift, some gesture or reading
would pop into it without effort, and later I incorporated it into
my performance. I couldn't see or hear myself, but relied on
others to tell me whether or not they were convinced, and thus
a burden of self-criticism was lifted. There was no product to
worry over. Acting vanished completely. It was all process, all
consuming and all consumed. But we faced a devastating loss
when the show was over.

After dress rehearsal Sada and I were cleaning off our faces in
front of the mirrors surrounded by little bulbs. I confessed to
her that I felt sheer power. My experience of drawing portraits
before an audience had not prepared me for this. Drawing separated me from the crowd, but acting offered a collaborative
relationship with it, and when I was good, I did disappear, and
Jenny Diver took my place. A power beyond my careful control
worked for me.

Maxine Lipper telephoned me one afternoon. She sounded
chastened, but I resented her voice, nevertheless.

"Henry has asked about you," she said, "I've had a string of
no-shows and this Thursday is desperate. *Would* you consider
coming—"

"I'm sorry. I'm in a play. It takes up every free minute."

"A play? Really? I'll come and see it!" she cried, as if that
would give me more time. "May I? You don't mind, do you?"

"Of course not. Anyone can come," I said tactlessly.

"Oh, I'm thrilled. Listen, I've framed your pictures of Henry.
They're so lovely, so true to his nature. Several times I've been
on the verge of telling Sarah Jenkins about you. She's only
going to be around for another year and I thought you might
like to meet her—is that too pushy? Oh, I'm trying to take over
your life because mine is so dreary—"

I cut her off, saying I had an appointment. My relief was
enough to frighten me. Was I a monster? I did want to meet
Sarah Jenkins, but not through Maxine. I felt her helplessness
was infectious.

On opening night I suffered an attack of stage fright that was no less than terror, but after a few minutes on stage, became a glutton for audience response. It was all I could do to keep from augmenting the performance I'd rehearsed and set. Afterward the breathless, giddy cast was thronged backstage. The dressing room doorways were clogged with people who called out congratulations while we swiped at our faces with cold cream, leaving enough makeup on to maintain a showy allure. A girl burst in and threw her arms around me. "You were divine!" she cried. "Incredible!" Sada's boyfriend Roger fought his way through, holding high a gigantic bouquet. His face was drawn and reverent, as if he'd had a cleansing shock. "Roger is gaga," someone observed. "He can't be trusted." I looked around for Jack Lang. He had disappeared, probably with his dancer.

Philip had arranged for us to have a party in an off-campus house. We straggled along the street, reminiscing already about what had just taken place. The discipline of the performance would give way to the joyful slackening of the celebration. I drank some beer and instantly conceived a dizzy urge to dance with Jack Lang. I dared myself to approach him when he showed up. There he was, then, in the kitchen, alone. He caught me looking at him and winked. He flipped the cap off a bottle of beer and offered me the opener.

"Salut, Jenny Diver," he said. *"Why is she smiling so?"*

I tipped my head demurely. He came closer, his perfectly white teeth gleaming. A lock of curly dark hair fell over his forehead. He put his face close to mine and glanced back over his shoulder. My heart raced.

"You were sensational," he murmured. "You knew not to make it pretty. I think you understood that better than anyone." He sipped. "Listen," he said, and his eyes fell to my bosom. "I have something to ask of you." I didn't breathe. His eyes flicked back to mine and he cocked his head. "There's a marvelous woman over there in the corner, talking to Billy Rosen—do you know her name?"

I couldn't do a thing about the expression that spread over my face. I was devastated. He seemed not to notice. I turned. "That's Cornelia Kemp," I said. He nodded, touched my arm in a comradely way, and walked off to speak to her. The show had made me greedy. I wanted everything. I nearly wept.

Rebecca appeared at my side. "How do you feel?" she asked, and guided me out into the hall.

I forced my thoughts away from Jack. "Good. It was a lot of fun."

"You should feel good. You were excellent. Can we talk a little?"

We were standing in a long pantry lined with cupboards. A yellow slicker hung at the back door, over a pair of ·wading boots, as if a person were eavesdropping in costume. Muffled party voices were no more than sound effects.

"I'm proud of you," Rebecca began, her chin low and the ruffles on her dress seeming to float on an already matronly bosom. I'd have preferred the attentions of Jack Lang at that moment, but I was glad to have won her over. I respected her opinion. "I think you and I have a lot in common. We seem to share a rather special handicap."

I looked brightly at her. "What's that?"

"We're expected to succeed because we're smart and talented and we're our father's daughters."

I bridled. "What do you mean, *our* father's?"

Rebecca dug into a pocket in her skirt and took out her cigarettes. She tapped one against the counter and lighted it. "I'll explain," she said, exhaling. "*Our* fathers, Miranda, are ambivalent about success. It's an American thing. They wanted to pretend they didn't care about it, or that it would compromise real art, but when they didn't achieve it, they transferred their ambitions to us."

"Not in my case," I said. "My mother's the one who wants me to amount to something." I was thinking that Jules had done all right—why was she suggesting he hadn't succeeded? And he believed in himself. That was what really mattered. Desmond's fatal weakness was self-doubt.

"I'm quite certain that your mother was disappointed in your father," Rebecca said, tapping her cigarette. "She put pressure on him, I assume. Mine certainly did."

"That's true," I admitted. She blew smoke out of the side of her mouth.

"Look, all I'm saying is, I'm ambivalent about success too. I want to be part of the culture, and at the same time, I don't. I'd rather be the lonely artist doing only what I please, but I want to be a success. And God help you if you flop, in this country! In a way, I envy Philip. His father was at the top of his field and he's dead. Philip doesn't have to worry that if he succeeds, he's murdering his old man, and if he fails, he's breaking his heart."

The old snapshot of Desmond as Toby appeared in my head. He laughed, his eyes shut when the camera clicked, at just the wrong moment. . . . He was in costume, ready to entertain the folks. He must have been on top of the world! He was so young. "I don't know if my father really cares what I do," I said.

"But *you* do," she snapped.

"Sure. But I don't think about success. I just think about whether or not I'll—" I was about to say "fail," without thinking. I laughed. Rebecca snorted.

"Well, you're good at acting," she said. "What the hell. It's a gas, isn't it? You're high, you feel pleasure, you see that the audience is pleased—and you want more." She gave me a keen look. She was right. I had wanted more, I had been drunk on the audience's pleasure. "But then it's over and you're nothing without it. We both grew up around people like that. You know what I'm talking about."

One of the crew poked his head around the corner. He grinned and waved a beer bottle. "Philip's looking for you," he said. Rebecca threw me a last piercing glance.

"Rebecca, listen. I have no intention of becoming an *actor*," I said.

"That doesn't matter," she shot, turned, and went into the kitchen.

I ran my hand along the battered counter. The conversation was frustrating. I was reminded of the night I'd met Rebecca and her challenge to both please her and compete with her. Her opinions were killjoy ones. I wanted to celebrate, not be diminished by her perception of our common dilemma.

I went to the bathroom, and when I emerged, Sada was there in the hall.

"Pinch me," she said. "Roger's such an angel. He lets me carry on with everybody and just smiles like a big dog." She took my hand. "Miranda, you're my woman of the world. Should I do it, tonight?"

I laughed. "Do what?"

"For God's sake, do *it*, with Roger. That's what he wants. He's like Gordon Craig with Isadora. God, it's what *I* want. . . . Should I?" She shivered and rubbed her arms. *"Yes* is the answer. Will you cover for me? What do you think?"

"Of course I will."

I watched them leave. Someone was singing "Barbara Song" and I felt mildly violated; it was my number. Jack and Cornelia were head to head on a window seat. I probed a pile of coats in a bedroom and found a boy and girl obliviously clamped together.

The night was high and cold and glittering and seemed an enclosing arc that linked me to places and events I had no knowledge of, but would if I kept moving. The crisp air struck me forcefully after hours in the stuffy, crowded house, and it, too, was a revelation of my solitude. Alone, I could see everything clearly and at my leisure, and not be distracted by someone else's need to see differently. I turned to look back at the lighted windows of the house and the complicated silhouettes of the tree branches. A new record started up, lost momentum, and became garbled noise. Behind me, someone asked, "Had enough?"

It was Tom Batter in his peaked cap, standing like a sentry. "If you're walking back to campus, I'll join you."

We set off together. "They liked you, didn't they?"

"Were you there?"

"Oh, yes. I'm going to record the show—Philip scheduled the session for day after tomorrow. You're going to be my favorite band on that record."

"Thank you," I said. But a record would be an artifact. It could never evoke the performances and how it had felt to be on the stage. It would be like Desmond's boxes and Muriel's hoardings of the clothes she had worn to glory, years ago.

"Your friend coming to see it?" he asked.

I didn't know who he meant until I remembered he'd seen Hugh in Philadelphia. "No. Nobody is."

"Ah."

We walked in the middle of the street, past houses darkened for the night. On the campus, lights cast a cold glow. I was wide awake, entertaining an impulse to sit with Tom Batter on the curb and tell him the story of my life and ask him what he thought of it. But I wasn't capable of making objective sense of the past. I was used to drawing for clarity, and I wanted to render my life that way, too, without sentimentality. I broke away and said good night.

Sada didn't arrive until the rest of us were already putting on our makeup and costumes for the second performance.

"What are you looking at?" she asked in mock exasperation, then supplied an answer: "A woman fulfilled." She hummed while she painted her face.

We waited for the overture. Sada peeked at the house. "Full," she reported. "They look happy. Miranda, your Professor Brava is out there. He looks braced for the event."

I gasped. Brava, who could spot *el duende* or its absence! Jack and the band began to play. We all looked at each other, exhaling simultaneously. Was it courage or cowardice that made me wish I could embrace Muriel and Desmond now and ask them to wish me well?

After the show there was bedlam again in the dressing room. Philip was taking a night train to New York and left hastily, after assuring us that we had been even better than the night before. Sada and Roger mooned in the doorway. I dressed slowly and stared at myself in the mirror. Then I sidled between well-wishers in the hall. *"Miranda!"* That was Rebecca, calling from somewhere beyond the heads and the babble. "Miranda, here." I glimpsed her face.

"Well, look who's *here!*" This coy peal was entirely out of character. She beamed a confusing mixture of smugness and alarm. I searched the surrounding faces in vain. Then someone stepped aside and there he was, the fact of his presence amazing: Desmond.

Desmond here? It had been so long—my adult facade fell away and I struggled to gather it round me again. Love and misgivings poured out of my heart. But why shouldn't he be here? It was his setting, the clamorous backstage crowd, the hoopla, the earnest popular entertainment, the aftermath of illusion. I gave a little cry and threw myself at him.

"Hello, darling," he said, just as he always had, no matter what might have happened since we were last together. His cheek was rough and felt slack to my touch. His hair was gray around his ears and he staggered a little when I hit him, holding his lighted cigarette up out of the way. He smelled the same, a pungent scent that I associated with dry breezes on autumn nights. His eyes were lustrous.

"How did you know?" I asked.

"I heard about it from Jules," he said. "We just decided to come." He had on a blue polka dot tie I remembered, a pale yellow shirt, and my favorite oatmeal tweed jacket. Its padding made him look frail. Now that he stood before me, I remembered Portia's disquieting report of his "vagueness."

"Jules came too?" I looked for him and Rebecca.

"Oh, yes. Didn't you know we were your biggest fans? We'll go well out of our way to see you work." There was no edge to his voice, but I felt obliged anyway to offer a soothing explanation.

"I didn't tell you about it because I was nervous. I didn't want to make it a big deal. You know."

"Sure, sure. It's the function of underestimation," he said, fumbling in his pockets. Then he glanced at his watch, pushing his shirt cuff carefully with his hand.

"Where is Jules?" I asked.

"Somewhere about. I saw Rebecca. That was Rebecca I saw?"

"Yes, it was."

"A sweet girl. She was very gracious to you while I was busy with Jules, do you remember? She showed you the ropes up there. You were both pretty cute."

He seemed to have forgotten how old I'd been that summer. He searched his pockets again. "Did you lose something?" I asked, and regretted my tone. It was as if I'd been assigned an elderly foreigner to take care of.

"What?"

"What are you looking for?"

"My penknife. I may have dropped it. Well, so what. Why don't we find Jules and Rebecca and get a bite to eat? Do they roll up the sidewalks here? Shall we drive out along the Main Line? Jules rented a car. We're in a motel in Bala-Cynwyd." He pronounced the name elaborately, as if it were the punch line of a joke.

"I'll look for them," I said. Desmond strolled toward the stairs and descended to the wings. I watched him peer at the

light board, his hands clasped behind his back, and then squint
up at the flies. He tugged gently at one of the hanging ropes.

I darted into the girls' dressing room. Only one girl was left,
holding up a costume with one hand and beating at it with the
other.

"I found this on the floor and ten million people had tramped
over it," she said in a fury. I heard voices in the green room.
Rebecca and Jules were there, sitting on the old sprung sofa,
face to face. When I appeared at the door, they both turned to
look, their mouths open.

"Hi, Jules," I said, and hugged him. "Well, Miranda," he said
warmly. "Weren't you sensational, though."

"Thank you. Dad thought we might go get something to
eat."

"Of course. We have a car." He rubbed his hands together
with his old host's bonhomie. I asked how Poppy was. "Oh,
grand," he said. "She's so sorry she couldn't come. At a convention. She's gone into library work. Loves it. . . ."

"I'll get Dad," I said.

Desmond had vanished. Both dressing rooms were deserted
and he was no longer in the wings. I knocked at the door of the
men's room, my heart knocking too. There was no response. I
went down the steps to the side door of the auditorium and
into the empty, darkened house. Its laden atmosphere settled
around me as if all that had been projected from the stage that
evening was distilled to vapor. The place was eerily quiet and
the seats like tombstones.

Desmond was half sitting on a railing on the set, gazing rumi-
natively in the direction of the follow spot. I thought his lips
might be moving, but it was too dim to be sure. He lifted a
hand and called, "Cheerio."

Very softly, he began. " 'All the world's a stage and all the
men and women merely players.' " He gave me his old challenging look. " 'The world's a theatre, the earth a stage, which
God and nature do with actors fill'—well, darling, that's Hey-
wood, on whom Shakespeare wrought certain poetic improve-
ments. 'They have their exits and entrances, and one man in his
time plays many parts, his acts being seven ages. At first, the
infant, mewling and puking in the nurse's arms.' Miranda, you
were a particular mewler. I wore a cap and gown in the labor

room—didn't look like a doctor or a graduate, looked like a kosher butcher. I had the primitive father's pain—*couvade,* they call it. Or maybe it was the eighteenth century *sympathique* of my generation. Outside the hospital, hooligans were tying down car horns because it was Halloween."

Muriel had complained that Desmond was out drunk somewhere the night I was born. His mention of Halloween clarified things: he was recalling Portia's birth.

"I remember the day you learned to wave," he continued. "You turned and looked and registered that hand with perfect comic timing. It was a new appendage, a thing apart, you'd never noticed it before. Timing is something you're born with. It can't be taught."

Jules was calling us. Desmond ignored him. " 'And then the whining schoolboy with his satchel/And shining morning face, creeping like snail. . . .' You and Portia, hand in hand, going off to school."

But he hadn't been there! He remembered some artist's conception, or some writer's—maybe his own. Our morning kitchen had been a bunker in wartime, Muriel the general, Desmond the deserter, and no one creeping like snail. Desmond scraped at my sores with this invention of erstwhile family life.

"Jules and Rebecca are ready, Dad," I called softly.

He looked to his left, then to his right, straightened his tie, and abruptly yielded to his feet, tapping and shuffling across the stage in his old soft-shoe routine. He was about to click his heels for a finale, but he stumbled instead and grabbed at a piece of the set for support. We were both panting for breath. I ran up and thought to hug him, but diffidence and distaste slowed me down. He recovered and we looked into each other's eyes and then away. "Coming, Jules," I called.

We drove out Route 30, Desmond recommending various roadhouses and Jules vetoing them, until we found a brilliantly lighted Howard Johnson's. It sprawled over its plot, and inside there were more waitresses than customers. A sign indicated it would stay open until one A.M. We scooted into a booth and one of the waitresses approached.

In years past, Desmond would have bantered with her, but he was subdued that night and silently read his placemat, which told the story of Valley Forge. Then he went to work on the menu and read most of it aloud to the rest of us while we read our own. "Are oysters in season?" he asked me, since the waitress had backed off while we decided. I didn't know. "They were always famous for their seafood," he said sadly.

The waitress took our orders, and Jules excused himself to go to the men's room. Desmond leaned over and summoned the waitress. "I think I'll have a martini," he said artlessly.

The generalized anxiety I had been feeling, which might almost have been excitement, sank heavily to my gut and lay there as fear. The waitress brought the drink as Jules slid back to his seat.

"Is something the matter, Miranda?" he asked. I flushed.

"Let's toast these superb girls of ours," Desmond said. "I won't even say 'chips off the old blocks.' I'll say, 'tributes to their sex.' " He drank, and the rest of us sipped from our water glasses.

"It's a grand college, is Swarthmore," he went on. "There's real heartache in a scene like that one tonight. It's such fun to be young." He gazed over my head, visualizing. "The academic profession is the last great aristocracy we have," he said.

I watched him miserably. What might he do to humiliate me? How much control had he over body and soul? But Jules and Rebecca looked unconcerned. She asked Desmond about the college in New Caledonia.

"It's a dump," he responded cheerfully. "The spit and polish school of learning. Well, they like me. They encourage me. I'm writing a book, you know, and getting paid while I do it. Say, Jules, whatever happened to that young actor who wanted to tell me the course literature was going to take?"

Jules couldn't remember who he meant. Rebecca prompted him and he came up with the name. But nobody knew what had become of Mark Yates. Desmond sipped his drink until it was gone. He began to look around the room. *"No! No more!"* I wanted to cry. What was the matter with me? Then he took off his glasses to clean them on his napkin, and suddenly the night in the kitchen returned. I saw him blindly wielding the bread knife, playwright rampant, but letting Muriel script the scene. Of course he couldn't get the facts straight about my childhood. He'd been under attack most of the time, and no one could think clearly in that state. I had learned, that night, that despite appearances, he was no danger to me. But I was left with the worry that he was a danger to himself. He gave me a mild smile.

"What's your book about, Dad?" I asked.

His eyes twinkled. "You know, I don't think I'll tell you. I've never been one to coddle the muse, but in this case I'm going to." He glanced at Jules. "I was recalling the old script for Adah," he said. "I can't find a copy."

Jules frowned. Rebecca said, "For the show?"

"The radio script I wrote first," Desmond said. "I couldn't convince the network that a highflying nineteenth century trollop would attract sponsors. That was when I took the idea to Jules, do you remember?"

"Of course," Jules said. Rebecca looked surprised. Had Desmond never been acknowledged as author of the original idea? I felt a surge of admiration. He looked as if he'd settled a little score. He looked fine, an old salt riding the waves. Maybe all of his endeavors need not end in a shambles. Maybe he really was writing a book. I chastised myself for suspecting, when he wouldn't talk about it, that it was just a boast.

The food arrived and we wolfed it down. I was losing my post-performance momentum, the famous "high," and felt abruptly depleted. Jules asked me if I would encourage Portia to apply to Swarthmore. Desmond spoke up. "She ought to. She's a first-rate mind. Maybe a legal mind—I may not have mis-named her, after all. . . . She organized my house for me on a visit earlier this year."

We learned that Charlotte wanted to be an actress. No one mentioned Muriel or Lou. They had probably discussed them in the car, coming down. I wished Muriel could have heard Desmond talking about his Adah script. I would not be able to report to her. She'd be devastated if she knew that Desmond had come to the play and she'd not been asked. But neither had he! He'd come on his own! As we left the Howard Johnson's, I asked Jules, "How did you happen to mention the show to Dad?"

"He checks with me pretty regularly, wanting news of you." My cheeks burned. How had I believed that he didn't? I hurried to put my arm through Desmond's. Of course he cared what I did. From now on, I vowed to inform him myself. When we got into the car, the gin and vermouth on his breath were so marked I wondered if he'd had some earlier too. But he was docile, not the obstreperous drinker I remembered.

We nestled together in the backseat. It was cozy, listening to Jules's and Rebecca's droning voices ahead and watching the comforting lights flash by. Desmond sighed. His shoulder against mine was heavy; but I could distinguish that weight from the inertia of life itself. I was happy to support him for a few minutes. A rumbling in my ear turned out to be his voice, singing snatches from "Pirate Jenny."

"I thought you were tone-deaf," I whispered.

"Oh, I learned that one years ago. I met Brecht a few times, you know. He was really okay despite what you heard. He wasn't a bastard." He winked at me. "He *wanted* to be a bastard. . . ."

Rebecca lived on another part of campus, so Jules dropped Desmond and me at my dorm first. We ambled arm in arm to the door, our footfalls reverberating off the walls.

"Dad, I'm so happy you came. I'm sorry I didn't tell you. I should have." I couldn't remember ever confiding a difficult feeling to him. "Listen, Dad. I thought it was great when you asked Jules about the Adah script. I never really understood that it was your idea to begin with."

He made a dismissing gesture, peering intently into the darkness. "It's one of those things," he said. Then he took my wrist in his hand. "Darling," he said hoarsely, "I could hardly watch you tonight, you were so like your mother—" I took a step backward. His eyes were milky with anguish. He cleared his throat and went on with an inflection that sounded rehearsed. "You must know that I love her very, very much." Had he come, after all, to tell me this? Didn't he know what she thought of him? Where was his self-respect? I was barely aware that he had wounded me, that I wished to be the center of his attention and not, again, to recall my mother! I shut my eyes, picturing them together, and the sense of loss was overwhelming. There had been life in their battles. Since they'd split up, neither had held a real shape. Desmond was himself only when contending with her, Muriel only when railing against his "weakness." Now he seemed slack and hopeless again. It made me angry.

His eyes pleaded, but there wasn't a thing I could do. He

knew he had lost the war. Another man might try starting over
again with someone new, try remaking himself and avoiding
past mistakes. But not Desmond. He loved what limited people.
He admired the grace of a man who carries his loyalties to the
grave.

But then it occurred to me that he hoped I might carry the
message to Muriel. Could that be?

"I'm sorry, Dad," I said.

"She's never forgiven me," he said. "But you know, we
speak, now and then. We poke the lifeless form, and it
twitches." He grinned a lopsided grin. "I wanted you to know."

I hugged him. He wanted me to know that he loved my
mother. "I love you, Dad," I said, feeling delivered from love.

"Thank you, darling." Headlights lit up the street behind us
and we separated.

Jules called softly, "Desmond?"

"Will you come back in the morning?" I asked.

"Jules has to go back to the city," he said. "I'd better go
along."

I walked to the car with him and leaned in the window to
kiss him good-bye. He settled himself, and I waved and waved
at the back of his head until the car was swallowed up in the
night.

I slept in an empty room again. Sada's bed showed evidence
of Sada only in that a skirt, blouse, and stockings lay on it in a
heap.

In the morning someone knocked insistently on the door.
"What?"

It was Cornelia Kemp, her eyes wide and her mouth set righteously. "Have you heard?" she asked. "I guess you couldn't
have."

"What?"

She sat on the foot of my bed. "Sada's been suspended."

I sat up. "Oh, no! Why?"

"They caught her in Roger's bed. With Roger, naturally.
Early this morning. She was hauled off to Dean Chapin and
told she had to get out for the rest of the semester. She can
reapply in the fall. I thought she'd be in here packing. I know
she called her folks."

"Sada . . ." I said. Cornelia shook her head. Sada, caught

enjoying life—what a bitter irony! She was the last person one would expect to be punished for that!

"I never trusted Roger's common sense," Cornelia said.

"And he was about to graduate with high honors," I said.

"He still is. That's the worst part. There is no rule that says *he* can't have a girl in his bed, only a rule forbidding the girl to be there."

It was sickening. I even considered turning myself in to win clemency for her. The *Threepenny* cast was outraged. We persuaded Sada to perform one more time, and made the evening a passionate tribute to her. Her solo stopped the show. That night a rumor circulated that Roger's father had complained to the dean that his son had fallen prey to a "hot-blooded Mediterranean type." The heinous euphemism made us laugh cynically.

Hugh was there when I went home for spring vacation, transplanting shrubs. The house was going on the market again.

There was still lots to sort, get rid of, or pack. Muriel and I went to the basement. Years before, we had bought metal shelves and assembled them. They were loaded with the coffee cans in which she stored nuts, bolts, and odd pieces of hardware. We began looking them over.

After a long silence I decided to risk confiding in her. She bent over a heap of items she had once had plans for, and saved on the assumption that life would go on in a predictable way. She hummed under her breath. Her face sagged and the curls flying from beneath her scarf had lost their burnish. I longed to reveal something of myself to her. Hugh, out in the yard, reminded me there were dark secrets I dared not expose, and they included Desmond's declaration after he'd seen *Threepenny Opera*. But surely his persistent tender feelings for her were not my burden. Muriel must know all about them. I did wish I could blurt a hint of the rapture I'd felt when performing—wouldn't it bring us together? We were picking over the basement miscellany, as separate as if she spoke only French and I spoke only English. But I was afraid to tell her.

Mulling over the play turned my thoughts to Sada, and I summoned the courage to relate that story instead, praying that Muriel wouldn't belittle me for choosing "naive" friends.

She surprised me. "That's shocking!" She straightened up

with an expression of dismay. "I thought it was a liberal school. What will she do now? Will she try to go back?"

I explained the situation. Muriel clucked impatiently. "Well, I know what it's like," she said darkly. "Your father was a dormitory lover." She seemed to wait for a response. I gave none. "I was lucky. In those days, my whole life might have been destroyed if we'd been caught." She said this without irony. "I was considered above reproach because I was a top student. Appearances were what counted." She flashed me a warning look. "I want you to make something of yourself. It's the only protection in life. Be grateful for a painless lesson."

She went back to sorting a box of washers and nuts, assembling a collection to take to the new house, wherever it was. I understood that she'd never give up. It was her duty to have nails and screws and half-empty cans of paint and remnants always handy. That was how she kept possibility alive.

I imagined her surrendering, back in her dormitory (but it must not have been literally her room), to passion and romance. I saw her as a maiden with boundless energy and a Rabelaisian appetite for experience and excitement, for something different and flattering. Desmond had been so charming, persuasive, and talented, she'd joined forces with him, sure that nothing could stand in their way. For the moment I couldn't imagine a surrender not involving loss.

Portia called down the stairs, "The Salvation Army is here." Muriel sighed, as if it meant troops had invaded, wiped her hands on her thighs and mounted the stairs with a heavy tread. I heard the rumble of a masculine voice and scraping as the boxes we had stacked by the side door were removed. I hoped that Muriel would be rewarded for her courage. She would miss this house so much more than Portia or I would. She had chosen it, pressed her very being into its crannies, and now come to see that she must leave it behind.

The shelf I was clearing was lined with newspaper. I lifted a jar and a headline caught my eye: BROODING ISOLATION CREATES SENSUOUS STATEMENT. There was a faded photograph of a woman I'd never have recognized, but the caption beneath it was clear: *Painter Sarah Jenkins.* I carefully picked up the sheet and read what remained of the story: . . . *gave new meaning to the "shifting sands of time." Miss Jenkins says she intended her*

*work to be erased by the wind. "If we all disappeared tomorrow, would nature
mourn?" But the work attracted more popular attention than she desired, and
now a period of retreat has resulted in a new show of landscapes that are
stripped and rebuilt . . . systematically and yet sensuously wrought. . . .
Patterns that underly the particular surfaces . . . ask, how we react to
"landscape." . . . A struggle to reconcile the bias of mind against the evidence of the senses.*

This was a truly remarkable coincidence. The sand work was
evidently the one Maxine had mentioned the day I'd seen Jenkins at the stables. I looked for a date, but it had been torn
away. It wasn't likely that Muriel had replaced the shelf lining
within the past two or three years. How amazing that this record of Jenkins's achievement had become part of Muriel's museum of industry, now we were clearing out. I placed the clipping in the bottom of a carton headed for the new house. It
would be a good-luck charm, a curious connection to an artist,
and might illuminate our new lives.

Across the room the old canning cupboard door had swung
open, and the tattered Freedom from Fear poster fluttered in the
little breeze that entered a window overhead. There it had hung
since before we'd moved into the house, and there it would stay
when we left, a marvel of banal iconography and excessive
technique.

"Miranda, what are you up to, down there?" Muriel called.
"We haven't got time to waste," she added, sounding just the
same as always.

10

I watched Woefflin's face fixedly, but it didn't reveal what he thought of my work. It was an interesting face, a little spongy with age. He wheezed, poked out of habit at an empty breast pocket, and waggled a shelf of eyebrow. More coarse gray hair sprouted from his nostrils and the sides of his head. He wore a shirt a shade darker than the inky blue-black of his jacket, and with a narrow, lopsided tie, he looked like a minor underworld figure. Outside, men were breaking up the pavement with jackhammers. The intermittent racket rattled the high old windows while I waited to be judged.

Woefflin taught the graduate painting seminar at Pratt, which offered it through the School of Education—training for earning a respectable living, just as Muriel thought it should be. After the "liberal education" I would have felt bereft without, I had come to New York that summer and found nothing but a minimum-wage job. Every evening I had made paintings and drawings, and finally conceded to myself that I needed a formal context in which to develop, teachers, and fellow students. I wanted to be a painter. It seemed to be a thing I couldn't help.

Out in the hall more applicants waited to show their work. They had all brought boxes of slides. Only I had as many boards, canvases, and portfolios as I could lug on the subway. I felt utterly foolish when I realized my ignorance of the practices of artists. Here were students auditioning for Woefflin as if he were a dealer. I thought I must be the only one with semesters of art history behind me, noting that Woefflin's name was the same as that of the author of the classic text on "later art"—meaning the Renaissance and Baroque. Why would it have occurred to me, after studying so many slides of the Old Masters, to have my work photographed? And yet the mood of restless arrogance out in the hall was my mood too. I knew I was good and expected Woefflin to agree.

He conducted his interviews in a little studio made of masonite partitions that gave the light a creamy cast and were smeared here and there with the variegated strokes of my predecessors. Woefflin grunted when he saw what I had brought with me, but said nothing disparaging. I showed him three paintings of Desmond and Muriel as small-town performers, based on photographs, and a series inspired by some Rauschenbergs I had seen in a gallery. Their combination of precise drawing and collage reminded me of how Muriel worked with whatever ingredients fell into her life, and now I seemed to, too. Because I was afraid not to include my proven strong suit, I also brought some portraits and the city sketches I had made all summer.

Woefflin took his time. Finally he said, in a jaded tone, "This was once a neighborhood of shoe factories, did you know that?" I said no. "When you go outside, notice the chimneys, the smokestacks, the design. We were set up so we could convert at once to the manufacture of shoes if this enterprise of educating artists failed. . . ." He grunted, and I returned his steady gaze. This was some teacher gambit. He sighed. "Your work is intelligent," he said. I relaxed my spine. This was what I wanted to hear. "Intelligent, strong, assured. You will do okay here. Good luck."

I didn't look at anyone on the way out, but I knew they were looking at me. My face shone. The trip back over the Manhattan Bridge from Brooklyn on the D train was the same thrilling experience of access I always had coming into town. Muriel had objected to my living on the Upper West Side, because I would miss out on campus life, but I wanted to be on my own in the real New York. I had left her new little house with two suitcases. Our lives were emptied of most of the goods and nostalgia that had burdened us and lent what passed for élan to our lives. She had handed over some once-chic clothes, and I went on affecting an eccentric appearance that would probably be run-of-the-mill at art school.

But the pleasures of the city had an undertow that might belong to the past and might augur the future. Success in school was one thing; what was to become of me from now on was another. I'd arrived in the present by hurrying through every phase of my life. All that summer, too, I'd been in a hurry to learn my way around and be an old timer. I had combed West Eighty-seventh Street for a trace of Muriel's Arts Club, but there was none. Desmond's midtown world, by contrast, was superficially intact. The towers, cornices, pediments, the brass and the stone were glories of the universe. I remembered that he'd shown us how to comb the area, too, without ever setting foot aboveground. I explored the subterranean passageways, and memorized the subway system. But when I tried to find the old *Clapper's Corners* studio at the radio station, everything seemed to have been remodeled and I was no insider, but only a trespasser.

I began to glimpse Desmond ambling toward me in a crowd, through ripples of heat that rose from the pavement. He was dapper in a well-cut suit, and his elbows bent as he whittled. My heart would leap in the split second before he became a stranger. He seemed to know me, too, and he looked as if he owned New York.

When I got home after my interview with Woefflin, Portia was perched at the top of my stoop. She'd been in the city longer than I had, having chosen Barnard College, even though larger scholarship offers had arrived by telegram from Bennington and Sarah Lawrence, the schools Muriel was pushing. She'd told me she couldn't bear, finally, not being in New York. "And the Barnard application was the only one I filled out entirely by myself. I was damned if I'd go to a college that chose me on the basis of an autobiographical essay ghosted by my mother!"

Over the summer, while I'd worked as only the biller in a paste-up studio because the old-timers thought a college girl couldn't master their craft, Portia was employed by a midtown law firm. Once in a while she called with a complicated, entertaining story about celebrity litigants, and as Muriel had used to, we had a regular date to go to the theatre. There I would sit, a secret sister to the actors.

Now Portia ran down the steps to give me a hand with my artwork. "Did you get in?" she cried, looking very pretty with sun-bleached curls and a tan. More than one lawyer had taken her to the beach or out in his boat.

"Yes. I forgot you knew it was today."

"Sure," she said, surprised. "Oh, that's terrific!" I handed her a portfolio.

I lived on the second floor, in the front, in a narrow room about the length of three men lying head to toe. A window with a shallow balcony looked out on the street. I'd have been happy, too, with a rear window, an acanthus tree, and the back-side of impinging lives, but the more formal traffic in front made me feel settled and well-placed. When I put my key in the lock, a door down the hall opened a crack. Portia frowned a question.

"That's Boris," I said under my breath. Inside the spattered zone that was my kitchen, I imitated Mr. Deschenko's accent. "The super has assured me, 'Do not be alarmed. Boris is just crazy Russian.'" The building was full of Russians in exile. Deschenko lived on the ground floor with his wife. He wore one chicken-skinned arm in a sling and when he wrestled with garbage cans his wife gave a cry and ran out to restrain him, throwing accusing looks up and down the street. "He is artist, he is hurt," she said. He had been a violinist in Russia. When he'd lived on my street for a year, a brick had fallen from a roof and landed on his shoulder. He would never play again. I al-ways ran down to help, when I was at home, and she baked me a weekly batch of cookies. I had not laid eyes on Boris, who lurked behind his door.

"I like this," Portia said of the picture on my easel at the window. It was based on Central Park drawings I'd made under the influence of a Pissaro in the Museum of Modern Art.

"You'd make a good picture, there in that light," I said.

She smiled, "Any time."

She was studying French, of course, political science, English poetry, and—guess what—art history! "You've influenced me," she said.

I told her I would have a theory seminar at Pratt, a studio of my own to paint in, life drawing, and some dubious-sounding education courses. My advisor was an old dog, a painter and a critic. "So he's part of the art world. I'm not just crawling back to an ivory tower."

I made some tea. Portia paced the room. I had thrown a cover and pillows over my Salvation Army cot to make a couch, but she didn't sit until I did.

"I still can't make up my mind about graduate school or a job," she said. "I hope some kind of revelation will come."

"Leave yourself choices," I said over my shoulder.

"Do you remember once, when I was about three years old, you wrestled me to the floor and sat on my chest and I screamed, 'Miranda, you watch out! When I grow up and I'm you, I'm going to beat you up!'?" She shook her head. "*When I'm you.* That's what I thought it meant to grow up."

"I got a letter from Dad," I said. "He asked me to show it to you. He probably made a vow not to write more than one, or risk spending the whole month corresponding with everyone on the engraved stationery." Desmond was at an art colony at last, finishing his book, a fictionalized memoir of his boyhood. He had sent me two chapters to read and they'd made me weep. He wrote from an open vein, without sentimentality or apology —and it hadn't been commissioned by anyone.

"'I've been giving readings,'" Portia read aloud. "'Unlucky Mr. Dylan Thomas made our evening's entertainment back in Old Chatham into a national industry.' God, do you remember that awful night?" I nodded. "Mother doesn't know he's there, does she?"

"Nope." I had been tempted to tell her, for the satisfaction, but Desmond's victory wasn't over Muriel. She was back in school, too, taking her Master's degree so that she could teach full time. Sometimes she called for help with a paper. She took too many notes and was too jittery to organize them. It was strange and gratifying to make her an outline and suggest an opening paragraph, while she listened obediently. She allowed herself "study treats"—cookies in a jar, a glossy Italian magazine, a new nightgown, and her house was as efficient as a little cabin cruiser. The money from the sale of the old one was invested in the stock market, and the stocks were on the rise. She lived as frugally as before, but now there was an undercurrent of suspense: When was the right moment to take a profit?

I put Desmond's letter away in the carton that served me as a file cabinet. Some children started up a ball game in the street.

Portia checked her watch. "I'd better get going." I didn't ask
why. When we had something to do, just for ourselves, it suggested a guilty secret. This was the legacy of all those Saturdays
spent at chores. She lingered at the door.

"I hate writing to Lou," she said. Lou was in Hollywood, a
big producer out there. "I never know what to say to him. How
do I justify myself? I can't claim I'm studying to please him."

"You shouldn't try. That can't be what he needs."

"But what does he need?"

I shrugged. "We can't do anything about it."

She departed with a wave of her hand. We never embraced,
as if expressions of physical affection was how bargains with
outsiders, like Hugh, were struck.

After she was gone, I felt lonely and the room clutched at me.
At some point during the summer my aimless search for Desmond had become a search for Hugh. I never imagined I saw
him, but never doubted that I would. In a scarcely conscious
way I believed that I wouldn't know all about myself unless I
knew about him. In the last years we had met less and less
frequently, and finally one night, he had picked me up at
Muriel's new house and taken me to a bar out on the highway
to hear a piano player he liked. She was a boozy, maudlin performer who winked at him and dedicated a song to "the love-
birds," but had used up her voice long ago and played mechani-
cally. I ignored this acquired taste of his and took comfort in
the enduring one for me. He was still sitting in on classes at
NYU and was waiting on tables on MacDougal Street. The job
was wearing thin, but he had no plans for another. He was
vague about everything until we kissed rather chastely in his
car and he said, "We've grown past this scene. There'll be a
better place and a better time," and started the ignition.

Late in the summer I had begun taking the subway downtown after work, stopping in a café or two, sketching for a
while, then circling Washington Square Park. I drew a pair of
jugglers practicing. It was time to select "mature" themes, and a
juggler might be a twentieth century equivalent to Watteau's
"Gilles."

Muriel's nostalgia for the Village had rubbed off on me, and I
had read many accounts of its artistic heyday. They indicated
that anyone who had hung around the right crowd there would

eventually wind up in the cultural history of the place. One needn't so much prove oneself as endure. It was a safe, mutually reinforcing community and continued to lure newcomers with the bohemian notion of a "purer" success that required failing the crasser uptown tests. My nostalgia put me on guard.

But I thought Hugh might turn up there any time, appearing without a word. There was no urgency to this feeling; it was a slow-burning appetite that never expired. We had surrendered only to instinct, and always in sheltered places, safe from the world's judgment. Only we knew how good we were. It was a union that demanded too little to dissolve.

I began at Pratt with what I knew well and could be sure of. The long hours I spent painting in my studio, in the labyrinth of studios, everyone else painting all around me, satisfied the old desire to be at the center of things. The pleasure of laying my brush to the canvas was utterly simple, especially on sunny days, when light poured through the grimy windows and even the jackhammers outside were an envelope and my room was fit for nothing but work. The whole building was uniformly utilitarian and shabby. Some students decorated their studios with talismans and souvenirs, but I liked mine as it was.

I attracted casual visitors. Painters came and leaned in the doorway to watch and comment. Woefflin praised my work in class and more students dropped in, so that I was always receiving. But the pleasure I took in this was flimsy, no more than conceit. Underneath it, *promise* lay like a pentimento. Absurd as it was, it seemed to me that every day my promise wasn't fulfilled was a day of failure. I circled and circled, waiting for permission to land, expecting to be made whole in the very next instant.

I wasn't the only one looking for magic. Next door, Ginger labored on huge acrylic "color field" works that never satisfied her and drove her to my studio several times a day. She was like a cosmos flower, thin, her hair in drifts, and she spoke in a vague, drifting style, always about herself. She had been raised on the Main Line and defied her family to study art. She'd wandered around Europe the summer before, sleeping with artists. She envied everyone working in New York, everyone exhibiting, and for a rich girl, seemed strangely eager to earn her way by her brush. She could afford to be any sort of person she wanted, I supposed, and to try anything out.

"I know the work is all that matters. I know the struggle is what the picture is about. . . ." She sank into the folding metal chair that was my furniture. "I'm too impatient. But so is everyone." That was true. In theory class people got up and wandered around the room or even left while Woefflin was talking; it didn't seem to matter. We agreed that we were performing necessary but meaningless exercises. No one could be taught to paint. We were passing the time until we could match ourselves against the best the world had to offer.

"When I came back from Italy, I consulted a psychic," Ginger told me. "She said, 'Work, it's a sin not to work, to want success and glory without working for them.'" She sighed. "But I know oodles of painters who became successful because of a fluke, or luck, or timing, or knowing the right person or being a shit. . . . She said I was a child of the sun. I have a thirty percent chance of being happy on the Mediterranean, fifty percent north of the Equator, and only twenty percent in New York! Can you believe that?"

We went together to the galleries in Manhattan, and I could see that what I was doing at Pratt bore little resemblance to anything shown. Ginger was tempted to imitate the many abstract surfaces. "I've never been able to draw," she said.

"What made you decide to be an artist?"

"It's what's in me that wants to come out," she explained. "These are my intuitive marks, these strokes. But I'm so at sea. You know what you're doing."

I denied it. The motionlessness of painting, its enforced single point of view, were beginning to frustrate me. I wanted to show events over time, to render coincidence and causation. How could I put all of my experience into my paintings? I began a work of serial moments, some blurred, some sharply drawn. Delacroix had written of "the fetish for accuracy that some people call the truth," and it stuck in my mind, with its superior tone. I wanted to paint as no one else did, but still be accountable to an observer's standards. It was a dilemma. If I tried to be realistic, I might succumb to illustration. To avoid that, I employed a flamboyant technique, thick pigment, large ambiguous areas. I liked the way my accidents looked and resisted working them until there could be no mistaking what they stood for.

A Chinese boy named Kenneth Wang liked to spar with me. "Realism panders to the mass taste," he pronounced. I told him I'd be pleased if everyone understood what I was trying to do, but he had caught me between two poles. He painted colored squares and chevrons and could talk about them in terms of paint alone, for hours. The finest draughtsman in our class was Oswald—I conceded that he drew better than I did. We worked from a model named Journey. The instructor had taught just that class for generations. He hung my work and Oswald's on the wall and commended it. "Look at them biscuits," he cried, holding his hands to Journey's buttocks. "These two have drawn them." Oswald reminded me of Hugh. He frowned and sat by himself and blurted his few contributions to class discussions: "Intention isn't what counts. Conviction is."

I saw him on the street with a girl who hung on his arm, chattering and rising on her toes while he glowered at the sidewalk. He disappeared for a week in November. When he reappeared, it was with bandaged wrists. Ginger speculated excitedly. The girl, a fashion student, had left school. She must have gotten knocked up. Brilliant Oswald had seen his career on the verge of ruin and tried to kill himself. We never found out if the theory were true.

We discovered that our drawing instructor, Briggs, would sit over coffee in the cafeteria, surrounded by rings of students, discussing art and life. He wore chains around his neck and homemade shoes, had studied with Hans Hofmann, known Thomas Hart Benton ("what a son of a bitch"), and cut his artistic teeth in Paris. He liked to tell us there was a right way to live, but few discovered it early enough. He had fathered many children in his youth, and all were grown and troublesome. Relationships don't endure, he remarked, the woman always devours the man. "Women go to my head"—then a twinkle of his eye. He was so cute that it wasn't hard to credit his attractiveness. He quoted Eakins: "Paint from eggs to learn the nicety of drawing, learn color from pure colored ribbon and muslins. . . . Simple studies make strong painters." We would giggle, this literal injunction was so far from what any of us wanted to do, now.

"You don't realize how recently artists have made direct statements," he said. "In Rodin's day everyone had copiers." And, "See the whole in many parts. Leonardo's lichen make a complete landscape." I was grateful for his quaint learning, and for all his scoffing at women, he never made me feel that my sex was any impediment to becoming an artist. Quite the reverse: He even used to say that women had the tactile sense, and the persevering passion. "They have the drop on us," he'd say to the men.

Ginger and Kenneth proposed we go to the Cedar Tavern. "To see the action painters in action." They thought I was too stuck in the past and should see live practitioners at their watering hole. I remembered Muriel's scorn for Desmond and Luks at the Rubicam, but I agreed to go along.

We behaved a little foolishly on the train, shouting over its racket, flaunting our paint-spattered clothes. It occurred to me that I was fully myself only when I was alone.

Ginger's face took on a startling avidity when we entered the tavern. I wondered if Kenneth and I were mere accessories to her wild impulses. She was impatient to attach herself to artists, by way of becoming one, too, and sex was her tool. Kenneth's was his sense of style. "When I look at nature, I see a Newman or a Rothko," he would say. "It's all been looked at and done." The various interpretations informed his vision, and he kept abreast of every development. There were too many for me; I tried to ignore them. Such a proliferation of high art images created as much clutter as the mass-produced ones did. They clarified nothing for me. I wanted to see with eyes unclouded by the visions of others, but it was impossible.

I watched Ginger's glance fly around the tavern, never lighting for long. If no one attracted her, we might be spared witnessing her seduction of some big painter in order to be artistically enlarged, herself.

We sat at a little table, drinking beer and Coke and keeping quiet for fear of being overheard. There was nothing we could say that wouldn't betray us. A midafternoon, all-male crowd was lined up at the bar. There were lots of cowboy boots and jeans. No one paid us any attention. Two men behind me discussed a dog one of them had taken in off the street. The dog had contracted an infection his owner was treating according to some theory he had, and the other man disputed it. Ginger whispered, "There's nobody here!" Kenneth trained a thoughtful look on the ceiling. After a few minutes Ginger suggested we go to a nearby gallery and look at pictures until it was late enough for some famous faces to gather in the bar. We pooled some money and paid for our drinks.

Just as I reached the door, trailing the others, someone clutched my arm. I whirled around and peered at the face that presented itself. My whole body responded instantly. It was Hugh, wearing little round spectacles and a massive padded coat, with a black scarf thrown around his neck, a negligible smile on his face. He was lean and his hair was already thinning.

"Glasses!" I said. They made him look impudent.

"What do you think?" he asked. "I found them in a pawnshop." His eyebrows tilted up the same way. "I've missed you," he avowed.

Ginger poked her head back in the door. "What's going on?" she demanded. Kenneth's face showed over her shoulder, wearing a dignified look of inquiry.

"This is an old friend," I said to Ginger. "Hugh—Ginger, and that's Kenneth out there. From Pratt. I'll see you tomorrow, Ginger."

She gave Hugh a long onceover, said "Sure" resignedly, and left.

"You look so young," he said, grinning.

"Young? I *am* young. So are you."

He pointed to the top of his head. "I'm losing it." His vanity surprised me. Yet his cheeks were stubbled, as if he'd shaved carelessly. I stared at the side of his face when he turned away, the slant of bone, the tilt of brow. He ordered two beers, holding up his fingers and gulping the rest of the one he already had.

"I never dreamed I'd see you here," I said.

"It was a good bet."

"I've never come before." My heart was pounding. Aimless prowling in Washington Square hadn't prepared me for his flesh. We stared stupidly at each other for a while and then began to pry information, in a haphazard way, pausing to study the rows of bottles ahead. So many murmuring voices finally encouraged us to talk, and the traffic of customers to let our shoulders touch. As time passed we leaned together, like old lovers. Hugh told me he was still borrowing Gaylord's studio. "I doubt he even pays the rent anymore. No one comes around to collect. I never see a soul." Gaylord had stopped painting.

"Stopped, why?"

"He's found a way to make more money," Hugh said with a cynical laugh. "He's dealing."

"I hope you're careful," I said.

He looked pleased. "I never see a thing. But Gaylord's big time."

Soon we would leave and walk to Elizabeth Street to his "studio." Yet we stayed put, talking in spurts, touching shoulders. Once, he covered my hand when I put it on the bar.

"I have a new job," he said. He was stretching canvases for a painter, meeting a lot of new people. I was envious. The painter was Ad Reinhardt, he said offhandedly. I looked at his face. He stared ahead. Could he be making it up?

"It was Gaylord," he explained. "He studied with him out in Brooklyn; he was offered a job and he didn't want it, once he connected with his source. So I got it. Come on, let's go."

The day was still bright, to my surprise. I felt wanton and uncoordinated after three beers, but drink seemed to deepen Hugh's natural gravity. I was a huge flower blowing down the street with a rolling stone. I could hardly wait to see what he'd been painting. I grabbed his arm, smiling goofily. How funny we were, walking along, pretending to be city strollers, when really we were racing to tear off our clothes and twist and twine until we were weak and dripping.

The landscape grew increasingly barren. It contained, in fact, reminders of the Meridian Avenue Station and looked unlike any part of the city I knew. Houston Street stretched broad and desolate, and we turned in the direction of low, deteriorating buildings that receded all the way to the eastern horizon. A vacant lot on the corner was overgrown like a field and littered with bottles and battered appliances. Grit and bits of paper were borne on the wind. Everywhere windows were boarded or gaped empty, yet we came to a fenced alley with a limousine parked inside, gleaming. A tiny restaurant next door sent clashing smells into our faces. The door opened suddenly and a man lurched into me. He poked out a grimy finger. "Sorry, hon' " he mumbled, his blurred eyes on my midriff.

"Harmless," Hugh said in the same register.

We came to a tenement building with a rickety fire escape twisted along its face. The doorway and street wall were encrusted with layers of repulsive brown paint. Hugh pushed the door open and I thought instantly of rats and hung back. He looked sardonically at me.

"Is it safe?"

He laughed shortly and touched my cheek. "You've come this far. It's empty. You just have to watch your step."

I was ashamed to be afraid and reliant on Hugh in the unknown. We traced a narrow hallway to the rear and went up the stairs. The walls and ceiling were covered with stamped tin, fringed with putty spotted with old gilt. Hugh kicked a squashed can and it clattered down the flight. He took the last steps with catlike leaps and vanished around a corner. I decided his ease in abandoned places was a pose concealing ordinary fears, but his inscrutability attracted me, and I didn't challenge it. How could one ask a cat where it has been, when it comes scratching at the door again? I followed him and vowed not to ask nagging questions. We passed a toilet stall without a door and came to the end of the corridor.

"This is it."

"No one else ever comes here?"

"Not as a rule."

"Where do you live?" I couldn't bear to think of him sleeping in the building, dressing and undressing, or in his clothes, waking to those walls and their silence—but it wouldn't have surprised me if he did.

"Different places. I'm still looking for the right one." He blinked behind his glasses.

I listened, rats still on my mind. The quiet was harrowing. I followed him into the room and was struck by a shock of light, blasting from the windows, the white walls and ceiling. A mattress shone eerily on the floor. Out on the street a truck rumbled over the potholes. I looked out. A man was walking sideways, looking back apprehensively. Hugh glided up behind me, put his face against my neck, and brought his hands around to my thighs. Waves of pleasure broke where he touched me. My

head fell back to his shoulder. After a while I revolved slowly
to kiss him. How easy it was to sink under the weight of it, how
clear my memory of the times we had done this. But there was
something else—

"Let me see your paintings," I whispered.

"Not now—"

I laughed and pulled away. Our bold embrace and the beer
encouraged me to toy with him, and I really was eager to have a
look. I scurried to a row of square canvases the size of card
tables, stacked along the floor, and pulled one away. Hugh
sighed behind me. I stared at this first picture, let it fall, looked
at another, and then another. All of them were painted a thin
coat of uniform black.

"Whose are these?"

"They're mine." He leaned against the opposite wall and
folded his arms. His glasses glinted obnoxiously.

"You're joking." He didn't smile. "They all look like little
Reinhardts, don't they? What are you, the most faithful disciple?"

"They are my meditations," he said solemnly. "They're statements of pain. No, of painting. Of surface."

I shuffled the rest of the stack. "You do this over and over
and over again, every one exactly the same—why don't you
lose your mind?"

"What *don't* you do in life, over and over and over again? You
fall out of bed, put one foot in front of the other, zip your
pants, eat a banana—"

I had noticed a row of paint cans in the corner—Sherwin
Williams, gallons. "Is this what you use? House paint?"

"I don't go to art supply stores anymore," he said, his lips
curling slightly. "They're full of tourists."

"Come on, Hugh." I stared at him. "What's the explanation?"

"There isn't any. That's the point. They can't be translated,
they're reduced to their essence."

"Hugh," I said in a coaxing tone, "where are the images that
used to be in your head?" That head looked pale and vulnerable, a gourd with flesh stretched exquisitely over it, and that
thinning, golden hair.

He stood at the window. "Look out there. There's nothing
worth looking at. There's nothing worth painting. You have to

invent." This didn't sound very different from what Kenneth said, but coming out of Hugh's mouth, it shocked me.

"*Invent!* Black washes? Who besides you could make anything out of this?"

"Content is too sweet for me," he said.

I pressed my lips together. We stared across the room at each other. Finally I said, "Well, I expect to go on looking. I can find plenty to paint. You used to look to your imagination. You were inspired."

"I seem to remember you said it was like stuff in museums," he countered. "None of that will outlast us."

"*You* said people would charge admission to see it."

"The event is what matters. The act, not the image."

I sat on the floor and gripped my ankles. My shoes looked wretched—an old pair of Muriel's I had neglected to polish. They were scuffed and worn down at the heels.

"I read it in Baudelaire," Hugh said. "It's an old idea. *The New.*"

"Listen!" I thought I heard footsteps echoing in the bowels of the building.

He stared at the door and I expected it to fly open. "People pass through," he said indifferently. There was a thump, as if a heavy object had been dropped. A nauseating suspicion seized me: Could Hugh be involved in Gaylord's dealing? He seemed, now, to be susceptible to anything that came along. Or he might be using drugs; how would I tell? They would make him willfully obscure and his paintings monotonous.

"I don't think Baudelaire had this in mind," I said.

"Did he have professional training in mind?"

My mouth fell open. "Is that what gets you? You think I feel superior? What could be more elitist than these black things? You have to learn a whole new language to even talk about them. There's nothing to recognize, nothing of the world, of humanity, beauty, even ugliness. . . ."

"Recognition is a distraction. I'm not an illustrator."

"Who is? You don't have to wipe out everything just because illustration exists." But of course he had identified my dilemma. No wonder I was defensive. I demanded of myself subjects and themes worthy of the masters of the past, who hadn't had to agonize over what to paint. I was always in danger of illustrat-

ing, and always in need of a subject. It was a self-defeating
cycle, and outside that cycle everything might well *be* a uniform
black, for all I knew. It was a struggle for me to begin a painting, and a struggle to end it. Hugh had neatly avoided that
problem. It was easy to see how he could begin the paintings
here. A phrase of Bertrand Russell's, read in a course at
Swarthmore, popped into my head: *"The truth is usually dull."*

Hugh was smiling smugly, but this bickering would be painful for him too. If he was serious about these paintings, it must
be the result of an almost religious conversion. And my admiration for him was inseparable from my passion. Now we were
fighting instead of making love.

"You're upset over nothing," he said.

"I don't think you believe that."

"Come on, come here."

"Oh, Hugh, I don't even know if you're all right—"

"Of course I'm all right."

I dared not ask him if he was selling drugs. "I care about
you," I said in a tiny voice. He walked to a paint can, knelt,
pried the lid off with his thumbnail, and stuck the thumb in the
paint. He raised a stream of salmon color, to my surprise, leaned
over and traced a heart on one of the paintings, then an *M* in
the center.

"There's my content," he said. "That's as far as I'll go."

I laughed. He pretended to put his thumb in his mouth, then
wagged his tongue at me.

"Oh, God, I have to pee," I cried. "The beer. I'm bursting."

"Out in the hall," he said.

I shivered. "I can't, out there."

His eyebrows shot up. "It's all I've got."

I listened for sounds. "Guard the door, then, please." I was
overcome by shyness. I remembered a Rembrandt etching of a
woman squatting in a field, holding her skirts up, exposing her
genitals streaming urine. Rembrandt had been sympathetic, but
he *had* turned a woman into an unconsenting subject. I shuddered with shame at the prospect of abasing myself before
Hugh in this austere, black phase. . . .

But I hurried into the stall. The toilet was seatless, and after a
cursory glance I hunched over it. The splatterings of filth
looked neutralized by time, and the cubicle might be an angry

Dada exhibit. Around the corner Hugh whistled. I shut my eyes and released my flow.

When I looked up, he was standing in front of me, his hands hanging at his sides. For an instant his face was vacant, and the expression I read might have originated in my imagination. His hands looked humble and caring and my eyes found them first, then his eyes, which had surely deepened with a suffusion of tenderness. His lips parted.

"Okay?" He held out a hand. I pulled up my underpants and tugged at my clothes. This was the same ordering we had managed together in his car or the shed, but all hint of artfulness or violence or greed were bleached away. I had risked intimacy and was safe. We returned to the room.

He lay down on the mattress. I took off my clothes, standing over him. He pulled down his pants and peeled off his shirt without rising. His hipbones were pearly white. I touched them and his kneecaps and stroked the golden hair on his legs down to their pink-tipped toes. His eyes were shut away in hollows. His genitals looked huge and highly colored, as if borrowed from a larger man. The color and swelling suggested pain, and we proceeded with excruciating delicacy.

Afterward he said, "It's always perfect. You should remember that. And don't cut your hair again."

I touched it. "I thought you hadn't noticed."

"I have a confession," he said. "Those paintings aren't really mine."

I twisted to confront him. "Calm down, calm down," he said. "Reinhardt had the idea someone should make a painting for his show, to see if any of the critics noticed."

I whooped. "You see? It's a fraud, the whole thing is a fraud!" Barry Lipper would love it, I thought.

"It isn't at all," he said earnestly. "He's a great man. He'll outlast most of what's done. He's a master. Anyway, the idea was dropped."

"But he's admitting what's wrong with his ideas by thinking of tricking people." Hugh lay back and shut his eyes. There was no use continuing this argument. "What do *your* paintings look like?"

"You'll see. People are keeping them for me. I couldn't leave them here. It isn't safe. I sold one to a collector." He opened his eyes to see how I would take that. I smiled. "It lives in a posh apartment on Ninth Street. I want you to see it. Burt's giving a party and he asked me to come. I can bring you."

My reaction was complicated, although my smile remained simple. "When is the party?"

"Next weekend. Can you come?"

I thought it over. Following Hugh into deserted places was one thing; involvement with the people who attracted him was another. I was frightened of any society he had chosen after all our years by ourselves.

"It could be wild," Hugh said. "Lots of possibilities."

"I'm interested in limits," I said automatically.

"The truth is, I never go to parties," he said. "But there'll be artists. Burt knows them." I was relieved. It put us on an equal footing.

He walked me to the subway, but didn't go down into it. I refrained from asking if he intended to return to the building and stay there in the dark. On the way home an idea for a painting came to me: Hugh's body, and mine, the deep color where we joined. I saw a field of umber, a few bold, sensuous lines tracing hips, thighs, wrists, then a flaring of light. Hugh would disdain it. The particular image trivialized experience, according to him. Perhaps the flaring of light was evasive. I drew in a penis, to see. But it broke the movement of line and color and riveted the eye on itself. Here, then, was the problem! How to depict, without placing false emphasis on the particulars and skewing the whole? I wanted to work in a way more abstract and more real, too, than any black field. I wanted to suggest everything, not nothing.

11

Kenneth and Woefflin tangled in class. Kenneth was like a coiled snake, his voice pitched high, his fists clenched. He was no longer interested in our remarks about his brush strokes, his color placement, his choice of texture. He wanted to know how his work "stood up." He meant, of course, against work being shown in galleries, work in museums.

"You must not be afraid of formal criticism. It doesn't hamper expression. If something is formally wrong, it is also symbolically confused," Woefflin scolded drily. "We need discussion when the work does not convince." He sat like a great cat. For once we were all present, straddling our little paint benches, ranked in a wedge aimed at him in his folding chair with his hands clasped over his belly and smiling without warmth. "You must make statements of importance to yourselves. . . . I will give you an assignment. You are to create ambitious autobiographical works. This is a chance to sum up your lives, to discover your own personal iconography. Reject simple solutions —for example, a self-portrait would not be satisfactory. On the other hand, you may not assume that anything you make is autobiographical. I want large-scale works. You have six weeks. This is a task of limits, but limited can mean deeper. In a corner, you dig down. You are there because something is close to your sensibility. All powerful acts are focused."

A pause, followed by the scraping of benches. Ginger flew to Woefflin's side to ask a confiding question. I headed out the door, very excited. The assignment was made for me! What had

I pondered more than my life? What interested me more than
iconography? The problem of beginning was solved—I had
only to gather, sort, select, and transform what existed already.
I hurried to my studio to make some notes.

I decided to quote from the works of art that had meant most
to me—*Las Meninas, The Garden of Earthly Delights,* Piero's Queen
of Sheba; even some Hoppers, to amplify the images I selected
from my life. I would try to use allusions as if they were words.
I usually hesitated over a style when I began work, but this
time the collage method I'd experimented with asserted itself
over all other possibilities. Some areas would be precisely
drawn, others blurred and skewed to suggest ambiguity and the
distortion of memory. Degas's compositional techniques be-
spoke chance, Rembrandt's compassion. The Masters hovered
while I thought about how to signal language, sound (radio,
music), performance. Rauschenberg had actually set real radios
into a work I'd seen. A series of works would do what a single
one could not—show the passage of time, the working of influences, and the idea about life that interested me most: its para-
doxes. *The more you hang on, the less you have. You always hurt the one
you love,* and I had never forgotten the Armenian restauranteur's
toast: "The things we lose will increase us."

I worked furiously, scribbling, collecting memories, recording
dreams, making cartoons and pages of faces like the old "expressive" ones of my childhood. I was determined to make a
significant work. Ambition stiffened my hand and I fooled myself in order to loosen up. The central paradox had always been
that I worked best when I didn't try to. I subjected watercolors
to the shower, and the faint images that survived were surprising and elicited a fresh response when I reworked them. Accidents stimulated new gestures. I made monotypes to interpose
more process between eye and hand and drew with the hand I
never used.

Both studio and apartment were choked, by the end of the
week, with memorable images. I had stirred myself to a boil,
preparing. At the end I looked forward to the party with Hugh.
I longed to see him and to be seen with him—in black, what
else?

The night was chilly and clear, and the walk from the West
Fourth Street subway stop recalled another time. The area still

looked the way it had in John Sloan's etchings, and I pretended I was a shopgirl in one of them, dressed to the nines for adventure, my whole life ahead of me and New York aglitter and friendly. Hugh waited at the corner with his shoulders hunched, spewing little clouds of vapor from his mouth.

"I'm making sense of my life," I bragged. "You'll be in the picture too." He grimaced and took my arm. Of course he wasn't interested in school assignments. I would show him the work when it was finished.

We entered a house at the ground level, as if we were visiting people who lived where the Deschenkos did, in my house. Coats were piled up inside and cool jazz played at a high volume. The room we entered was two stories high—the belly of the house had been cut away and a balcony ran around it above, giving on to more rooms. We headed for a massive table spread with platters and tureens and furiously burning tapers. People plucked morsels with their fingers and lifted them to their shiny faces. Others stood in the shadows beyond, or drifted about. No one looked at us.

Beyond the table the room was dim and oddly menacing. In a moment I recognized the shapes that loomed on the walls. They were primitive objects: spears, shields, headdresses, tools, masks, baskets, carved statues, strings of beads, charms, and lengths of fabric. In this setting they had a repellent effect. I revolved in place, looking from one thing to another, half believing that captive spirits glowered back.

"Oh, yeah," Hugh said. "Burt travels a lot."

"It's eerie, isn't it? They seem resentful. Where is your painting?"

"Upstairs. Off the balcony. I'll show you." He was unknotting his tie, the first I'd ever seen him wear. "I'll get you a drink," he said, and plunged toward the table. Someone stepped aside with an amused expression, and Hugh ladled punch into some cups. When he brought one back to me, his hand shook. The stuff was sweet and sharp. We drank, looking around. Hugh had turned pale. "I don't see Burt anywhere," he muttered.

"What do you think?" said a rasping voice. I turned to a short man with a face like a woodblock and an uncontrollable blink. His thin frame was fitted into an outlandish pink suit, ruffled

shirt, and black tie. I reached for Hugh and he backed away
with an expression of apology.

"Clifford Hallow," said the little man, taking my hand. "And
you are . . . ?" I told him. "Charming," he said, ignoring
Hugh's retreat. "I would like your opinion on an ethical question." He blinked. Did I approve, he wondered, of this wrenching of objects from their native context in the name of conser-
vation?

"I'm not sure how I feel about it," I ventured, scanning the
crowd at the table for Hugh. "Where are they from?"

"The Marshall Islands, the Carolines." He pointed. "New
Caledonia . . ." I started at this reminder of Desmond. *He*
would have had the wit to manage this fellow. ". . . the Mar-
quesas . . . ah, there's a little African one. We take the phallic
figures and make them at home anywhere, don't we? Do you
think it's American, this mania for souvenirs? Do you remember the craze for Napoleon busts in the last century—an entire
industry sprang up in France, just to meet the demand here! We
collect anything! Is it greed, sense of mission, fear of death?
Does the work of savages comfort us, somehow?" He smiled
and folded his hands across his belly. Hugh was gone, the vic-
tim of some infirmity. Was it shyness? I worried, but the challenge Hallow presented was more immediate. He seemed to
mock me, for no reason that I could discern.

"It had a big influence on modern art," I muttered. "Picasso—"

His eyes widened and he stepped back to admire all of me.
"Of course! The Old Devourer, our Pablo! Let me tell you a
story: Apollinaire threw a party and invited Picasso and the
Douanier Rousseau, who made a toast to Picasso: 'You are the
foremost painter in the Egyptian style and I am the foremost
painter in the modern style.'" Hallow blinked. "People are said
to lose access to their unconscious at an early age—around
seven or so. Artists have to reopen that connection. Primitive
objects, phalluses, war masks, totems, used to allow our fore-
bears to manage the feelings we repress. It's no wonder, then, is
it, that they are collected? And they offer a model of spontaneous design in a time when spontaneity is such a struggle—
because we *know* so much, don't we? After all, what we set out
deliberately to express says so little. . . ." He put his hand be-

neath his chin and let his eyelids dance for me. "But what is your interest in Picasso?"

"I'm a painter. Well, right now, I'm—"

"Ah," he interrupted, lowering his eyes solemnly. "That is a difficult life." We both sighed. "So terribly difficult. One might say that no life is ever easy, but—"

I noticed that a woman with thick black circles painted around her eyes, garish cheeks and mouth, and a black spangled dress was observing us from a few feet away. She stuck out of the crowd like an Ensor mask. Her expression had the vacant, omnivorousness of a hungry animal. She and Clifford might be man and wife; no one else looked as bizarre. I couldn't remember ever having to master my repugnance to a person because he was interesting, but I managed to stand my ground.

He told me that he dealt in works of art, for corporations, who purchased them for the tax benefits. "This is the new patronage, you know. I am the sole agent for the work of Colin Hewes. He was lacking in genius, but he had a certain persuasiveness and was amazingly prolific—a drawback, while he lived. People took advantage because he drank. I was present, nearly at the last, trying to reason. He'd taken to his bed in his squalid digs; you can picture it, I'm sure; rinds and crusts and wads and jugs, and a *smell.* His wife, equally besotted, was present as well. He had a pisspot, but when he felt the urge, he just grabbed his thing and shot all around the room. He had become famous, you see; he was collected. I brought a doctor to see him, a woman from the National Health. " 'Ow 'bout a fuck?' he said to her. She will not soon forget that visit. He died. Then the surprise: His thousands of works were worth millions of pounds. His dying made my fortune."

Hallow blinked and posed. He wore me down. What had happened to Hugh? There was a name for so extreme a reaction to a crowd of people. Suddenly the painted woman shot over to us. "Oo 'ave we 'ere?" she inquired in the comedian's broad French accent.

"This is Miranda, my dear," Hallow said smoothly. "Burt's new friend." Her face glowed and her lips shaped an *O.* "This is Blossom, my wife," he explained.

She inserted herself between us and tugged at my arm.

"Come, come, I will tell you everything. . . ." She pulled me to the wall.

"Your husband is mistaken," I said. "I'm not a friend of Burt's."

Blossom laughed as if I had made a grand jest. She, too, betrayed a facial tic. Hers froze in an extreme grin after every sentence. She leaned on my arm in order to turn her shoe this way and that. "What can I do? I cannot fit my foot in this city. . . ." She gave me an apologetic look. "I know, I must be patient. Don't tell me. I am famous, in Europe. I write songs and I sing them and everyone sings them—but I cannot transfer this reputation to New York. It is a cold and marvelous place. I have hired Bill as my publicist. He works so hard to help. They love me over there. They will love me here, won't they?" She pursed her lips and blew me a kiss. "Have you seen the house across the street? It is a voodoo den. White clad figures stream in and out. I adore New York!"

Clifford came after us. "Blossom, let me take Miranda around. We'll meet some painters. I know what she wants." His smile was a rubber band snapping. Blossom pouted, but someone called out her name, and she whirled about. A young plump blond woman wearing a low-cut dress and very high heels tottered toward us, followed by a tall man in a tuxedo with the puffy, irritable look of someone rudely awakened. He nodded at us with strained civility, and waited for his turn to embrace Blossom. Clifford steered me away, putting his arm through mine.

"I have to find the man I came with," I said. "He felt ill, I think."

"We'll find him," Hallow said. "On our way, I will narrate the party for you." Behind us, Blossom and the couple whooped.

"That was Annie and Bill," Clifford said in an undertone. "Our dearest friends. Over there is the painter Janet Gloat. You don't pronounce the *t,* as in Margot. She is trying to talk Bates Jones into something, but he hates to talk to women unless they are beautiful girls. He thinks only of himself and therefore dislikes no one else—but how can a woman know that? None of that poison transmitted by people endlessly analyzing the behavior of others. . . ." We circled the room. He pointed to a frail, elegant man leaning on a cane. "That is Lindstrom, the poet/critic. He is immensely supportive of younger artists, very eclectic, very encouraging—he hasn't a powerful vision of his own to block other people's. Blossom accuses me of hankering after him, but he is in love with the burly fellow he is talking to, and that is the fellow's mistress, there. . . ." I drew this group in my head, seeing the complexities of their relationships in the juts and angles of arms, legs, and heads, the negative spaces they cut. How much juicier was Hallow's analysis of the composition than what I was used to reading. "And yonder," Hallow said, "just disappearing through that doorway, so that you see only her magnificent back, is Sarah Jenkins."

I halted abruptly. Hallow stopped, too, and gave me a bemused glance. Sarah Jenkins, here! Was this a sign of some sort? Surely it was a challenge I could not ignore. Hallow seemed acquainted with her, but the last thing I wanted was to be introduced as his companion. The prospect of meeting her alone made me perspire already. Oh, for a reputation, so that I would be instantly interesting! I told Hallow I had to go to the bathroom. He directed me to follow Jenkins through the door and proceed across the next room. The man called Bill was approaching us, anticipation spread across his wide features, and I fled before we could be introduced.

The next room offered a contrast in mood, with soft light glowing from low lamps, a couple of couches and fat cushions for sitting scattered about the floor. I saw little groups of people conversing and then I saw Hugh, sitting with his back to me, one knee up and the other down, motionless, at the feet of a woman whose face was shadowed, but whose inclining torso expressed tender attention. I froze, instantly imagining that this was a lover he had arranged to meet. What motive he might have had for bringing me along, too, did not occur to me—I was crazed, susceptible to illogical extremes. How suave he looked, as he had never looked to me before! I felt helplessly drawn to him and profoundly put off.

"Disgusting!" a man said loudly from the couch next to me. Then a woman laughed sharply, and I saw that it was Sarah Jenkins, sitting on a cushion nearly at my feet, talking to another woman who shook her head vigorously and held up a restraining hand. I sank to the floor and leaned close to listen.

"Oh, you try to get at the truth," the woman was saying, "and how can you? There's a certain self-loathing that makes it hard even to put a pot on the stove, and then you think *you're making art,* and you free yourself a little—enough, perhaps, to do it. . . ."

A hubbub broke out to my right. A man rose, teetered on his feet, and launched into an imitation of someone everyone else knew. He was applauded enthusiastically and sat down again, tears streaming over his face. The woman with Sarah Jenkins was saying something about "losing the volume of the figure." She demanded, "And what is to replace that?"

"I don't see the human figure as a noble subject," Jenkins said. I drew a breath, instantly provoked. "Men are at odds with the landscape. They're upright, they don't fit the curves and the slopes, as animals do. Isn't that our trouble? We have to set people off by themselves to make them heroic. It's no wonder, when you think what science and progress are all about. Animals don't suffer from narcissism. And what does that leave *us* with? That awful fear of death. . . ."

The point seemed inarguable, but it was in our nature to paint ourselves as noble, I thought. I'd never have dared to speak aloud, but I felt as if I were tangling with her, part of the exchange. The other woman was saying, ". . . You fight to the death. When chance truly connects you to something and experience strengthens that connection, you have to stay with it. . . ."

On the couch, someone cried, ". . . We live in an exceptionally ugly time. . . ."

A tall, handsome man, his face framed by curtains of white hair that swung at his cheeks, bent to address Jenkins and her companion. "Sarah?" he asked in a New England twang. "And Mary? Is it really Mary Clarke too?" Yes, yes, they took his hands, exclaiming happily. When had they last seen each other? How was this friend and that one? Before long he was telling them about a painter whose wife had died. "He's the only true genius I have known, wouldn't you say? And how he suffered! We were all so concerned. Before long he took to hiring beautiful models, filling his studio with them and yet painting his usual muted squares, his meditative abstractions. People were shocked. He was making himself a laughingstock. He defended the practice. 'But I *like* having naked women all around me while I work!' "

The women whooped with laughter. "Yes, yes, we can live like peasants, with so little comfort, but for our work, we always need *something,*" Mary Clarke said. Soon the white-haired man took his leave. Someone poked my shoulder. A man leaned over and whispered, "Is Clem here?" I said I didn't know and his eyes turned spiteful. The women were talking again, in low voices. I didn't want to miss a word! Hearing what they said was worth years of floundering on my own, wasn't it? Here was the *sense* of being an artist!

Sarah was saying, ". . . I went tearing around, I was mad, riding the subways, staring at awful people, and in the end, it was all right there. I just hadn't seen it."

"Yes," Mary Clarke said feelingly. What was? I had lost the thread of this.

"You pay too much attention to what people think and you no longer hear that inner voice, what you're trying to hear in order to work at all. No one else will hear what you're saying until some famous critic utters it first. . . ."

At that moment I glimpsed Blossom Hallow hovering in the door, throwing her wild glance around the room. Afraid she was in search of me, I ducked my head and half lay on the floor behind Sarah Jenkins and Mary Clarke.

"I can't bear this," Sarah said sharply. "I don't know why I came. Burt doesn't even show his face. Where do you suppose he is? I ought to say good-bye, at least." She became aware of me and turned, looking down into my face.

"Hello!" she said brightly. I hastened to sit upright, my face throbbing.

"Excuse me," I stammered. "I've seen you before. With Maxine Lipper, in Pennsylvania. The stables."

She looked blank. My skin prickled and I avoided Mary Clarke's eyes. "Ah," Sarah said at last, drawing it out. "Maxine. . . . Really!"

I stole a glance at the doorway. Blossom was gone. A couple flounced across; in the other room people were dancing. "And you're her friend," Sarah said wonderingly, as if it were the solution to a riddle. She reared back to put me in perspective.

"No. A student of *his.* Now I'm painting at Pratt, in the graduate school." She continued to give me a scrupulous examination.

"Are you really! Mary, here's a painter from Pratt. Mary's a painter."

"I know," I confessed humbly, nodding at Clarke.

"Baker's still at Pratt, isn't he, Mary . . . and Henry Woefflin. Do you know him? What's your name . . . ? Miranda Geer. Of course, you know the likelihood you'll find any women leading seminars out there—" Mary Clarke guffawed and stood up, glancing at the doorway. But Sarah Jenkins was all attention, beaming her eyes on me. What I wouldn't do to please her, I thought.

"I overheard what you said about the human figure—" I began, and faltered. "It's what I paint most. I can't imagine—"

"Of course," she said easily. "You must." I felt a terrific tension leave my own body. Mary Clarke said she was leaving and Sarah turned to talk to her. I waited for my chance again. It might be that her interest in me was a call I'd unknowingly kept myself in readiness for since I'd first lifted a pencil. Sarah Jenkins, whatever the details of her struggle (". . . tearing around, mad, riding the subways . . .") was working on what would make her complete—figures, landscapes, whatever, and I could tell she was generous. She would help a younger person to begin. Clarke walked off and Sarah turned back to me.

"So, how do you get along with Henry?" she asked. I said he was all right. He liked what I did.

"I'm not sure his paintings quite justify their lofty titles," she observed. This offhand candor flattered me, but I didn't want to discuss the faculty at Pratt.

"How do you decide what to paint?" I blurted.

She looked surprised, and reflected for a moment. "The question doesn't address what happens," she said. "I follow what my eye follows. What makes me feel good when I wake up in the morning." She thought again. "Look, if you start casting around for something that's worthy of your talent, that will have lasting significance, forget it—that's not what it's all about. Immerse yourself in your life—live it out, learn from it, learn it through and through so that every gesture you make is part of your history and part of your possibility. . . ."

"I see," I said, and believed that I did. But when I thought of my autobiography, a wave of dread washed over me. I *did* know my life, through and through, but recreating it was still a painfully self-conscious effort.

"Sarah!" cried a man with thick glasses.

"Oh, hello, Burt, I was just going," Sarah said. "Do you know Miranda?"

He pumped my hand. "Oh, let me see you for a moment," he pleaded to her.

Sarah said to me, "I'm glad we talked," as if she had profited. How gracious that was! He took her away and I stood alone, giving thanks for the felicity of the encounter. It seemed so full of meaning and charm that for a moment I was blind to the room. Then I remembered Hugh. He and the woman were gone. I felt sure I was about to learn something painful.

"Hello," said a deep voice. It was Bill, who had come in with Annie. He bowed. "Clifford sent me to see you," he said. "Why don't we sit and get acquainted?"

"I've lost my date," I said.

"People are leaving. Are you sure he's still here?"

"He was a minute ago."

"Well, if we stay put, perhaps he'll find you." His voice had a hypnotic timbre, nearly an added dimension, as if it were amplified electronically. Next door the music switched to rock 'n' roll. A pair of dancers reeled into the room. Blossom followed, pawing good-humoredly at their bodies. She winked at Bill and me. Two of her teeth were smeared with her luscious lipstick.

"She's terribly sexual," Bill confided sotto voce. "You see, Blossom has a heart of gold. I don't want you to be alarmed by any of us. We've all been together for years, you know. We have a special sort of love among us, a way of expressing in the most beautiful possible way what we feel for one another. . . . It is utterly without reservation and the prohibitions of society at large. . . ." I watched his thick lips shape these words. His diction carried me all the way back to childhood. He sounded like an announcer, one of those disembodied voices everyone had trusted. I could think of nothing to do but change the subject.

"Are you in broadcasting?" I asked.

"Heavens no. I'm a press agent. Do you know what that is?

I'm trying to create opportunities for Blossom. She's a sensation abroad, but unknown here."

Blossom rolled her eyes at me and glided near, laughing lewdly. "Behave yourself, darling," Bill said mildly.

Blossom looked me up and down. "Oh, you're the sexual one, aren't you?" she cried, with no particular accent. "You can see it in her face, can't you, Bill? Oh, look at her blush. She loves it, don't you, pet?" She circled the room, peeking over at me. "But she doesn't want the world to know, does she?"

My face burned. The room was nearly deserted, but the dancing couple stared. Blossom chortled. "Loves it, loves it," she chanted.

I tried to smile agreeably, like a good sport, but my humiliation seemed complete. I seethed with anger, and in an unkempt corner of my soul, was perversely pleased. I stood with as much dignity as I could muster and walked through the door that Hallow had said led to a bathroom.

There was a short hall and then a bedroom. Hugh was in it alone, sitting stuporously on the bed. He looked relieved to see me.

"Hugh!"

"Here you are," he said feebly.

"Here you are. I've been right outside. What do you think you're doing?"

"I'm waiting. I'm sorry. The whole thing just hit me. I had to be alone for a while."

"What did?" He was silent. "Who were you sitting with?"

He brightened a little. "It's strange," he said. "That was some woman who runs a gallery. She wants to see my work. To 'bring me along.' Maybe have a show."

I had readied myself so thoroughly for a confession of infidelity (as I put it) that this revelation rendered me speechless. "I guess Burt sent her to see me," he said.

Hugh was young and inexperienced. How impossibly grandiose to have a show in a gallery! Would it be pastiches of Ad Reinhardt? Hugh ran his hand around the back of his neck and then reached for me. "What's the matter?"

"I've had a hard time," I said. I wouldn't tell him about Sarah

Jenkins. He didn't deserve to know. "I met some charming folks. They have a sex network and they want me to sign on."

He looked blank.

"Where is your painting?" I asked savagely. What if Hugh were about to become famous and have a great success? What would it do to him? Envy and common sense told me it would ruin him. But if it happened to me, if I were instantly to vault that hurdle to fame and recognition, I'd be able to relax and work at my leisure for the rest of my life. . . . He led me out of the room and up a little circular stair to the study over the tribal museum.

He pointed to a canvas hung over a desk. It was small, no more than eighteen inches square, and looked at first to be entirely white. The paint was thickly laid. I leaned closer to examine it, but I was already disappointed. It confirmed the worst. Hugh went to look down from the balcony, where the party sounds had diminished.

The painting, I saw, was not devoid of content. The impasto formed ridges and sworls that hinted at imagery as they caught the light. I made out landscape elements, figures, and even weather. All the marvelous variety of the station walls was mysteriously alluded to, but nowhere explicit. Or did I invest the painting with these things? Another look yielded nothing but smears, applied probably with Hugh's usual unconventional tools: a thumb, knife, fork, matchsticks. I blinked, stared hard, and the images returned. It invited a trancelike viewing.

"It's very evocative," I said. "Full of illusion. I see all sorts of things. Did you intend—"

"I don't *intend*," he said sarcastically. I supposed he was superstitious. He refused to explain himself, but took life as it came, without plotting a course. So long as that worked, it was bad luck to analyze it.

I went to stand next to him. Burt and Clifford were sitting directly below in a leather hammock. Blossom, Annie, and Bill circled the table, gaily feeding each other with remnants from the party. "Have you done a series like that one?" I asked Hugh.

He put his arms around me. "You'll see," he said.

"What did I tell you!" Blossom shrieked, her face turned up

to us. "Come down here, you two." Hugh turned to me for guidance.

"Are you coming home with me tonight?" I asked. He frowned and looked away, like a character in a melodrama. "What's the matter?" I demanded, my suspicions revived.

"I want you to come to me," he said. "I don't have a place yet, but I'm working on it." I didn't know what to believe. "We'll get out of here," he promised. "Just stick with me."

We descended to the room and were surrounded. Blossom gave Hugh an impudent grin. Bill shook his hand gravely. "Don't go yet," he said. "We so admire your little picture."

Blossom poured us huge glasses of Scotch and then she dangled a little sausage in front of Hugh's mouth. To my surprise, he let her put it inside. Burt swung his arm up around Hugh's shoulder.

"Just want to tell you a little about absorption of dealer discounts," he said. Clifford laughed. "Don't let Lily have everything. String her along a little," he said. Hugh let himself be drawn to a corner.

Blossom leaned over the table, chewing with her mouth open and gulping from her glass, so that liquor dribbled down her chin. She kept her eyes on me, showing that I was the object of her antics. "She's sly, isn't she, Annie?" she asked. Annie shook her head tolerantly and sopped up the remains of a pâté with a hunk of bread. "Look at that profile, will you?" Blossom snapped, turning her head for me to see. "Isn't it gorgeous? It's known all over the Continent, you know. I've got Bill working on my case, but so far, *nada.* . . ." Her lower lip shot out. "But I'm grateful to be with my pals, while I wait." She had begun to sound midwestern, or what Muriel had always said was midwestern. *Her* diction was professional, like Bill's.

"We're that close, you know," Blossom added. Annie perched on the table. The men talked in their corner, telling Hugh how to manage his career.

"You mustn't hide your fire, darling," Blossom said, grinning and narrowing her eyes. "What are you afraid of? It's all there in your face, what you are . . . you ought to become one of us. You can bring your friend." Watching me, she laughed. "She's shocked, Annie, she's truly shocked!" Then Blossom planted her red lips on Annie's. Conversation stopped across the room.

"Darling," Clifford called, like a man who can't find his second sock. Blossom tossed her head. "It's just love," she said. Then she yanked one strap from Annie's shoulder, pulled Annie's right breast from her dress, and probed the nipple with her tongue, rolling her eyes gleefully at me. Annie looked down with a little resigned smile.

"That's enough, darling," Clifford barked. Blossom stood back and pouted.

"These good people are not prepared for such a demonstration," Bill said smoothly. But they were all smiling.

Hugh said, "Let's split." Burt let us out of the house.

"My apologies," he said. "She's drunk."

"It's all right," Hugh and I said together.

We could see stars in the sky and it was such a relief to be under them that I nearly howled. Hugh walked with his head bent.

"What a scene!" I said.

"I'm sorry. I had no idea—"

"It was an experience." Sarah Jenkins seemed to belong to an episode from the distant past. I groped for memory of her, but Blossom intervened, and it seemed no accident that I had crossed her path too. Her words had been like an incantation. My face burned again, harboring, as she claimed, my "secret." There was something to that, having to do with the way I let myself go, with Hugh, with art, but only in part. I was never of a piece—always a collection of parts, including the part that "drew like a man," as someone had said, and the part that analyzed the events of my life as if they were happening to someone else. If I presented myself to people as I thought I did, Blossom would never have noticed me. She proved that I could not control what people saw, when they looked—and that had been a point of pride.

"I have some money. Let's get a cab," Hugh said.

"Where are you going?" I asked peevishly, but I was really too disappointed in him to care.

"A friend's." He had his own life. I had better attend to mine and stop trying to corner him. We rode uptown without a word, and when we pulled up in front of my building, he got out too. For an instant I thought he had changed his mind and would have welcomed him, but he kissed me quickly and set off in the direction of the park. It was just as well. I was grateful to be by myself.

My head teemed with images as I lay trying to sleep, the last being that of the grieving painter who surrounded himself with naked women while he worked.

12

My work on the autobiography was complicated by what seemed to be new influences I must swallow whole in a very short time. I couldn't remember much about the Sarah Jenkins clipping I'd seen on Muriel's old shelf, so I went to the library to find out more about her.

There had been a spate of articles a dozen years before, when Jenkins was little older than I was (or Hugh!). Critics said she was outside all categories, in a time of rigid categorization. But years passed without any mention of her. I imagined her in hiding.

Jenkins herself was quoted in a newspaper piece. "You're moved by particulars and inclined to opposites," she said. (Now I could hear her rapid delivery and the inflections in her voice.) *"We learn from what attracts us, of course—you remember what Ortega says about it"*—I made a note to drag out my old copy—*"but these are biased attractions, they have to do with our deciding to be excited about something and they don't feed the fitting into the world that art has to do for us. We can't let attractions take over, can't impose our own little frames on what's outside. Instead, we must learn to understand the laws to fit in. When you find what excites you, that will be what's easiest for you and you can put it aside and begin to unravel the real mysteries."*

A dim illustration accompanied the interview. It looked like a pair of nude figures—*human figures.* They reminded me of Hugh's wrestlers and also of the picture I'd wanted to make of him and me. It might have shown me, had I seen it, how the subject could be handled without falsification.

I could find no reproductions of her recent work, and reviews indicated that it was more abstract. She was quoted again: *"Reality must be discovered by acts of the imagination. Society covers it with clichés to make it intelligible. The task of the artist is to break them down. . . . All things in nature undergo a similar process: An eddy swirling, water boiling, clay cracking, skin wrinkling, smoke rising and whorling. If we look hard enough, we can see the process and understand its laws."*

An idea that embraced all change was irresistible. But I couldn't visualize it. Perhaps Turner had come close, or Leonardo. But my assignment was different—a *life,* narrative episodes, drama, and my instinct, still, was to paint the dramas that excited me.

Every day produced aspiration and misgivings. My head swam with what I ought to strive for and what I must avoid. I knew that if I stayed in touch with the painting, every gesture would count. But if I lost touch with it, the result was a mess. What was important? Fragments of experience threw me off course. I enjoyed painting the old pink Studebaker so much it nearly turned the work into a piece of pop art. When I recognized passages that worked, I was wary. It might mean I had seen them before and was bowing to someone's authoritative vision. As much as I desired to be original, I wanted to be approved.

I spoke nearly every week to Muriel, so it was a surprise to hear described the beginning and end of a romantic involvement in a single phone call. First, she interrogated me and then said "Well, I hope that mulling all this over means you're learning about life. It isn't natural for parents to allow children the luxury of thoughtless bliss for long. Maybe we begrudge their happiness. Maybe it's ironic revenge for the guilt we feel when they *aren't* happy. . . . All great artists had unhappy childhoods. Someday you'll thank me."

This statement preoccupied me so that I was startled when she told me about a man she'd been dating. They'd met in the anteroom of her brokerage firm, where people could come in off the street and watch the ticker tape machine. "We went to dinner. I came home. I had hopes. But he wasn't interesting. He was just a man. I would take almost anyone, I think, sometimes. There's something about it, about another person, sharing what happens; the things that happen are so cruel. I want to laugh a little during the lulls. Make meals for someone and have him bring me coffee in the morning."

"Au lait. And croissants," I said. "It would be nice."

When we hung up, I found myself dwelling on Desmond—it was often the outcome of Muriel's laments. I had always been frightened of what could happen to him, and her scorn disguised that fear, so that it was a surprise. He was so mild, so dear, and the chapters he had sent were such elegant constructions, meant to please and to affect, even to fool one into believing in the universe he had made up out of intelligent recollection and craft. Writing invented what had not previously existed. But painting was supposed to break matter and relationship down, and reveal what was innate to things—not to show what anyone could already see. Perhaps Desmond's writing resembled what I had admired in the Eakins paintings, the execution so beautiful it overshadowed its subject. Nobody painted anymore like Eakins; the ideal lay at the other end of the scale, where a naive brushstroke was the one that convinced, and the subject of painting was paint. Presented with perfect realism and fine writing, these days, people tended to question the artist's sincerity. Desmond prided himself on being able to write anything and on not taking himself too seriously. Writing was a gentleman's skill—*Muriel* had been the self-styled bohemian, clacking her castinets in his ears, trying to get him to concede.

One afternoon, carrying a bag of groceries on Broadway, I saw Tom Batter buying a newspaper. He greeted me warmly. "Are you living right around here?" he asked. I told him where. "That's great! I'm up at Teacher's College. I live on One hundred-twelfth Street. We have to get together!" I told him that I was studying painting, and he looked so pleased that I laughed. "I hadn't any doubt, you know," he asserted. I laughed again. "I've had to revise my perfect baby ideas," he went on. "I'm learning to teach the disabled—retarded, emotionally damaged. We do a lot of hugging. I seem fitted for the job." Our exchange was so charged that passersby turned to look at us and smile. I thought of suggesting that we have a cup of coffee. He glanced up the street. "Here she comes," he said happily. A dark-haired young woman with a sweet expression came up, and he introduced her. There was no mistaking them for anything but lov-

ers. We lingered a moment longer and then I went home. Tom
had fostered an envy of happiness, and the encounter left me
feeling foolish. Sadness was no spur to creativity.

Curiously, our habit at Pratt of dropping in on each other's
studios abated while we produced our autobiographies. A
strange respect for privacy prevailed. There were rumors: I
heard of conceptual works such as a rack containing vials of
tears shed on different occasions, a pup tent filled with equipment for life. Ginger told me she was sticking to color field,
after deciding against a photographic collage of her family
archives. Oswald, we heard, was making an immense mythol-
ogy, based on a Poussin, substituting characters from his life for
the gods and goddesses. I worked both at home and at school
and concentrated better at home.

Hugh called me. He had borrowed a place to live and wanted
me to see it. I was hesitant, but I ended up going. The attraction
was deep. The place turned out to be two small rooms on East
Third Street, belonging to his friend Denise, who was clearing
up family matters for a few weeks following the death of her
mother in Winnetka. Denise was an education major ("You
have that in common," Hugh said wryly), and was a "tough
friend" who did favors and already knew her way around the
school world. Hugh thought she could get him a job teaching
art at a progressive preparatory academy. He wasn't working
for Reinhardt, and the gallery had some pictures but had not
committed itself to any sort of show. "It's nothing," he assured
me, as if he knew that I was disapproving.

Denise had a cat with thick gray fur, a chunky, sullen face,
and a loud, protesting voice. The cat shadowed us, and even
minced indignantly over our naked bodies when we went to
bed. The bed was a pullout couch in the living room; Hugh said
it made him uneasy to use Denise's little bedroom. He occupied
only a few square feet of the apartment and seemed even more
reticent than usual, as if anything we said would accumulate
and clutter the place.

We were tentative in our caresses, but gradually we gave way
to shared knowledge and made love with abandon until the cat
joined in. She inspired a bout of silliness. We wrestled and tickled and Hugh fell off onto the floor, taking the morose animal
with him.

His hair was disarranged and a very long strand hung below his ear. It looked as if he'd let it grow to comb over the thinning places. When he noticed that I was staring at his scalp, he got up and went to the bathroom, emerging with his hair carefully restored and an aggrieved expression that made me laugh.

"What are you really afraid of losing?" I chided. His face hardened further and I felt a slight remorse. He asked me coldly if I wanted some coffee, and stood at the stove while the water heated. I was puzzled and hurt. He must be worried about something more than passing youth and comeliness, but what was it? He'd always resisted conventional "maturity." It was odd to see him leap ahead to a fussy, brittle bachelorhood.

"I didn't mean to hurt your feelings," I said.

"It's okay," he grunted. I might have asked him to explain himself, but when had he ever? All warmth between us was gone. We drank the coffee and I left soon afterward, feeling I was the loser.

During the week before our autobiographies were due, I gave thanks for the magical power of perseverance. My work began to achieve unity and consistency and pleasure in the doing rose, sometimes, to ecstatic peaks. Either I managed to do what I intended, or my intentions adapted to the work itself and brought a lessening of tension that was, paradoxically, exhilarating. When I looked at the painting, which I did for extended periods of time, I found tiny perfecting refinements possible, where once there had been the awful challenge of nothing at all.

Our presentation was scheduled for a Friday afternoon. All eleven of us milled around various parts of the building, avoiding our studios. Woefflin had sent us surprise notes, announcing that a visiting artist was to conduct the criticism. Kenneth was jubilant, evidently expecting to be discovered by someone with more worldly connections than Woefflin possessed. We were all unspeakably nervous and trying not to succumb to panic. The atmosphere was killing.

We filed into the seminar room at one o'clock and set our works on the wainscoting that ran around the wall. Woefflin supervised gruffly, more one of us than he had ever seemed, as we waited for the visiting critic. He made a circuit of the show.

"Very interesting," he pronounced. "It looks quite strong and diverse, I must say. Some of you have taken surprising turns. I am pleased." He looked at his watch. As he did so, Sarah Jenkins strode in, wearing jeans, a loose shirt, a leather vest, and hobnail boots.

"Sorry I'm late," she said. She threw us a quick smile. "Henry." She shook his hand vigorously.

"I have the honor to present Sarah Jenkins," he said. "I hope you all know her work. I kept you a secret," he added impishly. Jenkins frowned. Around the room there were a few blank faces and some fawning anticipation.

I felt as if my blood had changed course. This was the nearest I had come to panic since my college stage fright. Her arrival was so unexpected and now so portentous—would she remember me? I leaned forward to grip the battered old paint bench I was riding, as if otherwise my pulse would lift me off it.

Jenkins and Woefflin conferred in low tones and then she told us she would discuss each work with no response from the artist, but afterward we were to comment or protest. Woefflin nodded and walked to the back of the room.

"I want to make a little speech before we begin," Jenkins said. "I have feelings about teachers and about critics—I'm sure you all do." We tittered. "For me to take on both roles and to be an artist as well, looking for my own truth, as you are, means that I have to offer a few cautions. We all know right away what's wonderful and what stinks. It's the range in the middle that confuses us. The trash eventually goes. . . ." I felt a new quality of attentiveness in the room. "You may paint what you see. If you see around and through, and let us know that you see how it works, why it is that way, we will trust you and be granted that serenity one has before a wonderful work." She paused. We were totally silent. "In a way, you're obliged to betray anyone who has ever taught you or influenced you. You must deny all of them. The mistakes you make are what force you on to something new. Think of art as opposed to the din of the world. We can't look at everything. We focus on what speaks to our spirits. Authentic change is what relates to you and me—to anyone who isn't stupefied by the way we live. . . ." She laughed and the class sat like zombies, quite overwhelmed by her. I certainly was. She turned to look at our display.

"Well," she said. "We seem to have the entire contemporary kaleidoscope. . . ."

My concentration was only fitful; Jenkins talked about formal values, beginning with Kenneth's abstract, shaped canvas, painted with delicate calligraphic marks and the colors of classical Chinese prints. Another piece was mildly condemned as "too tasteful," but most of what she said was generous. As she neared my painting, I held my breath. Woefflin had never attacked me in class. I wondered uneasily if there were people in the room waiting for Jenkins to do so. But when I glanced at my piece, I felt the weight of what I had put into it. Surely she would too. She studied it silently for some time.

"Let me make a few general remarks," she said at last, "based on this work, but they apply to all of us. When you find your way, it's like looking into the mirror for the first time. Here, the artist is hiding. I don't see a true impulse. Something doesn't want to come forth." I let out my breath—it was audible, and people turned to look, although Sarah Jenkins did not. She continued to stare at the canvas. Woefflin looked at his watch.

Jenkins said, "The drawing is accomplished, the color is good. But there's a quality both facile and careful—do you see?" She indicated a passage. "What I see here is that the artist was excited by ideas, visions, but the excitement was biased and got in the way. Usually only part of us is attracted by an idea, or a vision—the part that has a fantasy already, already wants to respond. There aren't any answers in that." She paused, folding her arms. "This work is planned," she said. "We know that— the plans come across, but they were all in the artist's head to begin with; they don't derive from the experience of making the painting. Reality is what teaches a course. We make reality actual." She glanced briefly at the class. "There's a mediocrity that's a kind of sedative—you give them what they want, what's already evident, and if you continue to work that way, you'll be bored by it. There's so much intelligence here and I see a search for truth, but it doesn't leap out from the painting. It's been implanted in it. We can't use intelligence to make a work intelligible, to interpret for our audience. You see, we grasp all too easily what's going on here—it has satisfied our expectations, even as it set them for us. The life is shaped and fitted."

Two people next to me looked sympathetic, and even angry, but that only increased my humiliation. It was always easy to grasp at praise and dismiss criticism. The silence in the room was thunderous.

She had said more about my work than anyone else's, all of it condemning. What a distinction! I dared look nowhere but at my hands, grasping the bench. All of my being was concentrated on keeping still until the session ended. Finally Woefflin invited Kenneth to open the discussion, and as soon as I heard his wavering, contending voice, I stood and bolted from the room, from the building, from Brooklyn, on the subway.

Raging impulses dragged me this way and that—I let a train go by, then boarded another, then thought of throwing myself off at the next stop. Gradually I calmed down but angry tears spilled over my cheeks. Across the aisle a young woman in a suit, with a briefcase open on her lap, looked away from my face. A black youth in brand-new sneakers danced past, humming tunelessly, heaved open the door at the end of the car and held it for a blind beggar in layers of rags, coming the other way. The beggar, thrown from side to side, tapped his cane along the car, crying out in a falsetto voice, jingling the coins in his cup. He wore a clumsily lettered sign—HELP ME GOD'S CHILDREN—and smiled an eerie, challenging smile. The train emerged to daylight and lurched over the bridge, stopping every few feet, throwing me onto the shoulder of the man next to me, finally crawling into the maw of Manhattan. Suddenly we picked up speed, an insane speed: The car was a tomb, racing to certain destruction. The motorman was crazed. All of us would die. I submitted to this fate, still weeping.

At Broadway-Lafayette I got out at the wrong end of the immense station, Piranesi dark and deserted. Three stairways were chained off, the passages above like exercise runs in a prison. I heard a strange thudding sound. A dazed, shambling youth was dragging his dead hand along the fence as a child might drag a stick, for the mischief-making noise. I threw myself up the last stairs, along more cold corridors, past the token booth, to the street. A derelict teetered at the top. I rushed past him and a cinder blew into my eye. I clawed at it, and thought of lying down in a doorway and slowly expiring there. Had anyone ever stabbed me as Sarah Jenkins had?

All around me there were artists in lofts. I stumbled toward the Bowery, to the building Hugh had worked in—or hadn't worked in; I wasn't sure. The door didn't give. I banged on it, calling his name to the windows above, but there was no response.

The afternoon was bitterly cold. I trudged north, bent at the waist. Every step seemed a product of something deeper than purpose. The building on East Third Street had a set of bells. I rang the one I had rung before: D. Biaggi. Presently, Hugh appeared on the stairway and raised his eyebrows at me through the glass in the front door. Then he let me in, smiling ambiguously.

The apartment smelled stale. His clothes now lay on chairs and the table, and the bed was unmade. A coffee cup and saucer full of cigarette butts sat on the floor next to it. Hugh looked unshaven and disheveled. I guessed he hadn't been outside in a week. I burst into tears—what help could he be?

"What's the matter?" he asked, sitting in the chair.

"I'm no good," I said, and walked to the window. It was a phrase out of a moralizing romance. I heard a match strike behind me. "I'm discouraged," I said.

"I'm discouraged too," he said. "What do we do about it?" I didn't want him to laugh at me. It seemed suddenly clear that we might never again see each other. Hugh had offered me temporary oblivion for years. What would I do without it? I turned, went to him and kissed him. He responded—he might even have been pleased to be the object of lust cum "discouragement." We worked so hard at transport, I nearly blacked out, yet each of us withheld some endowment and tantalized the other with its possibility, parceling out surrender and satisfaction. Finally a dreamy blandness spread across his face, as if he had gotten to me at last. I lay back and examined him. He must not have bathed in days—his breath was foul, his fingers stained yellow and the nails black, and the creases of his body were filled with contamination.

"Did you get what you wanted?" he asked.

I carried my clothes to the bathroom, washed myself and dressed. A glimpse of my face in the mirror produced no surprises: It wasn't the first time I had seen myself, and I was the same.

"You know where to find me," he called from the bed. We exchanged a frightened look when I emerged.

On the street I flexed my fingers and toes, as if climbing out of a wreck and checking for amputations. Could I really walk away from his obfuscations and my fear of failure (his or mine) so easily? Something in Hugh, tiny and fertile as a seed, had appeared to be inspiration. But most of his other qualities, familiar as they were after so long, were ones I didn't like at all. Intimacy had attracted me in the partial way that Sarah Jenkins had warned of—it was a limiting thing, a snare, a fixation. No wonder we had let ourselves be flooded by passion; to have remained conscious would have been to see the truth. I wondered, though, if he would remember me with any respect. Then I wondered what he had done with the cat, and the thought made me smile.

I bought a bottle of cheap sherry on my way home. After two hours of sitting and drinking, I set a large pad of paper on my easel, took up a stick of charcoal, and made a series of sweeping, slashing strokes, drawing nothing at all. I ripped sheet after sheet away and threw them aside as soon as they were filled, without glancing at them. I kept this up for hours, until I was exhausted. The angry slashes didn't seem to ease me; rather, they drew further fury from my soul. I hadn't yet revealed myself. Sarah Jenkins had taken me more seriously than I ever had.

Blossom Hallow's face romped through my brain, leering and provoking me. I drew her portrait. Drawing had always been a way to control and make things intelligible. Blossom's spectral figure seemed dimly connected to Muriel's vanity and self-loathing, the dark, repellent feminine force I had fled, robbing myself of another form of expression. My choking rage recalled the old bouts with Muriel, as if a more powerful adversary, who would forever have that relation to me, blocked my escape. I had wanted to make a direct autobiographical statement, but had failed, because I wouldn't give in to something larger than myself.

I fished among some old drawings and admired them, nevertheless. Few people would dare to do what Sarah Jenkins had done. Her intention was not to destroy me, just to challenge me. Surely there was hope in that. She must have faith in my willingness.

When sleep came, it was guilty. Whom had I failed? My shameful flight lay like a stone on my breast. But in the morning, the thought of slinking back to Pratt propelled me from bed and into the shower, to be purged by fire and water.

I decided to go for a walk. In the hall I heard an irritable voice: "Who is there? Miss?"

"What?" I barked.

Boris was leaning out of his doorway, holding a dressing gown over his pajamas. He stared blindly in my direction and beckoned.

"What is it?" I demanded to know.

"I need your help. I have misplaced my glasses. Perhaps my cat—" He gestured helplessly. "I have looked everywhere. Can you—"

I followed him into his apartment. He stood with his eyes unfocused and frantic, with an unkempt beard and florid skin. "I put them on my bed table. I never lose them. They aren't there." There were cartons all over the room, books and magazines on every surface, and on the walls a shocking display of paintings of nude women in lewd positions in a folk style and brash colors.

"Where do you think they are?" I asked, picking my way to the interior.

"I have told you! On my little table!" He wrung his hands. His bed was crammed in under a heavily draped window, and a little table was piled high with reading material. A lamp over the bed was awry, and the place reeked of something composite that I couldn't identify. A woman in the building had complained about Boris to me once. He had been hired to tutor her friend's child, and after one session had proclaimed the child hopelessly retarded. She had twirled her finger around her ear. "Coo coo," she muttered. "And *mean!*"

I looked back to see what he was doing. He stood in the doorway, flexing his fingers and his brow. I lifted a few of the magazines off the table—*The Nation, Foreign Affairs, Bulletin of the Atomic Scientists*—found no glasses, and knelt by the bed. Great mats of dust had collected about its legs. I peered beneath it and cried out. A cat, its eyes gleaming dully on the light, gazed malevolently back at me.

"What, what?" Boris demanded.

"Your cat startled me." The cat slunk quickly away and wreathed itself around Boris's legs. It was slender, tan-colored, with a long foxy face. I bent again and shook the corner of sheet that hung below the bed frame. The glasses fell to the floor with a little clack.

"Here they are."

"Ah, ah, give them to me. Thank you, I am grateful, ah, you cannot know the panic, when I am not able to see at all—" He snatched them out of my hand and set them on his nose to look at me. We had a moment of mutual study. "You are the young woman," he said at last.

"Miranda Geer," I said. "People have told me who you are."

"They cannot have," he said. There was a short silence.

"What are you working on, here?" I asked, edging toward the door.

"I am writing a history of the American State Department."

I reflected a moment. "Really." He continued his piercing examination of me. "What's your point of view on it?"

He laughed from his throat. "It is an exposé." He frowned and pulled his robe tighter. "I cannot talk. It is *top secret.*" Then he chortled again. "You are a student?"

"Yes. I am studying painting."

His face brightened. "Ah! You see I am collector! What do you think of my paintings? They are my companions," he added, and with a wave of the hand, "with Ninotchka, of course." His companions! It suggested a perversion. I shuddered slightly.

"They're not quite what I like, but they're interesting," I said. "Where did you get them?"

"In Fort Myers, on the sidewalk. They were a bargain. The artist was destitute," he said with immense satisfaction. "Do you have a father?"

"Yes," I said.

"What would he think of you in here, with me, an old man in his pajamas."

"I'm sure he wouldn't mind at all," I said, stepping away from him.

"Ha ha ha ha. Well, I wonder about a young lady like you alone in this city. I see many of you, just girls. I wonder about your fathers—you understand. What is it you are looking for?"

I squared my shoulders. "I want to be an artist."

He laughed slyly. "I know what that is," he said. "So you have the artistic temperament. So that is it." I was offended.

"I have to go."

"Wait. You look for things to paint—" I was afraid he wanted to commission more erotic pictures, but instead he said, very feelingly, "I have a wife. An artist as well. She is an opera singer. Very gifted, very beautiful." His voice cracked. "But we have tragic situation. She is Yugoslav, sings only in her native tongue. Here, there are no roles for her. Here, I have my work. She must travel, travel, travel." He sighed mightily at this implacable wanderlust. "It is difficult. I know that things happen. . . ." He looked cannily at me. "She is human. I know. But I love her, in spite of that." He held out his hands, for me to inspect them and see that it was true. I wondered how many roles there could be, anywhere, for a Yugoslavian opera singer, but nodded sympathetically. He narrowed his eyes. "For an artist, there is always struggle."

The cat sat at his feet, righteously licking its belly.

I took a breath. Boris shook his finger at me. "Let me tell you a story," he said. "Once, in the night, a man came in that window, there, where I have hung the curtains! An addict, in my house, with a knife!" He pushed his face close to mine and gestured menacingly. "This," he said huskily, "is the desperation of the city! Aha! But he was more afraid than I! He saw me here, on this spot, and his eyes rolled in his head and he turned and climbed out again. I thought he would fall to the ground, but he didn't." Boris glared at the cat, remembering. "I called the police, of course. I do not want police here, but there is no protection." He made a spitting sound. "They wrote and wrote in their books. They said, too bad, too bad, but I was *lucky.*" He spat again. "They went away. I warned people, but they want only comfort of ignorance. I warn you now. It isn't safe." He waggled his finger at me.

I stood my ground, hearing him out. He gestured sharply toward the pile of work on his table. "You see, I have work to

do. I am busy. There is little time. I do not like to be interrupted."

The switch was so unexpected that I stood stupidly where I
was, surprise on my face. "Thank you for your help," he said
with sarcastic formality, and began to shoo me out. He opened
the door, grumbling to himself. I stepped past his arm, over the
threshold, and he latched the door three times behind me.

I shivered a little. The old goat had been trying to frighten
me, had been envious of my youth, my freedom from assault,
my innocence. I *was* afraid, not of the city, not of the infirmities
of old age, not of sentimentality, but he had churned up another dread. An odor of obsession and futility clung to my
clothes. Boris had adapted to narrowed horizons and chronic
apprehension and would probably work on his "exposé" for
life. The terrible lesson had been preached again: human beings
could get used to anything. *I* could get used to my own mediocrity and shape my future to fit it!

I ran down the stairs and into the street. The day was unex-
pectedly springlike after a week of cold, and something buoyant in the air had summoned a stream of Saturday families to
bask in the sun. They hurried toward the park to rest and
wander and display affection for each other. I fell into line,
hoping to be consoled by their normal happy talk. Partway
down the block my head cleared and I realized that the large
party around me was chattering in Puerto Rican Spanish and
none of it was intelligible.

I took a certain imbecile pleasure in the family pushing a
stroller loaded with provisions, shouting, laughing, bickering,
and chasing the littlest ones skittering ahead. I was invisible,
enveloped by loneliness.

Massed clouds raced down the sky, and the heightened mood
of my companions seemed ironic. The weather looked like one
of New York's staged attractions. I passed three men with side-
burns and loud jackets, examining the wreck of a car, caressing
its flanks, poking at its innards. Urchins careened past in a pur-
loined grocery cart and an old woman shrieked after them,
shaking her fist. The Puerto Rican family laughed and laughed.
We drifted into the park, and when they took one path, I took
the other. The tree trunks were black and the delicate sprays of
a willow glinted in the sun and swung like golden tresses. I

hiked to the top of the lake and stood like a general surveying casualties on the great plain. It was bounded by the towers of commerce and gain—possibility within limits. I shut my eyes for a moment and walked on.

Children were scaling the rocky hill to the Belvedere Tower. It had been a favorite perch of mine, but I felt I had lost the right to command it. Climbing to a view was once a powerful and rewarding instinct; now I imagined vertigo. The tower was a romantic place, suitable for dreaming. I watched three boys collar a little girl who might have been the younger sister of one. They were persuading her to hide from them and loomed over her, battering her with their enthusiasm. She looked from one to the next, her little fists clenched with excitement, her face shiny and gullible, and then she dashed away down the path. The boys, suppressing their merriment, took off in the opposite direction, through the trees and over the field. I wanted to tell the little girl she'd been duped, but she had hidden herself so well, there was no sign of her.

Dogs romped on the rocks and in the grass. People threw sticks for them to fetch and wrestled with them on the turf. A sedate party on horseback cantered along the bridle path. A gray squirrel approached me, its eyes intelligent and demanding. I backed away. Someone had told me most of the squirrels in the park were rabid. My flesh felt weak. Soon I came upon a man standing near a bench, his face turned up to the sky and his arms outstretched like a crucifix, holding a bag of peanuts in either hand, while a dozen or more squirrels scrambled over his body. I gave him a wide berth.

Any other day I'd have sketched him and the various vistas, but I had brought nothing with me and the things I observed no longer seemed to be subjects.

The zoo lay ahead. I passed the brick, turreted arsenal, which, like so many structures in the city, was modeled after an original meant to press at frontiers or measure someone's mastery and here sat like part of a giant child's kingdom. The underpass to the primate house emitted a vile smell. I paused with the throng hooting at the sea lions. People had gathered for distraction; they taunted, jostled one another, and threw bits of food to stir the creatures up. A man held high a sickly baby who cried piteously. Other children hurled themselves up and down

the walk, bumping into people and jeering. Cracker Jack and
pieces of hot dog and ice cream cups and sticks littered the
pavement. A mother smacked a little boy dripping chocolate.
The sea lions romped and barked, looking neither fish nor animal, but arrested at a limbless stage that fit them only for this
entertainment. I hurried past cages where exotic birds screeched
and preened their gorgeous plumage in the stinking air. Outside, the movement of the crowd was continuous and vivacious.
I let it bear me along, but the shabby, weather-beaten cages and
the liveliness of the mob filled me with a superior despair. The
zoo seemed to attract a singularly hostile, unstable, and cruel
lot, who drew perverse consolation for the human condition
from the press of their own kind and provocation of the help-
less beasts of the world. Then I came to the lion's cage.

I had been remembering a time when Desmond brought Portia and me to ride the carousel. The excitement had been almost more than we could bear, and we jumped up and down, clamoring for more rides, then, when he absolutely refused, a look at the zoo, especially the lions—we loved the MGM lion and used to leap out of the dark upstairs hallway to roar at each other. "No," he had said, and justified it by telling us it wasn't safe. "The keepers carry rifles," he told us solemnly, "the cages are so flimsy." We had gone on to an East Side hotel and sat in a dim lounge drinking ginger ale—or Portia and I had. It might have been true, about the lion keepers, at one time, but I knew the whole zoo had been renovated, and if anything, the lions were in greater jeopardy from the people than vice versa. The ancient Chinese emperors, Desmond had told us in the hotel, had called their menageries, where lions were allowed to roam, "parks of intelligence."

The beast I saw in its cage that day was an enormous buff-colored female, stretched out calmly on the floor and gazing steadily out over our heads, past us, to the universe. She seemed to possess all knowledge, to embody all dignity and grace and enjoy a private superiority over the benighted humans outside, we who were puny and feckless, trivial and transient.

How did she survive this life? Her sleek coat, powerful shoulders and limbs, great chunky paws, placid, noble head, and incarnate capacity for violence, found a deep response in me. A man stopped to roar foolishly, showing his fright and disrespect. She didn't blink. I felt more caged than she, longing to fathom a secret she seemed to safeguard for me. If she could survive this life, she could pass the secret on. I stood worshipfully for a few minutes, knocked from side to side by passersby, and then I ran home to get some paper and a pencil.

I returned in time to see her snarl, for no obvious reason. The livid show of mouth and fangs was followed by a yawn, and then she stood up, stretched, and paced briefly before she lay down again. I drew, copying, as I had copied masterpieces as a child, to learn from them and incorporate them in my gestures. People noticed what I was doing and interfered, asking questions, leaning over my shoulder, offering criticism. I shook them off, praying for Gottfried Mind's gift for likeness, his poor simple brain and his elevated soul.

The burlesque continued to play around me and the lion to rest stoically. I drew and drew, until the sun sank below the buildings on Central Park West, and then I went home to look over my sketches.

I poured some sherry and sat down on my couch. The pictures were bitterly disappointing. There were no answers contained in them, only the look of a lion. What hint of life showed up was no more than a reflection of the silly one that pitched and lurched along outside the cage—the "reality" that had attracted me all my life, demanding faithful representation. The essence of my respect was not there, nor the bestial power, nor the secrets of the feminine. But I couldn't describe what I had seen in her—it was something that the senses, if properly tuned, responded to instinctively with excitement and calm. Sarah Jenkins had remarked that animals are given their reality and men must find theirs. The lion was not a subject for me, she was a clue to a way to be.

It called for an act of faith. Some things weren't logical, but paradoxical, and were not understood, but accepted. Certainly, I had to believe in myself. I had failed to please Sarah Jenkins and been forced to abandon the practice of pleasing anyone. It had set dreadful limits on my capacities. Living with paradox meant setting out blindly, not knowing how something would end when I began it, not drawing as things ought to look, but as they did look.

I tried doing the lioness again. I would make what I wanted to make and nothing less would do.

After a few more large charcoal sketches, I wound up buying a can of black spray paint, with a nod to Hugh, who wouldn't have hesitated, as I did, to use a medium over which he had little control and was designed for, say, touching up an automobile. I remembered the drunken Brit, pissing all over his bedroom before he died, a dead rich man, and I let loose, full of fear and with no idea how to judge the results. A process had been reversed: rather than stare at the light, I groped in the dark. Every gesture was new—when I found myself duplicating old ways, I stopped. Finally an image appeared that I recognized as resembling what I had felt about the lioness. I had put something from inside me onto an outside surface and weathered its possible failure.

This was Sunday. It was growing dark, and the scattered city noises were muffled and soothing; the soft lights across the street signaled a warm, domestic restfulness. I left my final picture on the easel, and while I seldom looked at it during the evening, but sat reading from Delacroix's *Journal,* it seemed to radiate calm at its end of the room and to be an intermediary between me and the world.

It would be necessary, in the next week, to meet with Woefflin, find out what my grade had been, what we were to do next. I wished to meet all of my adult responsibilities. Someday I hoped to see Sarah Jenkins again and show her what I could do. I was sure the opportunity would arise.

I hoped that Muriel occupied herself that evening with some solacing task. In a little soaring fantasy, her old suitor Hubbard Moseley appeared out of the blue; his wife had died, his children were grown and married and had good jobs or promising businesses of their own, and he wanted a taste of a life with some of the qualities of the novels he liked to read. He thought often of Muriel, wondered how she was, if she still sang like a lark, still smiled an alluring smile. He had put all the hardware stores in the hands of trustworthy subordinates and allowed himself a month to savor metropolitan pleasures and desired Muriel for his guide and companion. Like any wish for someone else, this was both magnanimous and self-serving, and I refrained from calling her, for fear of betraying myself.

I did call Portia. "Do you remember—you may have been too little—when Dad took us to the carousel in Central Park and then wouldn't let us look at the lions in the zoo?"

After a moment, she said, "We went to a hotel afterward. It was springtime. I wore my blue coat and had a straw purse. Forsythia were blooming, but there weren't any leaves on the trees."

"Well, I saw the lions yesterday, or one of them. There was just one, for some reason. She's magnificent, the queen of beasts. I thought you might like to see her too. Can you come down tomorrow afternoon?"

The next morning a letter arrived from Desmond. He was quite a celebrity, he said, on the campus, and enjoying it thoroughly because once his book appeared, the reviews might not be kind. He did *hope*, however, for kindness. The publication date was now set officially for early April, and he would come to the city. His editor was taking him to lunch and he'd asked that Portia and I be invited to join them. I was terribly touched. We should plan some sort of family celebration to mark the occasion too.

"Did you hear from Dad?" I asked her when we met on my stoop.

"I did. What do you think?"

"I think we should have a party!" I cried, surprising myself. A party? What an idea! But Portia's face lit up.

"You're right!" She grew thoughtful. "And invite whom? Jules and Poppy . . . Lou . . ."

"Of course Lou. He might even come. I'll write to him. I want to, anyway," I added ambiguously. I did want to write to Lou. I felt that I had a lot to report to him, if I could manage to convey it. "He'll give us other names." We could appeal directly to Desmond's old associates and clear the air. They would be enthusiastic. His troubles had been shrouded in mystery; we had been ignorant children, divided in our loyalties.

Portia was studying my face. "What about Mother?" she said dubiously.

"Here's what I think," I said. "Let's just ask her to come, and see what happens!" I beamed at her.

Portia hesitated a moment. Then she said, "Okay, why not?"